Advance Praise for
The Housekeeper

"Mesmerizing suspense . . . Readers will relate to the very human Anne as she struggles to gain her emotional balance."

—*Publishers Weekly*

"Suellen Dainty has created such a sense of place and life-style here . . . I was entranced. The fact that there was also a rip-roaring story of shocking betrayal and childhood trauma underpinning the whole thing was just the cherry on top. I loved, loved, loved this book and cannot recommend it highly enough."

—Lisa Jewell, *New York Times* bestselling author
of *The Girls in the Garden*

"Dainty writes with such nuance that I felt completely sub-merged in the Helmsleys' world. I couldn't help but fly through the pages. Gorgeous writing, wonderful characteriza-tion, immersive atmosphere, and a final twist that I did not see coming!"

—Kate Moretti, *New York Times* bestselling author
of *The Vanishing Year*

"A compelling setup, intriguing characters, expertly han-dled plot, full of sharp details and insight. I couldn't stop reading it!"

—Lottie Moggach, author of *Kiss Me First*

"*The Housekeeper* is a tense, compelling story of memory, madness, and family secrets. Dainty's lush prose drew me into an orderly, domestic world where eerie images of the past lurk beneath charming, polished surfaces. You will fall under this novel's urgent spell—page by page to its shattering betrayal—and will not be able to pull yourself away."

—Karen Brown, author of *The Longings of Wayward Girls*

"Suspenseful and intriguing, wise, funny, and shocking. Beautifully written, this is a thriller for an age obsessed with celebrity—and all too ready to give its heart away to glamorous gurus."

—Elisabeth Gifford, author of *The Sea House*

ALSO BY SUELLEN DAINTY

After Everything

The Housekeeper

a novel

Suellen Dainty

W

WASHINGTON SQUARE PRESS

new york   london   toronto   sydney   new delhi

Washington Square Press
An Imprint of Simon & Schuster, Inc.
1230 Avenue of the Americas
New York, NY 10020

First Washington Square Press trade paperback edition February 2017

WASHINGTON SQUARE PRESS and colophon are registered
trademarks of Simon & Schuster, Inc.

For information about special discounts for bulk purchases, please
contact Simon & Schuster Special Sales at 1-866-506-1949 or
business@simonandschuster.com.

The Simon & Schuster Speakers Bureau can bring authors to your
live event. For more information, or to book an event, contact the
Simon & Schuster Speakers Bureau at 1-866-248-3049 or visit our
website at www.simonspeakers.com.

Interior design by Carly Loman

Manufactured in the United States of America

10 9 8 7 6 5 4 3 2 1

Library of Congress Cataloging-in-Publication Data

Names: Dainty, Suellen, author.
Title: The housekeeper : a novel / Suellen Dainty.
Description: First Washington Square Press trade paperback edition. |
   New York : Washington Square Press, 2017.
Identifiers: LCCN 2016032542| ISBN 9781476771403 (paperback) |
   ISBN 9781476771427 (ebook)
Subjects: LCSH: Psychological fiction. | BISAC: FICTION /
   Psychological. | FICTION / Suspense. | FICTION / Literary. | GSAFD:
   Suspense fiction.
Classification: LCC PR9619.4.D33 H68 2017 | DDC 823/.92–dc23
LC record available at https://lccn.loc.gov/2016032542

ISBN 978-1-4767-7140-3
ISBN 978-1-4767-7142-7 (ebook)

For my family

1

∞

What moved me, in the first instance, to attempt a work like this, was the discomfort and suffering which I had seen brought upon men and women by household mismanagement.

—*Mrs. Beeton's Book of Household Management*, 1861

The bus was about to pull away as I turned into Park Lane, but the traffic lights suddenly changed. I raced across the road, dodging taxis and motorbikes, and jumped on just before the doors closed.

I stumbled down the aisle, past a sleeping woman and some boys jostling each other, and fell into a seat near the back. The couple in front of me were experimenting with ringtones. Joyful upbeat jingles alternated with thumping drums and pealing church bells. The man opposite sighed with irritation and drummed his fingers on his knee. I turned away and stared into the cold January night. The pavements were almost empty apart from a few people striding along with their faces muffled by scarves and the usual group of chauffeurs clustered around their limousines outside the Dorchester Hotel.

A couple walked towards one of the cars. The woman had her head on the man's shoulder and he was caressing her hair, their faces bent towards each other. A chauffeur rushed to open the rear door. The interior lights snapped on, and I recognized them from the restaurant earlier in the evening. They'd sat at table 12, the best in the room. Pretty much everyone who came to the restaurant was good-looking, so I didn't notice them because of that. I noticed them because they seemed to be so much in love with each other. They'd ordered lobster, one of the most expensive dishes on the menu. Anton and I had arranged it on their plates with a sprinkling of chervil and decorative pools of saffron sauce, everything in careful symmetry designed to please. It's what Anton and I do: stand shoulder to shoulder every evening, preparing food to make people feel happier, sexier, bolder. We try to make everybody feel like somebody.

The bus moved along Bayswater Road, Hyde Park on one side and elegant white stucco buildings on the other, before slowing for late night roadworks. The man opposite sighed again. I didn't mind the delay. After working in a basement kitchen for so many hours every day, I liked being above-ground, glimpsing other people's sitting rooms and strangers sitting safely at home, even though the underground would have been much faster. The couple in front of me stood up, ready to get out at the next stop. There was that familiar smell of stale alcohol and scent that came from people at the end of their evening out. Anton always smelled like sun on sheets. I wondered what he was doing, if I should call him.

Someone had left a newspaper on the seat beside me and I picked it up, looking for distraction. In between pages of blingy advertisements for New Year bargains, grim-faced politicians warned about trade deficits. Another African country was about to be torn apart by civil war. I kept flicking until an article with the headline AN ISABELLA BEETON FOR THE 21ST CENTURY! caught my eye. Isabella Beeton was a heroine of mine. I admired her pronouncements on family life, cooking, and housekeeping. Order. Discipline. A place for everything and everything in its place.

The bus lurched to yet another halt and cold gritty air blew in through the doors. Normally that kind of thing annoyed me, but this time I hardly noticed. I read on. There was a photograph of a woman leaning against a marble fireplace. She had long blond hair and she was smiling at something or someone to her left. Her look was elegant and self-assured.

"It's all about organization," the woman told the interviewer. "Every working adult—men as well as women—needs to put aside time to plan their domestic life in the same way they plan their business life. Both are equally important and both feed into the success of each other." Her name was Emma Helmsley. She'd been a psychologist but had left counseling because "I was much more interested in modern day household management and the way it could affect people's lives and their happiness."

I'd never heard of her, but apparently she was England's answer to Martha Stewart and Oprah Winfrey. Her books sold millions, and her inspirational lectures ("oh please, more like informal chats") were always sold out months in advance. She was in her middle forties and married to a psychologist called Rob ("twin souls, like swans, we've mated for life") who wrote books as well and hosted a popular late night television program. They had a son aged fourteen and a daughter aged sixteen and lived just outside Richmond, in Petersham, near the river.

I dropped the newspaper on the seat, suddenly envious of this stranger's perfect life, her handsome husband and her happy marriage. I wished I was back in Mayfair with Anton. Maybe I should call him, just to say good night. I fished my phone out of my bag and dialed his number. No answer.

My attempt at distraction hadn't worked. If anything, I felt more ill at ease. Everything that had happened before I left the restaurant jumped into my mind like a flashback in a film. I saw myself climbing the stairs to Anton's apartment above the restaurant, hanging on to the idea of some quiet time, just the two of us away from the crowded frenzy of the dinner service. I was longing to see him in his usual place on the sofa with his chef's jacket flung on the floor, to feel his reassuring bulk as we embraced. All day as I'd chopped and diced and tasted, I'd reminded myself to keep my voice calm, my conversation light and cheerful, and to be the person he fell in love with.

But Anton wasn't on the sofa where I wanted him to be. He was in the bathroom wiping steam from the mirror, a flush along his cheekbones from the shower. I stood behind him in misted focus, still in dirty work clothes, hair scraped into a tight ponytail. I should have changed and put on some lipstick and mascara after my shift. I should have taken the time to make myself look prettier, less like the dependable sous-chef.

"Why are you going out?" There it was, that tone in my voice again. I tried, but I couldn't make it disappear, not entirely. "It's so late." It wasn't late at all. It was only a bit after ten thirty.

"Investors. Money. The competition at my heels. I can't afford to stand still." After thirty years in London, a French accent still lingered around the edges of his sentences. He fiddled with his shirt buttons and smoothed his hair, the small preening gestures he always made before taking on the outside world.

He studied his reflection from different angles. Anton wasn't conventionally handsome—his nose was too large and his face was too wide for that—but he had brown eyes that danced, a shock of gray curls, and a body that moved with surprising elegance. He was very fastidious about his clothes and grooming, as if he was on show in some way. I guess he always was on show. Anyhow, people tended to look twice.

He opened the wardrobe door and studied a line of black jackets. "All part of my job, my life," he said. But I just want to be alone with you for a few hours, I thought. I want you to stop staring at that row of coat hangers. I want to go back to the beginning and start again.

He chose a jacket from the middle and shook it out with a whoosh of air. I went to help him put it on, but he had already fastened the buttons and was moving towards the door. "I might bring them back here afterwards." He reached for his wallet. "Downstairs, to the restaurant and the kitchen. Maybe up here for a drink. Show and tell. You do understand, don't you?"

I nodded and arranged my mouth into a smile. Of course. I understood. I shouldn't have complained. I know the business. The fierce competition. The famous but fickle customers. Sometimes I thought they followed the paparazzi rather than the other way around. Lately, there'd been talk of opening another restaurant near London Bridge. Anton et Amis, however well established, had its limits. Restaurants always needed more money, even ones as well known as this, with its bronze front door often in the newspapers framing the entrances and exits of minor royalty, actors, and supermodels. There were still paparazzi outside the front door, but not as many as a year ago. A successful New York restaurateur had recently opened a chophouse in Marylebone, luring away many of our regular customers.

Anton picked up his keys. I leaned against him, feeling the curls of his chest hair under the thin cotton of his shirt. I started to put my arms around him, but he slipped away.

"See you tomorrow," he said. "We can talk after the dinner service." Then he was gone. I picked up his chef's jacket, idly rubbing at the crusts of leftover food on its sleeves. A quick tidy up and then I'd go home. I didn't like being alone in his flat. Anton never said anything, but I think he didn't like me being alone there either. I didn't mind him minding. Being there without him made me feel lonely, and there was always the thought of the other women who'd been there before me.

By Mayfair standards, his place was modest, but still much bigger than my own little box miles away in the non-gentrified part of Brentford. Anton never stayed there. He got fidgety if he moved more than a mile away from Hyde Park, and he always said his flat was far more convenient for our work and our life than mine.

I'd been with Anton for just over two years, and nothing in his relentless bachelor decor had changed in that time. Everything was brown and gray and hard-edged. I used to joke about bringing in some floral cushions to brighten things up, to leave some small trace of myself, but I never did. I tossed the dirty jacket in the laundry basket, keeping the lid open longer than necessary so I could inhale the scent of him: cooking, soap, and sweat, and under these, a vanilla odor with a bit of cinnamon somewhere. He must have been trying out a new recipe. I went downstairs again. Dinner service was almost finished. The porters were already sluicing down the floors and scrubbing the counters. In the locker room, I changed my clothes and left, buttoning my coat as the cold air bit my face after the warmth of the kitchen.

By now, the bus had juddered and swayed its way across London. Small workers' cottages and late night kebab shops had replaced the large terraces of Bayswater. I was nearly home. The bus lurched to a halt and I stepped onto the pavement. A young boy was playing hopscotch, nimbly dodging late night commuters. A group of boys in padded jackets milled about the pizza café, passing around cigarettes and cans of beer. Smoke spiraled in the frosty air. A sprinkling of girls stood to one side, biting their lips and giggling. There was the faint tinny sound of rap. I caught my reflection in a shopwindow. The breeze from the bus had whipped my hair into a frizz. My face looked tired and pinched. I made myself smile, surprised by how easily it came, how natural it looked. I might have been a wife on her way home to meet her husband, an intimate evening ready to unfold. I walked past the pawnbroker and a row of empty shops, their windows covered by metal shutters emblazoned with graffiti, then turned into my street.

After I locked my front door behind me, I changed into pajama bottoms and a T-shirt, made a pot of chamomile tea, and lay on the sofa, trying not to think about Anton and what he might be doing. There was a time when I would have opened a bottle of wine at that point of the evening and finished most of it. Maybe all of it and then opened another. But alcohol brings out the worst in me. Bleak depression. Dreams of howling. Waking up with a jolt, not remembering where I am or what I've done. These days I stick to the one glass at a time rule, and only when I'm with other people.

I sipped my tea and contemplated the fat cream-colored moon that hovered at the top of the window. My flat was nothing like Mayfair. If I was lucky enough to remain solvent and employed, it would be mine in about twenty years, all 540 square feet of it. I'd never have been able to scrape up the deposit on my own, not in London, but Gran had left me enough for a down payment, carefully squirreled away to avoid it being used up by the nursing home bills, and I'd moved here just before I started working at Anton et Amis. I was on the third floor, with people above, below, and beside me. The sitting room had comfortable armchairs and a sofa covered in pale blue linen. A motley collection of framed prints from Tate Modern hung on the walls. Matisse, Klee, Mondrian, nothing unusual. The kitchen had a new oven and refrigerator. In the bathroom there was a full-size tub, again new. No moldy speckles in the grout.

Other people might have left the teapot and mug in the sitting room until morning. I wasn't one of them. After I scrubbed everything clean and wiped it dry, I checked my emails—nothing of interest—and then, because I wasn't quite ready for sleep, I did a quick search on Emma Helmsley. She had a lot going on. Numerous magazine and newspaper interviews, the usual Twitter and Instagram accounts as well as a website and a blog. There was even a tip of the day, called "Taking the Moment," sent straight to your inbox. Why not? I thought. I entered my email address for her daily update. It wasn't the kind of thing I normally did, but there was something about her that interested me. Maybe it was the way she revered order and organization, just like Isabella, just like me.

I picked up my battered copy of *Mrs. Beeton's Book of Household Management* and went to bed. I'd found it in a charity shop on the main road, soon after I bought my flat, and thought it might be amusing to flick through recipes for boiled fowl or advice on plucking grouse. But it quickly became something of a bible to me. I had to explain to Anton who she was: that she was the eldest of twenty-one children, who had started writing about household management in her early twenties; that her book had sold two million copies when it was first published and was still in print today. Anton roared with laughter and asked what a Victorian housewife had to do with the way we lived now. As usual, he had a point, but that didn't discourage me.

I turned to it most nights before sleep, opening a page at random and reading about the duties of butlers, housemaids, and laundresses. After the jangling of the kitchen all day, the comfort of their ordered life soothed me. Occasionally I imagined myself moving through halls with wooden floors waxed to the color of honey, adjusting flowers in vases to the best effect and snipping off any tainted blooms.

More often, I imagined Anton and me in a house together. An unassuming, comfortable place in a street where you could go for a walk in the evening and peer through the windows to see families having supper together, or children doing their homework. We would stroll arm in arm before turning for home to enjoy a quiet drink in our garden, just the two of us. Sometimes, but only very rarely, I allowed myself the luxury of even more delicious imaginings: as we strolled arm in arm, I was wearing one of those papoose slings strapped around my waist, with a baby's head, covered in dark wisps, bobbing happily against my heart.

I woke the next morning with a start, one arm searching for the outline of Anton's warm bulk, as if my sleeping body had refused to accept his absence. The sheet was dotted with spots of blood. I must have scratched myself during the night again. My pillow was clammy with perspiration and my quilt was twisted around my legs like a straitjacket. A prick of nerves ran along my spine. I thought I'd gotten over all that.

After Gran died, it happened a lot. She had brought me up single-handedly after my mother died when I was five years old; I couldn't even remember my life before her. It seemed that there had always been just the two of us, even after I'd left home for London. Without her I had the feeling of being a child left out in the rain and not able to find my way home. The word that came to mind was "abandoned." If I'd tried to explain that to Anton, he'd have patted my arm and said I was exaggerating. I would have agreed with him. Gran was eighty-six years old and had been ill for some time, confined to her bed in a nursing home in Dorset, near where I grew up. No one ever left a place like that to start a new life somewhere else. But for all the advance notice, it still hurt, much more than I'd expected. Most people I knew had parents or grandparents who had passed away, and after a while they managed to function perfectly well without making themselves bleed in the night and wake up shivering.

Luckily, Anton slept like a person entombed. He always set three alarms on his phone and woke cheerful and oblivious to my nightmares and nerves. I never said anything. I didn't want him to think I was needy, like some of his others had been, or so he said. I was determined to be bright and lighthearted.

Outside, streaks of orange light flickered over the horizon of tower blocks and office buildings. There was the dull roar of planes queuing to land at Heathrow and the grating gear changes of early morning buses. In the bathroom, I dashed cold water on my face. The bloodstained sheet went into the washing machine. I did all the usual things to calm myself. Tea. Toast. A long shower with the water drumming on my head. I told myself that I had Anton now. He was my family. I fixed my mind on seeing him later in the restaurant kitchen, how the sight of his head bent over the enormous cooking range in the middle of the room always calmed me, like I'd come home after a long journey.

If people didn't say it, I knew they thought it. I wasn't Anton's usual type. Jude, my closest friend, told me that right from the beginning. "Don't you mean his former type?" I snapped back. Even Anton was keen to make a distinction between me and the others. "Glamour is boring. *Jolie laide*, the way you are, is so much more interesting." His former type was likely to be someone with a professional blow-dry and daytime stilettos, the kind of person whose job was more of a hobby to fill in time rather than an actual way to earn a living. Not that I'm some kitchen skivvy who only gets a glint in her eye when she's faced with a pile of carrots to chop. There are plenty of those around and I'm not in their club. Still there's no denying that I come across as someone more practical than glamorous. But that's not entirely accurate. I do have lace underwear, pretty dresses, and pairs of high-heeled shoes to put on when I want Anton to think of me in a different way, as someone who's not always chopping and slicing and tasting and stirring. I just don't wear those things to work.

———————

Spring, two years ago. "I'm not sure," Anton said. "You're not my usual type of employee. Most of my people have worked in France for a while, Lyon usually." We were in his tiny office with a glass door looking onto the vast basement kitchen. He wore a crumpled blue linen shirt and baggy black trousers. A clean chef's jacket hung on the doorknob.

He propped his elbows on his desk, scattering piles of old-fashioned order slips held together with rubber bands. Behind him were rows of shelves crammed with books. There was a row of dog-eared classics—*Larousse Gastronomique, Le Cordon Bleu, Cooking with Pomiane*—and more recent books by chefs like Ferran Adrià, Thomas Keller, and Alice Waters. Right at the top were the ones that he'd written: *Anton Richell's Classics Made Simple, Beginner's Cookery*, and all the others, dating back to the time when his hair was still dark brown.

I'd already known what Anton looked like from photographs and his television series. He wasn't famous enough for mainstream prime time. But I'd seen him late at night on cable, cruising along French canals in a longboat, rustling up local delicacies on a makeshift stove at the end of each day. And here I was, barely two feet away from him, close enough to touch his face, to see the tiny shaving nick on his cheek, the spring of the curls in his hair.

"Do you want me to cook something?" I asked, trying not to let my nervousness show. The night before, I'd worried about what to wear. I wanted to look neat and capable, so finally I chose a man's white shirt over jeans and sensible thick-soled shoes. My knives, already sharpened in their leather roll, were in my bag on the floor. Most chefs carried their own knives. Anton might have thought I wasn't a true professional if I'd left them behind. In the bus on my way to the interview, I'd worried that I'd forgotten my favorite paring knife and upended my bag onto my lap to make sure I'd included it. The woman sitting beside me flinched and glanced towards the emergency button. "I'm sorry if I scared you," I said. "They're for my interview—a new job." She stood up in a rush and moved away.

Now, perched on the edge of my chair, I shifted my bag closer to my feet. "Really," I said. "I'd be happy to prepare anything at all." Behind me, I heard the revving of the kitchen as it geared up for lunch. The crash of pots and the thunk of chopping, the slop of water in buckets as porters sluiced down the floors. Overlaying everything was the smell of simmering stock, the antiseptic tang of rosemary, the licorice of basil and star anise.

Anton shook his head. "No need, not just yet." He propped his hands under his chin and stared at me, as if he was deciding how to test me. I prepared myself for anything he might throw at me. Rare ingredients? Unusual recipes? Cooking techniques? I was confident of my knowledge about such things. I could make proper filo pastry, each sheet so thin you could see through it. I could bone a pig's trotter in less than five minutes. But his question, when it came, was unexpected.

"Tell me what you eat and I will tell you who you are." There was a smug smile on his face. He expected me not to know what he was talking about.

"Easy," I replied. "Jean Anthelme Brillat-Savarin. Eighteenth-century French lawyer and politician. Extraordinary gastronome who said eating chocolate was good for the brain."

Anton erupted with laughter. "Not bad at all. In fact, pretty damn good. Now, here's the thing." The laughter was gone. He spoke seriously. "When someone is going to work for me, they need to taste things in the same way that I taste them. Otherwise, we don't know what we're talking about."

"I understand." I didn't really. I only knew that I was attracted to this man, already leaning towards him like metal filings to a magnet, as if my body was aware it was drawn to him before my mind organized that impulse into a thought. I brushed the feeling aside and reminded myself that this was the job I wanted more than any other. I'd have more chance of being hired if Anton saw me as a responsible sous-chef rather than yet another starstruck kitchen flirt.

Besides, I really *was* a responsible sous-chef. I never called in sick and I never drank on the job, or took drugs, like so many others in my world. I took my work seriously and I liked it more than anyone else I knew. I liked the fifteen-hour days, the curious dialect of gestures and grunts incomprehensible to everyone but us. And I loved the magic of it all; the way I could put on my sensible shoes and my chef's jacket and stand at the same station every day, weighing ingredients to the gram, mixing them in the right proportions and the right sequence until they were transformed into something else altogether that could change people's lives.

Really. It's true. It's not fanciful exaggeration. Businessmen and -women shake hands on deals worth millions of pounds, lovers resolve grievances, and parents bond with their children over a particularly fine lunch or dinner. Believing that I was creating a kind of magic spell pushed me through the long shifts, the aching legs, and the fatigue. It's not something peculiar to me. Most people who work in restaurant kitchens think like that. It's what we share in our mongrel world of Polish engineers, Afghan refugees, PhD dropouts, recovering junkies, and former Buddhist monks. Right wing, left wing, Oxford, Princeton, Cambridge, people who can barely read or write their own name. We're a profession without borders. An empty plate is all we need for job satisfaction.

Then there's the wonderful science of cooking. Flour plus butter plus milk, in the correct quantities, added in the correct stages, will always make a béchamel sauce. If you fail to stir it, there will always be lumps. If you press a piece of beef or lamb, and it's soft to the touch, it will always be pink. These things are unalterable truths.

But how to explain all that to Anton in less than two minutes, in a way that would set me apart from everyone else who wanted this job? I knew about Brillat-Savarin, but was that enough to make him take his hand off his chin, stop appraising me with his clear brown eyes, and say yes, the position was mine, and ask when could I start?

"Ask me anything," I said, sitting up straight. By now, I'd gotten that uncalled-for impulse of attraction under control, although my hand itched to reach across and touch the small bead of dried blood on his cheek.

"Do you want me to cook something? Anything at all. Do you want me to go through where I've worked?"

"No," he said. "I've read your CV. But it doesn't tell me what I need to know. I need to know that people in my kitchen experience food the way people out there"—he gestured towards the dining room—"experience it. As a whole, not as a series of ingredients." I was beginning to understand what he was talking about. "So let's eat together." He tucked my résumé under a pile of papers and looked at me, cool and appraising. "Then we'll see."

"Sounds great," I said. "Whenever." I shifted in my chair and uncrossed my legs. The knives clinked in their bag by my feet. I told myself this wasn't a dinner invitation. It was just an unusual method of interviewing. Anton probably didn't want to discuss his tasting menu with absolutely everyone in the kitchen, but it made sense that the people who worked right by his side should share his ideas on food.

"Tonight?" Anton leaned back in his chair. It wasn't a question, because he already knew the answer. "Not really an exam as such. Nothing serious. Just a little test."

I scurried back to my flat and spent the rest of the day flinging every garment I owned onto the bed in a fever of indecision and excitement.

The plain black dress with the low back? No. I looked like a nun from the front and a call girl from the back. I was neither. The red skirt? Too tight, too obvious. The last time I'd worn it, I'd drunk too much and ended up in bed with a man I didn't even like, a coke-sniffing American called Joe. That dress with the frill down the front? Too hippy-dippy-girly. It was almost dusk when I decided on a pair of black trousers and a white silk shirt. Smart, but safe. I would add high heels and those glittery earrings I'd bought on a whim and never worn. With a bit of luck, I wouldn't look too much like an upmarket waitress.

I opened a bottle of amber-scented bath oil, my last birthday present from Gran, and immersed myself in hot water. My knees and breasts emerged like pale islands above the soapy foam. I shut my eyes and lay without moving until the cooling water stirred me to jump out. From the bathroom cabinet, I took out my box of smoky eye shadows and blush-colored lipsticks and set to work. In my bedroom, I put on my clothes and slipped on my shoes, the black suede ones with kitten heels. They transformed me, those oils and lotions and pots of makeup, those pieces of lace and silk. In an hour, I was no longer the hardworking chef in the serviceable clothes. I was an excited thirty-three-year-old woman about to meet a desirable man for dinner.

Waiting for the Uber car outside my building, buffeted by the herd of commuters heading home in their uniforms of hoodies and trainers, I felt an alien in my own neighborhood. Too coiffed, too scented. All dolled up, as Gran would have said with a sniff. But as the driver pulled away from the lines of fast-food shops and down-at-heel pubs, and crossed the series of roundabouts leading to Knightsbridge with its designer stores and jewelry shops, I felt less strange. My surroundings and my appearance caught up with each other and began to merge. By the time we reached Shoreditch, I was at ease with my other persona, the one I had put on and smoothed down when I got out of the bath. I glimpsed myself in the rear vision mirror. Men might give me a second glance. Anton almost certainly would.

There he was at the bar, waiting for me, an ice bucket with an open bottle of champagne beside him. He was standing side on, and right away I noticed his belly. It wasn't one of those silly little pots that middle-aged men so often try to hide by wearing their shirts hanging outside their trousers like some kind of smock. Even if I'd never met Anton, I'd have known that this was a confident man just by the unashamed high swell of that belly. It was large and round, and for a moment before I walked over to join him, I imagined how good it would feel to rest my head against it.

The day disappeared and I entered the fantasy world of a good restaurant. This one was a mixture of an art gallery and high-end chophouse. It was seductive and I fell for it, even though I recognized the relentless front-of-house smile and knew all about the furious industry in the kitchen, the sweating and the swearing, the totting up at the end of each night before the venture broke even.

We talked like old friends, in a meandering, inconsequential way, about the food. Was my pigeon breast a touch overdone? Did his loin of venison lack seasoning? And the cheese? Ripe enough or perhaps a little too salty? This was the way we familiarized ourselves with each other. He didn't ask me where I'd worked or what I'd done. I didn't ask him about the business of owning and running a restaurant. There were none of the usual interview questions about cooking techniques or the restaurants where I'd worked.

At some point during our meal—I can never remember exactly when—Anton shifted closer to me. His hand brushed my thigh and my skin leaped at his touch. He poured more wine with his other hand and studied the label. "A Pinot Noir from Patagonia. Who'd have thought? I must order some of this for the restaurant. It's very good, don't you think? Is everything all right?"

"Everything is perfect," I replied.

We shared a pot of mint tea. By the time we left, and by the time we reached Mayfair, we both knew that I would spend the night with him. I forgot that I would have to wake in the early hours and go back to my flat, so the staff wouldn't spot me when they came into work. Until then, I had him beside me. I was protected by his bulk, the food he had fed me for the past three hours, the wine he had chosen for me to drink. Afterwards, I lay awake and watched him sleep, hypnotized by his steady breathing, regular as a metronome.

I was so in love with Anton, entwined with him in a way that would have been impossible if we weren't working together as well as sleeping with each other. After that first meal together, we spent every day side by side in Anton et Amis's basement kitchen, finishing each other's sentences, knowing the state of each other's moods by a gesture or a look. Mayfair playboys on the street above us revved their Ferraris so loudly that the wineglasses trembled on their shelves. Nothing shook us as we snatched exchanges and checked our timings. The whole kitchen worked as a team, but Anton and I worked as a pair. But now I worried that we were drifting apart.

2

∞

All of us love and laugh sometimes and all of us
hurt sometimes. And it's no fun! But if you're brave
enough to examine that hurt and learn from it, you
will be a wiser person because of it.

—Emma Helmsley, "Taking the Moment," January 29, 2016

I hopped down the basement steps to the kitchen, already thinking about the small change I wanted to make to our tarte tatin.
It was one of the restaurant's better-known dishes, but I thought
it needed updating with a smidgen of star anise or black cardamom. Recipes don't stand still. They ripen and mature, like
wine or cheese. They need tweaking every now and then.

In the locker room there was that familiar smell of last
night's wine and food mingled with the freshness of the early
deliveries of mushrooms and strawberries, parsley and basil.
Unusually, the room was empty, and I stood for a minute, ap-
preciating the silence before the beginning of my working day.
I was shaking out the creases from my jacket, about to put it on,
when I heard footsteps, then laughter.

"She has to know by now." I recognized the voice. It was Ed,
the kitchen porter, the one who was always smirking. "I mean,
the whole of London knows about Anton and . . ."

I slammed the locker door shut and wheeled around to face
him. Two others were behind him, looking surprised. "Knows
what about Anton?" I slipped one arm into my jacket, then the
other. It took longer than usual to button it up.

"Knows what about Anton?" I repeated.

"Nothing," mumbled Ed. He glanced away. A flush crept along his cheeks. "It's nothing. Just stupid gossip, that's all. Forget I said anything."

I jammed my hands into my pockets. I tried to think of a clever retort and couldn't. All the tired clichés of deceit that I'd refused to recognize for the past few months flashed into my mind. That flicker of annoyance on Anton's face. The nights he said he couldn't see me because of business meetings, or saw me only briefly. The mumbled phone calls. That smell of vanilla on his clothes in the laundry basket. The sharp tone in Jude's voice whenever she spoke about him. She was trying to tell me and I wouldn't listen. Everything whirled and flashed like knives in the air and settled into the inescapable fact that Anton had someone else. The air disappeared from my lungs like the aftershock of a silent bomb blast.

"It's late," I said, surprised that my voice sounded so steady and clear, ringing out around the room. "I need to get started." I brushed past them and strode into the kitchen. I tied an apron behind my back. There was a fierce desire to lose myself in the routine of work. If I made one unfamiliar move, I would fall apart, sugar on the floor.

The day passed in a numbed haze. I sensed, rather than saw, Anton enter the kitchen an hour later, and I forced myself to look up and give a cheery smile. He looked surprised and smiled back. I returned to the painstaking job of filleting and boning a large turbot. It wasn't my usual job, but we'd been short-staffed all week because of a particularly vicious strain of flu. I was grateful that the task required so much concentration that there was no time for thought.

All around me were the noises of a busy kitchen gearing up for service. This was the time of day when I found comfort in the low chatter, the sound of meat sizzling, and the steady rhythm of bubbling pots of stock. I felt like I was a member of an orchestra about to perform in front of an appreciative audience. But as I slipped my knife along the spine of the fish and felt along its length, as I pulled away each fillet with one clean movement and checked it for bones, I knew I was an outsider now. I was the one who was the last to know, the one they would joke about when I left the room.

"They look great." Anton was behind me. The spine of the fish and its head were still on the counter. One glassy eye stared at me above a grim down-turned mouth. I swept everything into the bin. My knife was smeared with blood and strings of slime. I rinsed it carefully before turning around to face him.

I expected him to look different, in the way that you viewed a puzzle differently after you knew its solution. But he looked like he always did, with his shock of gray curls reaching below his collar and the swell of his stomach under his jacket. There was the same feeling of homecoming when I finally met his eye. Maybe I'd got it all wrong. I always was prone to the odd spot of exaggeration. But then he glanced away and I knew I hadn't made a mistake.

Behind Anton, everyone peered across at us, expecting shouts and tears. I was determined to disappoint them. "Thanks. The new fishmonger is really good." I wanted to scream that I was the one who'd found him, who'd cajoled him to drive up from Devon and supply the restaurant exclusively. "I need a minute with you later," I said. "Just need to go over a few things." He blinked quickly. I'd read somewhere that excessive blinking was a sign of anxiety or lying. "Maybe later, when things are quiet?"

"Sure."

"Shall I come upstairs?" It was the first time in two years that I'd asked that question. It was always understood that his flat was where we went after our work was finished. But I wanted him to know that something had changed and that I was aware of it. Anton laughed and blinked again. "Of course. That's what we always do. I'll look out a good bottle from the cellar."

"Terrific." I remembered to smile before wiping down my bench and moving over to the main counter to supervise the sauces.

"Everything OK?" asked one of the apprentices.

"Perfect," I said, tightening the knot on my apron. "I just need more eggs and butter."

The rhythm of cooking dulled the pain. I forced myself to concentrate on my work, not to allow anything else to enter my mind. After the dinner service ended, I waited until the locker room had emptied before going in to change. My apron and jacket were dirty and smeared, and I tossed them into the linen basket. I put on a clean shirt. I untied and brushed my hair before the mirror and rubbed in some lipstick. My unremarkable face stared back at me. The harsh fluorescent light accentuated the circles under my eyes and the lines beginning to form from my nose to my mouth. Now that I'd taken off the armor of my work uniform, I wanted nothing more than to slump on the floor and scream and sob. I thought of leaving without seeing Anton and sending him a savage text from the bus. But some part of me that I didn't recognize, that needed to know the truth, held firm and propelled me up the stairs to his flat and through the open door.

I perched on one of his uncomfortable armchairs and accepted a glass of wine. A Saint-Estèphe, he announced with some pride, from one of the best vineyards. He sprawled on the sofa, lamplight playing along his smooth olive-skinned cheeks. I hadn't eaten all day, and the smell of the wine almost, but not quite, undid me. I didn't mess about.

"What's going on?" My voice was shrill, stretched to breaking point. I sounded like someone else, an actor playing a role in my life.

"I don't know what you mean," he said. There it was again, that nervous blinking. "There's nothing going on."

"Don't lie to me."

"I'm not lying—I don't know where all this is coming from."

"What's her name?"

"There's no one else."

"I deserve to be told the truth."

"Honestly, there's no one."

I drank the wine. It tasted like rotten fruit.

"Who is she?" I was determined not to cry, but my mind was a zone of chaos: structures collapsing, fires flaring, things sinking. I asked the same questions again and again. I made the same accusations. The high, tight pain somewhere in my center intensified, and my hands shook so much that I slopped some wine onto the floor. I had an overwhelming urge to leave but couldn't manage to stand up.

"It's just that I need a bit more freedom," he said after a small silence. "It's not you. I'm under so much stress right now. Please understand. It won't be forever."

"Tell me the truth and I'll go."

"All this worry about new investors. You know how it's been."

"The staff think you've already got the investors. How could you lie to me like that?"

Another silence. "It's not signed yet, so it's not certain."

It was nearly midnight. Sounds of laughter and shouting drifted through the open window. I went to the window and looked out. A couple, arm in arm, bounced down the street. They stopped under a streetlight to kiss. I slammed the window shut and leaned against the glass. If I concentrated on the chill against my forehead, perhaps I wouldn't have to feel anything else. Behind me, Anton said, "Maybe we need a break for a while. It's hard working together and being with each other all the time. You must agree. It gets . . . well . . . a bit claustrophobic."

I heard him stand and move towards the door. So this is it, I thought. This is my lover, the man who had slept naked next to me for two years, about to leave me. This is my life and my livelihood falling apart. It had taken less than fifteen minutes. There should be another language for words that wound more than others, that turn your world in the opposite direction. I managed to turn and face him.

Anton ran his hands through his hair, that gesture I knew so well. There was that familiar giddy feeling rising up, unwanted and unexpected. I never loved him more than at that moment. Mad as it was, I would have gone to bed with him right then and wiped from my mind everything that had gone before. I would have made it my life's work to forget. But he began to talk in a low, determined voice that I'd never heard before.

"I'm sorry. Yes, I lied to you, but only because I didn't want to hurt you. I care about you. I felt terrible lying to you."

"Do you want me to feel sorry for you?" I asked, bewildered and then angry for the first time. "What about me? I was the one you lied to. All you can think about is how bad you feel?"

He turned away, but not before I could see the look of relief on his face. Now that I'd forced him to tell the truth, he was free. I'd done him a favor by confronting him. "Sometimes these things just happen," he said. "They come out of nowhere. It wasn't intended."

There was nothing left to say. I managed to push past him and make my way downstairs and onto the street. An icy wind rushed through me. I was too stunned to cry or think about anything except getting back to my flat as quickly as possible. It began to rain at Shepherd's Bush Roundabout, hard like needles. People boarding the bus brought with them the smell of wet clothes and stale food. In the window, my reflection dissolved into misted rivulets. This is what I am, I said to myself again and again. I am a woman whose lover has lied to her and left her, whose job is over. I shut my eyes, not wanting to look at myself.

"Hey lady!" It was the man sitting next to me, maybe twenty, with earbuds and a greasy topknot. I'd leaned against him, my head practically on his shoulder, without realizing, and he was trying to shrug me off.

"Sorry," I said and drew back into my seat. Two stops away from home, my phone pinged and I grabbed it out of my pocket, almost dropping it on the floor in my haste. Anton. It had to be him, contacting me so late in the evening. It would be an apology, a misspelled text written in haste, begging me to come back, that he'd made a terrible mistake. I picked up my bag, ready to jump off the bus and hail a taxi for Mayfair even before I read the message. But when I scrolled down, I retched with disappointment. It was Emma Helmsley's thought for the day. I flung the phone back into my bag.

In the off-license opposite the kebab shop, I bought as much wine as I could carry. I strode back to my flat and hurried up the stairs, unscrewing the top of a bottle as I went, swigging straight from it before I'd unlocked the door. It was cheap and harsh and smelled like varnish. I didn't care. I needed something to stop the pain. I drank the whole bottle, slumped on the sofa and staring at the pictures on the wall until they multiplied into an alcoholic blur. I lurched into the bathroom and was violently ill, the smell of sour vomit all around me as it pooled on the floor in a murky stipple. I stared at the mess for some minutes, stood up, and left it. In the kitchen, I wiped my mouth and opened another bottle, crawled into bed. At four a.m., I woke with a dry, foul-tasting mouth and that sound of howling in my ears. It became clear, with another stab, that I had been only a part of Anton's life, but he had been everything in mine. I lay on my back, imagining him with another woman, making love to her in that slow assured way of his.

I missed Gran and the gruff sympathy she would have given me, how her hand would have reached out and rubbed my shoulder. I should never have come to London. What a mess I had made of everything.

My friend Jude rang, as she did two or three times a week, either before or after dropping the twins, Charlie and Amelia, at their nursery. "Top of the morning to you, my darling bestie. I'm telling you, I need a new wardrobe to keep up with those style fascists at the nursery gate. I counted five Chanel jackets this morning. Dearie me." Her friendly voice and her fake Irish accent over a background of cheery pop music made me burst into tears.

"It's over," I sobbed. There was a click. She'd switched off her radio. There was only the muted sound of sirens and traffic.

"Are you still there?" I asked.

"Yes."

"You knew, didn't you?"

"No," said Jude in her normal kind voice. "I didn't know. Although I had a suspicion that something wasn't right. You know I'd never lie to you, or keep anything from you. I didn't want to upset you for no reason. It's just that people have been talking. You know what a small town London is."

I gulped back tears. I was going to be sick again.

"I'm so sorry, dear one. But I don't know anything more. Anyway . . ." She paused. ". . . maybe it's best to leave it. It's over."

"I need to know who it is."

"What does it matter who it is now?"

"It does to me."

Jude sighed. "OK. I'll do my best. I'll call you back. Where are you?"

"In bed, feeling sick. I think I'm still drunk. I've been drinking since it happened."

"Stay there. Shut your eyes and keep breathing. Don't drink anything more."

She rang back half an hour later. "I put some pressure on some people I figured would know." I closed my eyes and registered the rasp of my breath, the scratching of my fingernails against the phone.

"It's the daughter of one of the new investors for the second restaurant. Everything about the money has been in place for a while now. It's been going on for three, maybe four months. I'm sorry," she repeated. "You don't deserve this. I'll book a babysitter for tonight. Let's meet in Covent Garden and talk about it properly. You can't stay in that flat on your own getting drunk. He's not worth it."

"He was worth it to me," I said. "He was my life." I hung up and rushed into the bathroom again. This time I managed to clean up my mess, wash my face, and brush my teeth before stumbling back to bed. The movement of the morning sun dancing on the ceiling made me giddy. I drew the curtains over the closed window, sealing off the outside world. Darkness was better, but I couldn't stop shivering. I wrapped the quilt around me in a futile attempt at some kind of comfort, not moving until it was time to meet Jude.

We sat in the corner of our usual wine bar. Jude ordered me a hamburger with French fries and made me eat it before allowing me to drink anything. "Maybe it was just the stress of business," I said, trying not to cry again. Anton. Anton. Would there ever be a moment in my life when what he thought or did, or what he might have thought or might have done, wasn't my first point of reference? I couldn't imagine a life without him. "Maybe now the restaurant thing is fixed, he'll come back," I said, wanting Jude to agree with me, to give me at least some illusion of hope.

Jude surveyed me from behind the rim of her glass. Under

the choppy Knightsbridge haircut, and above the designer leather jacket, her eyes had the same appraising gaze as they'd had when we worked together in that Chiswick restaurant and began sharing all our secrets. "Sometimes you just have to accept that relationships are over. It'll only hurt more if you keep pretending to yourself. And you've still got me. I may be busy, but you can talk to me anytime." She leaned over and took my hand.

"It just hurts so much," I said. We fell silent. Then, because there was nothing more to analyze or weep over, and because talking about Anton had begun to hurt more than not talking about Anton, I changed the subject. "Where's Philip?" Philip was her rich property-developer husband, who usually liked to keep her close by his side.

"He's in Berlin this week—that spa hotel," said Jude. "It's his new thing. He's crazy for it. He gets to charge top whack to people who aren't drinking and eat almost nothing." She drained her glass. "I miss the way things were back in Chiswick. It wasn't so bad, was it? At least no one broke your heart then. It was the other way around, as I recall."

I had to agree with her on that. Back when we worked together, at the end of the dinner service we'd hunker down on the kitchen floor, swilling from the leftover bottles (we could never believe what people left behind, opened and often almost full) while we decided who we'd sleep with for what was left of the night. There were quite a few to choose from: American Stan from the Bay Area with his energetic speed habit, Henri from Lyon squinting behind his glasses with his crazy black curls drawn back in a plait, or Alex from Edinburgh, his arms puckered with livid burn scars.

These days Jude could afford the unopened bottles, whole crates of the stuff. It was all go-go gloss and cashmere up there on Primrose Hill. I heard the slight intake of breath most days when we spoke, the clacking of her Louboutins on the marble floors, as she talked for five minutes and then said she must fly. Lunch. Gym. School run. See you soon, love you.

I knew she did, but I missed the easy early days of our friendship, before Fat Wallet Phil, as we used to call him, took one look at Jude plating up a mille-feuille. He couldn't stop staring at her tumble of blond hair and her pale skin, and began his dogged pursuit of her. We used to laugh at his extravagant presents, how he waited in his Porsche for her to finish her shift, then whisked her away to his fancy house. It was only a matter of time before she succumbed. Jude was the oldest of six children. There had been the alcoholic father, the hectoring mother. It had not been calm. Philip adored her and made her feel safe. It was so easy to return his love. Six months later, she moved in with him, and by some unspoken agreement we began to call him Philip. About the same time, she left the restaurant. Philip didn't want her cooking for strangers when she could be at home doing the same thing for him.

Jude checked her watch, a Patek Philippe that she wore loosely strapped on the underside of her wrist. She saw me looking at it. "I know, it's ridiculous for him to spend so much money. I liked my old Swatch, but Philip has this thing about showing off his cash." She shrugged. "I guess we should call it a night."

On the way out, she flung her arm around my shoulder. "You may not know it, but you're strong. You'll survive this and meet someone else. You'll get another job, a better one. But you need to stop drinking and focus on something else other than bloody Anton."

I hugged her goodbye and wept all the way home. In the sitting room, the green light of the answering machine winked at me. One message. "I feel bad," Anton said over the bustle of the kitchen. "But in time you'll see it's for the best. I didn't mean to hurt you. I hope you'll understand one day." The last bottle of wine was in the kitchen, a rough Rioja, half-empty. Not enough for total oblivion, but it would help. I had it to my mouth, just about to swallow, when I remembered Jude's advice. She was right. I emptied it down the sink before I could change my mind.

Anton continued to call every couple of days. I didn't call back. It would hurt too much to speak to him, to hear the pity in his voice when all I longed for was a passionate declaration that he'd made a mistake and that he was coming back. I kept telling myself that it was over. You only felt sorry for someone after you'd shut the door in their face. It was so shaming to be pitied.

"I've sent you a reference and two months' salary." A sucking noise. He must have started smoking again. "I've been considering things and it's the least I could do."

Oh really. We had something in common then, even after he'd left me. I'd been considering a few things as well. Like how I supported him and loved him without asking for anything in return, because that love kept me going and because I thought he cared for me. Like how I worked all those extra hours and sought out those suppliers from all over England who brought their flowers and herbs and fish and meat to the restaurant, all the things that lifted Anton et Amis above the competition, that made the food critics rave and people book a table three months in advance. I thought we were that old-fashioned thing, a team of two. Apparently all that counted for nothing when things got a bit tough and he came across someone prettier and richer.

Yes, Anton, I had her face on my computer screen seconds after Jude told me her name. A party girl with a Notting Hill address, rippling black hair, and a color-coordinated poodle, as well as a father willing to invest a million or two in your restaurant business. I spat on her image and then I threw up again.

Jude rang each morning on her way home after dropping off the twins at nursery. She listened to me weep for a fortnight and then she adopted the practical approach.

"I keep telling you that you'll move on. People usually do, if only because they have no choice."

I wasn't so sure. "I've never felt so alone. When Gran died, I had Anton. Now Anton is gone, I have no one."

"You're not listening. You have me," Jude said sharply. "And you need to get a grip on the self-pity. The best way to get over this is to get another job real fast. Times are much better now. There are restaurants opening all over London. It doesn't matter what they say about bankers' scandals and austerity. Philip says there's money to burn out there. There's a new place in Hoxton. You'd get a job there—anywhere. There aren't many people who are as organized in a kitchen as you are."

Jude was right. I did need a job. Anton's guilt payment wouldn't last forever. But when I looked through all the available positions—and there were quite a few—somehow I never managed to make an appointment for an interview. I couldn't face the inevitable gossip and sly asides that I'd have to stare down in any London restaurant kitchen. I'd have to prove myself all over again. Just thinking about it gave me the jitters. I couldn't shake off the memory of the last humiliating day in the restaurant. Everyone smirking. Anton's nervous blinking. Others might have stayed and put up a fight. I no longer had it in me.

3

❦

No matter how bad your day has been, no matter
the disappointments and failures you have encoun-
tered, be mindful that it is over and take time to
plan your triumphs for tomorrow. Draw strength
from all your past experiences and your early life,
everything that has informed you.

—Emma Helmsley, "Taking the Moment," February 6, 2016

Now that I'd lost everything that made me a functioning adult—
the desirable partner, the job, the long hours, and the sense of
responsibility—the scared child inside me took over. I'd never
heard of this scared child syndrome before, but it was something Emma Helmsley wrote about in one of her blogs. Silly I
know, but in those blogs, I felt she was talking directly to me.

I was interested in the other things she wrote about on her
website, like work-life balance and successful networking, even
though they didn't have huge relevance for chefs. How to make
your mark in the boardroom. Leading a winning team. Tips on
time management. "Spend the first 30 minutes of every morning making a schedule for the day," she advised. "Before an important phone call, give yourself five minutes to think through
your strategy."

All I wore at work was a white chef's jacket and an apron, so
I wasn't her target audience for wardrobe advice either. Still, I
read what she had to say. "Keep colors neutral. You can always
add a bright splash with a scarf!"

"Plan what you're going to wear each day at the beginning of the week. You'll save loads of time!"

Her household tips sometimes made me smile ("Dance while you dust! You'll burn calories and be finished in half the time!"), but I always rushed through them to concentrate on "Taking the Moment." If she'd suggested meditation or some contorted yoga pose while staring up at the sky, I would have dismissed it straightaway. All that was too open-ended for me. I would have moped about and thought about Anton and the mess of my life yet again. But Emma asked her followers to put aside ten minutes every day and consider a specific topic.

She was big on the idea that as an adult, you should be your own boss and not allow the childish part of you to take control. It was so simple and apparently well known, but I'd never heard about it, or even thought about it. I found myself rereading what she'd written again and again. Emma said that often when people were scared about the future or lacking confidence in their jobs, they retreated into the childish part of themselves, the time when they were scared of the dark or frightened to be on their own. That was a mistake, said Emma. It held you back and stopped you from being happy. She wanted people to imagine one part of themselves as a nurturing parent, someone who would take care of the other part of themselves who was an unhappy child. This made me think of my own early years with Gran and the unremembered time before that. I'd never been keen to play psychological detective games with my own past, and people who droned on about their childhood invariably bored me. But maybe Emma had a point—and it wasn't like I was pressed for time.

Shaftesbury, Dorset, 1986. "I came top of the class today," I said, tucking my bag between my legs. I was six years old and

I'd just started school for the first time. But I got the hang of it soon enough, although I got lost between the toilet and the classroom twice in the first week and the others teased me because I'd never heard of hopscotch and didn't know how to play any games.

"Don't boast." Gran chided me. "Ladies never boast."

"But I did," I replied. "I always come top of the class. I'm good at tests." There was a loud crunch as she changed gears. The engine spluttered, then settled into its usual rattle. "Wretched car, always going wrong." She peered into the autumn rain through the slap of the windscreen wipers. "In any event, you mustn't rest on your laurels." But she couldn't resist a congratulatory tap on my knee. "Well done, Anne."

"Annastasia." I sulked, wanting something more than a tap on my knee for coming first, like a bar of chocolate or a brand-new schoolbag instead of a battered one with a broken strap. "My name is Annastasia—Annastasia Swan."

"Can you spell that name?" asked Gran. She swerved to avoid a pothole. Our lane was full of them. Gran had complained to the local council, but they never did anything. "Can you spell it out loud to me?"

I shook my head. "I can say it though. Annah . . . stahsja."

"Well if you can't spell it, then Anne is better, much less . . ." Gran trailed off. Her hands, covered in raised blue veins, gripped the wheel. "Much less fanciful. And even though your mother called you Annastasia Swan, her name was Marianne Morgan. And the name Morgan might be more useful than Swan, because Morgan is my surname too. If we have the same surname, then people will know we belong to each other."

Even then, I could see the sense of that, and I liked the idea of belonging to someone, somewhere. I knew already that I was an odd child, and I could see I was having an odd childhood.

No mother. No father. Not even a family pet. I worried that I might always be looking in from the outside.

"We do belong together now, because your mother isn't with us anymore." Gran made it sound as if my mother was somewhere else, which I thought for a while meant that she might come back. Eventually I understood that my mother was dead and any return was out of the question.

The time before Gran, when I was with my mother, was always blurred and never talked about. When I was young, vague stories satisfied me. By the time I was ten, my questions became more doggedly specific. But whenever I asked about my mother, or where my father was and why he never came to see me—and I did this often—Gran wouldn't meet my eye. She would clasp her hands together, so tightly that her knuckles whitened, and say that she didn't know and it didn't matter.

"Your mother asked me to look after you, because she wasn't well. She had an illness in her mind, something she'd had for a long time, even before you were born. Then she had a heart attack and died." Always at this point in my interrogations, she began chewing at the edge of her mouth. "It was very sudden and sad. I never knew your father . . . When you were little, your mother and I didn't see each other very much because you didn't live in Dorset. So I never got to meet him."

A thin line would appear across her forehead that made me fall silent. Was it something I said? I would think every time. Was it something I did to make you have a heart attack? Or something I didn't do, to make you go away?

"I'm sorry, but you never get anywhere digging about in the past," Gran would say, busying herself at the sink or the stove, her sign that the conversation, such as it was, had ended. "Because you can never work out what was true and what wasn't. No one can ever tell, so it's best to leave it. You live with me now."

Gran was a tall, thin woman with hair like the Queen's,

a gray bouffant helmet molded into shape each week with heated rollers skewered to her head after she had washed it. I often examined her long nose and sharp cheekbones, looking for signs of my own rounded face and pale green eyes. I never found any. Even our hands were different. Gran's hands were narrow with long bony fingers. Mine were square and my fingers were short and chubby. She was my protector and my provider, but it wasn't a role that came naturally to her. She always expected the worst. "I'm doing my best," she would shout sometimes, flailing at the floor with a worn-out broom. "I'm trying my hardest to make it enough."

Every now and then, I thought I might have more luck asking about my grandfather. "Oh, we're all right, just the two of us," she said, ignoring my interrogations. "We get along perfectly fine. We don't need anyone else." I wouldn't have minded a dog that slept on the end of my bed at night, but I knew that was out of the question.

The only thing I'd known with any certainty was my name. Now that that had changed to Anne Morgan, I began to feel that Annastasia Swan was another person who had very little to do with me. It was as if my life had begun when I was five years old, when Gran came to get me from somewhere outside Cardiff, and we set off for our new existence in Shaftesbury. But where exactly was I before then? I didn't remember. Sometimes I saw myself playing in front of a caravan, a pile of tractor tires against a tree. At other times I was running barefoot down a long corridor, the sun dancing on the floorboards. I recalled the pungent smell of a bonfire smoldering against a dull autumn sky and the sharpness of blackberries eaten from a hedge. I knew that my mother and I had moved around a lot, because Gran told me. But I never knew exactly where we'd moved, or why.

I had only one memory of my mother. In my head there

was a picture of a beautiful woman smiling into the sun with a cloud of long hair blowing behind her like a trail of gold dust. But that might have been because there was a photograph exactly like that in a silver frame on the bookcase behind the sofa. Next to it was another photograph of her sitting cross-legged on a picnic rug, holding me as a baby and smiling at whoever was holding the camera. My face was obscured by her arms, so I had no idea what I looked like. I was always sure that my father was the one with the camera.

There was also a ring that Gran said had belonged to Marianne. She kept it in a box, next to her pearls. It was turquoise and silver with two carved beetles on either side. Over the years, the silver had scratched and the heads and claws of the beetles had blackened. Whenever I took it out, I always expected the stone to be warm, like skin, and was surprised to find it cool and tacky. Later on, the ring disappeared, and because I wasn't meant to be snooping, I could never ask Gran what had happened to it.

We lived in a small redbrick house set right on the lane, next to a group of tall, gloomy pine trees. A wooden shed with a rusted tin roof stood to one side. It wasn't what I'd hoped for, all through the long drive from Wales, bursting to go to the toilet and too scared to say anything until I wet my pants. Gran had to pull over by the side of the road and take off my clothes. I didn't have anything else to wear, so she wrapped me in an old towel that she produced from under the backseat.

"Here we are then," said Gran as she bumped the car into the space in front of the shed. "This is where you live now." I picked up my wet clothes and clutched the towel around me as I followed her into a narrow hall lit by a dim lamp, with a small sitting room on one side and a kitchen on the other.

"I thought you might like some cocoa," she said, switching on the stove. "And maybe some toast." She produced a loaf of bread from a cupboard, cut two slices, and put them in a toaster. "But first, we'd better get rid of these." She took my trousers and underwear and threw them into a bin. "Don't do that again," she said. "Now, would you like to see where you'll sleep?"

I nodded, and she took me into a small room with a bed, a table beside it, and a chair in the corner. The walls were painted brown, like paper bags.

"Do you like it?" asked Gran.

"Oh yes, yes," I lied. "It's lovely." She nodded and we went back into the kitchen, full of smoke from the burned toast. Gran scraped off the black bits and buttered what was left. We sat on either side of the table and chewed in silence.

Most of our time was spent in the kitchen. The other rooms—the sitting room on the other side of the hall and another small room with no obvious use—were too expensive to heat in winter and smelled of damp stone in the summer. The house stood in the middle of a small garden that backed onto fields. Gran was too busy working all day and then too tired at night and on the weekends to do anything about flowers or color. There were a couple of evergreen shrubs at the edges and a stunted pear tree outside the back door.

Every day, Gran would negotiate the bends and potholes in our lane and enter the main road a mile or so before the local primary school. She dropped me off, then drove on to her job as secretary in a solicitor's office on Gold Hill in the old center of Shaftesbury. The school had a tarmac entrance with bumps on it that caused you to trip if you weren't looking, and an area of scrubby grass out the back where we ran around. It was full of tough-bodied farmers' children, travelers' offspring, and the dregs of the West Country. I'd been there for about two years when my teacher, Mrs. Armstrong, asked to see Gran after school. Mrs. Armstrong told me to sit in the library while she spoke to Gran, but I snuck back along the corridor as soon as I heard the office door close.

"The girl has an exceptional ability in both maths and English," I overheard Mrs. Armstrong say. "And a great appetite for learning."

"Oh," said Gran. "I thought you'd called me in because there was a problem. Bad behavior. Understandable under the circumstances." Teacups rattled. A chair scraped on the floor.

"Not at all," said Mrs. Armstrong. "I wanted to tell you her talent could remove her from all this into another level altogether. Not just yet, but at the right time. I think we should start preparing her for better things. I have in mind a full boarding scholarship at one of the best schools in the southwest. Stanton Hall. I've no doubt that your granddaughter will win one."

The kettle made its bubbling sound. I ran back to the library and banged rows of books up and down the shelves. I didn't want to be removed to another level altogether. I liked Mrs. Armstrong and I loved her lessons. Everyone else in the classroom was bored and couldn't wait to get out of the place every day. Not me. I couldn't get enough of spelling bees and rote learning and history dates and times tables. The certainty that two times three made six every time was thrilling. The satisfaction of knowing that encyclopedia was always spelled the same way made me grin.

I even had a best friend, Douglas, who stopped the others from teasing me about all the games I didn't know how to play. He was the tallest boy in the class and no one dared to challenge him. I was safe. Douglas's father cleared drains and septic tanks, and there was always a faint smell of toilets about him. Because it was overlaid by soap, I didn't mind. We sat next to each other all the time, even when we changed classrooms each year. He taught me to ride a bicycle when I was seven.

We practiced kissing when I was ten. How much better could it get?

"Such an opportunity," said Mrs. Armstrong, as she handed me a set of test papers during lunch hour, alone in the empty classroom smelling of dust and chalk, everyone shouting and playing outside. "A privilege to be even asked to do the exam," Gran had said the night before. After school that afternoon, I inched closer to Douglas. "I don't want to go," I whispered. He shifted away. The other boys teased him for being a pansy because we played together. He walked towards the bus stop, and I whispered to the bumping satchel on his back, "I don't want to leave you."

A month later, Mrs. Armstrong summoned me to her office. "You're in trouble now," said Douglas and everyone tittered. An envelope, already open, lay on her desk, and she drew out the page inside, like a magician drawing a rabbit from a hat. "Now your mind will be extended as it should be," said Mrs. Armstrong. I burst into tears, and she took me in her arms, patting my head against her bony chest. "It's a lot to take in, I know, all the excitement. It can be overwhelming."

Halfway through the summer holidays, Douglas and I returned home from tramping about the woods one afternoon to find Gran already in the kitchen, opening boxes on the table and placing clothes into various piles to take upstairs. On my bed, Gran laid out my new school uniform with reverence. Just below the pillow was a felt Sunday hat, then a white shirt with a round collar, a hideous maroon sweater, and a checked flannel skirt. Underneath the skirt were kneesocks with a little flag at the folded over bit, and on the floor were lace-up shoes. I understood in some way that I had to fill out these clothes. I had to make them my own. I felt like one of those old-fashioned cardboard dolls with paper clothes that you cut out and stuck on them in a game of dressing up.

"Let's see it, let's see it on you then," shouted Douglas. Gran ushered Douglas out of my room and shut the door. The weight of her expectation, standing outside in the hall.

I stripped off my shorts and T-shirt and put on my new clothes. The shirt buttons rubbed against my neck. The socks scratched. The shoes hurt my heels. Everything smelled of starch and chemicals, like a dry cleaner's shop.

"Come in," I said, and Gran and Douglas were beside me, Gran bursting with pleasure, Douglas scared and backing off.

"It's for the best," said Gran, worried about my friendship with Douglas. The future she wanted for me did not include drains and septic tanks, human waste in all its forms. I was only eleven years old, but already she envisaged an alliance with a boy from Eton or Harrow, a brother of one of my future classmates. She wanted a successful grandchild, payment due for all that hard work.

Stanton Hall was near Salisbury, twenty miles away. It had stone entrance pillars wider and taller than our house. The gates were black, shiny wrought iron, with an emblem emblazoned in red and gold on a circle: a lion clawing at a shield. We drove through. On the backseat, taking up all the space, was Gran's old brown suitcase studded with brass nails. There was a rasping noise as my shoes and clothes, each item identified by carefully sewn on name tapes, slid from one end of the suitcase to the other. The drive curved through clumps of tall oaks and past a dark lake edged with bullrushes. "Oh, how beautiful!" Gran exclaimed. "How lucky you are!"

We passed playing fields with white fences and hockey nets, then tennis courts. Gran crunched the gears around a sharp corner, and ahead of us loomed a gray stone building with a series of columns and wide steps leading to a terrace. Among all this, girls roamed in pairs or packs, wearing with ease the uniform that I had struggled to put on that morning. One girl had pushed up the sleeves of her sweater. She looked casual, almost elegant. Another had flung it around her shoulders, like a model in a magazine. How confidently they loitered, all the same, as if they had joined a club in the womb, a club that made them better than everyone else.

Gran pulled up and opened her door. "Remember, you're just as good as all these girls," she whispered. "Just as good."

A red-faced man heaved my suitcase onto a barrow and wheeled it towards the dormitories. "This way," he said, mopping his forehead with his sleeve. Gran gave me a brusque peck on my cheek and pushed me out of my seat. "It's for the best," she said, her voice quivering. She snapped on her sunglasses. "Remember that." She drove off, not looking back.

4

∞

Define your dream and work to make it reality. Never be afraid of what you might achieve right now, at this very second. The past and the future are beyond our control, so be mindful of the present and the joys it can offer us all.

—Emma Helmsley, "Taking the Moment," February 9, 2016

It wasn't my normal practice to hang about for a daily update from a stranger, but Emma's messages, delivered to my inbox punctually every twenty-four hours, had become one of the few reliable structures in my day. I'd even developed a ritual about the whole thing. I'd read aloud what Emma had to say and then sit cross-legged on the floor and set the timer on my phone for ten minutes. I just waited for thoughts to enter my consciousness. I'd always considered knowledge to be a collection of facts and conclusions that I could gather together, like herding sheep into a pen and shutting the gate. Boxes to be ticked. Right or wrong. Yes or no. This was completely the opposite. Sometimes I almost fell into a trance until the ping of the timer jolted me back into reality.

When I told Jude about Emma, she laughed and called it a girl crush. I suppose it was. I bought her books and looked at her Facebook page and the photos on her Instagram account. There she was with Rob at a Lucian Freud retrospective at the Royal Academy, their heads curved towards each other like mating birds. A handsome pair, fashionably disheveled. Soon after the Freud exhibition, there was Emma at a party for the London Book Fair, chatting to a Pulitzer Prize–winning author. The author looked as if he was laughing at something Emma had said. There were more pictures of Emma, on a government committee discussing the need for increased maternity leave, her finger pointing to an unseen person. There was a link to a recent *Vanity Fair* poll listing them as one of London's Top 20 power couples.

There were links as well to Rob's Facebook page and his website. Compared to Emma's breezy advice and multiple exclamation marks, his stuff was dull. There were lists of his academic articles, reviews of biographies he'd written of famous psychologists and psychiatrists. They sounded more like textbooks than something you might want to read on a bus or train. There were photographs of people he had interviewed for his BBC television program. The list was impressive. Paul McCartney. Stephen King. Bill Gates. You get the picture. He'd been presenting it for more than ten years. People compared it to *Desert Island Discs*, except guests talked about their fears and neuroses instead of their favorite pieces of music. As well as choosing either books or music to take with them to their favorite place, they could also choose parts of themselves to leave behind, like their fear of flying, or crippling social anxiety. There were reviews of the program as well. Critics said he was perceptive and insightful, that he had a chocolate voice and a way of making people tell him things.

In between reading Emma's advice and checking out her life online, I slept at odd hours for too long and found myself eating breakfast at midnight or lunch at dawn. Not that it mattered. For once, food was not my preoccupation. I tried not to think about the blankness of my life, the lack of a job, the absence of Anton. I missed the routine of the kitchen, the jokes and easy camaraderie in the run-up to the lunch and dinner service. I told myself that I was free for the first time in years, and I was. But that didn't make it any less lonely.

Every memory stung, like a bandage ripped off too quickly—the thing that was meant to heal you instead tearing your skin apart, leaving it raw and jangling. I guess it was inevitable when a person found herself unemployed for the first time in two decades, when she'd been accustomed to fifteen-hour working days with no time to think about anything except how to do her job as well as humanly possible. The interminable hours between morning and evening, how they seesawed between anxiety and boredom.

"Too much time on your hands," said Jude a fortnight later. "Is Anton still leaving messages?"

"Not so many now," I said. It was almost noon and I was still in pajamas. I hadn't washed my hair for a week. "Maybe one in the past ten days."

"Have you deleted them?"

I didn't reply immediately, but she knew me too well.

"Delete them. Right now. Then text him and tell him not to call you again." I did as she said and paced up and down. The small flat made me feel trapped. The thought of another day here on my own was unbearable.

I showered and dressed and set off on a long pounding run along the Brentford Locks on the Grand Union Canal. At first my muscles protested and my lungs burned, but after a while, I settled into my familiar rhythm. I enjoyed running, the pleasurable shock of my feet hitting the ground, the change in my rate of breath, the pull on my leg muscles. I liked the way I felt connected to everything around me—the smell of grass and cars, my own sweat, the air that cleared my mind as I pushed through it—and still felt so free.

The towpath was deserted. There was just the thump of my footsteps and the slap of the water against the banks, with an occasional splash from ducks paddling by. After about half a mile, a high stone wall replaced the bare trees. Halfway along there was the glint of a bronzed plaque, made iridescent by the reflection of the water. I stopped to read it and drink some water. Behind the wall was once the largest asylum in the world, built by the renowned master builder of the Victorian age, William Cubitt. Nearby was a bricked-up door, where coal and food had once been unloaded from barges for the inmates locked away from the world, so close to the river but never allowed to see the sun dance on the water.

It started to rain just as I turned for home, not a polite London drizzle, but a heavy winter downpour, like the Dorset storms of my childhood.

Shaftesbury, Dorset. 1989. "We can't go out in this," said Douglas. The rain was falling hard. We couldn't see to the end of the path and the leak in the kitchen had started up again. "So what are we going to do all day?" We'd already explored the downstairs rooms, and I worried that Douglas might become bored and not come anymore, so I took him upstairs to Gran's bedroom. I wanted to show him the jewelry box with Gran's pearl necklace and my mother's turquoise ring. This was before it disappeared. But Douglas wasn't interested in jewelry. "I'm not some bloody poofter," he said, looking around the room. "What's that up there?" He pointed to Gran's hatbox.

"Nothing much. Just boring old hats," I said. I'd never been tall enough to reach it. Douglas pulled down the hatbox from the top of the wardrobe and untied the navy ribbon. Dust puffed under his fingers. He dropped the lid onto the floor and began rummaging through Gran's straw hats and felt berets. He put a scarlet beret on one side of his head and danced about the room. "Hey, look at me," he laughed. "I'm a jolly Frenchman."

"Put it back," I shouted. "She'll find out and then we'll be in big trouble."

"Killjoy," he retorted, but he took off the beret and threw it back into the box. "What are those papers at the bottom?" asked Douglas. "Your Gran's old love letters?"

"Don't be stupid," I said. "No one's ever been in love with her. Anyway, they're private." But I took them out anyway. We sat next to each other on the bed and unfolded them.

The papers weren't anything to do with love. They were all about my mother's death, every detail neatly laid out in an official report from the Cardiff Coroner's Court. We had to look up some of the words, like schizophrenia, in the dictionary. A long-term mental disorder, we read, involving delusions and inappropriate behavior. "Gran always said she had an illness in her mind," I said.

"Bloody hell," said Douglas. "This means your mother was a bloody nutcase. She should have been in the loony bin."

"Gran said she was ill," I whispered. The shock and shame, to have a nutcase mother. "Ill in the head . . . You won't tell. I don't want anyone to know."

"Don't worry," he said. "Not a word, not even to Dad." He felt in his pocket and produced a half-empty packet of crisps. We ate in silence and read the report. Crumbs and grains of salt fell on the pages. I brushed them away, but tiny oily specks remained. The coroner, someone called Dr. Edward Langbridge, said a hiker had found my mother's body in an abandoned trailer in the middle of a wood outside the city. Dr. Langbridge said there were many aspects of this sad case that he found unusual and puzzling. Although there was a record of a diagnosis of schizophrenia (a sad and often tragic illness, he said) at eighteen years of age, and then a record of my birth (father unknown), there was nothing after that date. My mother had to be identified by her dental records, as she wasn't registered anywhere. There was no mention of her name on any electoral rolls, in hospitals or welfare organizations. It was as if she had moved through the world like an invisible person. Maybe that explained why I always imagined I was invisible as well, until Gran came to collect me and I could be seen again.

There was a statement from her (Mrs. Florence Morgan, Shaftesbury Dorset, England, mother of deceased, unable to attend because of work commitments and child care duties). Apparently my mother had rung her from a telephone box in a service station along the M4, just after the Severn Bridge, and asked Gran to pick me up and look after me for a while. The service station manager (David Llewellyn, Chepstow, Monmouthshire, Wales, also unable to attend because of work commitments) stated he'd found a young child in a distressed state wandering between parked lorries. He was under the impression that the child had been alone for some time. He was about to call the police when the child's grandmother arrived and took the child with her. The hiker (Chad Cooper, firefighter, Vancouver, Canada) wrote that he had telephoned the police as soon as possible after he found my mother's body. The discovery was shocking and he still had nightmares about it.

Then we heard Gran's car in the lane, and quickly put everything back into the hatbox before she walked in, gray-faced with tiredness and carrying bags of cut-price shopping. That night, I lay in bed, my mouth moving around the edges of the new word I had learned. "Schiz." My teeth closed against each other. "O." My mouth opened into a surprised circle. "Phrenia." My front teeth bit down on my bottom lip until I winced in pain.

I was odd enough already, the only person in my class with no mother or father, just Gran with her heated rollers and pursed lips. Now I had a nutcase mother who should have been in the loony bin instead of wandering around Wales like a shadow, leaving no trace of herself anywhere, except when she died. I held the pillow tight over my head. If only I could stop breathing and thinking. I remembered a magazine article I'd read in the dentist's waiting room once. The article was called "Making Boxes," and I thought it was something I might be able to do with Douglas. He liked woodwork. But the article was about another type of box, an imaginary one. See the things and memories that upset you, the article said. Imagine a box, something sturdy with a lock and a key. Open the box and put the memories and things that upset you inside. Take care. Don't hurry. Don't be distracted. Close the lid. Lock the box and throw away the key. Now throw away the box.

By the time I had run home, my arms were mottled blue with cold and goose pimpled. Even my socks were wet. I changed my clothes, but as I grew warm again, I became so drowsy that I fell asleep on the sofa and woke up hours later in a blaze of afternoon sun. The rays were skittering along the gutters and roofs of nearby buildings, setting the room on fire.

There was that fraction of time before I registered that I was no longer with Anton. It still hurt. But maybe Emma Helmsley was right. Maybe I should say goodbye to the scared child and her fear of abandonment, the one who hated boarding school and all those snobby girls who sneered at me because my house was smaller than one of their many garages. That was more than twenty years ago. Time to get over it.

I went to my computer. Among the lists of jobs for chefs in hotels and country houses, there was one for a sous-chef in a new restaurant in Knightsbridge. Before I could think further, I rang the number and made an appointment for the next morning.

The restaurant was in a redbrick building in a side street

behind Harrods. I'd expected the usual overdone velvet and plush and was surprised by the bright bare room with its pale wooden floors and the open-plan kitchen with the staff on show. But I had my roll of sharpened knives and I'd worn my sensible shoes. I was prepared.

"This way, please come," said the skinny head chef. His name was Lars. He was at least ten years younger than me and had a pronounced Danish, or it might have been Swedish, accent. His office was large, with pots of basil and thyme placed at regular distances on steel shelves. His desk was empty apart from a small open laptop.

"Yes," he said, examining the screen. "Very experienced, I see." I'd emailed my résumé the night before. "But here, we are different. Not so much butter and cream all the time. More foraging and natural cuisine."

"I can adapt, I think," I replied. "I mean, maybe." Behind his head, through the glass window, I recognized one of the pastry cooks. She'd started at Anton et Amis at the same time as me, but had left after about eight months. She'd flirted with Anton. I'd never liked her. She glanced across at me and turned to whisper to the man snipping herbs next to her. He looked up. They nudged each other and rolled their eyes. In front of me Lars was waiting for a more convincing reply.

"I'm not sure. I'm sorry," I said. "I don't know if I could cope. I don't feel very well. I have to go." I rushed out, my sensible shoes squeaking loudly on the wooden floors. When I reached the street, I saw Lars through the window looking perplexed while behind him people whispered and giggled. Shame rushed through me. I could never work there, or anywhere else in my former world. I'd been a fool to think I could.

5

Too often we look at our failures as the end of
something, when they can actually be a beginning
of something new and exciting. All of us can learn
positive things from our failures, but only if we
allow ourselves to.

—Emma Helmsley, "Taking the Moment," March 19, 2016

I emptied the washing machine and draped my damp clothes
about the flat. Of all Emma's messages that I'd considered so
far, this was the most difficult. It was almost annoying, as if
underneath all the empathetic words and pithy advice Emma
didn't have a clue about my life or anyone else's. I thought of
my meager bank balance and how the mortgage and utility bills
ate so much money each month. I wasn't rich and successful
like Emma. Perhaps many of her followers could hang about
waiting for something new and exciting to show up. I couldn't
afford that luxury much longer. Perhaps her followers went to
parties and dinners where they came across new and exciting
people who transformed their lives on a daily basis. I couldn't
remember the last time I'd been invited to a party or a dinner.

Apart from Jude, my most frequent human contact was
with Ahmed, the surly man who owned the corner store where
I bought my groceries. He was middle-aged and stocky with
cheeks covered in gray stubble, and he always grabbed the
money from my hand as if I was about to do a runner with my
loaf of bread and pint of milk. Last night, I walked in to buy

laundry detergent. There was an old woman in front of me at the checkout, carefully laying out her items. A small jar of instant cocoa. Two small cans of cut-price salmon. A large can of spaghetti hoops and, doubtless her special treat, an economy pack of chocolate bars. Ahmed drummed his fingers on his thighs as the woman counted out her money.

"It's been a nice day," I said, just to hear the sound of my own voice talking to someone other than Jude. Ahmed and the woman ignored me. I imagined her at home, taking time to open the cans with her swollen arthritic fingers, sucking on her chocolate bar in front of the television. She had almost finished packing everything into a used carrier bag when the can of spaghetti hoops rolled onto the floor. I picked it up and returned it to her. She grabbed the can off me, like she'd caught me trying to steal it. It was a warning of a possible future, one I didn't like the look of.

The next morning I sat on the floor, closed my eyes, and considered how to turn my failures into something new and exciting. It didn't work. There was nothing new and exciting about any restaurant job that I might apply for. I was either going to be the kitchen joke, the scorned woman who was so dim she didn't realize her boyfriend had someone else, or I would have to move away from that small circle of top London restaurants and get a job at some country hotel where the food was delivered in plastic bags and reheated to order and none of the customers even noticed. OK. I was exaggerating. But I was still rattled by my experience in the Danish restaurant, the scornful look on the pastry cook's face. I still yearned for Anton.

I told myself that I would look at Emma's Instagram page, go for a run, and then attempt the entire exercise again. I opened my laptop and scrolled down, admiring a vase of primroses that a fan had given her after a talk in Ipswich. Gran and I used to pick them along the lane where they grew wild beneath the hedges. Below the photo of the flowers was one of Emma wearing rubber kitchen gloves and looking in a bemused way into an oven. The caption read, "Housework and cooking not my natural calling. Am going to get someone professional to help me out, pronto!" It was clearly a joke, because no one in their right mind would wear rubber gloves to take something out of a hot oven. She'd probably post something amusing about it the next day.

I locked the door and set off for the river. Again, I found myself heading towards the river at Hanwell, past the asylum to the series of five locks. Those eighteenth-century engineers on the Grand Union Canal had managed to upend nature and raise the water level more than sixteen meters in half a mile. I liked that—the triumph of willpower over the gravity of water, the idea that you didn't have to succumb to those innate laws that governed the planet. The engineers had thought of everything; small side ponds to conserve water and even steps down to the canal, so horses that stumbled and fell from the towpath could be rescued.

It was a cold, bright day with a breeze that scudded along the water and lifted the tentative haze from the tops of the trees. I took my jacket from my backpack and wrapped it around me and sat down on a small triangle of grass in the last of the morning sun. I closed my eyes, expecting the usual sadness and loneliness to push up. I waited for the thought of Anton and his new lover, the thump that inevitably accompanied the surfacing of that thought. But there was only an eddy of cool air lifting the hairs on my arms. Maybe I wouldn't run home just yet. Maybe I would stay here and do as Emma suggested, think about failure and endings and beginnings. I thought about Huckleberry Finn and how he woke up one morning and decided to light out for the territory. It probably wasn't just a whim. He probably considered his decision more carefully than that.

I didn't get up from that patch of grass on the towpath think-ing that I could change anything about my life. There was no bolt of lightning, no Saint-Paul-on-the-road-to-Damascus type of epiphany as I ran home. There was, however, something that might have been a possibility of an idea, and it hovered on the edges of my consciousness, almost teasing me as it appeared and disappeared like shifting mist. All through the rest of the day, as I fiddled about the flat, and through that evening as I cooked my dinner of green beans and lamb chops, the possibility floated through my mind until it settled as a fully formed idea.

No, I couldn't. The whole thing was completely mad.

Yes, I could.

But I had no experience.

Yes, I did.

I had plenty of experience, if only I was brave enough to talk about it.

But was I brave enough?

Or was this idea of mine very stupid?

Or worse, could it more accurately be described as cowardice?

Running away, like I ran away from school all those times?

Not necessarily, I told myself as I watched a rerun of Hercule Poirot on television, my plate and saucepans washed and dried by the kitchen sink. This could be different. Outside, a burglar alarm blared. Someone shouted. A motorbike roared past. I closed the window and went to my computer. I quickly wrote an email and sent it, then went to bed with my copy of Isabella. I read how sprinkling tea leaves or freshly mown grass on rugs be-fore sweeping kept bedrooms clean and sweet-smelling, and that grates should be polished daily, before I fell into an uneasy sleep.

Emma's assistant, who introduced herself as Fiona when I rang the office the next morning, was hesitant at first to even offer an interview, saying I was overqualified. "We haven't even advertised the position of a housekeeper yet, although we are definitely thinking about it." She had a polished kind of voice, like many of the customers in the restaurant. "So do you mind me asking how you heard about it?"

"A friend," I replied. "Actually, a friend of a friend mentioned it the other day." I went for a lighthearted tone, something that might contain the hint of a laugh or an exclamation mark. "And I thought, why not! I'm ready for a change!"

Silence. I didn't want to tell this Fiona that I'd been following Emma's Instagram account and was practically addicted to her daily messages. She would think I was some weird stalker and hang up immediately,

"I'm sorry, I didn't catch your name."

"Anne, with an 'e.' Anne Morgan."

"Anne, yes. Now I have your email in front of me." More silence. "The thing is that if Emma does decide to employ someone, she'll want someone who'll fit into family life. You seem very overqualified for the job, and our fear would be that you'd get bored after a couple of months and leave."

I had my reply ready before she finished. "I can see why you might think that, but look at my work history," I said, careful not to sound too eager or defensive. "I've been sous-chef at Anton et Amis for two years, and I worked for five years at the same place before that. So you can see I'm not a person who chops and changes."

Then, something more, a plausible explanation for the career path deviation. "I'd like to take a different direction in my life. The working hours are very long in restaurants and I was ill for a while last year. Although fully recovered now. And chefs spend a huge amount of time cleaning and wiping down, almost as much time as they do cooking. So I don't mind housework at all. Of course."

Of course. Even on the telephone, remember to smile, don't purse your mouth. No one wants a sad sack moping about the house. "I know you must be very busy, but I'm wondering if you've had a minute to look at my references." At the other end, a barely audible sigh. It might have been a sniff. Again, silence.

Perched on the edge of the sofa, hair awry and wearing my oldest tracksuit, I pictured Fiona, no doubt chic and highly groomed, scrolling down my email and quickly scanning its contents. She had to be impressed by the whole Anton et Amis thing. Unless you had the unlisted number, you had to wait for ages if you wanted to eat after 6:30 p.m.

"So sorry to lose Anne—an invaluable member of our team, but it seems her mind is made up," Anton had written in his reference. "No one who employs her in any capacity will ever regret it."

"I'll call you back," said Fiona. "Maybe by the end of the week."

"Thank you," I replied, trying to swallow down the hammering in my stomach. A good night's sleep would have helped. "And if there is anything else, anything at all, please call or email me."

Jude, rushing to pick up the twins from kindergarten, sighed into her mobile when I told her. "I can't believe you've applied for a job as a housekeeper, of all things. I don't care if it's for your beloved Emma Helmsley. I wouldn't care if it was for God himself. I thought you were going to try that new place in Bloomsbury. Philip and I had dinner there the other night. It's had rave reviews and they're looking for staff. You'd make it to head chef in less than a year. Then you'd be looking at getting your own place, with your own investors. Wouldn't you like to see the look on Anton's face if you did that? You're ruining your career, all over some stupid man. What a waste of good cooking talent." Brakes screeched in the background. "The way these school mothers drive! Look, martyrdom is so last year, darling one."

I sawed at a jagged thumbnail with a worn emery board. "I'm not being a martyr and it's not all about Anton. I want something different, something quieter for a while. I want to take a bit of time to sort things out. And let's face it, I need to get a job."

"Get a new man, get a new life." Jude sounded exasperated. "Everything is out there waiting for you. You're not going to find it scrubbing someone else's kitchen sink."

I spent the next three days painting the sitting room in the morning and running along the towpath in the afternoon. The sitting room didn't need repainting, but its carefully inoffensive gray walls had been getting to me and there had been a special offer on white paint at the hardware shop on the main road. Gran would have said white was too cold and antiseptic, but its blankness appealed to me. Fiona had said she would try to get back to me by the end of the week. But she could be busy. She could be away with Emma, or taking some time off. I'd give it until Monday or Tuesday next week. Then I'd call again. If it didn't work out, I would call the restaurant in Bloomsbury. At least Jude would be happy.

On Thursday afternoon, I took all my mess—the empty cans, the trays and paint-spattered newspaper pages—down to the garbage bins at the back of my building. The couple upstairs had replaced their usual cut-price Côtes du Rhône with Chilean Cabernet Sauvignon. The bachelor in the flat below was going through a Thai red curry phase. I jammed my rubbish into the bin, made sure the lid was secure, and went back upstairs.

I made myself a cup of mint tea and saw the telephone machine light blinking. One message. "I'm trying to contact Anne Morgan," the voice said. "It's Fiona, from Emma Helmsley's office. We spoke to each other earlier this week. Could you ring me back please, when you've got a minute?"

It was just 5 p.m. Plenty of time to return her call. I played the message again, trying to decipher the tone of her voice. Was it inviting and friendly and therefore about to offer me an interview? Or politely dismissive, a courtesy call at best? Was I frightened? I wasn't sure. I only knew that I didn't want to spend another night on my own, disappointed after being told I didn't get the job, or that there wasn't one to get. It could wait until the morning. At least then I wouldn't look quite so desperate.

The phone rang again before I'd had time to drink my tea. I left it for a bit, then picked up the receiver.

"Hello, is this Anne?" The voice was newly familiar.

"Yes it is." I scratched hard at a spot of dried paint on my arm. The paint came off, but my arm began to bleed. I pressed it against my jeans, dark blotches blooming along my thigh.

"It's Fiona, from Emma's office. Sorry to ring twice in the one afternoon . . ."

"That's fine," I blurted. "I was out when you called. I was just about to call you back."

"Well, Rob and Emma are both free tomorrow, which is unusual for them, given both their schedules. It's short notice, I know, but they were wondering if you might be able to have a chat with them at home in the morning. I won't be there. It would be just you and them. Nothing formal. More a conversation than a proper interview, just to get to know each other a bit."

"Yes, I'd like that, thank you."

"Ten a.m.?"

"Yes, that's perfectly convenient. Thank you."

Of course I already knew where they lived from my googling, but not their exact address. I scribbled down the street and the house number.

6

Cleanliness, punctuality, order and method, are essentials in the character of a good housekeeper . . .
Like "Caesar's wife" she should be "above suspicion" and her honesty and sobriety unquestionable; for there are many temptations to which she is exposed.

—*Mrs. Beeton's Book of Household Management*, 1861

My bus arrived in Richmond far too early for the interview, and I walked up and down the high street peering into department store windows until it was time to catch the next one towards the river. Apart from two American tourists wearing hiking boots, the bus was empty. It made its way through a deserted winding road with woods on one side and cows and horses in their winter blankets grazing in a field on the other. It was hard to imagine that less than a mile away there was a busy town with cinemas and shops and supermarkets.

"Different air they breathe here, love," said the bus driver as I got off. The American tourists bounded past me, eager to explore Richmond Park. "You've got nearly twenty-five hundred acres of park on one side and the Thames River on the other. Film stars, rock stars—they love it," he went on. "No change from ten, fifteen million quid for any of these houses."

"I'm going for a job interview," I replied. "Wish me luck."

He gave a thumbs-up sign and drove away. It had rained earlier and there was a smell of damp earth and wet grass. A flock of feral green parakeets flew overhead, a neon streak in a pale wintry sky. The air was filled with their dinning, a strident, joyous noise drowning out the more reserved birdsong from native robins and wrens.

I'd checked the route the night before, but I made a mistake and got off the bus one stop too early. Then the walk took longer than I'd expected, and the houses were so huge and far apart from each other that I had to jog the last bit, my skirt riding up my legs, my tights making that brushing fibrous noise, and my toes cramping, unaccustomed to high heels. I almost missed it because I was looking for a street number and all the houses had names instead. It was only when I looked closer that I saw the numbers painted in brown below the letter boxes. I walked along until I found the one I was looking for, barely visible on a high brick wall. Above it was a bronze plate engraved with a name. Wycombe Lodge. I stood for a minute to regain my composure and wipe the mud off my shoes.

Along the wall was a pair of wrought-iron gates, each bar as thick as my arm. The bottom half of each gate was covered with a solid sheet of black metal, so I couldn't see anything of the house from the street. I walked along to a wooden door with an intercom next to it. I swallowed hard and pressed the buzzer. The night before, I'd wondered whether to announce myself with my usual "Hi" or go for a more mature "Hello." I thought the second option would be safer, but I didn't get the chance to say anything at all. There was no voice at the other end, just a buzz as the door opened and then a click as someone hung up the intercom.

I pushed through to a glorious square house built of wine-colored brick. It was either Georgian or Queen Anne. I could never tell the difference. A climbing rose, still bearing some of last autumn's hips, reached all the way to the roof, softening what might have been an otherwise austere exterior. Sunlight bounced off the bank of tall windows on the first floor, almost blinding me. When my vision cleared, I saw I was standing in a graveled forecourt edged by giant topiary balls. An empty stone pond with a fountain stood in the middle, in front of a portico with white stucco columns. The door was open. I glimpsed a flagstone floor and a flash of red from a rug.

I walked towards the door, my shoes with their flimsy leather soles crunching and slipping over the gravel. It was uneven, almost bare in some places. In others, weeds had sprung up and fell over themselves at odd angles. The bottom of the pond was littered with browned leaves. Two pots containing scrawny bay trees stood on either side of the portico. Tucked out of sight behind them were plastic crates of empty wine bottles and dirty dinner plates. A clump of old telephone books, their pages all curled up, lay heaped in a corner.

"Come in, come in," called an unseen woman's voice. I walked into the empty hall, my heels echoing on the checkered flagstones before being muffled by a worn patterned rug. A curved staircase led up to the higher floors. Along the hall were three open doors, and at the end a pair of closed doors. I had no idea where to go and paused next to a narrow table with a rectangular gilt mirror leaning over it. Piles of letters were propped against a vase of fading white roses, the water green and scummy. Blotched petals fell onto a pair of muddy trainers.

"We're in here," said the voice, and I followed its sound into the first door opposite the staircase. Emma stood against the fireplace. Embers smoldered in the grate. She was taller than I'd expected, and she looked younger than she had in the photos, with a small heart-shaped face, the skin tight and gleaming across the bones. Her head was cocked to one side like a curious bird's. There was a crosshatch of fine lines around her eyes. At first I thought they were green, but then the sun broke through into the room and showed them to be an unusual clear blue with a dark ring around the iris. She wore Converse trainers and what looked like a thermal vest over a long, trailing skirt, the hem torn in places where she must have tripped over it.

"Hello, thank you so much for coming," she said in a voice like silk. "What a mess we're in. I'm so sorry." She made it sound as if our positions were reversed, as if I was the potential boss and she was the one who was under scrutiny. "We had a few friends to dinner last night." She did this little fluttery thing with her hands.

Just then Rob walked in, his mobile glued to his ear. He waved and started to walk out again. At the door, he paused long enough to hold his phone at arm's length. "Hi," he said. "Back in a minute."

"Everything went on a bit later than we thought," said Emma. She moved a vase of fading lilies from one table to another, seeming not to notice the bright yellow pollen sprinkling everywhere. "We're a bit done in, so sorry."

I knew the feeling. I'd been up until midnight myself, finally deciding on an irreproachable Marks & Spencer black skirt and checked jacket, an outfit that Emma herself might have advised prospective job applicants to wear to an interview. The unapologetic light above the bathroom mirror had showed the dark rings under my eyes as I practiced answering the questions she might ask. Best pronunciation, all crisp consonants and inoffensive vowels.

"I haven't actually done this type of work before . . ."

No. Too negative.

"I'm sure I could do the job to your satisfaction . . ."

Did that sound overconfident, arrogant even?

"I've been working in restaurants for years, and in so many ways it's the same as running a house . . ." Yes, that might work. Remember to smile. Try to get some sleep. In bed, I lay on my back and listened to the rise and fall of my breath. A cab pulled up across the road, its brakes squeaking. The headlights swung on the ceiling as it turned around and drove away. There was the clattering of garbage bins and the urgent scream of a fox, like a person pursued. After that, there was no sound until the raucous ping of my alarm.

Emma was gazing at me, nodding as if she'd agreed with something I'd just said. But I hadn't said anything at all. I knew she was expecting a response, something that would indicate my suitability for the job, that I wasn't the sort of person to show up at an interview and not have anything to say about myself.

"You must be so busy," I said. "With your work and talks and everything."

Was it the right kind of comment? Too late now. I brushed specks of pollen off my jacket and concentrated on keeping my body still and formal so the nerves inside wouldn't show themselves.

"I hope I'm not late," I said, although I knew I was punctual to the minute.

"Of course not," smiled Emma. Gold hoop earrings danced about her face. "Would you like to take a seat?"

I went to sit down, but she kept standing, so I straightened up again, feeling ridiculous, as if I'd begun to curtsy to her but changed my mind. I smiled, hoping that it was the kind of professional smile that might convey competence and efficiency.

The sitting room was large and elegant, with high ceilings covered in elaborate plasterwork. There were two windows at the front and French doors leading onto a garden at the other end. I sensed its history of lustrous evenings and lively conversation. But now the room and everything in it were at odds with each other, like split personalities. I'd imagined something smarter, maybe some of those Italian modular sofas with walls in shades of muted beige, and abstract pictures hung at orchestrated angles; or classic squashy sofas in chintz with elegant armchairs and antique sideboards.

I didn't expect the old-fashioned 1980s egg yolk–colored walls, the cracked bamboo side tables, and the rickety furniture. A high wing chair stood on one side of the fireplace opposite a faded sofa. Strands of stuffing—it looked like horsehair, although I couldn't be sure—were coming through. Scattered about were pairs of those Edwardian armchairs with cane sides and mahogany legs, all scarred with bits gouged out of them. There were holes in the rugs as well, patched from underneath with pieces of duct tape. Bits showed through, dull silver like discarded coins.

The mess of it all! Empty wineglasses smeared with fingerprints crowded the side tables, and three plates gummed with hardened cheese were scattered on the floor. Emma didn't seem to notice. She didn't even pretend to be embarrassed about everything skewed at odd angles, the candles left to collapse into gray stalagmites on the mantelpiece. And me so anxious the night before in my little box with the cushions prancing en pointe along the sofa, the coffee table at a perfect parallel, mugs washed up on the hour.

There had been no need for the Q and A session in front of the bathroom mirror either. Emma only asked two things. When could I start and did I like dogs? Right then, a small hairy cairn terrier made his entrance and peed on the rug right in front of me. Although I could see he was a male, he squatted like a bitch. I'd have tapped him on the nose with a rolled up newspaper and put him outside, but Emma giggled.

"Poor Siggy. All my fault. I forgot to let you into the garden. I'm sorry, little boy."

The dog's urine began to spread from a puddle to a large wet patch while Emma smiled and waited for me to reply to her questions. All I could think about was the urine seeping through the pile and how it would smell. I scrabbled in my bag for a wad of tissues, bent down and began blotting it. Emma did another hand fluttery thing.

"I should have thought of that, how silly. Naughty Siggy."

The dog wagged his tail and she leaned down and scratched his ears before picking up a wastepaper bin, full of wine corks and old newspapers, and offering it to me with an apologetic shrug. I put the sodden tissues in it.

There was a whoosh of air behind me and Rob came back into the room. He pocketed his mobile and rubbed his hands together. His eyes wandered around the walls and came to rest on me. Behind the rimless spectacles, they were alert and appraising. His gaze moved slowly and unapologetically around my face and head. I wasn't used to being studied so closely, and I worried that my appearance would be found deficient because of its very ordinariness, its lack of definition. The nervous hammering inside ratcheted up several notches. The room was so warm, almost hot. My neck pricked with perspiration. I shifted my feet. A tiny piece of gravel rubbed against my heel.

His face crinkled into a sudden disarming smile. "Well!" he exclaimed, opening his arms like a concert conductor, waving them around. "I'm afraid you've caught us a bit unawares." His voice had a slight northern burr, and it really was chocolate, the way critics described it. He didn't sound afraid at all. He was taller than Emma by about half a head, with a handsome olive-skinned face and thick black hair combed straight back from his forehead. He wore a crumpled pale blue linen shirt hanging out over faded jeans. He was barefoot, with long brown toes, reminding me of a monkey.

Both of them had the untroubled, slightly vacant look that I associated with effortless superiority and moneyed ease. Together they were more attractive than apart. Rob's darkness made Emma's fair skin and hair less bland and predictable, and her pale, fine features lightened what might otherwise have been a sallow cast to his face. He moved towards her and touched her shoulder. It was an affectionate gesture, but not an intimate one; just enough to make me feel an outsider. Rob folded his arms. Emma leaned against him and put her arm around his waist

"So, what do you think?" she asked. "Will you take us on? We're not that bad, really."

As if on cue from some invisible film director, they smiled. They were so sure I would like them, and they were right. For that moment, both were completely focused on me, and I felt that they believed in me, that they saw in me qualities I'd never noticed before. It seemed they liked me more than I liked myself, although they didn't know me at all. The feeling was immediate and almost too peculiar to express. It was like walking into a strange room and finding it acutely familiar.

"I hope we haven't ruined our chances with this mess from last night," said Emma, still clutching the wastepaper bin. "We promise to try to be good. And Jake and Lily are practically grown up. They're at school every day and we're out of the house at work, so you wouldn't have to put up with us being under your feet all the time."

She sat down on a cane chair and stroked Siggy's head with one hand. He closed his eyes and lifted his head. If he'd been a cat, he would have purred with pleasure.

"We wouldn't expect you to start too early in the morning, or stay late in the evening," she continued. "But we need someone to sort us out, just a bit. Keep us on the straight and narrow. Rob's got this book to get finished and I've got all this other stuff to do. So . . . would you, I mean could you . . . perhaps think about coming to work here?" Her voice was diffident, like she was asking a huge favor from a random stranger.

"Please say yes," said Rob, beaming and nodding at the same time.

"Yes, then. Yes," I repeated, not quite believing my good luck, how everything was falling into place around me like blossoms from a tree. "I'd love to."

I almost leaned towards them on the way to an embrace, before remembering that both Rob and Emma had never set eyes on me before that morning.

"What do you think?" asked Emma. "Maybe start sometime in the late morning and leave about seven p.m.?"

"I hope that's OK," said Rob. He mentioned an amount of money.

"It's fine. It's great." I'd never worked such a short day, and the salary was a bit less than I'd earned at Anton et Amis. But I was frugal.

Emma stood up, still clutching the wastepaper bin. "What a relief! Thank you so much. Fiona said that if we didn't snap you up right now, someone else would and we'd regret it for the rest of our days."

Once the interview, such as it was, had ended, Rob and Emma both began questioning me, one after the other, often interrupting. Was it true that Tony Blair had dined at the restaurant? Yes, I replied. He'd ordered from the set price menu.

"Really?" said Emma. "How interesting." At first I thought she was being merely polite, but her intent gaze and frequent nods indicated otherwise. Maybe she was trying to decipher the psychology of Blair's policy on the Middle East by whether he chose à la carte or prix fixe. Did his choice indicate a man who knew his own mind and would not be swayed by cholesterol-raising heftily priced plates of Scottish lobster and hand-fed beef fillet, or a certain economic meanness and lack of original thinking? How did this illuminate his political decisions? I'd read enough of Emma's books and blogs to know that any detail of a life, no matter how small or seemingly insignificant, had its own interest.

"And what about Madonna? What did she eat?" asked Emma, her hands clasped, leaning forward, so close that I could smell her scent, something woody and herbal. I had to plead ignorance on that one, as it had been my day off.

"Do people really spend a thousand pounds on a bottle of wine, or is that an exaggeration?" Rob asked.

"Sometimes," I said. "Hedge-funders on bonus day. People whose horse had won a big race or who'd bought or sold a company."

"I do hope you won't get bored too quickly," said Emma. There was a worried look on her face and she stared at me. "We're terribly dull and normal compared to all the people you've been working for. No scandals in our life. We just plod along from day to day. We don't even own a car. Are you really sure you won't get bored?"

"Not at all," I replied. It felt so good to have someone think what I'd done was interesting. "Besides, I was working in the kitchen, not sitting next to them at dinner."

"Well," said Emma. "It sounds pretty glamorous to us." A phone rang in another room and she jumped up. "That's someone I have to speak to. I'm sorry. Everything is getting away from me this morning. I wanted to show you around the house, so you'd know where everything is. Can it wait until you start? Do you mind?"

"No, it's fine," I said.

She shook my hand. "We're so happy that you're going to take up our offer. Really happy." Then she was gone, her Converse trainers squeaking on the flagstones.

Rob showed me to the front door. "See you very soon then." He patted me on the arm. "You're one of us now. Let's hope you don't regret it." We laughed, as if he'd made a ridiculous joke.

"I bet I won't," I said. After he closed the front door with a solid thud, I stood on the porch and surveyed the curve of the gravel forecourt, the weathered stone of the pond and the massive topiary balls planted so long ago. Everything had an air of pleasing permanence, despite the peeling paint on the front door and the plastic crates behind the pots. It didn't matter if weeds grew and the place needed a sweep. Most people would admire its gracious beauty before noticing trivial things like that.

A bus accelerated around the corner and I jolted.

That was the thing with places like this. Their walls and gates and balustrades had stood solid for centuries, through wars and bombs and family feuds. It made you think that nothing could get in. It made you forget that three hundred feet away a number 65 bus was making its way to Kingston.

7

Try, as much as possible, to surround yourself with
people with a generous spirit who inspire you and
take you with them to a place of higher awareness.
That place of higher awareness is the starting point
for achieving your dreams.

—Emma Helmsley, "Taking the Moment," March 16, 2016

Jude tried to talk me out of it. "I don't understand. It's like you're deliberately aiming low."

"I'm not aiming low," I said, wiping the steam from the kettle off my kitchen window. "I just want a break from restaurant work. I decided I wanted something quieter for a while."

"Hmmph!" She sounded out of breath. "Sorry. I'm exercising in the park. This new trainer will be the death of me. Can't you think a bit more about it? You can't get anything quieter than being alone in someone else's house all day."

"I'm not on my own. There are the children—they'll be home from school in the afternoons. And there's a dog."

"A dog! That'll make all the difference."

"You don't understand," I said. A pigeon landed on the ledge. I banged the glass. It flapped its wings and flew off, leaving a dribble of pale droppings.

"I know I can get another job in a restaurant, and I know I'm good at what I do. What I need right now is something simple. I want the time to think about how to fix my life, and I think I can make Emma's life less complicated and stressful. I really do."

"If you say so," she said. "Uh-oh, I'm in trouble now. The trainer is wagging his finger at me. Got to go, love you."

I started at Wycombe Lodge the next week, arriving half an hour early on my first day so that Emma could show me around the house.

"Thank goodness you're here," she said when I pressed the buzzer. Again the front door was open, but this time Emma was in the hall, dressed in a tailored navy suit and a white silk shirt. She looked older, more imposing. Siggy sat by her feet, staring up at me with his head cocked to one side. "I had this terrible feeling last night that you'd changed your mind and weren't going to show up. Oh, it's so good to see you."

"I haven't changed my mind." I smiled. "And it's good to see you too. It's good to be here." Wycombe Lodge was just as I remembered, but a bit neater. The crates and piles of old phone books had disappeared, and someone had made a start on the weeds in the gravel.

Together we walked down the hall, Siggy's claws scratching on the flagstones in time to the clack of Emma's heels. We went past the sitting room where I'd met Emma and Rob, then past a study with two desks and a desktop computer. Next to the study was another smaller sitting room with a television and more mismatched furniture. There was an enormous cloakroom with the usual basin and toilet, but also two armchairs and an open fireplace full of half-burned logs and ashes.

"Isn't that the funniest thing," said Emma, as if she were reading my mind. "A fireplace in a room like this. But I guess when they built the house, they wanted people to be comfortable when they needed a pee. We still light it sometimes, for parties."

She opened the doors at the end of the hall, and we walked into a dining room with windows all around. A long, scratched oak table stood in the center, surrounded by odd chairs, some rickety and fragile, others large and imposing, as if specially made for overweight people. A pine dresser and sideboard stood against the walls. French doors led onto a square of muddy lawn bordered by high brick walls with a tall beech tree in one corner.

All the time Emma kept talking, telling me straight out that the house didn't belong to them. It was owned by her family under some complicated trust. She could live there as long as she liked, but it would never be hers. When she died or if she decided to move away, some other relative would live in it, or perhaps Jake and Lily might be able to take it over. I envied that about her, the way she tossed private family information into a conversation with a complete stranger. "You'll meet Jake and Lily this afternoon," she said as we walked through to the kitchen. "They've already left for school." From upstairs there was a thumping sound and the rush of water through pipes, then a clatter in the dining room.

Rob dashed into the kitchen. "I'm running so late for my production meeting," he announced to Emma. He pecked her on the cheek before stopping short and staring at me, as if he was trying to work out why a stranger was in his kitchen.

"It's Anne," I said, dryness in my mouth in case over the weekend he'd changed his mind about me and forgotten to discuss it with Emma. But the moment was over in less than a second. He patted my arm in an avuncular way. "Welcome, welcome," he said. "Anne! Yes of course. Here you are. I hope we don't let you down." He grabbed a half-eaten piece of toast from the mess of cereal packets and plates on the table. "My only saving grace is that I'm not going to be in your way when I'm working from home. I'm religious about not leaving the office during working hours."

Emma giggled. I hadn't noticed at our first meeting, but one of her incisors was crooked. It made her look less perfect, prettier. "Rob means his man's shed at the bottom of the garden. It's got everything, even a shower and a composting loo. Rob is the only one allowed in—it's a no-go area for the rest of us."

She gestured towards the garden in an elegant wave. In the center of the brick walls was a gate opening onto a long double border of tangled shrubs. At the end stood a miniature clapboard cottage painted duck-egg blue, with a pitched shingled roof, a porch, and a white front door, like an illustration from an old-fashioned children's book.

"Just as well no one goes inside," said Rob. Toast crumbs sprayed down his shirt. "I may as well tell you now. You'll find out soon enough. I'm an absolute slob around the house. The only thing I do is put out the garbage bins each week. I've tried to be neat, but I'm just not very good at it. So sorry, hope you won't mind."

"I won't mind at all," I said.

That was the thing with Rob and Emma. They had a great pleasure and confidence in their own dazzling selves, as if there were no sad dark places, no simmering secrets inside either of them that needed to stay hidden. Every nook and cranny of their personalities was out there on the shelf. Pick me up, they seemed to say. Turn me over. You won't find me wanting.

After Rob left, Emma showed me around the house. Up the first flight of stairs was their bedroom, a high-ceilinged room bigger than my entire flat, with a fireplace at one end and an oversized unmade bed at the other. Next to it was a bathroom with one of those Victorian iron tubs with claw feet set in the middle of the room. There was a walk-in shower in one corner and a toilet with a carved wooden seat, almost like a throne. I'd never seen anything like it. Next to their bedroom was another large room with four wardrobes, one in each corner, and a pair of armchairs almost hidden under piles of clothes; Rob's shirts on top of Emma's dresses, jeans flung over silk shirts.

"Sort of our dressing room," Emma said. I picked up a jacket from the floor and put it on a chair.

"Oh, thank you," she said with a bit of a giggle. "I try to be neat, but it's all got into a bit of a state. You'd think I'd know how to be tidy—I'm always writing about it." The dressing room led into another room the same size. It was empty apart from a rowing machine and a desk and chair. "This is meant to be an office for me, but I never use it. Don't know why."

On the next floor were Lily and Jake's bedrooms. Lily's was neat, almost uninhabited-looking. In Jake's room opposite, the floor was littered with pieces of paper, clothes, and books. It was hard to work out how he made his way to his bed at night.

"They're keen on their privacy," said Emma. "Like all teenagers, I guess."

Along the corridor was another room with a sofa and a television. The blinds at the window were broken and hung at an odd angle. There was another floor above, with more rooms full of old suitcases and discarded computer games and toys. "I keep thinking we should clear this out," said Emma. "Maybe one day."

"It's nice to have space to store things," I said. Despite the mess, everything had a pleasing air of stability.

We went downstairs to the kitchen, another large, square room flooded with light. A counter topped with pockmarked and stained marble separated it from the dining room.

"It used to be two separate rooms," explained Emma. "We knocked the wall down and made it into one. No one lives in that stuffy way anymore. Thank goodness. So stupid." She grinned at me in a conspiratorial way, as if to say that there were no such divisions these days at Wycombe Lodge and that we were all in it together.

The working part of the kitchen was full of stainless steel machines (two dishwashers and one of those glass-fronted wine coolers) crammed between battered cupboards, with an enormous Sub-Zero refrigerator at one end. Everything was expensive, but nothing had been planned for efficiency. It looked like someone had taken every machine out of its box and stood it in the first available place.

"And here's the laundry," said Emma, showing me a small room off the kitchen, next to a larder. There was an alarmed expression on her face when she consulted the washing machine manual, like she was explaining the Large Hadron Collider instead of an appliance in her own house.

"I hope it's OK for you," said Emma, looking doubtful. "If you need anything, just say so and we can get it." She checked her watch. "Late again. I've only got two meetings today, so I'll be back by the time Jake and Lily come home from school." She picked up her handbag and made for the door. "I'll try not to go on about it, but really, I'm so pleased you're here. We were using one of those agencies, but it was hopeless. Everything got lost, and we were in such a mess."

She had already opened the front door when I noticed her mobile and purse were still on the counter. I was about to call out to her when she reappeared at the door and I handed them over.

"Thank you," she said. "I don't think I've ever made it out the door without coming back for something I've forgotten. Stop and think! Stop and think! I wrote an entire blog about it once, but I can't seem to manage to do it myself. See you later. Don't work too hard."

I spent the next few hours clearing away the mess in the kitchen and working out where everything went. Apart from following me with his eyes, Siggy lay motionless in his basket near the kitchen door. Every now and then, as if the effort of moving his eyeballs was too much, he sighed and closed his eyes, not even twitching when I walked past. I'd never owned a dog, but surely they were meant to move about just a bit while waiting for their owner to return. Maybe he was waiting for me to take him into the garden? I tried to gently shoo him outside, but he burrowed further into his basket. I gave up and left him in his comatose state.

I moved through the house in a slow, pleasant haze, so different from my usual frenetic work routine. An hour passed, and then another, without self-pitying thoughts of Anton. I heard nothing except the measured pace of my own footsteps and noticed only the gradual movement of light through the house, how it played along the elaborate plaster cornices and bounced off the crystal chandelier in the hall. I'd always thought I thrived on the pressure and deadlines of a professional kitchen. Now, after less than a day in this new job, I wasn't so sure.

Just before Emma rushed back in (Siggy bounding out of his basket like Usain Bolt off the blocks), Lily and Jake arrived home from school. They had inherited the healthy self-esteem genome as well, with their firm handshakes and direct eye contact, their clear, well-modulated voices; the species of teenager who was used to strangers in their house and people clearing up after them.

"Hello," said Lily, dropping her backpack on the floor and rolling her shoulders back and forth. "Mum said you'd be here. Welcome to our madhouse." She had Rob's brown eyes and his broad frame. Her hair was thick and dark and captured in a ponytail. Not entirely successfully, as rebel strands had escaped and curled about her face in a chaotic frizz. Her face was arresting, with heavy eyebrows and a high forehead. One day she would be beautiful, but not just yet.

"Heavens, we're not that bad," said Emma, taking off her jacket and kicking off her shoes. She bent to pat a rapturous Siggy. "Anyway, we're quite normal, aren't we, Jake?"

"As normal as any family that names their dog after Sigmund Freud," he said, heading for the refrigerator. Jake was as thin as a stick, with Emma's golden coloring and high cheekbones. His hair was fine, the color of straw and settled in thin wisps at the base of his neck. He looked me straight in the eye, as if he'd been taught from an early age how to greet people. "How do you do."

They piled a plate full of food—peanut butter sandwiches, chocolate biscuits, cartons of orange juice—and went upstairs, leaving their backpacks scattered about the floor. I picked them up and put them to one side.

"I always think I should do something about healthy snacks when they come home from school," said Emma, surveying the chaos on the counter with a quizzical expression. Her brow wrinkled. She might have been trying to understand some Tracey Emin installation at Tate Modern. "But somehow I never get around to it." I cleared away, happy to have another small chore, a means by which to make my mark.

At the end of that first day, I decided to walk back to Richmond. My breath rose in puffed clouds above my head as I strode past the fields. It was fully dark by the time I reached the first houses. Along the pavements was the smell of wood smoke from someone's evening fire. I tried to remember everything Rob and Emma had said to me, although the cold made clear thinking difficult. "We'd like you to feel part of our family," Rob said. There was a tentative upward inflection in his voice, as if he was asking me a favor.

"And you must feel able to talk to us freely if anything upsets you, or if you need anything," continued Emma. She rummaged in a side drawer and produced a set of house keys held together by an elastic band. "I'm sure you'll figure out which ones work for which doors. We have an alarm, but we never use it. In fact"—she laughed—"I'm not even sure it actually works anymore."

Everything had been so easy, as if I was setting off down a path clearly signposted for me to follow. I picked up pace as I considered my new employers. It was clear that Rob and Emma were very comfortable, as Gran used to say. But they definitely weren't what Anton would have called high thread counts. I'd have despised them for that, just a little. Rich people were always so obvious. We used to wink when they came into the restaurant. Always a chink in the armor with a rich person. New money always that bit nervous, making them excessive spenders and good tippers but rude and demanding. Old money often so miserly, as if their first shilling from the Tooth Fairy had to see them out. But they were insecure as well, because they'd done nothing to earn it and so they would never know their own measure.

Rob and Emma weren't wallowing about in inherited wealth. But they weren't entirely self-made either, because of Wycombe Lodge and Emma's family trust that allowed them to live there. They didn't fit into any category I'd ever heard of.

8

~∞~

Hospitality is a most excellent virtue; but care must
be taken that the love of company, for its own sake,
does not become a prevailing passion.

—*Mrs. Beeton's Book of Household Management*, 1861

The climbing rose in front of the house was now covered in
fat buds and intermittent white blooms. I'd been at Wycombe
Lodge for almost two months. It had taken a while, but I'd
gotten the place into my kind of order. Emma had often gone
by the time I arrived in the morning, while Rob was still meandering about the kitchen, taking his time to leave for the studio
or his garden shed. The minute I had the house to myself, I
set to work. I cleaned windows sticky with grease and wiped
down skirting boards thick with dust. I scrubbed baths and basins. I mopped and polished floors. I even got up a ladder one
day and vacuumed all the curtains with a special brush attach-
ment I found somewhere. When I'd started here, everything
in Rob and Emma's dressing room was jumbled together, with
boxes of shoes and clothes that Emma had ordered online not
even opened. Now all their clothes were organized in color-
coordinated parallel rows, all the coat hanger hooks facing the
same way. Every wardrobe had been reorganized, its contents
lined up with military precision.

Downstairs in the kitchen, the cupboards were crammed
with pots and pans so battered that the lids didn't fit. But in
the laundry there was a stash of copper-bottomed saucepans

still in their boxes. Emma didn't even notice that I swapped them over. In my second week at Wycombe Lodge, I found a spare front door key in the freezer. Apparently Emma had read somewhere that it was a good hiding place. The drawers had been stuffed with an eclectic but useless collection of utensils—a cherry and olive stoner, but no potato masher, an oyster knife but no spatula. Knives that would be hard pushed to cut butter.

The laundry shelves were piled with a huge cache of liquids to clean floors, sprays to polish hobs, special bottles for windows and bench tops; each one so expensive and many not even opened. As each container emptied, I didn't replace it. Instead I bought bottles of ordinary soap and vinegar, tins of inexpensive powdered cleanser, the cheapest brand, from the back shelves of Ahmed's shop, and vials of tea tree oil from the health food store. Between them, they killed most bacteria, and the vinegar smell soon disappeared. I had even brought some of my own equipment into the house: my favorite paring knife, the expensive handmade Japanese knife that was one of my prize possessions, and the sharpening steel.

"I can't believe what we've done to deserve you," cried Emma, rushing out of the house one morning. "Everything is transformed." Silly, I know, but it felt so good to make a difference and to be needed. And really, all I was doing was putting Emma's philosophy into practice because she was too busy to do it herself.

As well as her work—everything growing so quickly that there was talk of another assistant to help Fiona—Rob and Emma were big entertainers. I'd never been to any of Rob and Emma's parties, although I couldn't help being curious about them. They had one every couple of weeks, either on the weekend or beginning soon after I left for the day; Emma running downstairs just before I said good night, dressed in floating silk pajamas, her face flushed from the shower and her hair still wet. She never heeded her own advice about making a daily timetable, right down to the number of minutes taken to apply makeup, and then sticking to it religiously.

The parties were always Rob's idea and he took them very seriously. Compiling each list could take days, adding some names, erasing others, sighing when Emma didn't pay attention. Apart from Rob's meticulous preparation of the guest list, there were never signs of any other planning. There were only the forgotten glasses in the sitting room the morning after and the crates of empty wine bottles and the boxes of dirty plates and cutlery outside the front door. All this was picked up by a van from the local deli and wine store that arrived promptly at noon. The driver was a burly Jamaican called Eric who said the same thing every time.

"Hey, good bottle count today!" He would whistle in admiration. "Fun night, I bet. I hear all sorts of well-known rich people come here." I would smile and nod, hoping he thought I'd been included among the guests and not wanting to admit that I hadn't been at Wycombe Lodge the night before, but alone in my flat watching TV. On the way home one evening, I walked past the deli, curious to see what it was like. Its windows were full of platters of salads, cold salmon, and rare roast beef. I went inside, thinking I might pick up something for my own supper. A woman in front of me, dressed in gym clothes and a fur coat, picked up two small containers from the counter. "That will be forty pounds eighty-five," said the salesgirl. I quickly walked out.

A few weeks later, as I walked towards Wycombe Lodge, I saw Emma, dressed for meetings in one of her suits, getting into a taxi. "Hello there," she said, clutching one of her oversized handbags brimming with papers. "I've been so busy and we need to catch up. Is everything going OK?"

"Everything is great," I said. "Thanks." I was about to say goodbye, but she shut the door and the taxi roared off in a cloud of exhaust fumes.

In the kitchen, Rob was wandering about the breakfast mess chewing on a piece of toast, his spectacles hanging on a cord around his neck. Unlike Emma, who rushed from room to room before collapsing in complicated huddles, Rob had an elegant slouchy way of walking. He was wearing his at-home uniform, faded jeans and an old David Bowie T-shirt, so different from the preppy jackets and button-down shirts he favored for his days at the studio, giving him the air of an Ivy League professor.

"Hi," he said, rubbing his unshaven chin. He leaned a hand on the wall beside him. His head blocked the morning sun, so that his face darkened while all around him the light blazed.

"Hello," I said. "How is everything with you? And the book? Going well?"

From snippets of overheard conversation and what I'd read on his website, I knew that Rob was writing a biography of some rogue psychiatrist called Rowan McLeish, who believed that the modern family was responsible for much of what passed as madness. He was the leader of some weird eighties commune in the countryside, and he'd died about a year ago. The name McLeish was vaguely familiar, but I wasn't that interested. What Emma wrote about was much more relevant to how I wanted to live.

I'd never struck up the same relaxed chat with Rob that I had with Emma, although he was around the house more than she was. It felt easier talking to Emma. The girl crush thing, as Jude called it. Rob was a bit more serious. I guess I took my lead from Emma, who was always so mindful of Rob's well-being and his work. It wasn't that she deferred to him all the time. It was more like she needed him to be happy so she could be happy. Maybe they really were twin souls, as she'd said in that newspaper interview.

There was also the realization that Rob was, superficially, pretty much the kind of man I'd always been attracted to. I'd always gone for a vaguely Mediterranean cast to features, way back to Douglas, who'd been more swarthy than fair. There was that thing about the texture of olive skin, smooth and rippling under the touch.

Rob shrugged and waved his toast about. "Everything's OK." He fixed me with that kind, direct gaze of his. "But how are things with you? The job I mean. Are you happy here, not too bored?"

"Yes, everything is good, great." I blinked and moved away from the light, and began clearing dishes. "And I'm not bored, not at all."

I could have said more. I wanted to say that I was so happy to be in the house, happy that he and Emma liked me, that the family needed me. I didn't say this. Of course not. I didn't want anything I said to be misconstrued or to embarrass him. He could easily think I was making some kind of sad pass. I wanted to step over and touch his arm, the way he so easily touched Emma and, occasionally, me. But I felt too awkward.

"Coffee before you go?" I asked.

"Any excuse to procrastinate," he said. "Oh, that sounds so rude. Thank you. I'd love some."

I looked about for the coffee I'd brought with me to Wycombe Lodge soon after I began working there. Two packets of a good Colombian single estate that had been on special. I disliked instant coffee, and Rob and Emma didn't seem to go in for real beans,. They hadn't succumbed to that caffeine neurosis thing we saw all the time in the restaurant, with customers asking where the beans had come from, how they'd been roasted, and what kind of machine we used. Anton called it coffee status anxiety.

Behind me, Rob gave a low whistle. "The genuine deal! It's

been a while since I've seen anything resembling an authentic coffee bean in this house. We went through a phase a while back where we tried to make proper coffee, but then we just forgot about it and went back to the stuff in a jar." He peered at the packet of coffee. " Emma wouldn't know what to do with that." He looked wistful.

"But you could try making it," I said. "A lot of men do. Most of the champion baristas are male."

"Maybe I will." He laughed. "Although as you've seen, we're not too trained up in the culinary arts."

"You could make a start by grinding the coffee." And there, just like that, we'd slipped from careful conversation into an easy banter. I heard my voice soften to rise and fall in tune with his, recognized the light and laughter in it.

"I don't think we have anything as sophisticated as a coffee grinder."

"Yes you do." I bent down and retrieved it from what I privately called the leftover appliance cupboard, full of machines worth hundreds of pounds. There was a gadget to dry fruit, something to cure fish, a pasta maker, a bread machine, and one of those mini grills. None had ever been used.

"It's pretty simple. You put the beans in, plug it in, and turn it on."

He crinkled his eyes. "Then what? We don't have one of those French press things. Jake broke it and we never got round to replacing it."

"I've got it covered," I said.

He poured beans into the grinder, spilling a fair few in the process, and turned it on. The grinder was too noisy for conversation and we stood in silence, our shoulders almost touching. He was so close that I could see the occasional gray bristle on his chin, the hairs in his nose, and the tiny glop of butter at the corner of his mouth. We watched the beans spin and break into chunks, and then into smaller and smaller particles, until they became something else altogether.

I filled the kettle and turned it on. Steam rose in plumes across the sunlight slicing through the window. I made the coffee in one of the simplest and best ways I knew. In the leftover appliance cupboard were some cone-shaped ceramic coffee filters and some filter papers. I found two clean mugs, measured the coffee into the filters, and poured the water over it. Immediately, the rich dark scent cut through the smell of charred toast.

"You need fresh water for good coffee," I said. "And the water should be just off the boil. Then you can drink it pretty much straightaway. With or without?"

"Without."

I handed him the mug and watched him sip it, anxious for him to like it, that my trite and obvious coffee-making lesson had worked.

"Terrific," he grinned, clutching his mug. "Really good." He had elegant hands, tanned, with long, straight fingers and neatly tended fingernails. Outside there was a loud screeching from the parakeets as they flew overhead, their flight path creating flickering shadows on the ceiling.

"They're so loud, those parakeets," I said. "Do you think they're forcing out the native birds? Poor things, they're so much smaller."

"Apparently not," said Rob. "Somehow or other they've worked it out between themselves."

He blew on his coffee and took another sip. Again he fixed me with that kind, direct gaze. "So, Anne Morgan, the person who's transformed life here at Wycombe Lodge, tell me something. Who do you go home to every night? There must be someone, surely."

I wasn't prepared for such a direct question. I hadn't

thought up one of those socially acceptable bland statements that people come out with after relationships end: it had run its course; we both wanted different things; our lives went in different directions. And then the lie. But we're still friends, of course. Of course.

"There was someone," I said bluntly, "in the restaurant. He was the owner and the head chef. We were together for two years, but he met someone else. Just before I started here."

"That sounds tough." Just three words, but his voice soothed me. I remembered what the critics said, about Rob having a chocolate voice and how he had a way of making people want to tell him things. There was a pang of remembered pain, almost a compulsion to tell him everything about Anton right then.

I might have been mistaken, but I thought he was about to move towards me and pat my arm the way he'd done once before, when there was a scrabbling at the kitchen door. Siggy had been snuffling about the garden. Now he wanted to be let in. Rob's face creased with annoyance. He didn't like Siggy. I sometimes thought he was jealous of the way Emma patted and fussed over him, never reprimanding him for bad behavior. Outside, Siggy began to whine. He was used to getting his own way. Any second now he would begin to bark. Giving in to him was the only one way to shut him up. I went to the door and opened it. When I turned around, holding a triumphant Siggy panting his meaty breath all over me, longing to continue talking, Rob had already put his mug in the sink and was looking around for his phone.

"I'd better start work," I said, putting Siggy down. I didn't mean it. It was just something to say, to disguise my disappointment that our conversation had ended. "I've taken up too much of your time already."

"No, no," he said. "We should talk more, really. But I guess it is time to hit the desk." He stepped outside and walked across the lawn towards his little cottage, leaving a meandering trail of footprints on the dew-covered grass. As I cleared the table, I saw him in his office, pacing up and down and then sitting at his desk, still on his phone. He looked up and waved. I waved back, holding a stack of cereal bowls with one hand, sodden cornflakes bobbing in their milky sea.

9

If you want to achieve something, try your hardest to succeed in getting it. Never underestimate the power of your own intuition. Listen to it and learn from it.

—Emma Helmsley, "Taking the Moment," April 19, 2016

As I set to work clearing the kitchen, I constructed a story whereby we hadn't been flirting, however mildly and harmlessly, but getting to know each other better because of Emma. He might have been curious about the person Emma chatted to so easily in the kitchen when he was still down in his office or reading in the study before dinner. Maybe she'd told him that she enjoyed my company, in the same way that I'd told Jude how much I liked Emma, and he wanted to find out why.

Last night's lasagna cartons lay congealing by the oven, and splotches of dried meat sauce covered the counter. Fiona, the assistant, had said that the job was general housekeeping rather than cooking, but Emma's schedule meant that she was too busy to manage even simple meals. As far as I could make out, the family lived mostly on takeaways or semiprepared meals from the supermarket. Judging from the contents of the kitchen bin each morning, Thai green curry was a favorite, then pasta and pizza.

That evening, I waited for Emma to come home, even though she'd texted me to say she would be late. She came into the kitchen and sank down on a stool. Her hair was pulled back with a clip and there was a dark smudge on her shirt. Above the sharp lines of her clothes, her eyes sagged with tiredness. Siggy danced about her feet and she bent down to pat him. When she sat up, her face was drained and bloodless.

"I've been thinking," I said. "I could take over the cooking and food shopping. It's just that, with everyone out of the house all day, I'm running out of things to do."

"But what about you?" She unclipped her hair. It fell about her shoulders in a tangle and she raked her fingers through it. "We can't have you working day and night. It wouldn't be fair. It would ruin your evenings, surely."

"I'm used to working in the evenings. I've done it since I was fifteen." My offer wasn't entirely altruistic. I wasn't doing anything else in the evenings except sitting by myself, and it would be easier to clean the kitchen then, instead of the next morning, when everything was crusted and hard to scrub clean.

Emma looked puzzled, and I worried that she might think this was a roundabout way of asking for more money. "I could start a bit later, if it suited," I said. "So the hours would be the same."

"It's not that," she said.

"Not what?" said Lily, walking into the kitchen.

"Anne says she could do the grocery shopping and stay on and cook supper," said Emma. "But it seems too much."

Lily grabbed a carton of orange juice from the refrigerator. "Mum, don't be totally mad. It's not like we're doing *MasterChef* or *America's Test Kitchen* every night down here. Just say yes!"

Emma turned to me. "Are you sure?"

I nodded.

"Well, then. I'll just say yes."

Lily lifted the carton in a victory salute, slopping juice on the floor. "Quick, in case she leaves her senses." She took my arm and marched me out of the kitchen into the study. "This is the computer for the shopping. Dad uses it as well, but only in the evenings. It's an old one. I'll show you how to log on. It's so easy."

Later, on the way home, nothing could penetrate my personal climate of well-being. I was so happy to be cooking for other people again. And not strangers, but people who I liked and who I thought liked me. It wasn't the same cooking solitary suppers for myself. Besides, like most chefs, I wasn't interested in anything more complicated out of hours than a good take-away curry, grilled fish and salad, or poached eggs on toast. The satisfaction came from feeding others.

Despite Jude's misgivings—"Chief cook and bottle washer now! Not to mention personal food shopper! You have moved up in the world!"—I was enjoying myself at Wycombe Lodge, even more than I'd expected.

Before I took over the food shopping and cooking, I saw that the Wycombe Lodge idea of buying groceries was to log on to the supermarket website every week, press click, and repeat the existing order. Whoever unpacked the bags crammed everything in front of last week's slimy vegetables and rancid cheeses with the edges nibbled away, and left slabs of raw meat on the top ledges with trails of dried blood congealed beneath them. In the wine cooler next to the refrigerator, I counted five open bottles of Chablis.

At the restaurant, we pickled carrot peelings, and made burgers from meat trimmings. We concocted flavored oils and butters from prawn and lobster shells. "I'd rather you stuck toothpicks in your eyeballs," Anton would shout, "than throw away something that can be eaten."

I saw the waste of everything at Wycombe Lodge, their careless domestic inefficiency, despite the constant bleats of no money and Rob rushing through the house complaining about Emma's late night Net-a-Porter habit. I didn't care. It made Rob and Emma seem more human behind their busy social media lives, their entertaining, and their work. I felt more connected to them.

Emma liked to chat in the kitchen as I prepared supper. She always wore the same type of clothes at home, some version of a tracksuit and thick-soled trainers as if she were about to go running. I'd gotten used to her style of dressing in reverse, Emma going out looking ready for bed, in thermal vests, or silk pajamas and some kind of flowing dressing gown, then lounging around the house in clothes designed for a strenuous workout. I'd learned as well to translate her office wardrobe. For meetings and public appearances, she wore tailored suits, silk shirts, and high-heeled shoes. If she didn't have to leave the office, she stuck to shrunken tops and trailing skirts, the type of thing she'd worn when I first met her and Rob.

"Chicken, how wonderful!" she exclaimed one night. "With broccoli and potatoes. Delicious!"

You'd think she was talking about a double-starred Michelin experience, the kind of thing we did in the restaurant, culinary still lifes with vegetable spirals and flavored foams, instead of a tray of baked chicken and potatoes with steamed vegetables on the side. Emma was big on praise, whenever possible. There was a whole section on it in one of her books. She called it "learned competence." The idea was that if you kept telling someone that they were good at something, then they worked towards excelling themselves, often without being aware of it. Apparently it was very effective.

Emma leaned against the refrigerator in that way she had when she wanted to talk. "I imagine you've worked out that we like to entertain a lot, in our own messy kind of way." She smiled. "Not that we expect you to do anything. You have enough to do, cooking and cleaning up after us. Are you sure you don't mind, about the parties? There's sometimes a bit of a mess the morning after."

"I don't mind one bit," I said. "A house like this should be used, be full of people."

"Good," she said. "I mean, we have lots of dinners and parties anyway, probably far too many for our own good. Although you've probably realized that we don't get too carried away with the catering. I just ask Fiona to call the deli place. They deliver and send people to help serve and clear up. Then someone comes and picks up the plates and stuff the next day." She fiddled with one of her earrings. "We're thinking of having something a bit bigger in a couple of months, better organized. Rob's working on this book, and well . . ." She paused. "Publicity never hurts, particularly for biographies, things like that. What I do is different. It's easier to sell."

Here was my moment to tell Emma I read her blogs and took to heart her daily messages. Up to now, there had seemed no easy way to insert this into our casual chats about what I was cooking for dinner or where I had walked Siggy that day. I could scarcely tell Emma that I'd ordered two organic chickens because they were on special and then all of a sudden segue into "Oh, by the way, your thing about dream diaries is really terrific. I've started one myself," before reverting to grocery deliveries.

"I think what you do must help a lot of people lead happier lives," I said carefully. I rinsed out the sink and turned off the tap. "I've looked at your website and your blog—you give great advice."

"Really? I'm so pleased." She shook her head, as if she couldn't believe what I'd just said. "That is very kind. Thank you very much." She brushed a speck of something from her sleeve. "Sometimes I think it gets a bit monotonous, so it means a lot to me that you like it." She shrugged. "Anyhow, what do you think? About the party, and parties in general?"

Emma always asked me what I thought, as if my opinion was a domestic deal breaker. I always told her what I thought she wanted to hear, but I was flattered nonetheless. I wasn't the most gregarious person in the world, but I didn't mind parties, the excitement of the preparation and the postmortem the next day. Often the before and after were more enjoyable than the actual event.

"I think it's a great idea," I said, peering inside the oven. Everything was browning nicely. I turned to get the broccoli out of the refrigerator, but Emma was in the way.

"Sorry," she said, moving to the sink just as I wanted to turn on the tap. A lot of people who don't cook are like that. They always stand in the wrong place in the kitchen.

"Sorry," she said again, stepping towards the refrigerator. "I never know where to put myself."

"It doesn't matter." A companionable silence settled. Sometimes I thought Emma might be lonely in spite of the dinners and her job, her life with Rob and the children. Not long ago, I overheard her saying to someone on her phone, "Rob and I are so fond of Anne, even though she hasn't been with us for that long. We feel she'll become a proper friend."

Future images frolicked in my mind as I filled the dishwasher. The three of us sharing a fresh pot of coffee in the mornings, the sun skittering through the kitchen windows as we had one of those meandering, inconsequential conversations enjoyed only by people who know one another well. Rob and Emma confiding in me about Jake and Lily, the details of their working days.

I skipped through the rest of my work that day with an energy I hadn't felt for some time. Flattery. It worked more often than you thought. But later that night at home, I told myself not to get carried away, that Emma and Rob had enough friends of their own without having to add another whom they paid by direct debit on the first day of every month. It was the sort of thing that people like Rob and Emma said all the time, a harmless yet endearing habit to make me feel at ease and not like just the hired help.

It was also a typically Emma thing to say. She was probably a little uncomfortable with the idea of having a housekeeper because it was too reminiscent of her own family. I'd seen the photographs in her bedroom of the honey-colored stone manor house in Gloucestershire, the ponies in the field, and the woodland picnics with her little gang from boarding school. I'd picked up the letters addressed to "The Honorable Mrs. Emma Helmsley." In more lateral London, married to Rob whose father was a butcher from Manchester, she didn't like talking about her privileged childhood.

Emma leaned against the refrigerator, pushing her fringe to one side. "We'll get proper caterers in for the party this time." Her fringe was far too long, down past her eyebrows. Under the strands of hair, her eyes were bloodshot. "Although you'd probably have a better idea than us of what to do, with all your restaurant experience. And it would be fun, have the house really heaving with people."

"I'd love to help," I said. "As much as I can."

Emma picked off a piece of broccoli and nibbled at it. A tiny floret caught on the corner of her lip. I wanted to brush it off, but scratched my own mouth instead.

She hitched up her tracksuit bottoms. Another thing I'd noticed since I began working here. Emma was too thin, hipbones jutting out, wrists too big for her arms. She only pretended to like food. A lot of the time she pushed it around the plate, and every night Siggy slipped silently under her chair, his tongue hanging out.

"It's such a busy time for Rob and me. And these days, I've got a mind like a sieve, can't remember a thing."

"That's not true," I said.

"Oh, it is," she replied. "Rob and the children are always teasing me about it."

I put the broccoli on the side of the sink. Emma did occasionally forget names and places, probably because she had so many other things to remember. There were her books, her speaking engagements up and down the country, all the children's activities, and everything to do with Rob and his job. I opened the oven and prodded the potatoes. They were still a bit hard.

"Everything will be ready in about fifteen minutes. I'll put the timer on, so you'll know. Then just wait until the water boils and put the steamer on top. About five minutes should do it."

"Thank you, Anne, for everything."

Emma said this every night, accentuating every word. Jude would have laughed if I'd told her, but every night I felt the same small ping of pleasure.

"I'll take the laundry upstairs before I go."

Emma jabbed her mobile. "Have a nice evening. Would you mind telling Jake and Lily that supper is almost ready?"

Lily's door was open, but I still knocked. She was straightening books on her desk.

"Supper's ready in about a quarter of an hour," I said, putting the pile of clean clothes on her bed. Her room smelled of patchouli oil. For a teenager, she was uncharacteristically neat. Her bed was always made, her clothes hung in color-coordinated rows. She made lists of things to do, dividing each day into quarter-hour chunks. *Wash hair. Finish history homework. One hundred sit-ups.* Things like that.

"OK," she replied in a flat voice, still moving her books about. "What is it?"

"Chicken."

"Not fried?" A note of alarm.

"No, I roasted it and you can take the skin off. There's broccoli. And potatoes, but you don't have to eat them."

"Hey," she said, fixing me with her steady brown-eyed gaze. "Thanks. Before you came, Jake and I thought we were going to overdose on takeaway. The MSG levels were seriously out of control. Everything is better now—the food, the house. The people before who came to clean chucked things out or stole them. We could never work out what was going on. The whole place was chaos."

I didn't expect to feel so pleased, but I did. "That's good, thank you."

"Mum says you worked in a restaurant, as a proper chef, like on all those TV programs."

"I wasn't on TV, but yes, I did. Do you like cooking?"

"I don't know," she said. "I've never tried."

"We could cook something one afternoon after school, if you like. I mean, if it doesn't interfere with homework."

"I'd love that," she said, her voice rising. "Really, do you mean it?"

"Sure. I'd like that too. Maybe some of your friends might like to join in. Anytime."

I looked across to Jake's empty room.

"He went out about an hour ago. He told me he'd be back in time for supper," said Lily. "Some film club thing." She raised her eyebrows. "So he says."

The floor around Jake's bed was scattered with clothes and shoes. He'd stuck some posters on the walls for bands I'd never heard of. Although all the members had long hair and some wore untidy beards, everyone had a wholesome, untouched appearance. Lily had told me that he didn't like people poking about his room, but I couldn't help myself. I found space for the clean clothes in his cupboard and started picking things up. A marker pen had fallen on some crumpled T-shirts, bright yellow blotches flaring like sunflowers. I searched for the top of the pen and saw it lolling in the binding of an open book on the bedside table. Of course I peeked.

It was more a thick pamphlet than a proper book, published by something called the Church of Eternal Truth: "*Death and Hell will deliver up the sinners in our midst. And every man and woman will be judged according to their works. There will be no exceptions and no excuses.*" I turned it over and saw that the church was less than ten miles away, in Southall.

It was probably something to do with their homework. Jake and Lily often had eccentric assignments that appeared to have nothing to do with the subject at hand: maths projects that required written essays and history essays asking for poems or short stories instead of facts and dates. It was a feature of their school, fashionable and alternative, popular with media types and actors. I dumped the T-shirts into the laundry basket and went downstairs.

10

❧

Cooking . . . is the progress of mankind from barba-
rism to civilization.

—Mrs. Beeton's Book of Household Management, 1861

Late April. One of those unexpected downpours, as if winter
were trying to beat back spring. The rain flung itself at the dining room window, splinters of light bouncing off the branches
of the beech tree. Emma was laying the table. She liked doing
it herself. She said it was the least she could do, when I offered
to stay on to serve dinner and clear up afterwards.

Every piece of cutlery was mismatched; bone-handled
knives, split and dulled from the dishwasher, next to modern
stainless steel, mixed in with proper old-fashioned silver forks,
every tine tarnished beyond cleaning. All the plates were different too; delicate faded floral patterns and cheerful rustic
earthenware thrown together with the occasional plain white
circle. On any other table it would have looked a bad taste jum-
ble. But somehow here, it seemed elegant, a style beyond fashion. That was Emma's gift, even though she sometimes didn't
lay enough places and occasionally even forgot the glasses.

But she always remembered to light the candles. There were so
many of them: tea lights in small silver jars on the table, fat cream
church candles on the side table, and tall, slim candles burning
in the wall sconces. Every candle burned at a different rate and
height. Sometimes I'd look up from the hob to see their heads suffused by a halo of light and all around them in flickering shadow.

Just the four of them tonight, plus Rob's friend Theo, and one of his girlfriends, a silent PhD student with lots of bedraggled hair. Theo was a psychologist as well and lectured at University College London, where Rob used to teach. He was a kind of ex-officio family member, always barging into the house unannounced like an extra from a soap opera.

"I just had to meet you on my own, have you to myself for a bit," he'd said when we first met. He'd bypassed the front door and squeezed past the bins down the narrow path at the side of the house, flinging his bag by the door and embracing me like an old friend.

"Rob and Emma haven't stopped talking about you, how you've transformed their lives. And isn't this the most fabulous house? Aren't we the lucky ones!" He stepped back and rubbed his hands together in pleasure, then gave a little jump like a small boy.

Theo had the appearance of a bouncy middle-aged leprechaun, with ginger curls flopping about his freckled face. "I'm a lost orphan in need of a family, so I'm almost a permanent fixture around here. Do you mind? No one else seems to. I'm Rob's friend although really I'm in love with Emma, always have been. That's why none of my women stick around for very long. But a man must follow his heart, don't you agree?"

He didn't wait for me to reply to any of his questions. Theo had an infectious enthusiasm for pretty much everything and often began conversations about the need for slate shelves in the pantry to keep food cool, or whether grass-fed beef was better than grain-fed. Not in a patronizing way, but as if he was really interested. He occasionally joined me in the kitchen after dinner, when Emma and Rob retreated to their computers and Jake and Lily had disappeared upstairs. I liked those moments, when he asked me about recipes and told me about plays and exhibitions. I had the feeling that we were the older siblings in an extended family with Rob and Emma at its head.

"We've got to get you out of that apron and into the wider world," he said one night. "It's only fair after everything you do for everyone here. You've got to see that play at the National—everyone is raving."

"I'll get there," I said, doing a last wipe down, hoping he might ask me to join him. But he began talking about something else. Maybe he was shy.

That night, I'd decided on mushroom risotto, then grilled sea bream and salad for dinner. Emma had finished lighting the candles and was wandering about with a smoldering match in her hand. Her hair, still wet, dripped down her neck. She wore a top I hadn't seen before, of oyster-colored silk with flowing sleeves and a complicated neckline. She'd either forgotten to take off her tracksuit bottoms or couldn't be bothered. The effect was schizophrenic, like she'd got dressed in front of two mirrors, each one showing only one half of her body. Her toenails were glossed black. On her feet she wore a pair of those flimsy disposable sandals that beauty salons hand out after pedicures. Siggy kept trying to nibble them. Finally she took them off and gave them to him. He wagged his tail and began chewing and shredding them everywhere.

She peered into the saucepan. "Rob and I once tried risotto, but it ended up like porridge and we had to throw it out."

"It's not that hard," I said, deciding that the tracksuit trousers probably had something to do with one of her blogs. Emma had been talking a lot about what she called "the naked self" lately and the freedom that came from doing away with elaborate social disguises of clothes and makeup. "I'm going to teach Lily how to cook it one day after school. After her homework, I mean." I didn't want Emma to think I was disrupting any after-school routine, but Emma just smiled.

"We're so lucky to have you. And I'll have to take your word for it about risotto. Far too complicated for me."

It's not actually. A lot of people think risotto is difficult, too last-minute, but you can get it to the halfway stage and then leave it until you're fifteen minutes away from serving. It's not a prima donna dish. Not like a soufflé. I don't get involved in that debate about butter or oil. If people don't like butter, they should cook something else. I like to use proper stock, not a cube. And carnaroli rice, not arborio. It has a firmer texture and keeps its shape better. The important thing about a risotto is the *mantecatura*, right at the end when you take the pan off the heat and whisk in the butter and Parmesan cheese. You need to put a bit of muscle into it, otherwise it won't be creamy and smooth.

Emma was always asking me to join them at the table, but I never did. I preferred to serve them from my side of the counter, watching them eat as I slowly cleared away, so I could hear their conversation.

Jake took the bowl of risotto to the table. He put it down and slopped some grains of rice on the table. Emma scooped them up in her fingers. A piece of mushroom covered in melted Parmesan dripped onto her shirt and she brushed it onto the floor.

Something else I'd gotten used to since I started work here. There was no polite handling of knives and forks at Wycombe Lodge. Gran would have been shocked. Rob and Jake reached over each other and grabbed food, sometimes abandoning cutlery altogether and eating with their fingers. Emma and Lily were less primitive, but often used their knives as forks.

Emma noticed my reaction and wiped her fingers on a napkin. "I'm afraid they've taken on my boarding school grab," she said. "I hope you're not offended." I wasn't. As usual, I envied her confidence in dispensing with such bourgeois notions as table manners and clothes that matched. When they finished, Jake brought the plates back to the counter. They were all empty. A warm feeling, like I'd done something right, the way we used to feel at the restaurant when the plates came back scraped clean.

At the table, Rob was talking to Theo about a program he was planning on cognitive therapy. He occasionally did documentaries as well as his *Desert Island* neuroses and fears series, and this was his latest idea.

"It shouldn't matter so much about what happened in your childhood," he said. "It doesn't have to be the determining factor. Because although you can't change your character, you can change your behavior."

Opposite him, Lily interrupted. "But how can you separate them? Aren't they the same thing?"

"Not necessarily," replied Rob. He mentioned this brother and sister he'd been reading about in his research. Their parents had been heroin addicts. They had been fostered and then abused by pedophiles throughout their childhood.

"They've grown up. They have jobs, families of their own," Rob said. "They're OK now. They haven't let what happened in their childhood dictate everything in their adult lives. Of course they're marked by events and the terrible things that were done to them, but they have survived. That's the idea here . . . You don't allow yourself to be tyrannized by past events, by the child that you once were."

It was an intriguing idea, like Emma's blog about the scared child. Was it possible to cut out a part of your life that had damaged you, like a lizard dropping its tail after an attack and then growing another one?

I patted the sea bream dry with a paper towel and scored the skin to stop it shrinking. All that was left to do was rub it with salt and a little oil so the skin would turn crisp, then put it under a very hot grill. Not for too long, because it keeps cooking after you take it out. People forget that, as if you can stop a natural process bang in its tracks, just by moving it from one place to another. Food and people have a lot in common. Both need care and time. Both need to collect themselves before presentation to the outside world.

The plates were already on the counter and the salad was prepared. I put a piece of fish on each plate, taking care that it didn't break. This time Lily jumped up and took everything to the table. The rain had eased and I could hear more of the conversation.

"Other people's neuroses are so exhausting," said Rob. "And it's only Tuesday. How will I keep going until the weekend?"

Theo laughed. "I feel sure you'll manage."

Rob sighed, a mock theatrical whoosh of air. The candles on the table guttered, throwing a flickering shadow on his face before steadying and burning brightly again. "I'm not so sure. I've still got the final part of this book to finish. Everything is taking so much longer than I thought."

He waved his fork as he spoke, scattering bits of fish around his plate. "I don't know why, but somehow I thought it would be so easy to find most of the people who lived in that community with McLeish. But many are proving hard to track down. I guess they're not the types to go on Facebook. Also, I didn't realize that all his papers were in such a mess, complete and utter chaos."

I scrubbed the pots. Cold water does a much better job than hot to remove starchy food. Grains of rice, speckled an oily gray from the mushrooms, blocked the drain. I scooped them out and flung them into the compost bin.

"McLeish sounds so weird," Theo's girlfriend said, speaking for the first time. Her voice was loud and grating. Even Theo flinched. "What was it like? You know, the place where they lived."

"I've got photographs," said Rob. "Somewhere in the study." He jumped up and left the room, returning minutes later with a plastic folder. "The house is called Kinghurst Place. It's in East Sussex." He delved into the folder and spread a pile of glossy color photographs over the table. "Here it is now. Quite the hedge-funder's paradise."

I finished wiping the pots and slid them into a drawer under the counter. I looked across and saw a large Edwardian-style house painted white, surrounded by swaths of perfectly striped lawn, a tennis court, and a turquoise swimming pool. Everything reeked of money. There were photographs of the interior as well: drawing rooms and billiard rooms and vast halls, all shiny and new.

"And this . . ." He pulled out a smaller cardboard folder and opened it. "This is what Kinghurst Place used to look like, when McLeish reigned supreme back in the eighties." He held up a grainy photograph of a gloomy liver-colored brick house standing at the end of a cracked tarmac drive. What looked like a giant yew tree, draped with torn flags, leaned against one side of the house.

The saucepan drawer closed and a faint beat started in my head, like castanets. Clickety-click, clickety-click, followed by the strumming of a banjo, or it might have been a guitar.

"What a depressing-looking place," said Theo. The clickety-click stopped, then started again, in time to a simple tune without words.

"It wasn't really gloomy," Rob continued, "because all the residents were free to explore themselves and their creativity. And don't forget this was during a time when governments had cut funds for mental health, and many sick people were going without any kind of treatment. What conventional society at the time saw as madness, which could only be dealt with by knockout drugs or being locked away in an institution, Rowan saw as an intelligent response to an intolerable situation. It was very humane. He was a remarkable man.

"Writers and academics came from all over the world to visit. It was famous and kind of glamorous in its own way. For a while, it was very popular with Hollywood actors and directors. It was incredibly hip."

Rob heaped his plate with salad. "I don't think I would have finished my degree if he hadn't been my tutor. He was absolutely brilliant, a professor before he was thirty. And a talented musician as well—nothing he loved more than playing jazz on the piano.

"He set up Kinghurst Place a bit before I became his student and moved between there and the university. The fact that he was such a respected academic and that he also ran what he called this experimental community meant he and his work got a lot of attention, but also that no one pried into the activities of Kinghurst Place. If anyone had investigated, they would have seen that he hardly ran things by the book. Weird goings-on. He was like a dictator with a harem on tap, and he wasn't averse to the odd psychedelic drug, long after most of the psychiatric community had abandoned their use for treatment. What he did was completely unorthodox, but everyone who knew him worshipped him like a god.

"He was a hero to the whole university—standing room only in all his lectures. *Rolling Stone* once did a cover story on him. His book, *Anti-Memoir*, sold about six million copies. It was on the bestseller lists for more than a year. And to think I was lucky enough to have access to his intellect and ideas. He blew my mind, as we used to say back then."

"Oh Dad, come on." Lily shook her head and grinned. "We're sheltered kids, we don't need to know about your druggy days back at university."

"Not that druggy," said Emma. "We both did well, remember. You don't do loads of drugs and get first-class degrees at the same time. We had to put the work in. Although I always envied Rob that he knew McLeish and I didn't. My tutor was so dull. No one would bother writing a book about him."

Theo turned to the girl. Her name was Amber. Judging from the puzzled expression on her face, she had no idea what anyone was talking about. "McLeish died a year ago, and left all his papers and stuff to Rob. A bit of a bolt from the blue."

"I didn't expect it," said Rob. "It was a complete surprise. Who knows why he did it? Because we lost touch with each other a couple of years after I graduated. The last time I saw him was maybe ten years ago, when he appeared on my program. He was drinking pretty heavily by then and his reputation was going downhill. Kinghurst Place was no more and he'd left academic life, said he was bored by the administrative nightmares and pettiness. But he still hankered after the Kinghurst Place days, said they were his finest hour."

"But if the people there were mad," Jake asked, "how could they look after themselves? Didn't they need treatment, medicine?" His voice was breaking and he kept his face completely still when he spoke, as if by doing so he could control the cracked sounds that sometimes emerged from his throat.

"So many things he did were wrong, but equally, so many things he did were right. Rowan believed in treating all people as sane individuals, in talking to them," Rob replied. "There's a fine line between being mad and being eccentric. He wasn't interested in drugging them like zombies with conventional pharmaceuticals." He scooped up the photographs and put them back inside the folder.

From the table, Emma turned to me. "Anne, dinner was delicious. But we've kept you too long. I hope we haven't interrupted your evening."

"Of course not," I said. The tune without words inside my head had stopped by now, and I'd been so caught up in Rob's conversation that I hadn't noticed the time. I looked at my watch. Not even nine o'clock.

"Good night," I said, gathering my things. "Would you like me to put the folder back in the study on my way out?"

"Thanks," replied Rob, refilling everyone's glass. "That would be terrific."

I picked up the folder and walked towards the study. Rob's desk was piled with pages marked with bright yellow Post-its. Lily and Jake always teased him about his old-fashioned way of printing out everything to do with his work, instead of storing it on his computer. I put the folder on the lowest pile.

Rob had forgotten to turn off the computer, and the screen was frozen on a blurred YouTube image of a man playing a piano with his back to the audience. I was curious, and clicked the cursor to play the clip. It was McLeish, at a jazz recital in Edinburgh in 2010. When he turned and bowed to muted applause, a lick of white, greasy hair fell over his forehead. There was an air of apology about him. He slurred his words as he thanked the audience, and he stumbled as he walked off the stage. I couldn't help thinking that Rob had chosen a difficult subject. Did anyone care what had happened back then?

An hour later, I was back home listening to the couple upstairs argue—"How could you lie to me like that?" the woman shouted. Oh, how I recognized the hurt and anger in her voice. But now I did so at something of a remove. Scar tissue, I supposed. There was an exasperated reply from the man. "It was nothing. Get over it." I heard a door slam and then stamping on the staircase outside my door.

11

∞

There is nothing more unreliable than memory and yet nothing more precious. Sometimes, even unconsciously, we perceive our memories as wounds that won't or can't heal. But the power to heal those wounds is within each one of us. Try considering a specific memory in a different way. What you see might surprise you.

—Emma Helmsley, "Taking the Moment," May 10, 2016

It happens to everyone, music slipping in through the cracks. Jude once sang "Roar" by Katy Perry for at least a fortnight, and Anton used to get stuck on Coldplay songs for days at a time. Most of the time, when a song gets embedded in my head, I don't mind. I've always looked upon it as some part of the brain having a rest, just playing something on a loop. But this tune, which came back into my head just before sleep, annoyed and agitated. I couldn't retrieve the words, even though it wafted about my head like a long forgotten nursery rhyme.

The tune wouldn't identify itself and it wouldn't leave me. I couldn't get it out of my head all the way to Petersham the next morning. At some stage on the bus, I must have started humming it again, because the man sitting next to me nudged me with his elbow. "Give it a rest, OK," he said. I apologized and got off two stops early to walk the rest of the way to Wycombe Lodge. When I opened the front door, I nearly collided with Rob, smelling of toothpaste and shampoo, with a whiff of last night's wine.

"I'm just off," he said. "Emma has already gone. Oh, but I've got something for you. I almost forgot. Hang on a minute." He dropped his bag on the floor and turned back towards the study. I stood under the columns, noting the weed-free gravel with some satisfaction. It hadn't taken that long to clear. Then Rob was beside me, brandishing a battered paperback.

"What's that tune you're humming?" he asked.

"Sorry," I said. "I can't get rid of it and it's becoming annoying. A man on the bus this morning told me to stop humming. I wasn't even aware that I was."

"Hmmm," said Rob, his eyebrows wrinkling. "Sounds catchy."

I shrugged. "I must have heard something like it somewhere. Lots of songs sound the same." I peered at the cover of the book.

"Oh, yes, this is what I went back for," said Rob. He handed me the book with a flourish. "I thought you might be interested. Take it home if you like. It's about the battle for nutmeg. Did you know that the English and Dutch went to war in the seventeenth century over nutmeg? A man called Nathaniel Courthope was besieged by the Dutch on an island called Run in Indonesia for four years before he died, trying to protect the seed of a single spice. Amazing!"

"Thank you," I said, irrationally flattered.

He checked his watch. "Why am I always so late when it's my recording day?"

"Who is it this week?"

"An outgoing department head of Goldman Sachs. He's leaving the corporate world to pursue a life of good works in Nepal. First world guilt to solve third world problems. Either that or he's about to be fired and wants to get out quickly before the proverbial hits the fan."

With that, he was gone. I closed the door behind me and

began my day's work. Upstairs, the bedroom was full of the usual morning mess. Pillows heaped everywhere, crumpled tissues scattered across the mattress, jeans and shirts littering the floor, and damp towels blocking the entrance to the bathroom. I picked everything up and put it in a pile for the laundry, folded back the duvet, bent to plump the pillows.

Then, something I hadn't noticed before. The mingling of Emma's special soap from Tuscany and Rob's sharper perspiration, the unmistakable musky, sweet, and stale smell of two bodies lying together, warmth rising out of them, skin to skin. Such an ordinary thing. I didn't expect to be undone by it, suddenly wanting to roll in the bed like an animal and claim it for myself. A ridiculous feeling and one I'd never had before. But I couldn't rid myself of it. I went to the window and leaned my head against the glass, felt the cool ribbon of air eddying upwards between the gaps until I was breathing normally again.

There was a scratching noise behind me, and I whipped around, scared of an intruder. But it was only Siggy on his daily pilgrimage through the rooms looking for his absent mistress. Cairn terriers were meant to be cheerful and clever, but so far Siggy showed no sign of either quality.

He fixed me with mournful eyes, then sniffed the carpet before flattening his brindled ears and flopping down in front of my feet. It was his way of saying that I was a poor substitute for his proper love. I thought he was a poor substitute for a proper dog, but I'd learned there was no point in shooing him away. He would only trip you up again. Siggy was cunning like that. I scratched his back for a bit then finished my cleaning. Tidied, dusted. Remade the bed, cleaned the bathroom. I liked doing things in the right order. Towels changed twice a week, bed linen once.

When I began at Wycombe Lodge, all I saw from this window was bare branches stretching up to the sky. Every now and then there was a tang of cold earth, almost like the country. Later, I realized that if I looked sideways, I could see the Thames, with ferries and small boats and an occasional lone sculler drawing in his oars as he paused on the bend.

Now that I knew the house better, Rob and Emma's series of rooms were not as opulent as I'd first thought. The backs of the curtains were water-stained and the lining was beginning to rot. The carpet was threadbare and the bedside tables warped and covered with ring marks from late night drinks and morning mugs of tea. In the bathroom, some of the old-fashioned black-and-white tiles were cracked and there was an ominous bulge in the wall next to the basins. They didn't care. Yet another thing that I admired about them: the way they concentrated on more interesting things than plumbing and lime scale in the bathroom basins, things that would bother me until they were fixed and scrubbed clean. I'd always been a bit obsessive about that sort of thing. Anton called it my control fetish. Whatever, any kind of disorder unsettled me. As I tidied their room, I thought of my own neat line of clothes, everything brushed and hung up the minute I took it off, the small piles of precisely folded sweaters and tops. I knew where everything was and the last time I touched it.

This was my favorite time of day, the house to myself, wandering around the sitting room, picking up the books and straightening the cushions. Sometimes, more often than I cared to admit, I imagined that I was the chatelaine, with my husband by my side and two children upstairs, that it was me flinging open the front door, greeting guests, another riotous evening about to begin. "Do come in. Sorry the place is in a bit of a mess." A smile, a small shrug. "Help yourself to a drink. Red. White. Anything you like. We'll eat soon, promise."

At other times, I just stood still and gazed through the French doors onto the walled garden. I liked to stand close to the windowpanes and tilt my head to see how the small distortions and tiny bubbles in the wavy glass changed my perspective. To the left, and the branches of the beech tree in the corner drooped. To the right, they grew strong and straight. In the wind they rippled and blurred into something completely different, a ballerina glittering in the sun, or hands outstretched for help in the rain.

Rob explained that these distortions were present in all glass made in the eighteenth century, because it was thicker in some parts than others. It was called drawn clear glass. The people who could afford windows hundreds of years ago didn't care that what they saw through the glass wasn't entirely real. They were happy enough to see a blurred version of the world, to have some light enter a room. Rob was thoughtful like that. He would see me looking at books or pictures and tell me about them, not in a condescending way, just as if he knew that I was interested.

I wandered into the study. Someone, maybe Jake or Lily, had been looking through the photograph albums. They were scattered all over the floor, their silver and black spines jumbled together. The photographs—Jake and Lily as babies, Emma and Rob proudly pushing prams—had been glued to the pages with neat captions celebrating childhood milestones. Emma must have been going through an organized phase, or it might have been Fiona. First steps. First solo bike rides. The early years at Wycombe Lodge. Emma with a frizz of crimped hair and Rob with a Western-style mustache. Everything neatly catalogued for easy reference. No chance of memories going astray here. Apart from that one photograph of the back of my head when I was a baby, I had no idea what I looked like before I went to live with Gran.

The front door opened and slammed shut. There were footsteps muffled by a dragging sound. I looked up to see Jake at the door, his backpack dangling from his hand.

"Hello," I said. "I'm just tidying here. Can you give me a hand, just to make sure I don't get everything in the wrong order?"

"Sure." He dropped his backpack and squatted beside me. He smelled of orange juice, sweat, and socks that had been worn a day too long. He picked up the album nearest to him. "They're all numbered, on the back page. It's Dad's thing. He's not very digital. Everyone else has their albums on Facebook or Instagram."

"But it's nice to have something physical, don't you think?" I asked. "A proper record of your life. No Photoshopping to make people's smiles whiter or their legs thinner. The real thing."

Jake made a noise somewhere between a laugh and a grunt. "Not so sure about that. There's that thing that the camera never lies, but it does all the time."

"I can't believe it would be possible to lie about your dad's mustache." I pointed to the photograph and we both laughed.

"You've got a point," he said.

"Let me get you something to eat—there's cake and fruit." We stood up. "Thanks, but I can get it myself."

"I know," I said. "But I'm not so sure if you'll clear up afterwards. When I first started here, I couldn't work out how you and Lily could make so much mess so quickly. I mean, really. It was an Olympic gold medal effort."

"I'm sorry." He blushed.

"Don't be," I said. "You're both so much better now. Besides, it's my job." A question about the Church of Eternal Truth formed in my mind. Just one, something mild and non-consequential to satisfy my curiosity. But he got up and walked out of the room. I put the albums back on the shelf, above the complete works of Jung and Freud and rows of hardbacks on behavioral psychology. John Dewey, Erik Erikson, Erich Fromm, Donald Winnicott. *How We Think. Childhood and Society. The Art of Loving. Home Is Where We Start From.* A complete history of the modern Western family, neatly filed and dusted.

12

〰

Everything that is edible and passes under the hands of the cook, is more or less changed, and assumes new forms. Hence the influence of that functionary is immense upon the happiness of a household.

—*Mrs. Beeton's Book of Household Management*, 1861

Good food, even plain good food, could create an inner calm, just the same as a well-kept house produced its own harmony. Some would say that people should find these things inside themselves rather than in a bag of groceries. But I thought cooking was more than science and the combination of heat and herbs. It had its own stardust.

I checked the refrigerator and the pantry for supper. There was going to be the usual weeknight fixture of Theo, and two others, Emma had told me the evening before.

"Rebecca and Christine," she announced brightly before supper when we were alone in the kitchen. "Rebecca is Rob's daughter, from before. I mean, from before we were married, but not that much before. And Christine is her mother. We were all at university together, and, well, now we're all good friends."

It was hard to know what to make of these bouncy announcements, particularly as a furrow appeared in Emma's forehead when she spoke. "Christine is very much her own woman now, but Rob likes to keep in contact with Rebecca. It's important for children, don't you think?" She didn't sound convinced.

"Rob and I, well there was a break for a bit, and . . ." She laughed. "Hey presto, Rebecca! She's a bit older than Lily. So Lily and Jake have a half sister," she said, removing one of her hoop earrings and pulling at the tiny hole in her lobe. With only one gold dancing circle, her face looked skewed. "Although we don't like that term, half sister or half brother. We just say brother or sister. It's really all the same. But don't get the wrong impression," she continued. "We're not one of those let-it-all-hang-out kind of couples. Rob and I have an old-fashioned kind of marriage. I always say we're the swans and the wolves of the human world. We've mated for life. All that social experimenting—the changing modern marriage, the blended family—it doesn't come home with us. We're old-fashioned."

She twiddled with her earring and fixed me in a steady gaze.

"That's good to hear," I said. Was she warning me? Did she imagine I had my eye on Rob and that I waited for her to leave each morning so I could begin a carefully orchestrated flirting session with him? No, she was just vulnerable. Despite all her success, she had her insecurities, just like the rest of us. It made me like her even more, to know that she had confided in me about her marriage.

Emma opened the wine cooler and pulled out a bottle of Sancerre. She wrestled with the corkscrew. "Will you have a glass with me?" I shook my head and she poured herself a glass, filling it to the brim. "I forgot to say that Christine and Rebecca don't eat red meat. And Rob says we should have supper early, so he can drive them home in good time. They live miles away, almost at Crystal Palace." She drank in steady swallows. "Although I don't see why they can't get the bus or the Tube. Do you mind, Anne? I hope it's no extra bother for you."

"Not at all," I said, about to add that it was no bother to be asked to finish work earlier than usual, when Lily and one of her friends walked into the kitchen. Unlike Jake, who seemed to have no friends, or none that came to Wycombe Lodge, Lily had an interchangeable group of sullen and spotty girls in a permanent simmering anger about pretty much everything.

"It's unbelievable," they muttered to each other, heads down and scowling as they gobbled fruit and cake in the kitchen after school before rushing upstairs. The focus of last week's anger was the illegal slaughtering of rhinoceroses. Next week, it could be female genital mutilation. From what I could gather, it was all about maintaining the rage.

"Who's coming to dinner?" asked Lily.

Emma reached for her glass. "Christine and Rebecca."

Lily turned to her friend and rolled her eyes. Lily had a particularly droll eye roll, slow, with a full circumference of her pupils around the whites of her eyes, accompanied by a slight rotation of her head and an exaggerated eyebrow lift. I tried not to smile.

"Why do *they* have to come to our house?" Lily demanded.

Emma clutched her wine. "Because Rebecca is your sister and she is Daddy's daughter," Emma said. There was a slight stammer in her voice. Maybe she was trying to convince herself as well as Lily.

Lily snapped back. "She's only a couple of years older than me, but she's always going on as if she knows everything. And Christine is a big fat pain. You don't like them either, I know you don't. Dad finds them difficult, I've heard him say so. The only person who wants to see them is Jake, and that's because Rebecca has always got her tits out on a plate."

"Lily! Don't speak like that. It's not true."

"Of course it is." Lily grabbed her bewildered-looking friend's arm. At the door, she turned and spat at her mother. "You're just too cowardly to say so. And you're jealous."

"Jealous of who?"

"Oh come off it, you're jealous of them." Lily glared at Emma, biting her lip as if she wanted to shout out something but didn't trust herself to speak. She stamped upstairs, her friend trailing behind her.

Emma turned to me, helpless and embarrassed. "Can you decide what to eat? I always seem to get it wrong," she asked.

"Sure," I replied.

Later, after dinner—one of their favorite tray bakes again, this time with cod steaks—I went upstairs with the day's laundry. Jake's door was shut, so I left his clothes in a basket in the hall. Lily was lying on her bed, reading.

"Are you still interested in cooking something with me?" I asked. "Maybe we could do an apple crumble tomorrow, for dinner."

"Why not?" she said, flinging the book onto the floor. "Oh, I'm sorry for being rude this afternoon. But I hate them. And I'm the legal one, not that bitch Rebecca."

I handed over the laundry. "Did you ever think it could be more difficult for her than it is for you? Just a thought. Anyway, tomorrow we'll have vichyssoise, roast chicken, and the crumble. Sunday lunch, except on a weekday evening. Is that so bad?"

At least I made her smile, just a bit.

It took Lily a while to learn how to peel an apple, but she got the hang of it. "You want the apples to be a bit sloppy for a good crumble," I told her. "It was one of the things my first boss, Mavis, taught me to cook in the nursing home in Clapham after I came to London. Mavis had a lot of rules about crumble."

"Like what?" asked Lily, scooping her peelings into the compost bin.

"Well, her first rule was that the usual mixture of butter, flour, and sugar was not good enough. She liked to add some rolled oats, or coconut and ground almonds, and she preferred demerara sugar." I put the ingredients, already measured, into a bowl and mixed them together. "And she said you had to have a good thick layer of crumble, so everyone could get their fair share. Mavis reckoned that food was very important, that it was the first pleasure to arrive in our lives and the last to leave."

"I've never thought of food in that way," said Lily. Siggy snuffled under our feet, hopeful for crumbs. A warm breeze carried the scent of grass and blossom through the open doors.

"Were you always interested in cooking?" she asked.

"Not in an obsessive way. I sort of drifted into it after school and then grew to like it. It was like going to a party every day and getting paid for it, because as well as loving the cooking, there's this whole subculture of misfits in restaurants and I fit right in."

"You're not a misfit," Lily said. "And is that really true? About the misfits?"

"Pretty much. In fact, it's hard to think of anyone completely sane in the catering business. First off, there was Sheila in the pub near Shaftesbury, my first job. She taught me how to pull a pint of beer and wore stilettos at all times, don't ask me how. Sheila also had a strong whiskey or two before breakfast every day. And then there was Charlie, who owned the first London restaurant I worked in—he was keen on things like mutton tartare and nettle pesto . . ."

"Mutton tartare! What's that?" asked Lily, layering the cooked apple in the baking dish.

"Finely chopped raw meat with bits and pieces thrown in."

"Disgusting," she said. "I could be sick."

"I agree with you, and hey, here's a funny thing. His place closed in under a year so off I went to other restaurants and chefs who knew a bit more about food."

"That still doesn't make you a misfit."

"Maybe not now so much, but at your age I was. I was packed

off to boarding school and I ran away—let me think now—maybe four or five times. Once I hid in the laundry truck, but the driver didn't unload it and I was stuck there all night with everyone's dirty sheets and towels. In the end, they didn't take me back. You're so lucky, coming back home every afternoon, having friends."

Lily wiped her forehead, leaving a smear of apple above her eyebrows. "But you must have had friends? Wasn't boarding school fun, being off on your own like in Harry Potter? Didn't you have, you know, adventures and crushes?"

September 1991. It was still so hot. Girls pushed past me. Perfect girls with clear pale skin, shiny hair, and pearled teeth. I was conscious of the freckles across my cheeks, the nervous rash on my neck.

In the dormitories, ramshackle by comparison to the grandeur of the school's façade, everyone unpacked her trunk, everything the same: pajamas with printed flower sprigs, silver frames with photographs of the girl's dogs and horses, and a large-bristle hairbrush. I had none of these things and hung about with no one speaking to me until a girl with long blond hair sat down on the bed next to mine.

"Did you blub when your mother left?" she asked.

"My mother's dead," I said.

"What about your father then?" She brushed her hair and began plaiting it.

I swallowed. Outside the window, light was falling. "I don't know where he is."

"My parents are divorced," she said, fastening her plait. "But we know where we come from. Everyone here knows that."

A bell rang. "Fabulous!" said the girl. Her name was Millie. "Supper." She turned to me. "Hurry up, otherwise there'll be none left." I thought supper was something people ate late at night. I didn't know it meant gluey potatoes and gristly sausages at six o'clock. I missed Gran's burned toast and her lamb casseroles.

At night I wept for my brown bedroom. I didn't belong there. I belonged at home, with Gran and Douglas. I didn't understand how I could be so lonely when I was never alone. I slept in a dormitory with nine other girls. I showered in a communal bathroom with only swing doors on the toilets. After school I studied in the library with the rest of my class and played lacrosse and hockey very badly. Everything was done in a team of which I was never a member. It didn't help that I was smarter than everyone else, although I tried to hide it. The other girls called me CLS, which took me some time to work out. It stood for Common Little Swat. The only surprise was that I stayed as long as I did.

"Throwing your life away," cried Gran. "Selfish child!" Long silences. Doors slamming then opening again. Earnest bedside chats.

"All those opportunities, gone forever," rasped Gran, too anxious to sit down, almost in tears. "I suppose all you can think about is that boy!"

"His name is Douglas," I shouted. "And I'll get a job." Alan, the publican, didn't care that I was only fifteen. He paid me even less than the minimum wage. Every night Douglas drove me home on his moped at the end of my shift. He'd left school as well, but hadn't followed his father into the excrement business. He plowed fields, mended fences, pulled weeds from rich people's gardens. For two years, everything was uncomplicated. There was pleasure and a sense of purpose, like it was the beginning of something, although I couldn't work out exactly what that something was. It was peaceful and I didn't have to satisfy anyone's expectations. But then Alan announced he

was almost bankrupt. The pub would close in three months'
time.

"I'll go to London and get a job," I told Douglas. "I'll work
in a pub there, maybe cook. Sheila says I could be good at
cooking. I'll come back at weekends, all the time. I won't miss
one, I promise."

I called him every morning from wherever I was living. The
hostel in Peckham. The room in Tower Hamlets, the studios
and the bedsits. Douglas told me if it had rained too much or
not enough, or if the hay was better this year than last. I never
really listened. I only wanted to drink in the regular beat of his
life, to wait for it to wash through me and sustain me through
those days and nights when the smell of cooking oil never really disappeared from my hair, no matter how often I washed it.
It was selfish of me to expect him to wait for me, like some loyal
Labrador, but I did. More than expected it, I counted on it.

One spring weekend in the cottage he'd rented for himself
outside town, he lay on his back after we'd made love. I traced
my fingers along his rough weather-beaten face down to the
soft skin on his chest. He rolled over and spoke to the ceiling.
"It's no good, being like this. It's not enough for me. I can't
hang about waiting for you to turn up once a week."

My fingers ran along the calluses on his palms. I'd always
admired his hands, their brute strength when he was working
and then their delicate touch when we were alone. I scrambled out of bed and walked to the window. My feet stuck on
the stone tiles. In the field at the end of the garden, a lamb
ran along the hedge. Up and down, up and down, tossing its
head, slithering in the mud and bleating in terrible broken
sounds.

"Can't we do something about that poor animal?" I cried.
The lamb slipped and fell on its side, its legs scrabbling and
failing to find purchase in the air.

"The ewe is dead," said Douglas in a flat voice. "The farmer will deal with the lamb soon enough. It can't survive without the mother, and there's no one with the time to bottle-feed one orphaned animal. You grew up around here. You know that."

In the reflection of the window, I saw my mouth grimace and tears run down my face. I felt as if I were suffocating. "I won't be in London forever," I cried. "But there's no work for me down here. Even Gran agrees with me on that one. I can't lose you," I whimpered. "I can't be without you."

I was only eighteen. I had no idea it would hurt so much.

I hadn't thought about that time with Douglas, or school, since the night about a year ago when I looked up from my bench at Anton et Amis and saw two of my former classmates drunk and tittering at a table full of leering red-faced men. I didn't have to turn my back. They wouldn't have thought to look into the kitchen.

"Everything OK?" Lily's question made me jump. "You were miles away."

"Everything is fine. I was wondering where Jake is—do you think he'd like to join us?"

"He's not here," said Lily. "Hard to know what he gets up to after school these days."

"He seems interested in religion—is there a school prayer group or something?" Again, I thought of the pamphlet in his room. "Or maybe he goes to a church?"

Lily snorted with laughter. "Hardly. Religion is not cool at our school, although there was one girl in my class who found God by the bus stop. But she forgot about him, or her, or it six months later. What makes you think Jake is interested in religion? If he was, it would be a first for this house."

"Oh, I don't know," I replied, deliberately vague. "Something he said maybe. I can't remember the exact details . . . but everything is all right with him?"

"Guess so." She handed me the bowl of crumble mixture and I spread it over the cooked apple. The counter around us was covered in a mess of apples and flour and sugar.

"Another of Mavis's rules was that cooks cleaned up after themselves," I said. "Start in a mess, end in a mess."

"Got it," she laughed and reached for a dishcloth. "Hey, this is good. Thanks."

"It's the wrong way round," I said. "Thank you. You've been a great kitchen buddy." I was about to tell her about Isabella's saying of a place for everything and everything in its place, but Lily would never have heard of Isabella Beeton.

Rob might not have heard of her either, but he would argue that Isabella's maxim applies to people as well. Rob had lots of theories about people's behavior. There was his point-of-chaos theory, by which he meant that everyone finds a place to store their mental chaos so they can remain sane during working hours. It might be the accountant who can do tax returns in his head but can't add up his restaurant bill, or the software engineer who can build entire digital systems but needs GPS to drive to the supermarket. He also thought people could work effectively for only three to four hours a day. The rest was just showing up or doing routine administration.

He'd say that this kitchen suited my psychological geography, another of his theories. Rob believed we have primitive responses to our environment. Some of us feel safe in the forest because there's always somewhere to hide. The rest fear the big bad wolf behind every tree and prefer open spaces where the enemy is more easily spotted. Since coming to Wycombe Lodge, I'd worked out that I was comfortable in the middle ground, with my back to the wall and a clear line of sight in front of me. In short, well defended.

By seven o'clock, everything was ready. Emma was home from work and Theo was in the kitchen chattering to me about definitions of happiness in various languages. "Did you know that Spanish has more words for happiness than any other language? Korean and Chinese have the fewest."

I wasn't that fussed about Korea and China. I was more concerned about happiness at Wycombe Lodge. I wanted my roast chicken and apple crumble to create family harmony and for Emma to lose that small furrow of anxiety on her brow.

The chicken was just out of the oven when a small, buxom, olive-skinned woman strode into the kitchen followed by an adolescent elongated twin of herself, with Rob taking up the rear.

"You must be the wonderful Anne." The woman bustled to the sink and held out her hand. I'd never seen a woman in her late forties with eyebrow piercings before, but she got away with it. "I'm Christine and this is Rebecca. Rob told us all about you. I have to say I've never smelled anything so delicious in this house in all the years I've been coming here. Lucky Rob!" Her voice was loud, yet husky. "And, naturally, lucky Emma!" Behind her, Theo rolled his eyes and made a funny face, like a nodding clown. I went to the sink and turned on the tap to hide my smile.

You could tell Christine was confident about her looks, the way she didn't wear any makeup and had let herself get plump, wearing a dowdy top and too tight jeans. Good-looking women were sometimes arrogant like that, regarding their beauty with the same nonchalance as rich women regarded their expensive clothes, like they were throwaway rags stitched together instead of designer fashion.

I saw it all the time in the restaurant. Oh, this old face, I've had it forever, can't think what to do with it. Christine pretended not to care, but she knew perfectly well that from the shoulders up she was an exact incarnation of those smoldering

French actresses, all almond-shaped eyes, sharp cheekbones, and hair chopped like the cat had been at it, her looks accentuated rather than marred by such a savage haircut.

Emma stopped lighting candles and rushed to greet Christine and Rebecca, stumbling over the hem of her skirt and almost falling into Christine's arms. Her fine blond good looks paled before Christine's forceful confidence and the bloom in her olive complexion. I thought of the face serums and creams beginning to multiply in Emma's bathroom.

"Wonderful to see you both," Emma exclaimed. "And Rebecca, don't you look lovely in that color!" Rebecca wore a sleeveless flimsy red gypsy-style top and jeans, with a skin-exposing gap in between. From her neck to her waist, the effect was cheery, almost festive, at odds with the scowl on her face.

"Where are those divine children of yours?" cried Christine. "Hiding away in the attic?"

Towering a full head above her, Emma pursed her lips. "They'll be down in a minute, probably just finishing their homework or something."

She had lit extra candles, so many that the dining room resembled an altar. Everyone gathered around the table. Lily passed soup plates, and Jake, returned from some unexplained outing, slid about in his chair, unable to take his eyes off Rebecca, who declined the vichyssoise because of the carbohydrates. After some hesitation, Lily did the same. The only sound came from the scrape of spoons on plates until Christine began rabbiting on about her job as a community worker, teaching teenage mothers how to look after their babies.

"It never ceases to surprise me," she said, "how the maternal instinct somehow always kicks in, even with the young ones, the thirteen-year-olds. But then, they're so much more physically mature than their mothers were. Some of the girls I deal with have been sexually active since they were about twelve." She made this sound like an admirable athletic achievement, like running a hundred meters in record time.

Rob snorted. "Don't you think it would be a better idea to hand out condoms at the school gate? A child with a child—never a good idea."

Christine's eyes narrowed. Her eyebrow ring glinted in the candlelight. "How very middle class of you, Rob, and how very prejudiced. It's a totally different world where Rebecca and I live. Not all of us aspire to the protection of fee-paying schools for rich kids. If I had my way, private schools would be banned. They're simply not necessary. They do more harm than good."

"I'm sure Rob didn't mean to offend," Emma chirped. The furrow between her eyebrows had deepened. "Gosh, this soup is good!"

Lily stood up and brought the bowls over to the counter. Soup slopped onto the marble, pale and slimy. She pulled her gray sweatshirt down to cover her thighs and picked up the bowl of carrots and beans.

"Oh, Rebecca could have helped," said Christine. Rebecca scowled, but Christine plowed on. "So lovely this, all of us here together." She raised her glass and everyone dutifully followed suit. I carried the chicken across to Rob.

"Ah," he said, determinedly hearty. "At last. The magnificent bird!" He picked up a knife and began hacking. He gouged out pieces of breast meat, waving each piece in the air, allowing it to go cold before tossing it onto a plate. Then he tore at the legs and wings, elbows raised to his shoulders with the carving action of a chain-saw killer.

Emma's wineglass had been traveling with a steady movement from her mouth to the table and back again, halting only for a refill. Rob glared in her direction as he picked up his water with a theatrical flourish. She ignored him and began talking about a house in Majorca that she was thinking of renting next summer.

"We'd love it if you could come, Rebecca," she said.

"Maybe," said Rebecca, flicking her hair. "I mean, thanks."

They began to eat, and somehow the atmosphere lifted. Rob and Theo had almost finished their first helpings and Emma was actually putting food into her mouth, not pushing it around her plate. They talked about films about to be released and a planned school excursion to the Royal Academy. Emma took care to include Rebecca and Christine in everything. Candles flickered behind Emma's head as she asked Rebecca about her favorite television series. *Breaking Bad?* Or *House of Cards?*

It wasn't exactly the free-flowing conversation I'd hoped for, but it was good enough. Everyone was carefully cheery and polite. They looked like a family. Not a perfect family. After a childhood searching for one of my own, I knew they didn't exist. But it was a functioning family nonetheless. Even Siggy was behaving like a proper dog for once, lying by the door in his basket, his head between his paws.

The tension in my neck and shoulders seeped away as I washed the last of the pots. I took the crumble out of the oven and placed it on the counter, thinking that one of the best smells in the world had to be roasting juices overlaid by the buttery sweetness of cooked apples. Emma took the crumble and a bowl of ice cream to the table.

"Lily helped Anne to make it," she said and they all clapped, even Rebecca.

My food had worked its alchemy after all. It was time to go home. Just a final wipe down and clear away, not too quickly, because I was enjoying the sight of everyone still sitting and talking at the table. Only Rob had slipped away, but he often went into his study straight after dinner.

"Good night," I said when I couldn't find anything else to do. "Enjoy your evening."

Emma jumped up and came over to me, still holding her

wineglass. "Thank you, thank you," she whispered. "You're an absolute lifesaver. I mean it."

"It's nothing." But it felt like something, walking through the hall towards the front door, hearing the easy rise and fall of their talk.

In the study, Rob was staring at the computer screen, wearing headphones. When he saw me wave goodbye, he whipped them off and motioned for me to join him.

"Have a listen to this." He handed me the headphones. I sat down and put them on. They were still warm from his ears. Such an unexpected thing, this transfer of physical heat. I brushed the feeling aside and concentrated on listening. At first I didn't hear anything except for faint static. After a few seconds, music began.

There it was, the clickety-click, then the banjo sound and after that, the tune I'd been unable to get out of my head. Except this time the tune had words, sung by a high, clear female voice. It was simple doggerel, almost, but not quite recognizable, like one of those nursery rhymes that you never quite remember and never quite forget.

> *I am you and you are me*
> *We are as one and one will be*
> *One or two, or even three.*

There was a chorus as well; more simple lines, but I didn't recognize the words. There was that same feeling that I'd had when I first walked into Wycombe Lodge, of entering a strange room and finding it acutely familiar. But this time there was no feeling of belonging or homecoming. This felt dark. I didn't like it. From behind the desk, Rob sat with his hand on his chin, looking at me as if I was a clue in a crossword puzzle.

"It's quite interesting," said Rob. "McLeish wrote that song.

He wrote lots of songs and this was one of them. But they weren't chart toppers by any means—they weren't even on public release."

"Odd," I said. "I guess it's just one of those weird coincidences."

As I stood up to leave, my eye fell on a black-and-white photograph on the desk. It was another photograph of Kinghurst Place, taken from a different angle, showing the side of the house and what looked like a small wood in the distance.

"There's a statue in that wood," I said without thinking, "of a little boy. And he's playing a flute. He's not wearing any clothes."

Even as I spoke, I knew it was gibberish, childish nonsense. I was even speaking like a child, about statues not wearing any clothes, when any sensible adult would have used the word naked.

"How stupid of me." I tried to laugh, but there it was again, that same feeling of fear and darkness. "All those big houses in the country—they look pretty much the same. Another of those weird coincidences. I must have gone to a house that looked just like that when I was a kid."

Rob gazed at me, his eyes magnified behind his rimless glasses. "Sure," he said. "It happens all the time. We get things a bit confused. Ghosts in the machine and all that."

13

~

Being strong doesn't mean closing yourself off from the world and pulling up the drawbridge. True strength comes from being open about your fragilities and weaknesses, to yourself and others.

—Emma Helmsley, "Taking the Moment," May 20, 2016

All the way home, I puzzled over my reaction to the song and the photograph. Unless I was going mad, which I very much doubted—I counted backwards from two hundred in nines and then in sevens and sixes, just to make sure—there had to be some rational explanation. As for my reaction—well, that could be anything at all.

If Gran was still alive, I could have asked her if I'd ever been to such a house as a child, or if I'd spent any time in East Sussex. She might not have wanted to tell me about my mother, but she would have told me about a visit to a house. No harm there. Even she would have admitted that.

The smell of drains rose up from the pavement as I walked towards my flat. The boy was playing hopscotch again on the street. He couldn't have been more than six or seven, but he was out here on his own in the dark. He sang to himself, a strange, tuneless song without words. Something about him drew me in. His cherubic face, at odds with the shadows under his velvet eyes that made him seem older. His neat black quiff bouncing up and down as he jumped from square to square, dressed in what looked like school shorts and a thin sweatshirt.

He kept licking his lower lip, which was swollen and chapped. His knees were knobbed and covered with chalk dust as he jumped neatly, legs together, landing like a dancer, softly on the balls of his feet. I was tempted to reach out and touch the warm nape of his neck and give him a tissue so he didn't have to wipe his nose on his sweatshirt.

"Hello," I said, looking around for a parent or a carer. Anything could happen to a boy that age left on his own. "Hopscotch is a good game," I continued awkwardly, trying to appear friendly, instead of sounding like a ponderous, aged aunt. "I used to play it when I was a child." The boy paused, balancing on one leg. "It's one of those games that children all over the world play," I added. His eyes were enormous, almond-shaped, with thick eyelashes, and he glanced around as if he was scared that someone might see me talking to him.

"I like it," he said in a croaky voice. He smiled, a polite smile, nothing more. He hopped into the next square, then stopped so suddenly that he almost tripped over me. I smelled the oil on his hair and chocolate on his breath.

"Sorry, sorry, Papa, I was just . . ." The boy was stuttering. I thought he was apologizing to me, needlessly, but realized he was staring at a point above my shoulder. A tall, thin man appeared from behind me. "Thank goodness I have found you," he said, embracing the boy. "I was worried, so worried." He stroked the boy's head with exquisite tenderness. "Anything could have happened." Although the man wore a shabby suit that bagged at the knees and slipped off his narrow shoulders, he had a distinguished air about him. In another life he might have been a professor or an eminent doctor, accustomed to authority. "Well, he's safe now," I said. "You must be relieved." The man nodded and walked into a building near the corner of my street, his arm around his son.

Jude rang just as I unlocked my front door. "You haven't forgotten about the twins' birthday on Sunday," she said.

"What sort of godmother would I be if I did a thing like that? I'll be there. Promise not to be late."

I changed into an old tracksuit and turned on my computer. There had to be an answer to the puzzle of that song and the photograph of Kinghurst Place. Less than a minute later, an explanation was on my screen. Déjà vu. Already seen. The illusion of having seen something before that is actually being experienced for the first time. So simple.

Next I typed in Kinghurst Place. There was the same gloomy picture of the house that Rob had showed me, newspaper and magazine shots of McLeish from various angles, and a series of McLeish portraits by David Bailey, moody and half-lit, looking like a gangster. Underneath these was an out-of-focus photograph of McLeish and some of his followers seated at a long dining table crowded with bottles and glasses and plates heaped with food. Groups of candles, placed at odd angles and heights, blazed. All around the table was dark. McLeish was gesticulating with both hands. He looked to be in midsentence, and everyone was leaning towards him with a rapturous expression. At the end of the table was a woman with blond, tumbling hair, her profile in shadow. There was something about the way she held her chin that reminded me of the photographs of my mother that stood behind the sofa in Gran's cottage, but I could have been imagining it. I looked at the photograph for some time, examining my reactions for signs of recognition of anything at all. Nothing. Nothing at all.

I scrolled down and read on. Many websites referred to the Kinghurst Place community as a cult and noted that McLeish, although a well-known academic, had no formal links to any government organizations. One site mentioned that he wouldn't have been able to escape close scrutiny in the present digital age. It pointed out that, although the Internet had existed in some form since the 1970s, it wasn't introduced publicly for at least another twenty years.

There were articles on McLeish, all of them echoing Rob's statements that he was brilliant, the most famous psychologist of his time and the charismatic leader of his very own Utopian community with no rules and no boundaries, a controversial mantra-maker back in the day of the sedative handcuff. Local newspaper archives reported complaints about noise and parties that continued all night. There was an interview with a retired teacher who referred to barbaric behavior and practices fit only for heathens. More recently there was an announcement for a biopic about McLeish starring an actor from the *Doctor Who* series and then another announcement that the project had been canceled due to lack of funds. There seemed no point in looking further. I clicked onto Emma's daily email. She wished her followers a happy and productive weekend. I ate the remnants of a vegetable curry and watched a rerun of *The Bridge*.

The next day I did my usual pounding run along the towpath, then drove to Primrose Hill on Sunday, the only day of the week with no parking restrictions. My old Peugeot hadn't gotten much use since Gran died. Before that, I'd drive down to see her in Shaftesbury every fortnight or so. M4. M25. M3. A303. The motorways rolled out, other drivers accelerating past me in scorn as I kept to my steady sixty-five miles per hour in the slow lane, along with the lorry drivers and befuddled old couples unfolding their maps, until I pushed past Stonehenge and its wandering circle of tourists. These days the car mostly sat in its space behind my building. So far, it had started every time, but not without protesting hiccups and coughs like an old man disturbed from a nap.

I parked and walked towards Jude's house. Its gate was festooned with blue and pink helium balloons. "No chance of gender confusion here," I said when Jude opened the door. The twins were hard to buy for. They had everything from initialed iPads to customized scooters. So each year, I gave Amelia an antique sterling silver table setting and Charlie some good red wine, stored for him at Berry Bros. & Rudd. They could do what they liked with them when they reached eighteen.

Inside, the house was heaving with overheated children wild-eyed from too much sugar. A pair of clowns tried to keep control as their parents drank champagne in the sitting room. Philip pecked me on the cheek and handed me a glass.

"It's only eleven in the morning," I said.

"You'll need it before the day is out," he replied. "Now, I have to mingle."

"With the children?"

"No, with their parents. Otherwise the twins won't have any friends. Who'd have thought I'd be working the room in my own house?" Under the conspicuous spending and relentless social climbing, Philip was a devoted father.

After the requisite one and a half hours, everyone left and Jude parked the twins in front of the television, where they immediately fell asleep, pink and blue icing dribbling down their chins. Philip went off to the gym he'd built for himself in the cellar, leaving Jude and me in the kitchen. I used to envy her that enormous, sleek room with glass doors opening onto a courtyard garden; the La Cornue stove, the custom-made copper sink, and the triple-door refrigerator. But now I'd grown attached to the kitchen in Wycombe Lodge. In fact, I preferred it, because I looked upon it as mine.

"So," said Jude, downing the last of her champagne. "At last I have you all to myself, face-to-face, I can interrogate you. When are you going to give up that job as a scullery maid and rejoin the real world?"

I laughed. "You're just like Gran—you never give up. I know it's hard for you to understand, but I like it there, and I like it more and more all the time. It's not for life, but for the moment it works."

"But who will you ever meet there, in the kitchen? Don't you want to get together with someone else? You're so good with Charlie and Amelia. Don't you ever think about children of your own?"

We'd had versions of this conversation before, mainly when we were both childless and the idea of motherhood was one of those what-if scenarios that probably would never happen. But now Jude had the twins, and as she'd pointed out to me not too kindly, the time for what-ifs was passing me by. I was approaching the what-might-have-been zone.

"Sometimes I thought about it when I was with Anton, of course. But I'm not sure if I know how the whole thing works. Mothers and daughters. I had Gran, and I know she loved me, but it never felt very maternal, if you know what I mean. I wouldn't know what to do with a child, and I'd be scared of messing everything up, scarring him or her for life. Maybe if it had worked out with Anton . . . but it didn't."

Jude leaned on the counter and took my hand. "Is everything better now? I mean, are you getting over it?"

"I think so," I said. "I'm not obsessed anymore, and days go past when I don't even think about him. And it wasn't all Anton's fault. He'd always made the parameters of the relationship clear. He was wary of saying the word 'forever.' I guess the end was inevitable."

"His loss," she said. "Hey, I've got something for you." She opened a cupboard. "Here." She handed me a Smythson notebook bound in bloodred leather.

I thanked her, but privately couldn't think of a more useless present.

"I can tell you don't like it much," she said. "But they're back in fashion right now, like those adult coloring books that are all the rage. Everyone is writing everything down in the old-fashioned way and you'll find a use for it sooner than you think."

"It's great, thank you," I said. "Really."

We hugged, her eyelashes fluttering along my cheek. I was about to tell her about the song and the photograph, how they could be my first entry in the notebook, but the twins woke and began throwing birthday presents at each other.

"Time for me to say goodbye."

"You've always got me," Jude said. "And Charlie and Amelia. We're not going anywhere."

The next day, I arrived at work earlier than usual. I wanted to ask Rob about my déjà vu experience, but he'd already left for the studio. It was a perfect early summer day with soft yellow light and gentle air. All the windows and doors were open. Fat bees hovered over the honeysuckle climbing the brick wall, and the morning light was steady without the usual jitterbug of sun and cloud.

I found myself circling the sitting room, eyes shut, trailing my fingers along the uneven surfaces of the pictures. Rough, hard whorls of paint from the children's efforts, fine brush marks for the family portraits, and powdery dust from the charcoal drawings. All the life going on below them, the clever talk, the casual wit, the food and drink, the children. Everything joining together in the family. If I were Emma, I'd stay here and manage my own house. I'd cook all the meals, be a wife to Rob and a mother to Jake and Lily. I wouldn't bother with the books and the hectic rush of her speaking engagements and interviews, promoting a way of life that she didn't actually have time to experience herself.

I dragged Siggy round the park for twenty minutes, my continuing but often futile attempt to make him see the attractions of behaving like a dog and peeing and defecating outside the house. He suffered my attentions—a weekly bath in the laundry basin, brushing his teeth every other day with a ridged plastic device that fitted on my finger, found at the bottom of a kitchen drawer—with a weary acceptance. His heart remained true to Emma. I didn't mind. I liked his loyalty, that he couldn't be bought off, like most dogs, with food or attention.

After that, I made my way through the rooms, clearing, cleaning, and making beds. The house held its silence. At the French windows, I blew clouds of condensation on the glass. The branches emerged into focus and then blurred again as I peered through a tiny bubble captured in the windowpane. I swayed from side to side, just a little. Blur and focus, blur and focus. The effect was hypnotic.

I wandered towards the fireplace mirror, an imaginary wineglass in my hand. I scraped back my hair, wishing I could do Emma's casual flick, halfway between a toss and a twirl, as she talked to people. It would have helped if my hair had been long and smooth instead of medium length and a coarse frizz. But, ever optimistic, I gave it a try. Tilt head to one side. Brush left hand across right side of head. It didn't work. I looked like an anxious hedgehog with a comb-over. I tried it the other way. A bit better, but in real life I would have spilled the glass of wine over my head. Behind me, reflected in the mirror, Siggy rolled onto his back. His legs scrabbled in the air and then flopped down. He farted softly and began to snore. I laughed to myself. It was a suitable response.

In the kitchen, the wooden floor was still streaked wet in places where I had mopped it earlier, and the air was cut with the smell of tea-tree oil and vinegar. Siggy appeared and sat down in front of the refrigerator. "It's not suppertime," I told him. "You'll have to wait." He stared in that beseeching way of greedy dogs, then gave up and ambled towards his basket. He turned his usual three circles and sank down with a heavy sigh, watching me as I sorted laundry. There was a pile of clothes for the dry cleaners: Emma's silk shirts, some of the tailored dark suits she wore to business meetings, and a bundle of Rob's jackets. One of our jobs at boarding school had been to sort the laundry. Some girls refused to touch other people's things. I didn't mind, either then or now. I was pleased that Rob and Emma trusted me enough to deal with the physical intimacies left on their clothes: salty circles of sweat on Rob's shirts, streaks of makeup on Emma's collars, and once a spot of menstrual blood on the lining of her skirt.

I checked Rob's pockets, retrieving crumpled receipts and old theater tickets. The last jacket was made of hairy tweed with a red lining. The side pockets were empty, but as I placed it on the pile, I felt something inside and shook it out. Pages torn from a diary, maybe fifteen or twenty, fluttered onto the floor. I picked them up and put them on the counter to shuffle them together.

Rob's handwriting was tiny, thin spidery italics. There were notes for program meetings, appointments with his publisher or lunch with Theo, dates of dinners and parties, and a kind of doodle on the top left-hand corner of some of the pages. The doodle was repeated about every week or ten days, and it looked like an ancient hieroglyphic. It was familiar, but I couldn't think how or why. I was sure I'd seen it somewhere before. A ragged memory of a dusty classroom, everyone except me tittering. The image floated, tantalizing my consciousness, then slipped away.

I put the pages to one side and began to chop carrots. The school day memory returned and settled into something I recognized. Everyone giggling as blushing Mr. Collins attempted to teach us elementary ancient Greek. We'd had the words for power and death and then came passion, or Eros. Ἔρως. I remembered that word more than the others because of the funny wiggle below the line.

That was the sign I saw repeated every week or so on the pages. An affair? I attacked the carrots with fury. Why else would Rob be writing that word, and in an extinct language few people understood? Probably some doe-eyed production assistant, pandering to his ego. Or Christine? Her relaxed social code probably wouldn't register an extramarital liaison as anything more than pleasure lightly taken. She might even think sex with Rob was perfectly acceptable, a way of keeping everything in the family.

I left the chopping board and paced the kitchen, banging my hip on the counter with each turn. How could he? What if Emma found out and divorced him? She wouldn't condone something like that. What if the family broke up? I slammed shut a cupboard door and kept pacing. I might lose my job. Everyone's lives would be changed forever.

Another fragment of memory surfaced. Mr. Collins hitching up his trousers and trying to restore order. "Silly girls," he said. More blushing. "Eros isn't just physical passion. It means life energy as well. Not everything is about"—and here Mr. Collins took a deep breath and almost shouted it out—"SEX!"

Oh, the relief of that memory. I was ashamed of myself for jumping to conclusions like a jealous girlfriend, especially when I recalled that Eros was in love with Psyche. Rob was a psychologist as well as a media personality. Like everyone else, he needed to write himself a reminder every now and then. Like many other busy people, he had his own special code to jog his memory. Perfectly normal. I took the pages upstairs and put them on Rob's bedside table. He'd never remember that he left them in his inside coat pocket. When we were next on our own in the kitchen, I'd make coffee and ask him about the déjà vu thing. He would know more about it than Wikipedia and random websites. Everything would be in its right place again.

14

Self-knowledge is the key to self-empowerment and self-empowerment is the key to a happy and successful life. Increase self-knowledge wherever and whenever you can. Try keeping a mood diary for a month. Write in it every day. You'll be surprised by what you discover about yourself.

—Emma Helmsley, "Taking the Moment," June 6, 2016

I actually saw little of Rob for the next fortnight. When I arrived at Wycombe Lodge each morning, he was either out or already in his office at the bottom of the garden. "Poor man, he's under such pressure," said Emma during one of our early evening catch-ups, with Rob in the study and Jake and Lily upstairs. "He could really do with a proper assistant at the studio. Things have changed so much. Everything is on a shoestring."

She had taken to sitting on the counter, drumming her feet against the cupboards. The noise was irritating, but at least she was stationary and we were not dancing our usual clumsy gavotte as she moved from one wrong place to another. "So many things have had to be put off. Like Christine and Rebecca. They haven't been here for ages. Normally Christine complains about Rebecca not seeing her father, but for once she's being understanding."

"That's good of her," I said, busying myself with a saucepan of leeks and chopped parsley. "And they can always come later when things aren't so hectic."

After dinner, just before I left for the night, Emma wandered into the kitchen holding the last of the dirty plates. "I was about to do that," I said.

"But you do so much, all the time." She peered through her fringe. Her eyes were bloodshot again, her face drawn. "Thank you, Anne." Her nightly chorus, regular as clockwork. "Oh, a favor. Would you mind very much putting the garbage bins out in the street when you go. Rob usually does it, but he forgot this week and I don't want to bother him now. He's so tired."

"Sure." I pulled the bins down the side path and onto the street. Rob must have forgotten last week's collection as well. They were so full that the lids wouldn't shut properly. Crammed on top of the usual black bags were smaller clear recycling bags full of printed pages. One of them fell onto the pavement and split, pages fluttering into the gutter. I'd have to pick them up and then I'd miss my bus. Very annoying.

An old woman with her aged Labrador meandering behind her walked towards me. "Are you all right, my dear?" she asked. "Do you want a hand?"

"Thank you, but no," I replied. "It will only take a minute to pick up." I stuffed a handful of pages back into the bag.

"Those bags split so easily. You'd think they'd make them stronger," she said and moved on, the dog snuffling behind her.

There was enough light left to see and I quickly scanned the pages as I picked them up, but with no real interest. It was all quite dull. Lists of footnotes and annotations. Academic titles about McLeish's peers and his early work. There were pages of chapter headings with question marks beside them and a folder of printed emails. The bus roared past as I picked up the last page from the gutter. It was crumpled and damp from spilt coffee, but the words, typed in italics, jumped out at me.

You are me and I am you
So we are one, but
Where are you?
If you are me and I am you
Then am I me
And who are you?

Everything slid sideways. I forgot about the bus and being tired and annoyed. I knew these words. I knew them like I knew the alphabet, like I knew my multiplication tables. This time I couldn't fob it off as something I might have heard or something that sounded like someone else. It was McLeish's song, one that Rob said McLeish wrote for his followers, one of their very own cult anthems.

I folded the page into my back pocket, tied the bag together, and piled it on top of the rest. It was late. I was confused. More than anything, I wanted to get home, sit down, and think. Perhaps I was imagining things. Or perhaps Jude and Theo were right. I needed to get out more, to think about something else except cooking and cleaning.

Back in my flat, I snapped on the lights and unfolded the page. Rob had scrawled something at the bottom, but the spilled coffee had made his writing illegible. I stared at the words, all the time hearing the tune in my head. I didn't understand. How was it that I, Anne Morgan, who grew up with her grandmother in Shaftesbury, Dorset, knew the words to a song that a rogue psychologist wrote more than twenty-five years ago in a gloomy house in East Sussex?

Was it possible that I'd been there with my mother before she left me at the service station and went off to that trailer in the woods? The coincidence of it all, that I could be working for a man who could know more about my early life than I did. To think that I was cooking his meals, washing his socks, and making his bed, not realizing a thing until now! I smoothed the page again and stared at it, hoping it might reveal something more. But there was nothing except a small rip in a corner where my thumb had snagged against the damp paper.

I missed Gran with a sudden fierce longing. I missed the way she pursed her lips when she didn't want to answer a question, her brusque affection that disguised an unfailing love. What a solitary life we had led, disconnected all three of us. Gran, an only child, with Marianne, an only child, with me, an only child. Three generations without husbands, or aunts and uncles and cousins. We could have done with a few more members to liven up things; a family joker, a chubby uncle who came over for dinner once a week, or a maiden aunt. And a cousin or two wouldn't have gone amiss. As far as I knew, Gran never had close friends either, just acquaintances that she kept at arm's length. So there was no one, not one person, that I could ask about my mother.

Gran didn't like me mixing with outsiders, except for Douglas, whom she couldn't deter. "Why don't you have some of your friends over?" she would ask when she picked me up from Stanton Hall at the end of term. She didn't fool me for a minute. Even if I'd had friends, she wouldn't have wanted them to see our little cottage, the way we lived. "It's fine," I would reply and she would look relieved. "There's such a thing," she'd say, "as too much company."

I paced the room until the man below banged on the ceiling. It was almost 1 a.m. Outside, the sky was half-lit, teetering between dusk and dawn. The summer solstice was approaching, a time of the year when sleep was almost impossible. I pulled the sheet over my head. Through the open window came the noise of garbage trucks, sirens, and buses. There was the screech of brakes and shouting. I got up and shut the window and listened to the sound of my own erratic breath until finally I fell asleep. When the sun broke through and woke me, I reached for my pen and notebook and wrote the first thing that came into my head.

Sunset. I'm knocking on the enormous black door. No one comes and I worry that I'll have to sleep outside on my own. So scared. I wet my pants, it's running down my legs, hot and stinging. Then a person—I'm not sure if it's a man or a woman—opens the door. Their face is painted like a clown, white with a big red mouth, but the red paint is running down their neck and it looks like blood. Someone is playing the piano. It stops and there is the sound of heavy footsteps, the smell of smoke.

I stopped writing and got out of bed feeling jittery, almost dissociated. The front of my T-shirt and the sheet were speckled with blood. I'd scratched myself in the night again, something I hadn't done for months. There was that prick of nerves along the back of my neck that I thought had gone forever.

I wasn't so sure about this notebook business, despite what Jude had said and Emma had recommended. The aftereffects were more confusing than soothing. I went into the kitchen and chewed on my muesli. I watched the bloodstained T-shirt and sheet revolve in the washing machine. The bizarre images that I'd scribbled down without thinking, the confusion and the feeling of missing Gran, were all to do with the mystery of that song. The only person who could help me solve that mystery was Rob. I needed to find him on his own one morning. He wouldn't mind if I confided in him, just a bit. It wouldn't take long and he was used to people telling him things. There was no need to tell him about finding the page in the recycling bag. He might think I'd been snooping. Besides, we'd already listened to McLeish's song together. He'd introduced the subject to me.

The morning was humid and overcast. When I arrived at

Wycombe Lodge, the doors to the garden were open. An eddy of damp, stale air hovered above the usual fug of breakfast. Siggy hauled himself out of his basket and wandered over for his daily ear scratch. And there was Rob, mooching about by the sink in the kitchen. My earlier anxiety fell away at the sight of him, just disappeared as if it had never existed.

"Hello," I said. "Want some coffee? You could hone your barista skills."

Rob laughed. I hadn't noticed before, but he had a crooked incisor, just like Emma. "My barista skills are pretty much non-existent."

"You can be my assistant then. It won't take a minute." I pulled out the coffee grinder and the packet of beans. "Here you go. You can't have forgotten already."

He hadn't, but there was something of a mess by the time he'd finished. I cleared it away and made two mugs of coffee. We stood on opposite sides of the kitchen, me leaning against the sink and Rob propping himself in front of the refrigerator.

"Thanks," said Rob. "The first decent coffee I've had since the last time you made some. Emma really is hopeless at that sort of thing."

"She's very busy and in demand," I said, excusing her out of loyalty, but realizing at the same time that I'd implied that Rob wasn't so busy, or so in demand. "I mean, you both are."

He smiled. "Sure."

"Actually," I went on. "I wanted to ask you something. Have you got a minute?"

He nodded.

"Do you remember when you showed me that photo of the house where McLeish and his followers lived? And then I said that weird thing about the statue. And then there was the thing about that song?"

"I remember."

"Do you think it was déjà vu? I mean, can you have déjà vu experiences about two different things, like the statue and the song?"

Rob walked around the counter and sat down at the table. Under the usual mess of breakfast, the surface was smeared with jam and spilled milk. Outside, a pair of robins pecked industriously in the cracks between the paving stones. Siggy snored softly in his basket.

"I did check if there was a statue of a cupid in the wood at Kinghurst Place, and yes, there was. You weren't wrong. Or mad." He smiled. "So you were either there, or you might have seen a picture of another cupid in some other wood, or been to another house where there was a statue in the wood. It's not such an unusual thing to see."

"I suppose so," I said. "It's possible I might have been in that house at some stage of my life, maybe before I went to live with Gran. But I don't have any proper memories of that time, only a few hazy recollections. And no one is around to tell me if I'm right or wrong." My words began to collide with one another. Rob put up his hand. It was a relief to stop talking, not to hear the anxiety in my own voice.

"Let's take this slowly and sensibly, OK," he said. "I completely understand that you're confused and curious. Anyone would be, so it's perfectly normal to have these thoughts." There was that chocolate thing in his voice and the curve of his shoulder as he hunched over his mug. I longed to rest my head in that curve. "And off the top of my head, there are so many possible explanations."

"Like what?"

"You could have gone there as a young child, maybe with your grandmother."

"Not with Gran. She never left Dorset. It was a point of pride with her."

"All right then," said Rob. "Maybe with your mother. Do you have any memories at all about her?"

"She died of a heart attack when I was very young, in Wales, near Cardiff. Her name was Marianne. I remember she had long blond hair, but that might have been because Gran had a photograph of her. Sometimes I think I remember disjointed things, but nothing that makes any real sense. I don't even know where we lived. Gran refused to talk about it and only mentioned a few times to me that she had been unwell. I read the coroner's report once, but that's it."

"You can't blame your grandmother for that. It's typical of her generation not to talk about anything upsetting. But it does leave you in something of a maze."

Unexpected tears pricked at the back of my eyes. "I know you're really busy, and Emma says you're under a lot of pressure . . . but is there any way you could find out if I was there? Maybe my mother and I visited and I don't remember. It's just that I've never had an opportunity to find out anything about her—she was an only child too."

"Of course I can check a few things. But look, Anne, the thing is . . ." He leaned forward and stroked my hand. "This book is about McLeish and his work, how and why he led his community. The weird things he did, and any recollections from his followers are included, but people came and went. He had relationships with some of the women, and some were more important than others, but your mother may not be among them. If she was, it would be fascinating for me, and no doubt an extraordinary thing for you. I can check, and I'll help as much as I can, but I might not find what you're looking for."

"Didn't he keep any records?" I asked.

"Yes, he did, but of his own work and theories, and his views about the people who lived there. But mostly they didn't use their real names, or he gave them pseudonyms. Keep in mind that these were people who might have run away from institutions and weren't keen to give too much information about themselves.

"Also, it was a private house, not an institution. Imagine trying to work out who'd come to Wycombe Lodge over the years. It would be almost impossible. We don't keep a visitor's book and neither did McLeish. No one checked in and out. And no one was looking at him or what he did at Kinghurst Place too closely."

Rob moved his hand away from mine and held the mug to his mouth. All I could see were his brown eyes, full of kindness and concern. He sipped his coffee slowly, then put his mug on the table. "But back to you and the mystery of were you there or weren't you there? Our memories are incredibly complicated, and there are so many different theories about how they work. People can remember things that never happened and people can forget things for all sorts of reasons. There are so many different forms of amnesia. Then there's PTSD—post-traumatic stress disorder. If something traumatic has occurred, you can get flashbacks and panic attacks, remember things that did happen, but are very distressing.

"I could go on and on, but all right, lecture over," he said. "Back to Kinghurst Place. I'll see what I can find. But, as I said, it's entirely possible that if your mother was there, she went by another name. It's also possible that you might have been there. That would explain the song and the statue, although those two things might not have any real connection."

He scratched his chin. "It goes without saying that our conversations are just between us. Jake and Lily needn't know anything, and Emma—well, I discuss everything with her, but not in such close detail. I want you to feel comfortable talking to me, about anything at all, and know that it won't go any further."

"Thank you. You're so kind. And I wouldn't mind about Emma. She says in her blog that we shouldn't be scared of the past."

Rob nodded. "She's right—and she told me that you sometimes read her. She was so flattered." He made it sound that, out of her many thousands of readers, I was the only one who mattered.

"I read 'Taking the Moment.' Some of the things Emma has written have made me think a lot about life and relationships. They've been a great help."

"Really," said Rob, sitting straighter with a proud look on his face. "Good. Anyhow, let me see what I can dig up."

I could have kissed him. "Thank you, thank you."

Rob looked at his watch and stood up. "It'll be a pleasure to do something for you, after everything you do for us. But it may take me a bit of time, maybe a week or more."

He handed me his empty mug. "See you later then. I need to get down to some work." He meandered down the garden, unlocked the door of his office, and closed it behind him. Through the reflection of the mangled shrubs in the window, he swayed from side to side before settling at his desk.

I slowly cleared the kitchen. In restaurants there was no time to think or remember. Everything was more relaxed here, with time for thoughts and feelings to surface, the frightening what-ifs of it all. What if my mother had been one of McLeish's followers? What if she had been his lover, his muse? And then—what if McLeish was my father and I was the child of a cult leader, a man disgraced? Everything in my life turned upside down and everything solved. It was both terrifying and exciting.

Before Jake and Lily came home from school, I sat at the kitchen counter and took out my notebook. It had rained in the afternoon, but there was a quick blare of sun that made me blink in surprise as much as anything else. Light flickered orange against my eyelids and there it was, another unbidden image.

I'm hungry and scared. It's dark in this hall, just a chink of light from the room where they are. I'm not allowed in. I'm meant to be asleep, and I can't make any noise. I sit down behind the door. The floorboards are rough and splintered against my legs and there's something beside me. I pick it up. It's a can of baked beans, already open. I scoop them out with my fingers, cold and slimy. The edge of the can cuts my finger. It stings and I cry but no one comes.

My writing was jagged and spiky, running off at angles across the page. There was that prick at the back of my neck again, although it wasn't completely frightening this time, right here in the kitchen at Wycombe Lodge, with Rob at the end of the garden. Part of me wanted to race down to him right then, give him my notebook, and ask him to make sense of it, to try to authenticate my early unknown life.

But these were only disjointed images, of no use to anybody. I didn't want to show Rob these scrambled thoughts, these half-formed things that brought with them a sense of shame, that came from some part of me that I didn't recognize. He might think I was an unreliable narrator, as they said these days. He might think I'd made them up to get his attention. Apart from anything else, they were intensely personal and I wanted to keep them private until I was more certain of what they meant. There was another thing as well. Disjointed and scrambled they might have been, but they made me realize for the first time how much I longed to know something, anything, about my mother.

15

Every daughter is entwined with her mother
and every mother is entwined with her daughter. In short, an emotional minefield.

—Rob Helmsley, *Madhouse: The Life and Times
of Rowan McLeish*

I wrote in my notebook each morning. Images came out more readily, almost like a flood. I didn't want to call them memories just yet. They were more a series of incoherent moments that had nothing to do with linear time.

I'm sitting on a man's lap, rubbing my cheek against the rough wool of his sweater that smells of tobacco. I smell earth and cloves, cigarettes and wine, and recognize the scent of my mother. I feel her hair, the way she rubs my back, the tips of her fingers tracing the knobs of my spine . . .

On my own. They've left me, all of them, gone away laughing, not noticing I'm forgotten. At night I hide in the cupboard by the kitchen with a knife, too scared to go upstairs. Something runs over my foot. Scream and scream and scream and no one comes . . .

Sunlight, dancing, the smell of hay and wild strawberries. Whirling around, hanging on tight to strong hands, the world upside down then righting itself, everything breaking into different colors until I fall over and crawl into the hedge . . .

The man has the knife again, the one with the sharp point, and he says he'll draw a picture for me, but he starts to cut into his face instead, so quickly that I can see what he has drawn before the blood starts dripping down his face. He has drawn a cat with a curly tail. The knife is covered in blood. I can smell it, sharp like metal. He puts the knife into his mouth and I run away, all the way up to the roof, where he can't find me.

The more I wrote, the more I cooked, concocting my version of a perfect family, dish by traditional dish: spaghetti and meatballs, roast chicken, lasagna, cakes and pies.

It was the middle of the school summer holidays. Emma said they usually went away in August to Greece or Italy, places with drinkable wine and reliable sunshine. But they were too busy this year. Jake and Lily didn't seem to mind being at home. They spent most of their time asleep or out of the house.

"I cannot say one more word about anything," Emma sighed as she came into the kitchen. She'd been in Bath all day promoting her latest book on how to build a corporate empire from the kitchen table. Her face was pale, and her smart linen suit was crumpled, with a dribbled coffee stain on the jacket. The smell of the city hung about her, gritty fumes from the train and a faint, stale whiff from being cooped up in a minicab all the way from Paddington. She disappeared upstairs and came down half an hour later, wearing a faded tracksuit and new fluorescent green-and-orange running shoes. She foraged in the wine cooler for an open bottle and poured herself a glass.

"Won't you? Just once share a glass with me?"

I shook my head. I didn't like drinking at work, where even one small glass was enough to unbalance me.

"Poor Rob, he's still working so hard," Emma said. Siggy rolled onto his back and she rubbed his stomach with her shoe. "Clever clever dog." His stumpy tail thumped on the floor. "Oh, he mentioned you might have spent some time near Kinghurst Place when you were a child."

"Yes," I replied, expecting her to ask about my mother, and almost looking forward to talking to her about it. Instead she wandered towards the door leading to the garden, Siggy dancing at her heels. "I never understand why people doubt coincidences," she said, examining her reflection in the glass. "To me, they're the most natural things in the world."

Dinner that evening was uneventful, with just the four of them. There was a goat's cheese and tomato tart, then cold chicken and salad. It was too warm for anything more complicated. All the doors were open to the garden. It was still so light that for once Emma didn't light any candles. Nobody said much. Lily was in a rush to get to the cinema, and Jake looked half-asleep, with spikes of hair sticking up at the back of his head. He yawned all through the meal and disappeared the minute it was over.

"I might go up and have a bath," said Emma as she brought a pile of plates to the counter. "To get rid of that train journey. I thought it would never end. Thank you, Anne, that was delicious." She'd barely eaten a thing. Under the wisps of her fringe, a blue vein pulsed on her forehead.

I tidied the kitchen and prepared to go home. Moths fluttered about the lamps. I turned the lamps off and waited for the moths to fly outside before shutting the doors. It seemed too cruel to leave them crashing against the light until they fell exhausted to their death. The house was almost dark. The only light downstairs came from the study, where Rob was working. I walked past and said good night.

"Hey, come in," he said. "Look what I found."

I stepped into the room, and he showed me, with something of a flourish, a photograph of Kinghurst Place similar to the one I'd seen online, but from a different angle and even more out of focus. Again, the room was lit by candles and most faces were in shadow, turned away from the camera towards McLeish, who sat at the head of the table. I stared at it, willing myself to remember something, but I didn't.

"There's a photograph a bit like this on someone's website," I said. Rob looked a bit put out. "But this is a much better one," I went on quickly. "McLeish's face is so much clearer here."

"Good," he said. "Now, there was a woman at Kinghurst Place for a while, who was close to McLeish. Some of the residents were jealous of her position. But McLeish and the others called her Mary, which could be a shortening of Marianne—or another woman altogether. Does Mary mean anything at all to you?"

I shook my head. What about me? I thought. What about me? Was I there with her?

Rob picked up his pen and began chewing on it. "This might be difficult for you—do you want me to go on?"

I gripped the edge of the desk and nodded.

"The woman called Mary was his mistress, his preferred mistress for some time." With his free hand, he produced another photograph from a folder and motioned for me to sit down. "This is a photograph of the two of them."

Something in the back of my throat made me splutter. Rob slid the photograph across the desk. I turned it around to see a bald, shiny-headed woman with shaved eyebrows wearing a long white dress, shapeless like a nightgown. She was barefoot and looked like an alien angel, certainly not human and certainly nothing like the woman in the framed photograph that used to stand behind the sofa in Gran's house and now stood on a shelf in my flat. Her hands were clasped behind her back and she gazed up at a man who I recognized as McLeish. His hair was long and curly. He wore a patterned Indian caftan and sandals and faced the camera lens with a broad, confident smile. His teeth crossed over at the front. A lit cigarette dangled from his hand.

Where were they? It was hard to tell. Maybe on the crest of a hill. The remnants of a picnic lay scattered about their feet. Summer sun blazed around them. They looked like they were about to float away.

"I don't know," I said. "She's in profile. I can't see her eyes. I can't see her hands."

"Why do you mention her hands?" asked Rob.

"She had a turquoise-and-silver ring. I would have recognized it." I traced the outline of her head with my finger. The photograph was faded, almost sepia. It was impossible to tell if her skin was fair or olive, what color her eyes were. "I wish there was something here I remembered." I heard the break in my voice, the disappointment it conveyed.

"It's because she's . . ." The woman in the photograph looked like something skinned alive. I thought of my mother's glorious blond hair, how it floated like a halo around her. ". . . shaved her head. Is that something they did?"

He reached over and slid the photograph back across the desk. The rasp of the paper on the wood made me start. "There was a time, maybe for six months or so, when all the women shaved their heads to prepare themselves for trepanning."

"The what?"

"Trepanning. It's when a hole is drilled into the skull, exposing the outermost layer of brain membrane. People did it to release what they thought were evil spirits, to literally let light into the brain. It's one of the oldest operations, goes back to prehistoric times. Sometimes it was used in conventional medicine to reduce pressure on the brain.

"At Kinghurst Place, they tried to do it themselves, in an effort to become permanently high. It was Mary—if that is her real name—and McLeish's idea. They believed it was a tool for mental enlightenment. McLeish bought an old dental drill and some books showing them how to do it. But the drill broke and it didn't work."

"But even if the drill hadn't broken, the women were willing to do that to themselves? To drill holes in their own heads?"

"Yes," said Rob. "They were willing to do anything they were told."

Silence fell between us. I struggled for a moment to imagine this, how a man could hold such power over women that they would shave their heads and try to drill a hole in their skull just because he told them to; how a woman would collude with such a man and help persuade people to do such a thing. It was madness, literally. Rob said McLeish had been a brilliant scholar; that his ideas, however bizarre, came from a place of caring about vulnerable, ill people, whom society had shunned. I didn't have a degree from UCL, but ordering people to drill holes in their heads sounded horrifying, like a twisted power game. Again, the thought, like a punch in the stomach. What if this man was my father? What if this woman, who Rob said was his accomplice, was my mother? I pushed this last image away. It could not be true.

From upstairs came the sound of padding footsteps and muted television laughter. Any minute now Rob would put the photograph back in his folder and say good night, and that would be the end of it. I would have to go home, no closer to finding out anything more about my mother and me. Again, it was as if Rob knew my thoughts.

"Just because you don't recognize the woman in the photograph doesn't mean your mother wasn't there," he said quietly. "I'll look through other papers and you can keep thinking about it, see what turns up in your mind."

"Can I see the photograph again?" He slid it back across the desk. This time I looked carefully at their surroundings, the plates and glasses on the ground next to the picnic basket. There was something in the corner, almost out of frame. A sandal, a child's sandal with the strap undone.

"Here," I said, showing it to Rob with a shaking hand. "This means there must have been a child there. It might have been me."

Rob put on his spectacles and peered at the photograph. "How crazy that I didn't spot that before. Now it makes sense."

"What?"

"In an interview I did with one of the residents, a man called Harry, he mentioned a kid several times. The kid got in the way, or the kid made him laugh. But when I pressed him on it, he said he didn't remember too clearly, and then he said the kid was his nickname for another man who lived there, because he was so small and slight."

He took my hand and patted it in the same kind way as before. "It's not very satisfactory, is it?"

I bit my lip. "I spent most of my life not thinking about this, not even caring about it—and now I can't seem to stop. I just wish I knew."

"So do I," said Rob. "Are you sure you don't remember anything else?"

"Not really. Just odd bits and pieces that make no sense and probably never happened."

"Well," said Rob. "I'm here, you know that. Talk to me at any time."

"Thanks," I said and picked up my things, ready to leave. It seemed as if I'd never be certain about anything.

Later that night, back home, hip-hop music rising from the street through the open window, the fag end of a breeze playing around my feet, I lay on the sofa and wondered why I hadn't pulled my notebook from my bag and just showed it to him there and then. I might have done so if it had been pages of neat handwriting with legible sentences and organized into days and weeks. But I was too ashamed. Such an antiquated word, but it was the only one that conveyed the way I felt. Everything was scribbled at odd angles and often upside down. Sometimes I wrote with such force that my pen tore the paper. Sometimes I wept uncontrollably as I wrote and my words were smudged and almost illegible. I didn't want Rob to see that manic part of me,

I closed my eyes. Images emerged. Dark eyes staring out from bushy eyebrows. A woman with her face turned away, shivering in excitement, like a dog. A door warped with damp and age, with a gap between the door and the frame, so that I could see into the room if I stood on tiptoes and cranked my head to one side. Holes in the wall where someone had stabbed an imaginary intruder. The screaming, the hideous soft thunk as someone's head pounded against the wall.

I jumped up and wrote it all down, everything, to get it out of my head and onto the page, a place where things would remain still and silent and not pound about in my brain. People whirling in white, like sheets in the wind, everyone untethered, screeching at a line of ants. The act of writing calmed me the way cooking and cleaning calmed me, made me feel sane once more.

That weekend, Philip was away in Berlin again, so Jude and I met for a picnic with the twins. We lazed under a tree halfway up Primrose Hill while Charlie and Amelia raced around us, chubby legs churning like pistons in the sticky air. We would have half an hour to ourselves before they got bored and demanded to leave.

"You were right about the notebook," I said. A wasp crawled over a half-eaten sandwich and flew away in search of something sweeter. "It is coming in useful. In fact, I'm writing in it almost every day."

"Good," said Jude. She lay on her back, her eyes closed. "With any luck you'll write yourself out of that job and back into the real world."

"But that's just it," I said. "It's the real world I'm after." My story rushed out of me, about the song and the statue, the fragments of memory that floated like smoke, and my growing feeling that I might have been there with my mother at the house, with the psychologist that Rob was writing about, and how kind and helpful he'd been.

Jude rolled over and pulled up a blade of grass. Charlie and Amelia had retreated to the shade of a nearby tree, where they were practicing handstands. "Have you told him about the notebook?" she asked.

"No—he might think I'm a bit delusional. I thought I'd wait a bit for something more concrete. And I suppose I'm a bit embarrassed. It's so personal."

Jude sat up. "I don't see where this is going to get you. You might never know the exact truth about where you were, where your mother was. So what good is all this going to do?"

"You sound just like Gran," I said. "It's different for you. You know where you come from. You've got brothers and sisters, and parents."

"Loads of people don't know anything about their family—refugees, orphans, people whose countries have been blown to bits. They just have to live with it."

I was almost in tears. Only the curious faces of Charlie and Amelia, bored with their handstands and wanting to go home, stopped me from weeping. "I've always lived with it. But the part of my life that I don't know anything about—it's become almost like an obsession," I whispered, "and I don't know why."

"I don't either. And now you've got the crush on Rob."

"I do not have a crush on Rob."

"Of course you do. You bring his name into every conversation. A dead giveaway. And you've also got the girl crush on Emma. It's not enough that you clean and cook for them." She brushed her hair away from her face. "They're not your family, you know. Rob's not your shrink or your father or your lover. Emma isn't your mother or your sister or your friend, and Jake and Lily aren't your children. You don't want to get too attached. They'll look after themselves first."

"You're talking as if we're on the *Titanic* and fighting for a seat on the last lifeboat," I said. "It's not like that at all."

We fell silent for a bit. You're wrong, I wanted to tell her. "They do look after me. Rob and Emma do care. Jake and Lily do like me. Even Siggy wags his tail when he sees me every morning." I gathered our picnic things together, ready to return to her house.

"And there's something going on," said Jude.

"What do you mean, something going on?"

"You're wearing makeup again. If I'm not mistaken, there's blusher as well, and lipstick and mascara. You're blow-drying your hair and you've stopped wearing that hideous plaid shirt and the jeans with the holes in them. So, something is going on."

"You kept telling me to make more of an effort, and when I do, you ask what's going on. Nothing is going on."

"I love you, whatever you do," she said. "But you could have fooled me."

Jude had suspected an infatuation with Rob. It wasn't like that. But we'd formed a habit of talking most mornings in the study over a mug of coffee that I made. It turned out he really was a rubbish barista. It was Rob who suggested moving into the study while we chatted. He said my wiping and clearing in the kitchen made him giddy. I got to prefer it as well. Something about walking away from the mess of breakfast made it easier for us to talk freely. Rob could sit behind his desk for ten, maybe fifteen minutes without moving. His stillness was soothing and exhilarating all at once.

We didn't always discuss McLeish and Kinghurst Place. I didn't always question him about my mother, or ask if he'd uncovered any more evidence, other than the sandal that might or might not have been mine. He told me all sorts of things, about Jung, and his theory of individuation, the process of integrating the opposites, including the conscious with the unconscious, while still maintaining their independence. He told me about Freud and sex and Piaget and learning and memory. It was another way, I thought, of trying to tell me that he understood.

In turn, I told him about cooking and Anton and Gran. I even got onto Douglas one morning, how I liked to feel his stubble. But I still hadn't told him about my notebook. Sometimes I read what I'd written, all the scribbled pages full of anguish and fear and loneliness. I wanted to show it to him, but I was wary of his reaction. I didn't want anything to change between us.

"Do you think it's possible," I said one morning—we were back onto McLeish and Kinghurst Place, my mother and me—"that Mary was Marianne? That we were there? I keep thinking about the child's sandal in the photograph. But then, why would she leave and go to Wales?"

"I can't answer any of those questions fully," said Rob. "Clearly a child was there, at least for that picnic, because of the sandal. And there is the odd mention of children or a child, but nothing that points directly to you. If I knew for sure, I'd tell you and I'd be writing about it in my book. But I don't, and I can't just make things up. It's a biography and a book of record, not a potboiler."

"What about the things I've told you? Only one other person in the world knows . . . my closest friend, and even she is skeptical. People might think I was mad . . ."

Rob looked at me carefully. He took my hand and placed it between his two hands. I felt a surge of something. Whatever it was, it wasn't sexual, but it was very intense.

"I can't include speculations of yours, or of mine, in the book, much as I might like to. All I can do right now is try to help you in whatever way I can. I've told you that everything we say in here to each other is between ourselves. These images, memories, whatever you call them, are disturbing, and you need to find a place where you feel comfortable and safe talking honestly about them. And I hope, because of everything you've done for us, and because of the way we feel about you, that you've found that place here."

I was ashamed for suspecting his motives, for my lack of trust. I looked above Rob's head to the shelf of photograph albums, all in the right order, from Jake and Lily's birth up to the present, the multiple rows of books, each one trying in its own way to explain who we were, the reassuring weight of their research and knowledge.

"Yes, I think I have."

16

∞

Mental illness is not always about breaking
down into chaos. It can be about breaking
through a barrier into freedom, finding a
way to a new creativity and order.

—Rob Helmsley, *Madhouse: The Life and Times
of Rowan McLeish*

An airless Monday evening at the beginning of September, the day's heat lying below a pallid sky. Emma and I were in the kitchen having one of our early evening talks. Did I ever think to tell Emma about the kaffeeklatsches with Rob in his study about Kinghurst Place, about McLeish and the woman, who might have been my mother, and my perennial question of whether I was there? Did I ever think to tell Rob about my catch-ups with Emma, her affectionate quibbles about him forgetting to pay the electricity bill, her complaints about his snoring? It never occurred to me. I only knew I needed to be there, to be part of their life. Each day seemed created afresh. Everything that happened at Wycombe Lodge had become almost as important to me as Anton had once been, as Kinghurst Place and my mother now were.

"Can you believe Rob actually doesn't know how to change a lightbulb?" asked Emma.

"It doesn't matter," I said. "I'm here now. I can do it."

She hopped up onto the counter and swung her legs like a small child. "Rob and I were wondering if you could stay on for our next party," she said in her tentative way. "Only if you're free. You might not want to. Not to work, of course not. I certainly want you to take off that apron you wear every day! But maybe to keep an eye on things as well as meet some of the guests. Rob and I tend to have to do the rounds, but Theo could look after you and it might be fun."

"Oh, I'd love to do that. I mean, I've almost nagged you to let me stay." There was an internal skip of excitement. I added a pinch of salt to the sauce with a flourish. My version of meatballs with tomato sauce. I've always liked the humble cuts. Neck of lamb, shin of beef, or minced beef and pork. Anyone can cook fillet steak or Dover sole. You just need to be able to pay for it. Heat the pan, wait for the butter and oil to start foaming. Slap, slap. And rest. You're done.

"I'll look forward to it," I said. In my mind, I was already at the party, wearing something other than jeans and trainers, moving through the rooms, smiling, helping where I could, Theo introducing me as a trusted family friend.

"It'll be good for Rob too, after all his work." She scuffed the cupboard door with her trainers, making a squeaky mouse-like sound. Siggy pricked up his ears then flopped into his basket again. "He has so much more gravitas than me. I don't think my books will ever be on the shelves of a university library. Not like Rob's."

She jumped down and foraged in a drawer for a box of matches and went to light the candles in the dining room and set the table. How many dinners had I cooked for them by now? More than a hundred? Or was it more like one hundred and fifty? Every time there was that prick of apprehension as I waited for them to eat their first mouthful. Was it good enough? Did it taste all right? Everyone apart from Emma helped themselves to more. Again, that good feeling, like I'd done something right.

A couple of days later, I came into the house from dragging Siggy around the block to find Emma sitting on the sofa with an overgroomed girl discussing canapé menus printed on laminated pages in a folder. "Thank goodness you're back," Emma cried. "Anne knows all about food. Anne used to work in a top London restaurant." The girl crossed and uncrossed her legs, quickly, like scissors cutting. Siggy inched towards her. I pulled him back by the leash, worried that he might practice lifting his leg on her shoes.

"This looks too studied," Emma said, flipping through the pages. "We want something more casual, more homemade-looking."

I looked at the pictures of shreds of beef stuffed into miniature Yorkshire puddings, morsels of risotto on antique silver spoons, and prawns on skewers. Everything a banquet in miniature; perfect, but three years out of fashion. These days, it was all slow-cooked pork belly and inside-out chicken wings. Ras el Hanout, za'atar. Szechuan pepper. I still kept up with that sort of thing late at night, browsing through restaurant and catering menus online, when I needed a break from my regular searches for anything to do with McLeish and Kinghurst Place.

"Except not homemade," I said.

"Exactly!" Emma slapped her knee.

The girl rolled her eyes and slammed her folder shut. I showed her to the door and said we'd be in touch. "Sooner rather than later," she snapped. "We get very booked up, months in advance." She strode down the path, adjusted her tight skirt, and slammed the gate behind her.

In the sitting room, Emma was peering through the window. "What a terrifying woman." She giggled. "I think we'll leave everything to Fiona and the deli as usual. It seems to work. I don't know what I was thinking. Well, I wasn't, as usual."

"You shouldn't be so hard on yourself," I said.

"Oh, I'm tougher than I look. Now, where did I put my bag? I'm so late."

I picked up her bag from the hall table. "I put your phone in it." Emma had left it by the toaster again.

"Thank you, Anne," she said, her daily litany. "Where would we be without you? Everything runs so much more smoothly since you arrived." Again, that small ripple of pleasure. Jude was my best friend and I loved her, but she was wrong about Emma and Rob.

The date for the party was set for Friday night three weeks away. Names came and went on Rob's invitation list. BBC executives, publishers and editors, writers and academics, talk show hosts and actors—the numbers kept increasing.

A week before, walking slowly to the front door, I overheard Rob talking to Emma in the sitting room, a thrum of excitement in his voice. "Call me starstruck, but how about this. My producer is bringing a guest—a famous guest! Apparently they were at university together in Cape Town."

"Who?" Emma's voice was distracted, almost sleepy.

"Dominic Butler." A barely disguised note of triumph in his voice. "Apparently he likes my program! I could do with a bit of extra publicity—I didn't tell you, but this week's ratings were down and there's some hipster kid sniffing around my slot."

"You mustn't worry," said Emma. "You'll be fine."

"I hope so. Anyway, the perfect famous guest, don't you think? He's incredibly intelligent, and charming. And he's been in therapy."

"That's wonderful," Emma said. A rustling of cushions, some version of world music playing softly. "Clever you, making that happen."

"Just the thing," said Rob, "to make this something out of the ordinary."

Outside, in the dimly lit hall, I smiled, as excited as if it were my party and Dominic Butler was my guest of honor. Butler was a big name. He'd headlined in sold-out plays on Broadway and in the West End. He'd been nominated for two Oscars. His occasional appearances in the restaurant created an almost audible head-swiveling.

I was about to open the front door when I remembered it was garbage night, so I doubled back and pulled the bins along the side path onto the street. Only one recycling bag this week, full of printouts from academic journals. Rob must have decided they weren't necessary for his research. But in the middle was a file I almost missed, with four pages of McLeish's verse and copies of some other documents. I scooped them into my bag to read later. I didn't want to stand there in the street, straining to see the pages in the dying light. At home, I took off my jacket and crashed down on the sofa. The folder was covered in Rob's usual coffee stains, and there was a blob of grease in one corner. The first page was a printed copy of one of McLeish's verses. He'd used an old-fashioned typewriter. The ink was smudged and some of the letters jumped slightly above the line.

> *Whatever you say*
> *Whatever you do*
> *Wherever you lay*
> *I am you*

I turned to the next page.

> *You are me and I am you*
> *So we are one, but*
> *Where are you?*
> *If you are me and I am you*
> *Then I am me*
> *And who are you?*

The next page read:

> *Follow you*
> *Following me*
> *We are one*
> *You are me*

I ran my fingers over each line, as if I could feel the faint indentations of each typed letter as it struck the page, even though I knew they didn't exist. They were only copies. On first reading, everything appeared to be simplistic childish doggerel, almost foolish. McLeish was no Walt Whitman or William Wordsworth. Yet I couldn't help feeling that there was something darker and more ominous there than mere play of words. Rob saw the verses as McLeish's way of describing the bond between parents and children, and men and women, but I thought they had a menacing personal ring, like an obsessive lover. There was a sense of wanting to control, to almost subsume the person McLeish was writing about. Who was that person?

The last page contained two more verses, very short and extremely angry. The first read:

> *You will not go*
> *I will know.*
> *My will grows as*
> *Yours does slow*

The second was three lines, repeated again and again.

> *You Do Not.*
> *You Will Not*
> *You Can Not*

There was nothing trained or intellectual about my response. It was only an instinct. It seemed that there was no skill or subtlety here, only childish anger and a cruel selfishness. The poems showed a desire to manipulate and encourage instability, not creativity. I put everything back in the folder. I couldn't think about it any longer. My brain spluttered with too many false starts and jangled images. Maybe Rob was right. Maybe McLeish was cleverly dissecting the human psyche. But somehow, I doubted it.

The next day was Friday, and Rob had already left for the studio by the time I arrived at Wycombe Lodge. I changed everyone's bed linen and washed and ironed and folded. Then I prepared dinner—fish cakes from leftover salmon and a carrot cake. Half an hour after Jake and Lily came home from school, Emma texted me: *We're back late tonight, so u may as well leave now. Have fun on the weekend!* I walked Siggy to the river and back, fed him, and left instructions for the fish cakes.

I spent Saturday morning finishing the book about nutmeg that Rob had given me months ago. I'd read to the halfway point and then somehow forgotten about it. Was Nathaniel Courthope's sacrifice worth it? I pondered that afternoon as I jogged along the Brentford locks, the brightly painted houseboats chugging through the murky water. A little grated nutmeg goes a long way in pretty much all its usual recipes: pumpkin pie, fruitcake, curries, and Middle Eastern food. I understood the wars over other things. I knew that Gandhi had marched against the British salt tax and that Britain and Iceland had gone to war over cod fishing more than fifty years ago. But to lay down your life for nutmeg? I wasn't so sure.

A couple with a small boy was sitting on the grass triangle opposite the bricked-up entrance to the lunatic asylum. I'd looked it up on Wikipedia after I'd first walked past it all those months ago. Hanwell was one of the first asylums to encourage patients to exercise in fresh air and to ban the use of mechanical restraints, a move that was considered radical at the time. But people had still been locked up behind these walls with no real freedom. Even McLeish's madhouse had to have been better than that.

I sat down on a nearby bench and gave a polite weekend smile to the couple. The boy stood up and tottered along in that beaming punch-drunk way of children who have just discovered how to walk. I foraged in my backpack and took out Rob's folder. I'd slipped it into the zippered section before setting out. I wanted to look at McLeish's verses again in a different place, to see if my reaction was still the same. But in my rush to read them the first time, and probably because of the dim lamplight in my flat, I hadn't realized that two pages had stuck together. Here, in the daylight, they were clearly visible. I carefully prised them apart.

The drugs were amazing. Not that sedative shit they handed out in hospitals to slow you down and mess up your mind. We used to call that stuff the lithium handcuff. The drugs McLeish gave us took you way up, with the best hallucinations, clean and clear. But some of the women didn't like it, in spite of the drugs. They complained about having to cook and clean, all the household stuff. McLeish was old-school like that. Women had their place. They'd leave and then they'd come back.

Oh, they were all in love with him. There was one woman, I don't remember her name. She was amazing looking and she cried a lot. McLeish was keen on her. The drugs didn't work for her. Bad reaction or something. I heard later she'd died somewhere and by then it was pretty much over. A lot of people left. Someone came and took us away and it was back into the old hellhole, locked in at night, for our own good, so they said. People said McLeish used us. Maybe. I didn't care. It was the happiest time of my life. Did I say about the drugs?

I shivered in the bright sun. This man, whoever he was, had said that McLeish handed out psychedelic drugs like chocolates to vulnerable people. The writer had linked the drugs to the death of an unnamed woman. I stared down at the page. The words blurred together. I read the last sentences again and again while an invisible band tightened around my chest. Why hadn't Rob mentioned this? Did he think I might not be able to cope, that I might become unhinged by such an account? I told myself to be calm. But everything had changed with the resident's story of reckless drug taking and the unexplained death of a woman. McLeish's experiments to unlock creativity had gone horribly wrong. He wasn't the head of an experimental free community set up to support vulnerable people. He was the controller of a warped drug-soaked laboratory.

A narrow boat chugged past, its decks gleaming with fresh varnish. Pots of red geraniums hung along the sides, and the cabin roof had been converted into a vegetable garden with late summer squashes and zucchini plants growing out of boxes. A floating home, growing food for a family.

I put the pages into my backpack and turned for home, where I spent the rest of the day trying not to think about anything at all.

That night, I dreamed that I was driving in congested traffic, hemmed in on every side, when a huge swan, its feathers glued together with oily filth, smashed through my windscreen and attacked me with flailing wings. Then suddenly it fell against me, a dead, stinking weight. In my dream, I was devastated. I cried like a child, not just because it was dead, but also because somehow it was my fault.

17

∞

Trust yourself and your instincts when it comes
to relationships. But to do that, you must strive to
know all about yourself. Take the time to ask these
questions. Why do I want this person? Do I want
this person, or do I need them? Do I like this person,
or am I merely attracted to them? Listen to the an-
swers. Use this knowledge to empower the choices
in your life.

—Emma Helmsley, "Taking the Moment," September 22, 2016

The day of autumn equinox came, an equal division of light
and dark as the sun crossed the imaginary line at the center
of the planet. White cloud-shaped seed puffs from the plane
trees clumped together on the pavement as I walked to work.
It was still so hot, a full Indian summer. The aftershock of the
unnamed man's statement and the nightmare resounded
through me with the thud of each footstep.

I walked into the kitchen and there was Rob, sitting at the
table, piece of toast in his hand, wearing a toweling dressing
gown. A blush crept along my cheeks, like I'd come upon him
naked. Rob had always been dressed before. Maybe dressed
casually, barefoot and in jeans and T-shirt, but never like this,
the sun glinting along the stubble on his chin, his hair up in
spikes and the smell of sleep about him, that musty smell from
their bed that I knew so well.

"Hi," he said. "Don't mind me. I was about to go upstairs.

But now that you're here . . ." He smiled and shrugged his shoulders.

"Coffee, now that I'm here? While I'm up? No problem." I smiled back at him, my embarrassment ebbing away and everything in a steadier place again because of the sight of him, his physical presence. Not in a completely steady place. But steadier.

"Coming right up." I walked past him into the kitchen. The collar of his dressing gown had fallen down, revealing the intricate whorls of hair on the back of his neck, disappearing down his spine. Five minutes later, I was back at the table with our mugs of coffee. Rob was already standing, and I followed him down the hall into the study, watching the curve of the muscles along his calf, how they tightened and relaxed with each step.

Just before he sat down, he turned suddenly and we found ourselves face-to-face, only inches away from each other. I felt a compulsion, like vertigo, to fall towards him. How long did we stand there without moving? Long enough for me to see the soft lines on his lips, the crusts of sleep at the corner of his eyes, the gray strands in the lock of his hair that fell over his forehead; long enough for me to want to touch the hollow under his collarbone, to rest my head on his shoulder.

The tufts of cotton on his dressing gown brushed my arm. My heart slipped. He tilted his head towards mine and I leaned closer, mirroring his movements and matching my breath to his. In and out, so very slowly. The air between us was thick, almost liquid. My lips felt swollen and sensitive to his every breath. I would have kissed him, right there, and done everything with him, without a thought of anything or anyone. But somehow we bumped into each other, awkwardly because I was still holding the mugs of coffee. I stepped back, bewildered by what might have happened and what didn't.

"Sorry," said Rob, tightening the belt of his dressing gown.

His upper lip was beaded with sweat and he wiped it clean. With that movement, the air thinned and everything disappeared. He sat down behind his desk and I handed him his coffee.

"So, how was your weekend?" he asked.

"Fine," I replied. It was as if the moment between us hadn't happened, as if my palms were sweaty for no reason and my stomach was churning of its own accord. "Quiet, but fine. I went for a long walk yesterday. It always clears the head. How's everything with the book?"

"Nearly done," he said. "And about time too." He ran his hands through the spikes of his hair and fixed me with that steady gaze I knew so well. Nothing at all hinted that we were almost in each other's arms less than two minutes ago. "I just wish I'd been able to help you more, to find out definitively if you and your mother were there. It's so tantalizing, but I can't say for sure. I can only say it's likely, because of the images in your mind. Our best clue was the photograph of the woman called Mary with McLeish, but that's not someone you recognize. Maybe when the book is published—although I'm not expecting a huge readership—someone might get in touch with more information. It often happens. I'm sorry."

I wanted to ask him about the man's statement, but he reached over and placed my hand between his two hands, like before, and I forgot everything except the warmth of his fingers and how he pressed his thumb into my palm, moving it back and forth in a slow, hypnotic rhythm. "But how's everything with you? Any more thoughts or images?"

I nodded. That morning, soon after I'd woken, an image had surfaced in my mind of a woman whirling in circles, humming to herself as her nightgown flew up like a ballerina's tutu, her pale legs unfurling in an elegant arabesque. I'd reached for my notebook.

*Drums beating so loudly. My ears hurt. Someone is playing a
piano. I can't see who it is. They're dancing now, the women
are jumping around the room. My mother is there, somewhere
with the others. They told me to go away, but I'm hiding outside
behind the door with the crack on the side so I can see. A man
watches, moves around like a cat with a mouse. A strange smell,
like metal mixed with sweat. I hear their labored breath, the
thump of feet on the floor. They dance on and on, their white
dresses clinging to their bodies, and then they fling them off
and throw them into a corner. The man moves between them,
touching breasts and bellies and legs. He lies on the floor. They
gather round him and sink down beside him. He gives them the
colored chocolates and they do those things again, the things
that make me feel sick and spinning. I want my mother, but I
can't find her.*

"It was a bit surreal and vague. A woman dancing." The idea
of giving Rob graphic sexual content so soon after that moment between us was too embarrassing.

"Just one woman?" he asked.

"I think so. Also, something else a bit vague—did McLeish
give them drugs?" I asked.

"Yes, he did. Not prescription drugs, but mescaline deriva-
tives, things like that. He thought it would free their minds and
make them more creative. It wasn't a new theory—there were
quite a few experimental studies way back in the fifties and
sixties, before drugs like LSD were made illegal. Even now, academics are still researching this link. There's research under
way at Imperial College, and the early findings indicate hallu-
cinogens have potential for treating depression and addiction.
It's not as radical as you might think."

"But wasn't what McLeish did still dangerous? I mean,
couldn't people have died?"

He shook his head. "No one died. Why do you ask?"

"I don't know."

"These images, these memories—you shouldn't worry about them. There is nothing abnormal or weird about what you're thinking, nothing at all. We'll make sense of it at some stage, I'm sure."

My eye traveled above his head around the room, across the shelves of books and the wall of paintings, all the things I knew so well by now, then down to his steady face and smooth olive skin. He took his hands away and left mine on the desk. After the warmth of his skin, the grain of the oak was coarse under my fingers and the butt of a nail rubbed against my thumb. Oh, I had wanted Rob in those few seconds of vertigo. I had wanted to lose myself in him. Now, away from the intoxicating smell and touch of him, I thought of Emma and the family I cared so much about. I couldn't have continued to work at Wycombe Lodge, to talk to Emma in the evenings and Rob in the mornings, if I had slept with him. The guilt, the sense of betrayal to Emma and Jake and Lily, would have undone me. Wanting him had blunted me to rational thought.

18

The first Friday of September, the day of the party, was warm with a drizzle of rain, but bringing a forgiving light that burnished the furniture and obscured stains and scuff marks. By early afternoon, the house was ready. Fresh lilies in the vases, their exotic scent everywhere. Surfaces polished and dusted. Floors vacuumed. From his basket, Siggy watched me as I walked through the expectant rooms, the sound of my footsteps echoing around me. The almost-but-not-quite moment with Rob had been deposited somewhere in my mind where I didn't have to think about it. As for Rob, nothing changed in his attitude towards me during our morning meetings, although they'd dribbled away to one or two times a week, because he said he was on a last-minute rush with the book.

By 5 p.m., everyone was back; Jake and Lily from school, Rob from a media lunch in Knightsbridge, and Emma from a book signing out of town.

"A quick pasta? Salad?" I offered.

"Thanks but we'll eat later," called Emma from the kitchen door. "I'm off to shower and change."

"Me too," said Rob.

"I'm going to the cinema," announced Lily.

"I need to be somewhere later. I'll get a pizza," Jake chimed in.

"But it's a school night," I said.

Lily grinned. "Mom and Dad won't even know that we're gone if they're having a party. At least, they never have before."

"Where are you going?" I asked Jake. "Anywhere interesting?"

Anger, or it might have been fear, flashed across his face. "Not really. But I need to hurry up, or I'll be late." He picked up his backpack. Seconds later, I heard the front door close behind him.

I was alone again. Above me, the pipes shuddered with the rush of water. There were footsteps back and forth, then nothing. In the foxed mirror between the kitchen and the dining room, I glimpsed myself, hair smooth and pulled back, my usual uniform of jeans and shirt exchanged for black trousers and a white embroidered linen top. I didn't look forlorn or put upon. I didn't look like the kind of person who might have spent her first five years in a cult, whose mentally ill mother might have been under the spell of a power-crazed psychologist; the kind of person who scribbled bizarre things in a notebook that might or might not be true. That pinched look I used to see every day in the mirrors of the locker room in the restaurant had disappeared. So too had the lines that were beginning to make their way from my nose down to the corners of my mouth. My night worker pallor had changed into the first suntan I'd ever had, the result of my daily walks with Siggy and runs along the towpath. I looked relaxed and normal, almost pretty.

Two hours later, the rain making everything outside wet and slick, a couple of men from the deli, sweating the way other people breathed, pushed through the front gate with their crates and trays. Three girls dressed in jeans and black aprons followed them.

"Sally," said one, introducing herself with an authoritative air. "Fiona sent us. To help with the drinks and things."

The other two strolled around the room looking at the pictures. "That's a Ben Nicholson," said one with awe in her voice. She looked stoned and spoke in a low drawl. "His pictures are in the Tate." I'd always thought it was an amateur landscape painted by one of Emma's relatives.

"OK," said Sally. "You can stop gawping and set up the bar. Open the red wine so it can breathe and put the white wine into the ice buckets. Pronto, girls, pronto."

"Perhaps I could help?" I asked.

"Good heavens no!" she replied. The men rushed past and slammed the door, leaving a pungent smell of sweat mixed with stale cooking oil. I retreated to the dining room. Fiona had ordered a glut of food. A whole salmon, its soft, pink flesh gaping under silver skin, lay in the middle of the table. Behind it was an enormous glazed ham studded with cloves. There were bowls of quinoa, spelt, and various other grains, and platters of roast beef and bread. There was cheese as well, far too many types and crowded together on the plate so that the overripe Camembert ran over the cheddar and down onto the table. Everything was festooned with chopped herbs, as if someone had dropped all the food on newly mown grass and picked it up again.

On the sideboard, teetering on the lumps of hardened wax left by all the burned-down candles, were four chocolate mousse cakes and a lemon tart, still in their cardboard boxes. It looked like a chaotic picnic, nothing like the elegant precise buffets we provided at the restaurant's private functions, everything polished and sculpted.

Just before 8:30 p.m., Rob came downstairs in jeans and a white linen shirt, a scrubbed gleam along his cheekbones. He stood at the bottom of the stairs, tapping his foot against the skirting board until Emma rushed down to join him. One of the girls in black handed them each a glass of wine and together they raised their glasses. "To us," said Rob, and kissed the top of Emma's head. "To you," she replied, moving towards him like a bird floating into a harbor. "And everything to do with you."

"Oh, and Anne," she said, turning to me and raising her glass again. "You've been so terrific. And you look so smart. Thank you for making an effort."

I felt myself blush. "You look lovely," I said, although I wasn't sure. Emma didn't look anything like her usual self. For once her hair was properly dry, and she had styled it in fashionable waves that reminded me of a drag queen's wig.

"I thought I'd make a bit of a change for tonight." She wore a new dress, not her usual floating silk pajamas. I'd seen it in her wardrobe last week with the tags still attached and thought it was something she'd bought by mistake and planned to return. There was nothing glamorous or smart about it, although it had cost nearly £800. It was dull brown and shapeless, designed by a stern Dutchman with an unpronounceable name who'd made his fashion reputation with asymmetrical inside-out seams decorated with dangling threads. Emma was wearing a pair of the designer's earrings as well, enormous triangles of orange resin swinging below blue buttons. Her shoes were heavy and black.

"That's more like it. I knew it would look good on you." Rob gazed at her with approval. So he'd chosen her clothes tonight. She'd certainly never worn anything like this before. She looked like a science teacher on acid, with too much coral-colored lipstick and her eyelashes clumped with black mascara. Her normal floating silk pajamas suited her so much better.

Rob drained his wine. One of the girls immediately handed him another glass. He looked around. "Where are Jake and Lily?"

"I'm not sure," I lied. "Probably upstairs doing their home-work."

"Do you think our famous guest will turn up?" There was that tapping of his foot against the skirting board again. "What a fiasco if he didn't show."

"He will," said Emma. "Everything will be good." She took his hand and together they moved into the sitting room.

It was still drizzling when the first of a steady stream of peo-ple began to arrive. I stood in the hall, taking people's um-brellas and coats and hanging them on a rail I'd found in the spare bedroom. An hour later, the house was full. Thumping drum music from some endangered Amazonian tribe pumped through the rooms on a brain-numbing loop. People hived off into groups, leaning against the hall table, slouching in both sitting rooms and the study, crowding around the table in the dining room. You could tell that most of them had been on holiday somewhere hot and sunny. The remnants of their sum-mer tans glowed through the gray evening light.

I'd always liked watching people, and it didn't take that long to work out where everyone fitted in. There was a silent state-ment in their clothes, their stubble or lack of it, the length of their hair and the size of their earrings. The television people were thin and dressed in black. The publishing people were also thin, but a bit older and more colorfully dressed, the women wav-ing their bronzed arms aloft. Their accents were different as well, polished, more like the academics, easiest of all to identify be-cause they looked older and more disheveled than anyone else.

Only Christine, striding into the hall with the late arrivals, couldn't be categorized. Her bottom half was clad in ill-fitting jeans. But above the waist, she wore a close-fitting vest embroi-dered with sequins low at the front and drooping down her back. The man in front of her stared without shame until his companion pulled him into the sitting room.

"Hello," Christine cried out, clasping me with both arms. We might have been close friends meeting after a long separation. Her hair was pulled back in an untidy ponytail with strands falling down her neck. "Rebecca couldn't come—some kind of summer bug." She laughed and fiddled with her eyebrow ring. "It happens sometimes; she's probably been kissing too many boys."

Emma came up behind her, bearing a glass of wine. All her carefully applied blusher and mascara, her dun-colored clothes, made her look old next to Christine's defiantly makeup-free face and sparkling top. "Emma, darling, thank you." They pecked at each other's cheeks and walked away. Christine had her hand in the small of Emma's back, as if she was the hostess and Emma the shy guest who didn't know anyone.

Waiters slipped between groups, offering glasses of wine and trays of miniature sausages and quail's eggs. Over everything rose the warm smell of food, perfume, and damp clothes, cut by slices of cooler air when the front door opened. Easy laughter floated through the rooms. The absolute untouchable confidence of them as they drank their wine and wandered about. Their voices ascended in clear lines; the sound of desirable postcodes, high-achieving children in fee-paying schools, and alpine skiing holidays.

". . . and I told my agent I'd rather stick red-hot needles in my eyeballs than do another book signing up north. Have you any idea what it's like to sit at a table for three hours and not have one single person show up . . ."

". . . frankly, if I was a university student these days, I'd sue for breach of contract. They're lucky if they see a tutor once or twice a term. I wouldn't bother with conventional tertiary education these days. I'd get a job and do MOOCS. Better an online lecture from an Ivy League school than some of the garbage they have to listen to these days . . ."

". . . we need to restructure the employment situation or it will be too late. What graduates can afford to live in London as unpaid interns unless their parents are filthy rich? Do you think there's a telly program in that . . . ?"

". . . It's already been done. Do keep up. And what exactly are MOOCS . . . ?"

". . . Massive Open Online Courses. It's the future of education. I just told you that. Another drink . . . ?"

And then. "Have you read it yet?" A woman with a savage bob and cat's-eye glasses walked down the hall.

"Which one? His or hers?" Her companion was older, with a salt-and-pepper beard.

"His, of course. I'm not interested in time management tips." Her voice was scathing.

"I think you'll find that quite a few people are," the man said. "Look at the bestseller charts if you don't believe me." Theo emerged from the kitchen to join them. "You can't compare the two books," Theo said. "Emma and Rob do totally different things." I moved to the sitting room door to hear more, but they had merged into the crowd.

I didn't hear Dominic Butler enter. I was in the dining room pretending to clear plates but really enjoying the play of air from the open door on the back of my neck. There was a ripple of hush, as if someone had turned the volume down on the radio or television before turning it back up again. Everyone was pretending not to notice.

It's what sophisticated people did when they saw someone famous. It happened all the time in the restaurant. There was never any overt sign of recognition. In fact, just the opposite. The small groups that had formed huddled closer, just a fraction, and their conversations became more animated. Nods of the head became more vigorous, and they tossed their heads that little bit higher as they laughed at each other's witticisms.

Anything to avoid acknowledging that a famous person, who they undoubtedly recognized, had just entered the room.

Everyone here—the television producers, the publishing executives, and the academics and writers—they were just the same. They had their own clearly defined rules of social etiquette. No gawping or brandishing their phones and asking the famous person for selfies. I was pretty sure they didn't do photo bombs either. They were far too urbane. They would think themselves above all that starstruck business. Not me. I stopped stacking the plates and slipped unnoticed into the sitting room.

Rob and Emma were parading Butler around the room. Butler was charming beyond all call of duty. "Hello," he said again and again. A lot of people here would have said they were immune to fame, but there was little evidence of it. Men straightened their shoulders. Women sucked in their stomachs.

"Yes, it's good to be here. And of course I remember you." Butler waved away the offer of a glass of wine. "Just water please. Where was I? I'm a great advocate of therapy. It saved me and my family, who are the most important people in my life. People often poo-poo psychology, but I think they're wrong. Trying to find out why we do what we do—well, any intelligent person should ask themselves these questions every day of their lives—and those are the kind of questions that Rob and Emma answer, in their various ways, in their various books. So here's to them!" He raised his glass and everyone followed suit.

I looked across to his shining brown hair springing off his high forehead, the friendly lines around his blue eyes. Everywhere Dominic Butler went in the room, the mood was lighter, the smiles brighter. Behind him, Emma and Rob linked arms, gilded by his presence before he slipped out the door half an hour later without anyone really noticing.

There was another momentary hush before the noise level

increased. "Something of a coup," said Theo, stopping beside me. "It's going to be a good night." We grinned at each other, witnesses to the winning game.

The perennial shadow in my mind, the shouting and the screaming and the wild, murderous threats, everything floated away. I was still alone. But I didn't feel lonely. I felt part of something: Rob and Emma, Jake and Lily. I knew their foibles, just as they knew mine, and I felt that we accepted one another like a family. Family. I said the word again to myself, just to feel the relief and joy it contained.

19

⁓

Sex—it's at the basis of everything and
all of us are nothing but hypocrites as
far as sex is concerned.

—Rob Helmsley, *Madhouse: The Life and Times
of Rowan McLeish*

There is always a moment in any good party, when people are no longer thirsty or hungry, when everyone's gestures become less theatrical and their laughter less shrill. They no longer look over the shoulder of the person they're talking to, in case they miss someone or something more interesting. Lulled by food and wine, they are content.

The heavy rain that was forecast did not arrive. After Dominic Butler left, people gathered around Rob in the sitting room while others made their way to the study or the dining room. The woman in cat's-eye glasses cornered Theo by the hall table. "Really, we should collaborate on a paper or something." There was a hopeful note in her voice. Theo smiled in an absentminded way. I could have told her Theo didn't go out with women of his own age and saved her from embarrassing herself, but she wouldn't have listened.

Emma moved easily from one group to another, threads hanging from her dress like cobwebs. "Heavens, how clever you are," she told the English professor who I gathered had written many unpublished novels. "I could never write even one chapter of fiction. All I do is bullet points." The professor beamed as she moved on to compliment the next person. "Three languages!" she exclaimed to a young editor. "I've only ever managed to say *frites* and *vin*! That's it. And with the worst accent imaginable."

I loved this hovering and eavesdropping. It didn't matter that I didn't know anybody. I wouldn't have known what to say to them anyway. I was happy picking up the odd empty plate in between being an observer and smiling at Rob or Emma or Theo when I occasionally caught their eye. "Can I do anything?" I asked Sally again as she and the two girls washed glasses and plates. "Good heavens no," she repeated. "We have our own system." She rinsed everything in hot water, very efficiently I had to admit. "But thank you anyway."

All I was doing was getting in the way. I went upstairs to get my coat and umbrella. On the landing it was dim and quiet, the light from the street lamp filtered through the mist of rain on the windows. The only sound was the murmur of conversation from downstairs and an occasional gust of muffled laughter. Siggy sat on the landing, his ears pricked and his head cocked to one side. He whined when he saw me. "Don't fret," I told him. "They'll soon be gone. You'll have the house back to yourself." He lay down and settled his head between his paws. His eyes darted from side to side.

I reached for my things. Something was different. There was a strange new odor, sharper, stronger. It didn't belong here. Every room in the house had its own smell. Upstairs was different from downstairs. At Wycombe Lodge, downstairs was redolent of food and wine and Siggy, of the pleasing fug of people gathering together, mingled with Emma's lilies. Upstairs smelled only of the family: Emma's French soap, Rob's male tang, and, on the floor above, Jake's mushroomy socks and T-shirts and Lily's herbal oils. I liked that, being able to move between the public and private spaces and know the difference.

Along the hall, there was an infinitesimal shift in the air, as if a door had just shut silently. Then, a barely audible rustle. I stood very still, certain that Emma or Rob wasn't up here. Emma was deep in conversation with another woman in the study, and I'd seen Rob not so long ago, sitting at a crowded table outside the dining room.

I crept along to their bedroom door, avoiding the creaky floorboard in the middle of the hall, and stopped outside, making sure I breathed quietly. There was a second rustle, then a gasp. The door was crooked and didn't shut properly. Sometimes it slammed in storms, but most of the time there was a gap of several inches between the door and the frame. I peered through. The room was in darkness, apart from a bedside lamp.

They were kissing at the end of the bed, caressing each other's head and face with slow delicate movements, as if they had all the time in the world. There was a wet slipping noise. I wanted to turn and run away, but didn't seem able to move. Lips traveled down a neck. A hand shifted, pressing closer. I stepped away and leaned against the wall, grateful to have something hard and solid behind me.

Everything fell into a chasm. My head grew hot, like when you wake sweating from a nightmare or when you are faced with something so hideous that everything swarms and melts into a sticky mess. It was the kind of heat that hurt, that made your face flush and swell.

From behind came the padding sound of Siggy trotting over the rugs in the hall. I knew what he wanted—quiet refuge and the comfort of a familiar bed, away from the crowds of people downstairs. Ridiculous, I know, but I scooped him up. I didn't want to watch him nose his way through the bedroom door while I stood stunned and motionless, not knowing what to do. I didn't want him to see Rob and Theo together. He licked my chin and I stroked his ears to quieten him.

"Shhh," I whispered into the musty furze of his coat. "Don't let them know we're here. Stay still." The hot feeling in my head turned into cold—frozen. Under the shock, my anger flickered and rose. My mind raced on.

The Greek sign for Eros that I'd seen in Rob's diary—Rob wasn't having an affair with one of his students or Christine, as I had suspected. Nor was he writing reminders to himself. He was noting his assignations with Theo in ancient Greek. I'd never have recognized the letter if I hadn't been the scholarship girl at Stanton Hall, where they were old-fashioned and snobby enough to care about subjects like Greek and Latin.

Below me the swell of the party was subsiding. Soon people would start hunting for their coats, looking around to say goodbye to their host and hostess. Siggy squirmed in my arms. I stroked him, but he kept wriggling and his tail began to thump against my ribs. There was only one person Siggy bothered to wag his tail for. Under the scratch of his claws against my apron, there was the clack-clack of high heels on the stairs. I was frightened that he was going to whine or bark and I let him down. He turned for the stairs, trotting faster to greet his mistress, his stumpy tail dancing from side to side, his whole body shaking in delight at the prospect that he might be patted or even picked up.

"Oh, there you are," I said, with more jollity than necessary, a false emphasis on every word. I stepped into the middle of the hall, pretending almost to bump into her, but at the same time barring her way.

Emma's eyes were glassy and there was a small wet stain on the front of her new dress. "I'm gagging for a moment on my own." She rubbed her forehead, rocking back and forth. "Just a quick five minutes, lying horizontal."

Under the hall light, she looked tired and drawn. Her lipstick had rubbed off. All that was left was a narrow coral outline at the corners of her mouth. Tiny black smuts of mascara gathered under her eyes. She always looked prettier without makeup. Siggy nudged her legs. She bent down to pat him, cupping his chin with one hand while she stroked his face with the other.

Inside my head, the cold switched back to heat. Everything would change if Emma pushed past me to the bedroom. Everything could stay the same if I persuaded her to go downstairs again. Like a camera, I registered everything about the moment: the wavering pattern of light and shadows from the lantern on the landing, the scuffed paint on the walls, the faded floral pattern of the rugs. I remembered the morning of my interview, how Rob and Emma moved together and smiled at me, how I had straightened like a sunflower at noon under their gaze. Tears began. I blinked them away. I looked straight at her. I kept my voice steady.

"I must have missed you downstairs. I came up here looking for you. Rob needs you, something urgent. He's in a bit of a flap. He thought you might be upstairs and asked me to go and check."

Emma looked puzzled. "But I haven't seen him for a while."

"He was in the kitchen a minute ago. He said he needs you down there. "

She slipped off one of her clumpy shoes and rubbed Siggy's back with her foot. He rolled over and she began scratching his stomach. "Maybe it can wait. I'm a bit done in."

"I know," I said, forcibly rearranging my face into a smile. "Still, everyone will be gone soon. But Rob wanted you because your agent is about to leave, and he needs to talk to you, something about a possible TV series."

I knew this house. I'd spent five days of every week here since the beginning of the year. I knew its idiosyncratic noises, that from Jake and Lily's bedrooms above, everything below was muffled, but somehow sound funneled and amplified from the hall into Rob and Emma's bedroom. Rob and Theo wouldn't realize I'd seen them, but they could hear every word.

I'd already lied. If Emma stepped past me, she would find that out for herself. She would think I was protecting Rob and had known about Theo. She might even think that I'd colluded with them about dates and times and assignations. "I think he was talking about a television series all of your own," I said, cajoling her. "It sounded exciting."

"OK." She sighed and put on her shoe. "Let's go." I followed her down the stairs, giddy with relief. In the hall, her agent, a red-faced man with bushy gray eyebrows, was weaving towards the rail, in search of his coat.

Emma swept her hair to one side and squared her shoulders. "Sorry to keep you waiting."

"But you never keep me waiting, my dear girl." He fumbled with a coat hanger. A glittery scarf fell to the floor and he stepped on it. Sequins spilled everywhere. I slipped past them towards the kitchen. Behind me, I heard Emma say, "Television! That does sound exciting. Are they really talking about a series or just the occasional appearance?" Her voice was determinedly cheerful. "Television? Yes, of course," he replied, sounding puzzled.

In the dining room, people sprawled around the table. Empty glasses, smeared with fingerprints and lipstick marks, were everywhere. Cutlery and dirty plates had been left skewed on side tables and on the chairs. One plate was tilted on a cushion, the fabric smeared with oil and pieces of ham crusted with rice. The woman with cat's-eye spectacles was digging out slivers of fish directly off the serving platter and tipping them into her mouth, even though there were utensils and a clean plate right by her elbow.

There was only a scattering of guests left. More than anything, I wanted to get out of the house before Rob and Theo came downstairs. But I needed to check on Emma first, to make sure she hadn't slipped away from her agent and gone upstairs again. I found her safely ensconced in the sitting room. The agent was leaning towards her, trying to stroke her hair and caress her face.

The front door was open and a breeze filtered through. A couple wandered off and then Jake and Lily were beside me. "We're a bit late," said Lily. "We missed the bus and had to get a taxi." She ran her eye over the empty glasses and dirty plates littered everywhere. "Wow, a good night, even by their standards. See, I told you they wouldn't notice a thing."

"You were right," I said, sick at what might have happened, them slipping into the house and going upstairs past their parents' bedroom. "There's loads of food. You should go and help yourselves."

I looked through the back windows onto the garden, wanting a moment not possessed by what I had seen. In the night reflection, I saw shadows under my eyes and lines across my forehead. I moved my head from side to side, the way I liked to do when I had the house to myself. Perhaps it was the darkness of the night, but nothing changed in my focus. It was the same series of shadows wherever I looked.

"Well well." I turned when I couldn't ignore Rob's voice any longer. I needn't have worried about the expression on my face, that I might have given something away. He gave that funny circus master wave with his arms, the same wave he'd given during my interview for the housekeeper's job, right here in this room, when I'd fallen for him, for them, the whole nine yards.

"Well," he repeated, with another circular sweep. Coin-sized rings of sweat bloomed in the armpits of his shirt. "What do you think? Did things go well?" How could he look so normal, like he usually did in a room full of people, full of confidence? His hair was neat, his face not even flushed. He looked so pleased with himself. Emma appeared beside him, running her hands through her hair with that careless gesture I tried so hard to copy. "How would you rate everything?" she asked. "You know you're our litmus test, that we rely on you to tell us how things are."

I made sure to look straight into her bloodshot eyes, behind the smuts of mascara and the eye shadow creasing at the corners. She had tried so hard to make the evening a success. "It's terrific," I said. "It's been a great party. Really."

The woman with the cat's-eye glasses tapped Rob on the shoulder. "A good evening," she said. A sliver of salmon, shining pink, had fallen on her black top. "A night to be talked about, along with many others. Well done."

Emma slid her arm around Rob's waist. "Thanks," she said. "We're so pleased that you could make it." They were seamless at that moment, smiling goodbye.

"I wouldn't have missed it," said the woman. "London's power couple does it again!"

For a second, I almost believed that nothing had happened, that what I'd seen was a terrible miasma. But there was a cold shiver at the back of my neck and a dry papery taste in my mouth. Everything was horribly and needlessly broken. I began picking up plates and glasses, but Rob took my arm.

"You've done enough, Anne, far more than necessary. Thank you. Go home now. The girls will clear up—it will all be back to normal when you return."

I protested, but not that much. Rob pressed a £50 note into my hand. "It's late," he said. "Call for a taxi, they never take long to come." My first reaction was to think that this was a bribe or the beginning of one. But Rob didn't know I'd seen them. He'd only heard Emma and me talking.

I said goodbye and walked out into the night. The drizzle had mixed with mist to dull the streetlights into a series of pinpricks. The pavements were black and slick with the drip of sodden trees. I rang for a taxi and gave the pickup point as the street corner nearest the bus stop, then scurried from streetlight to streetlight, my footsteps echoing around me. There was a moment, just before I reached the corner, when I thought I heard a shuffle and breathing and I ran into the middle of the street. At least I would have some warning of attack then. But it was nothing. There was nobody.

All the way home in the taxi, I kept hearing the gasp, the wet slipping sound. I saw Theo's hands running through Rob's shock of hair, the dim outline of their bodies bending towards each other. I smelled their sweat and felt the currents of air in the room, like electricity.

"Everything OK, love?" The taxi driver kept glancing at me in his rear vision mirror. "You look a bit done in."

"It's been a long day," I said and closed my eyes.

If I had hoped that my flat would provide calm, I was wrong. Its neatness mocked me, the vacuumed stripes on the carpet visible in the dim light of the lamp, the dishcloth folded into a perfect square in the kitchen. I opted for the Lady Macbeth response to the evening and ran a bath. I lay submerged in hot water, inhaling my neighbor's cigar smoke, exhausted by the effort of not thinking.

Everything banged around me in so many discordant emotions. Anger at Rob and Theo. Sadness that I could never again see Theo as a friend, that his professed adoration of Emma had been a complete lie. Fear that Emma would somehow find out. My desire to protect her and the children. The memory of them in the bedroom played in my mind. I could sniff the sex, almost viscous.

The lie of it all—why did Rob and Theo need to carry on

with this secret affair? It wasn't like people had to keep being bisexual or gay secret anymore. People were comfortable with being gay, transgender, sexually fluid, or whatever. Caitlyn Jenner, Ellen DeGeneres, Elton John—the list of famous people went on and on. Gay men and women got married, had children. So why did they keep up this pretense of heterosexuality? Why not be out and proud like everyone else?

One a.m. Sleep was impossible. Swaddled in a bathrobe, whiskey slopping in my glass, I paced my tiny room, not knowing what to do. Despite her success in the world outside the house, Emma wasn't cool and urbane when she was at home. Even with the house, her money, it was still Rob she cleaved to for assurance. There was that tentative way about her, her anxiety to please and her incessant thank-yous. I wanted to protect her, but that seemed impossible.

Two a.m. I decided there was no need to tell Emma. She needn't know a thing. We could continue our presupper chats in the kitchen about her day. And I could keep up with my morning conversations with Rob. I could even manage to talk recipes with Theo after dinner. Five seconds later, there was every need to tell Emma. I couldn't keep such a thing to myself, seeing them together every evening and having to greet Theo when he came to dinner. Ten seconds later, I would do neither of these. I would say nothing and leave Wycombe Lodge quickly, with some trumped-up explanation. I would discover what happened at Kinghurst Place on my own, without Rob's help. My thoughts spun in a whirring circle.

Three a.m. I slumped on the sofa, spilling whiskey on my bathrobe. The noisy hiss of car tires on the wet roads came through the open windows, then the faraway beat of music. Maybe I didn't have to tell Emma after all. Maybe I didn't have to leave Wycombe Lodge. All this might be a shock reaction, like when you saw a car accident or a street fight and you couldn't help yourself. You needed to talk about it. You turned to the nearest stranger, you grabbed their arm, and you said, "Did you see that? Wasn't that dreadful! What will happen now? What can I do?" And then you went home. You didn't actually do anything at all. I didn't want our lives to change; me, Emma, Rob, Jake, and Lily. This house had given me a place in which calm had begun to grow. Rob had given me an inkling of my past, with the possibility of much more to come. I did not want to be working in another restaurant kitchen, getting home after midnight, not knowing anything further about my mother and me, why she'd left me or who my father might have been.

Outside, a weak light spread over the horizon. I left the half-full glass of whiskey on the coffee table and went to bed, for once not bothering to plump cushions and wash up. I fell asleep and dreamed tense, inescapable dreams, a volley of screams and thumps, and woke gasping, not knowing where I was until the footsteps of the couple upstairs reminded me. I lay still for a minute, the hair at the back of my neck twisted and damp. It didn't take long to make my decision.

I would return to Wycombe Lodge. Do nothing, I told myself. Ignore it. Pretend it didn't happen. I was good at that. For the best part of thirty years, I ignored my own early life. I could do it again. I wanted to protect Emma and Jake and Lily. I wanted to continue being the housekeeper. I would keep writing in my notebook, keep trying to find out about my mother, and everything could stay the same.

20

∞

People say at Kinghurst Place the lunatics
have taken over the asylum. Absolutely, I
reply. Who better to run an asylum than
those who need it most?

—Rob Helmsley, *Madhouse: The Life and Times
of Rowan McLeish*

The prism through which I saw everything changed after the night of the party. The house was empty when I arrived on Monday, and I didn't see Rob until the next week. Something about changed schedules and extra programs, said Emma. He had to be at the studio by 8 a.m. But the next Monday, he was mooching about the dining table in his usual way when I walked in, ruddy-cheeked, like he'd just returned from a long health-inducing run. I managed to find a part of his face that was not quite his eyes and not quite his chin, and smiled hello. It was surprisingly easy to close off the image of him and Theo, as if I could turn the prism at will from a piece of glass that refracted a chaos of violent patterns to another angle where all was white and clear.

"Hey," he said. "Haven't seen you for a bit. For one of the very few times in my life, I've had to put the hours in." I hadn't thought of it before, but he didn't work that hard. Not like Emma, always gone before I arrived and rushing back in hours after Jake and Lily got home from school. "You were such a help at the party. Thank you."

"A pleasure," I said.

"I can't think what we did before you arrived."

I smiled and made coffee. But this time I didn't hang about waiting for an invitation to join him in the study. Instead I took my mug and disappeared into the laundry, piling clothes into the dryer and washing machine, adding detergent and color brightener and fabric conditioner, everything promising jasmine breezes and fresh cotton sunlight, a metamorphosis courtesy of modern chemicals. I paired socks into shapes like fists. I folded towels and ironed pillowcases and sheets into stacks so neat they might have been encased in invisible boxes, so intent on my straight lines that I didn't notice Siggy's whining until he began to bark and paw at my legs.

I clipped on his leash and set off for the river. It was high tide. Milky froth washed against the rocks under a sallow sky. I let Siggy free. He shook himself and began cantering about, looking back every few seconds to make sure I hadn't disappeared. We walked aimlessly for a while then turned around. I liked being back by the time Jake and Lily got home from school so they didn't come into an empty house.

An hour later, the front door opened and slammed shut. Lily and Jake rushed in for their smash and grab from the refrigerator. My attempts at healthy snacks—things like homemade muesli bars and oat biscuits—had failed. Jake refused to budge from his peanut butter and chocolate regime, while Lily crunched her way through apples and carrots and then succumbed to a packet of crisps half an hour before dinner.

Jake piled a plate with food and disappeared upstairs. Outside the chaos of his bedroom and the pamphlets with their warnings of damnation and calls to prayer, there was little trace of him in his own home.

"No homework pals today?" I asked Lily.

"They're coming home tomorrow," she said. "You don't mind, do you?"

"Of course not," I said. "But don't they ever want to stay on for dinner?"

"Not really." She chewed for a bit. "Besides, Mum and Dad prefer to have their own friends to dinner. They're not that interested in mine." Her matter-of-fact tone discouraged further conversation. She disappeared upstairs. I cleared away their mess and began chopping onions and tomatoes.

Everything was easier to understand now. I watched over everything at Wycombe Lodge with a sadness, as if I were looking at photographs of a country in which I'd once been happy. I could spot the difference between the tables that were French and valuable and the ones that were Edwardian junk. Under the residual smell of dog and fading lilies, I recognized the refined, dry smell of money. When I gazed through the French windows to the garden, the autumn leaves dropping like oversized petals, I saw as well the reflection of my own round face, giving nothing away.

Jude told me to leave. "Get out of that house," she puffed into her mobile during her morning boot camp in the park. "Leave them to deal with their dirty secrets. Nothing to do with you if they refuse to live honestly."

"I will. Soon, but not just yet. Something might come up about my mother. Rob might find out something more."

"And pigs might fly," she said.

As I walked to the river each day, Siggy doing his best to trip me up, I saw how Rob and Emma didn't notice much of what went on in their own home, although they spent most evenings there. Rob was preoccupied with his work. He was oblivious to Jake's unexplained absences and Lily's obsession with lists, her concern about her plumpness. It had taken a while, but I finally understood his concentrated gaze at Jake and Lily across the table. It wasn't that look of pride or adoration that parents often bestow on their children. It was almost abstract. He was looking at them in a professional way, analyzing some aspect of their behavior or speech in psychological terms.

I felt more protective and fond of Emma than ever now, but I'd become aware of her vagueness, the way she sometimes forgot to close the front door when she came in at night; how she loved her children, but seemed to regard them as two strangers who had somehow taken up residence when she wasn't looking. Couriers arrived at least once a week with clothes she'd ordered online for Jake and Lily, always too small for her and too large for him, and completely unsuitable as well. What sixteen-year-old girl needed a knee-length leopard print pencil skirt? What fourteen-year-old boy wanted a navy Ralph Lauren blazer? Where did she think they would wear such clothes? To the cinema? To Starbucks?

"I'm sorry, I've got it wrong again," Emma would say dolefully each time, peering into the boxes as Lily and I carefully rewrapped the clothes in their layers of tissue paper, ready for return. "I'm such a fool."

"No you're not, Mum," Lily would reply. "And after all, it's the thought that counts." After that, they would hug each other in a brisk fashion and Lily would retreat upstairs wearing the jeans she had bought for herself at TK Maxx.

I realized as well that Rob and Emma burnished their image of the successful in-demand couple whenever possible. Everything I'd thought was so casual and serendipitous—the mentions in glossy magazines, the attendances at opening nights and private viewings—was carefully planned. Emma had her own publicist as well as the efficient Fiona. I also saw that an invitation to Wycombe Lodge required more than a winning smile. Rob's favored guests were those with influence: academics who'd written popular books, about-to-be-big-time artists and editors. And more than once I overheard Rob blatantly cadging invitations to parties and opening nights.

Was it a week later? Or a fortnight? I don't remember exactly. Emma foraged in the wine cooler for an open bottle and poured herself a glass. "Christine and Rebecca. I couldn't put it off any longer. I kept hearing the rumbles of discontent. So tomorrow night, it is. At least they're going to get here on their own steam. It'll give Rob more hours in his day." She waved the bottle in my direction. "Won't you? Just once share a glass with me?" I shook my head.

"Shall we have the same dinner as last time? It seemed to work," Emma continued. "It'll be just us. Plus Theo on his own. The latest girlfriend seems to have gone the way of the rest."

I was nervous about seeing Theo again, about keeping an impassive face in his presence, even though I kept telling myself that he hadn't seen me. Still, on the bus the next morning, the thought of the evening ahead put the wind up me. Lily was of the same opinion, but for reasons of her own. "Bloody hell, them again," she muttered as she dropped her school backpack on the kitchen floor. "Tits reunited. Jake won't be able to help himself."

"They're not that bad," I said lamely. "And where's Jake?"

"Who knows? I'm not his keeper." Lily rolled her eyes, gathered up her crop of apples, and made for her bedroom.

I had my back to Theo when he bounced through the kitchen door three hours later, asking if he could light the candles.

"Thank you, but no," said Emma. "It's my favorite part of the day."

There was a creeping flush along my cheeks and I was tense and dry-mouthed, as if I were the guilty one.

"Anne," Theo said to my back. The force of his voice, jovial, yet commanding, was strong enough to turn me around. "Good to see you! We haven't caught up since the triumph of the party." He kissed my cheek with an exaggerated smacking noise. "How are you?"

On the bus that morning, I'd wondered if he would appear different in some way, more the type of man who was having an affair with a married man, whatever that looked like. But he was the same. If anything, he reminded me even more of a bouncing leprechaun. I busied myself at the oven, checking that the chicken was ready. He sidled beside me, and forced his face close to mine. "Everything smells delicious," he said. "As usual. We're all so lucky to have each other." He turned to Christine and Rebecca, who had just come in. "Don't you think so?"

"Think what?" asked Christine.

"That we're lucky to have each other."

"Luck." She sniffed. "It doesn't come along like a bus. You have to work at it. And it's so much to do with socioeconomic factors." Behind her back, Theo made one of his funny faces. I couldn't help smiling. From the sitting room came the mournful thump of drums and the high, wavering notes from what sounded like an out-of-tune flute. Rob wandered into the kitchen, greeting Theo in that usual blokey way of his. A slap on the shoulder with one hand, a mock feint with the other.

In the restaurant, everyone, even the washing up crew, knew which customers were having secret affairs. Despite the pretense of business meetings or magazine interviews, there was an inevitable glance that continued a moment too long, or a subtle mirroring of each other's movements, like a private dance. We caught it every time. But here in the kitchen, with Emma lighting the candles and Christine holding forth on educational inequality, there was no tiny gesture or look to indicate there was anything other than solid heterosexual friendship between the two men. Candles flickered above their heads, softening the outline of their faces. The memory of Theo and Rob embracing in the bedroom faltered. Did it really happen? Then my brain righted itself.

"Yet another spectacular meal," said Theo in the kitchen after dinner. There was that familiar grin. All the times we'd stood right here in this same spot by the counter, all the fuzzy moments I'd seen the two of us as some kind of siblings. All of it disappeared. "Good," I replied. "Very good." The pots were already clean, but I kept scrubbing them.

As a prize to myself for having survived the evening, I decided on a takeaway curry. It was past 9 p.m., but it wouldn't take long to drive to my favorite Indian place in Southall, where I knew they ground the spices freshly each evening and the kitchen had a proper clay tandoori oven.

At the restaurant, I picked up my lamb *dhansak* and *saag paneer* and headed towards Brentford, already salivating from the smell of ginger and cardamom. As I pulled away from a pedestrian crossing, a scarlet baseball cap caught my eye, and then the back of a figure wearing a T-shirt blotched fluorescent yellow above baggy low-slung jeans. The figure hurried across the road and ran up a flight of steps into a small dilapidated church adorned by a skinny cross and a banner reading FOL-LOW THE CHURCH OF ETERNAL TRUTH. SAVE LIFE! I'd driven along this road so many times and never noticed it before.

The figure looked like Jake. I thought of the pamphlet in his bedroom, even more chaotic than when I first saw it; clothes flung everywhere, everything covered with pieces of torn-up paper, like confetti. The pamphlet was increasingly well thumbed, and the pages were dotted with yellow from the fluorescent marker pen. The most recent underlined page read: *The nonbelievers, the liars, the impure and the infant murderers—all of them will be cast into the lake of fire, to the death they deserve.*

The ink had seeped into the margins and onto the next page. "Does Jake's class study comparative religion?" I'd asked Lily when I left his room.

She rolled her eyes. "Why would they do something like that?"

I parked the car and followed the figure up the steps. I'd never liked churches, and this one was no exception, even though it was modest, with a small wooden dais at the front and none of the ostentatious statues of the chapel at school. There was another banner of the cross, this time in purple, and a row of lit candles underneath, their dim gold light just visible against the high wattage overhead. A high, clear tenor filled the room and I looked around for the singer. But there was only a ghetto blaster at the side of the dais.

The church was hot and crammed full of people squashed into rows of fold-up seats. There were families, with the children's hair in neat box braids fastened with bright ribbons, next to old men wearing flat caps and women with mauve-tinted hair. I thought I saw Jake's scarlet baseball cap three rows ahead of me, but after craning my neck in both directions, I realized I was mistaken. The cap was more orange than red, and the back of the neck underneath was dark and covered in angry spots. But there were more baseball caps in the rows nearer the front of the hall. Some of them were red and Jake could have been among them. I peered and turned, but I couldn't see him anywhere. The woman next to me glared disapproval at my fidgeting. Suddenly I was no longer curious, merely embarrassed by my mistake and my intrusion into a place where I didn't belong.

As I got up to leave, an old man shuffled to a table behind the door, set up with a chrome urn and piles of cups. He was struggling to turn on the faucet of the urn, and I walked over to help him. It was simple enough. Milk and two sugars, biscuit on the side. He smiled through an array of tombstone teeth and grabbed my arm with surprising strength.

"My dear," he stuttered after the first few sips and mouthfuls. Biscuit crumbs gathered at the corner of his mouth and his breath smelled of yeast and sweet tea. "You must join us, at least for a little while." He steered me into a seat and sat beside me, his nails digging into my arm. I thought of my congealing curry. I'd stay for five minutes and then excuse myself. I could reheat my supper.

A plump woman who looked to be in her midforties hauled herself onto the dais and switched off the ghetto blaster. Her lipstick was too red and her blond hair was set in corrugated waves. But she had authority and everyone fell silent. She shook a cordless microphone from a pocket and started working the room.

"I'm standing for purity and the way of Him." She nodded her head. For a moment, I thought a juddering hank of hair would break free from its corrugations, but it fell back into place.

"I've given up my whole life, my entire existence on this earth so that you . . ."—she paused and jabbed a finger at one of the red baseball caps that jumped up as if it had been hit—". . . so that you, and yes, you . . ."—another jab, another baseball cap jumped—". . . can know the truth, the whole truth, so that you all . . ."—her arms were windmills; her sweater lifted to reveal a roll of belly flab—". . . have the opportunity, the God-given opportunity to stop being phonies and hypocrites, bad people outside this Church, swearing, drinking, fornicating." This last word was drawn out for some time.

The acrid smell of anxious sweat filled the room. The preacher's voice rose and fell on the beat of her words, like a giddying seesaw. The older section of the audience nodded approval, but it was clear from the direction of her hands and the sweep of her gaze that they were not the lucrative mother lode. It was the young at the front of the church that she desired.

The man beside me loosened his grip and began to stroke

my hand with calloused palms. I wanted to pull away, leave them to their prayers, but couldn't seem to manage it. In the front pews, I saw rows of shoulders heaving, quivering as if an electric current had passed through them. One red basketball cap shook more than the rest. The neck underneath it was pale and thin, with wisps of blond hair, just like Jake's. But I had been mistaken before.

As I removed my hand and motioned goodbye to the old man, a girl rushed onto the dais. She looked no older than fifteen, dark hair pulled into a vicious ponytail. Her face was wet with tears, with flushed dots high on her cheekbones. She took the microphone. The only word to describe the sound she made was keening. In her high-pitched, strangled song without words, there was such longing and pain. Tears coursed down her face as she halted for breath. The others clapped and murmured as the woman preacher embraced her. The girl's head fell against her oversized breasts, and the woman stroked her head. The baseball caps nodded in unison.

I had reached the door when the girl began to speak, low and faltering. "It's hard to believe in Him, and sometimes I don't. Sometimes I don't even believe in His Word and then I feel dirty and guilty." She leaned back and forth, as if her doubts about Him had removed her ability to stand straight. They leaned towards her, a tight-knit group of maybe ten or twelve. The baseball caps were waving, poppies in the breeze. Their hands stretched out like war-torn orphans waiting for a food drop. Behind them, the older members of the congregation nodded and smiled.

I'm meant to be upstairs, but I'm peeking through the crack in the door, watching them eat dinner. The way they look at him, like he's the father or a god or both and they're the children who worship him. They imitate his every movement. He laughs and they laugh. He leans forward and they do as well. The only time they don't copy him is when he talks. Then they fall silent and nod like those clowns you see at the fairground. Wild shouts, cigarette smoke, buttery spicy smells float towards me, but I'm not allowed in.

A drumbeat interrupted my reverie and the congregation began to sing, quietly at first. By the time they had reached the end of the first verse, everyone was in full throttle. The preacher stood to one side, nodding in a determined fashion. "Yes," she seemed to be saying to herself. "Yes, I have washed these children clean and He will enter their hearts." I shut the door behind me, as quietly as I could.

It was raining and blowing hard as I went to my car. I was grateful for the sting of it against my face, taking me back to my own meager world. All the way to Brentford, the windscreen wipers thumped to and fro in the same hypnotic rhythm of the woman preacher's speech. My lamb dhansak no longer made me salivate. There was just the smell of turmeric and garlic. I wasn't even hungry.

By the time I got back, there were no parking spaces anywhere in my street, and I had to drive two blocks to find one. Walking along the main road, I saw the boy again. This time he wasn't playing hopscotch by himself. He was weaving back and forth on the curb, far too close to the road. He had his feet close together, and he crouched like a surfer on the edge of a wave, moving his arms like wings right next to the cars and buses that whizzed past, steered by drivers with no thoughts for small boys imagining that they were hanging five toes somewhere sparkling and blue in the Pacific Ocean, far away from inner-city grime.

I dashed over and hauled him back to the safety of the pavement. He was too surprised to struggle. "Sorry to grab you like that." His huge almond eyes were terrified. "The thing is, you could have been run over. There could have been an accident."

We stared at each other, my hand still clutching his sleeve as we breathed in the fume-laden slipstream. "Where's your dad?"

The boy inclined his head in the direction of my street.

"Does he know you're out here?"

"He's on the phone." His voice was even huskier than before, with a slight lisp. "He'll be angry."

"You can't blame him," I said. "It's dangerous out here on your own."

He shrugged.

"What's your name?"

"Faisal."

"OK, Faisal, let's get you home."

Faisal's building fronted onto the main street, a brutish brick block with a side entrance. I passed it every night, but I'd never really noticed it. The front gate hung off its hinges. Weeds sprouted from between paving blocks, and the glass panes of the front door had been smashed and patched with black tape. Less than a hundred meters away stood my building, freshly plastered and painted, glossed green front door, smart brass buzzer plates.

"We live so close to each other. Maybe you might visit me one day, with your father." I didn't mean it. It was just something to say to break the silence. "So, what number are you?"

He pressed number 3. "It's broken," said Faisal. "He can hear the buzzer, but we can't hear him speak. He'll come."

After some minutes, the hall light switched on. There was a clattering and the sound of locks being turned. The door swung open and tiny shards of glass fell onto the ground. The hall smelled of urine and garbage.

Faisal's father looked at his son and then at me. "You were inside," he said to Faisal. "You were inside watching television, just minutes ago." He checked his watch, as if to make sure of the time. "I don't understand how . . ."

"Well, here he is now," I said cheerily. "Safe and sound. No harm done." I let go of Faisal's arm to shake his father's hand. "I'm Anne, Anne Morgan. We met before, kind of. I live nearby, just down the street."

"I am Imran," he said. "Come in, come in, off the street, please." He had an around-the-world-in-a-sentence kind of accent, mainly Middle Eastern, but with English and American overtones. He was taller than I remembered and he wore the same ill-fitting jacket.

I stepped into the hall. We stood in an uneasy triangle. Imran kept glancing from me to Faisal and back again. "It is hard to keep an eye out for the boy," he said. "I was on the telephone, to my sister in Lahore. The line kept dropping out." He smiled, showing square white teeth below shiny gums. "Not your fault, though. Will you?" He pointed to the open door behind him. I saw a sink, a square table with two chairs, and a neatly made bed jammed up against the wall. It was hard to imagine how Faisal had escaped. There must have been another room with a back door somewhere.

"Thanks," I said, swinging the bag of cold curry in my hand. "Just for a minute. I should get home. I have a load of things to do."

Imran poured me a glass of water and motioned for me to sit down. "It is very kind of you to look after Faisal. Thank you."

"No problem," I said. I drank some water. An awkward silence settled. "Where are you from?"

"Originally, we are from Afghanistan, my family. My wife and I taught medical students in Kabul. But it became hard to stay after she died. A stray bullet." He spoke in a matter-of-fact tone, but his fingers curled into a fist. "So we, my sister and Faisal, we went first to Lahore, and then Faisal and I applied to come here. And soon my sister will visit us."

"I'm sorry about your wife," I said. "Maybe when your sis-

ter comes, you might like to visit me . . . maybe for dinner."
The words spilled over without me thinking. "Just a thought," I
stumbled on. "To keep in mind."

"Thank you," said Imran. He looked surprised and pleased.
I immediately regretted my invitation. It was the sort of thing
that Rob and Emma did all the time. They finished one conversation by saying they'd like to have another. When they wanted
someone to leave, they mentioned something about getting together very soon. It meant nothing. It had taken me months to
work it out, so I couldn't expect Imran to understand. "That is
kind," he said.

"Come by anytime," I continued. "I live in the white building
down the street. Number twelve. My name is on the buzzer." I
shook Imran's hand again, and he walked me through the hall,
our shoes crunching on the broken glass.

At home, no longer hungry, I put the cold curry in the refrigerator. Maybe Imran would forget about my casual invitation. I hoped so. I turned on the television. Rob's program, this
week about a disgraced politician, had almost finished. When
I first started at Wycombe Lodge, I watched it most weeks.
But with the image of him and Theo never fully extinguished,
the sight of that earnest look on his face and the sound of
his carefully phrased questions angered and saddened me in
equal measures. I hadn't watched it since the party. Instead,
I'd become addicted to crime TV and all its cheesy mysteries.
I liked to think I was making up for decades of lost viewing
hours while I was working in restaurant kitchens. But the truth
was that I liked its constancy. On some station or other, at any
time of the night, you could always find the same cast of men
and women in New York or Los Angeles or Miami fighting for
justice without ever once asking for overtime or needing to
brush their hair.

And if I tired of them, I could turn to one of those obsessive

Scandinavian detectives with complicated relationships and alcoholic pasts, skidding around in their Volvos in the snow and the dark, everything always solved in each program and series by the time the final credits rolled. Later, another mystery solved, I picked up the file I'd taken from Rob's recycling bag last week. I reached for the third poem at the bottom of the pile.

> *Whatever you say*
> *Whatever you do*
> *Wherever you lay*
> *I am you*

The page fell on the floor and I picked it up. It was like all the others, a copy of the typed verse, still showing the original smudges and creases. Maybe it was the angle of the light, but it looked different. In one corner, there was what looked like rubbed out writing. I peered closer and turned the page around, examined it from another position. I picked up the lamp and shone it on the page like a torch. Yes, there it was. I was sure of it. Handwritten letters, almost but not quite erased. The fat, looped curves of the letter M. Underneath it, to one side, was the triangle of the letter A. The beginning of my mother's name. I moved the page closer, then farther away to sharpen focus. I did it again and again, until I was dizzy. I went into the kitchen and turned the kettle on, then listened to its panicky bubbling, watching the steam float against the windows until the sight of the streetlights and building opposite dimmed into misted shadows.

Back on the sofa with my mug of tea, I picked up the page again. I moved the lamp closer, making circles around the page until I could smell the paper beginning to scorch. I hadn't been mistaken. I could see the first two letters of my mother's

name, written in pencil. The lines were blurred, but I hadn't
made a mistake.

The other poems were in my bedroom. I got up and grabbed
them. I held each one under the same close light. There was
nothing on the first two pages, but on the third, the same two
blurred letters appeared again. There were more faint lines
and etchings. I looked closer and turned the page around. I
couldn't be sure, but when I turned the page upside down, one
series of lines looked like a stick man, the kind of thing a child
would draw.

An image came to me, fully formed for the first time. I
reached for my notebook.

Warm sun everywhere. We're in the room with swirly walls,
yellow and blue, all the way to the ceiling. She puts her arms
around me, she's helping me to draw something on the floor.
There's a piece of green chalk in my hand, all powdery and
dry. Her hand guides mine. Up we go with the curve, then
down with the straight line. I lean against her, burrow into the
softness of her stomach. I hear her laugh, magical, musical.
We keep making patterns along the floor. More curves and
straight lines until she puts her hand over mine and together
we draw one last swirl. "Look, darling girl, look. This is your
name, this is who you are. Annastasia Swan. I've given you
a name all your own. A swan is a beautiful bird that is loyal
and loving and true to its mate forever. And Annastasia means
Resurrection." I don't understand what that means, but it feels
so lovely and it looks so pretty that we smile and keep looking
at the marks on the floor, how the sun dances off my name that
belongs to me and no one else in the world.

And then the woman comes in, the one who stinks because
she covers herself in pooh and never washes. She screams like a
monkey and starts flapping her arms. She terrifies me when I'm

on my own, but I'm not scared today because my mother tells her to go away and for once the stinking woman disappears and I am safe.

I shut my notebook and lay back on the sofa, exhausted by the force and clarity of the memory. I must have been at Kinghurst Place after all. This was the clearest indication I'd had so far that all the things I'd been writing in my notebook could form a blueprint of my mother and myself. I longed to ask Rob about it. But we were no longer intimate.

21

∞

Each of us is made up of an inner and outer self.
Never ignore the inner self, the true essence of you.
Let it inform how you present yourself to the world
through your outer self. Try to be brave enough to tell
the truth about who you are. That way freedom lies.

—Emma Helmsley, "Taking the Moment," September 21, 2016

"I forgot to tell you," said Emma, swinging keys around her finger, suddenly shy. "I'll be back early today. A film crew is coming to interview Rob and me for that series, you know, *For Better or Worse*. It's only afternoon telly, I mean not many people will be watching, but it's silly to miss the opportunity. Particularly as there might be a series for me in the future, if it all goes well today. The producer told Fiona it's a kind of trial run."

So that explained the sharply tailored gray suit, the neat regular waves in her hair, the eyeliner, lipstick, and blusher; everything making her look older and more hard-faced.

"I'm sure to look like a rabbit in the headlights. Rob is so much more accustomed to this sort of thing than I am. I've gotten used to the public talks and the meetings, but on the whole, I like to hide behind my blog and my books."

"I'll make sure the sitting room is extra tidy," I said. "And you shouldn't be so hard on yourself. If they thought you had nothing to say, they wouldn't be interviewing you."

"I'm not sure," she said. The vein in her forehead pulsed underneath the wisps of her fringe. "Anyhow, today I'll have to lie and pretend I'm some kind of domestic high priestess. I won't be able to say what I really want to, which is that I can't manage anything without your help."

How many times had Emma told me this? And still my response was to almost salivate like Pavlov's dog, although I tried not to let it show. "Of course you can. You managed perfectly well before I arrived."

She fixed me with eyes like Siggy's. "No I didn't. It was always a terrible mess. And we all like you so much. I mean, you're just the perfect person for us. We couldn't be luckier. Rob is always worried that you're going to leave and find some much more glamorous family in Notting Hill or Chelsea. Bankers or Russian oligarchs." There was a forlorn expression on her face. "Oh, I almost forgot to tell you. Rob said something about Theo and a couple of his friends coming to dinner tonight. Is that all right? I mean . . ." Her voice trailed off.

"That's fine. And there's no need to worry about anything," I said. Then she was gone, the front door slamming behind her. Rob was already in his office and I was left to my morning routine. Cool air rushed in when I opened the window in their bedroom, cutting through the smell of them, their bed linen and their discarded clothes.

Lily's room, as ever, looked uninhabited. She had taken to tucking her duvet under the mattress in hospital corners. Her desk was empty except for a mug of newly sharpened pencils and pens. Jake's room was even more chaotic than usual. Two red baseball caps hung off the doorknob. Socks shiny with dirt, jeans, and T-shirts littered the floor. Around them lay pages torn from an exercise book. Some were screwed up into tiny balls. Others were ripped into rough pieces. Flung under his bed was a hard, round cushion with two indentations.

I set to work, putting the clothes in the laundry basket and picking up the pieces of paper. All had yellow marker pen scrawls on them, crossed out and impossible to read. The pamphlet from the Church of Eternal Truth lay open on his bedside table, one section highlighted with such force that the page had holes in it.

> *For He has suffered so much since the beginning of the world, and made so many sacrifices for His followers. Put away sin and dishonesty. Lies, whether to other people or oneself, are sins in His eyes.*

I thought back to that woman preacher, the way those teen-agers bowed to her will. If I said something to Emma, it would be an admission that I spied on her children. It would be so much easier if she occasionally ventured into their bedrooms. But she was always in a rush.

As usual, I distracted myself with food. Half an hour later, *pollo alla cacciatora* was simmering on the hob. The thing with stews like these is not to overdo the tomatoes. You need an equal balance with the celery, onions, and carrots. Some people use red wine, but I prefer a splash of white, some thyme, and a bay leaf. It's not traditional silver spoon cooking, but it's hard to think of any meat dish not improved by these herbs.

I'd almost finished clearing away when Rob bounced into the kitchen wearing one of his preppy button-down shirts, ready for the television interview. Like a light switched on, an image of him and Theo flashed before me. My foot began to jitter, but I made it stop. I switched off the image, something I was getting good at.

"You look happy," I said.

"Well, I am," he said. "Things are good. And you? We haven't spoken properly for ages, and I wanted to ask about how everything is going—the images and how you're feeling about them. I felt we left things slightly in midair."

I closed the dishwasher door. "I'm good," I said. "And you?"

Before he could answer, the front door opened. There was the clack of Emma's high heels in the hall and then her voice. "Just in here." Then she was in the kitchen, covering Rob's cheek with feathery kisses. Siggy flung himself out of his basket and jumped up on her. "Not on my good skirt," she said, pushing him gently away. I picked him up. He squirmed in my arms, his heart racing under his coarse coat until I calmed him by tickling his ears.

"The crew is here for the program," she said, looking pleased and embarrassed at the same time. I offered to take a tray of tea and coffee into the sitting room.

"No," she said quickly. "I'll come out in a minute or so." I got it. She didn't want the interviewer to know she and Rob had a full-time housekeeper, and it would be clear from the way I presided over the kitchen, stirring and tasting, that I was more than a casual cleaner or grown-up au pair. Emma needed to give the impression that she was competent in all aspects of her life. It was part of her job.

I prepared the tray, and clipped on Siggy's leash for yet another drag around the block. The hall was barred with a camera box and a tripod, so we went out the back door and along the side path. When I unlocked the front gate, I saw that the cameraman had taped opaque paper over the front window. There was a bright light behind the paper. Rob and Emma's profiles were sharply outlined like characters in a shadow theater.

Siggy followed me dutifully along the street. While not exactly bounding about, he was more accepting of exercise these days. He had stopped cringing when other dogs passed and occasionally wagged his tail as I bent down to pick up his droppings. We headed for the river, following the faint smell of mud at low tide.

A bus stopped on the corner and a group of teenage boys rushed onto the pavement. Siggy cowered as one of them stopped in front of us. His school blazer strained over his shoulders and pimples broke through the fuzz on his cheeks. He was carrying a bunch of wilting yellow chrysanthemums.

"Sorry, lady." His voice cracked like Jake's and he went to pat Siggy. He backed away, his tail between his legs.

"He's a bit shy," I said.

The boy smiled. "No need. I like dogs." His friends had already crossed the street, gathering at a corner piled high with bunches of fading flowers. Posters were taped one on top of the other. WE LUV YOU BROTHER and NO MORE GANGS. The words were written in neon yellow spray paint. A week ago, a gang from a nearby school had chased a pupil chosen at random, and stabbed him to death as part of an initiation rite.

"Was he your friend?" I asked. The boy didn't reply but his chin wobbled. "I'm sorry," I continued, but he had already dashed across the road, waving his flowers like a flag. I walked down to the river, scuffing my shoes with each footstep, despondent that the need to belong in a group of boys had caused the death of another. Wasn't that what gangs were all about? Needing to belong to something, somewhere, so you weren't prowling the perimeter like a lone wolf? Jake wanted to belong somewhere. Somehow, I had to make Rob and Emma aware of this.

I reached the towpath. Sometimes Siggy liked to chase seagulls, but today he pulled on the leash to get home. The opaque paper was still fixed to the window, so we crept in through the back door. After I inspected the chicken, I hung about the entrance to the hall. A querulous female voice told Emma and Rob to relax.

Then a young male voice called, "Testing, testing . . ." and the interview began. I sidled into the hall.

"So, Rob." The female voice was no longer querulous. It had turned into a soft lilt. I imagined the interviewer as being sharp and urban, with a well-groomed charm. "A successful television program, another book about to be published, and a committed family man. Who or what gets top priority?"

There was that pause that worked so well on television. It was hard to know why, because the pause was impossible to comprehend. Did it mean that Rob was thinking carefully about his reply because the question was so clever? Or was the question so stupid that it took time to formulate a comment that was neither insulting nor condescending? Lately I'd concluded the whole thing was just an act, but a plausible one nonetheless.

"Impossible to answer that," replied Rob. "Because everything feeds into everything else. I couldn't do my television work or write my books without Emma's support, and I hope she'd say the same about me. And I just couldn't imagine life without my children, which is the main reason I work from home as much as I can, so I can spend time with them."

Was there an afternoon when he'd been in the house waiting for them when they came home from school? I didn't recall.

"And Emma, what about you?" the female voice asked. Emma cleared her throat.

"Oh, I'm sorry, I'm taking too long to answer. Should we start again?"

The female voice said it wasn't necessary. Any mistakes or pauses could be edited later.

"Do you follow your own advice? You must be very well organized." The voice was seductive, inviting confidences. I stood bolt upright, like a stage mother in the wings, wanting Emma to give a good performance. I thought of the effusive way she thanked me at the end of each day, as if she was scared I might have second thoughts in the night and not return the next morning. Behind me, Siggy turned in his basket. I recalled the chaos everywhere when I started. Clothes flung on the floor, food left to rot, overflowing laundry baskets.

From the sitting room, Emma spoke in a clear, authoritative voice I'd never heard before. "Organization is absolutely vital in every house," she said. "Everyone here does their share of housework. A family is just like a small business. We all have to pull our weight. I live by my lists."

There might have been an impostor in the sitting room, someone so skilled at playing this charade that I almost believed her.

"But Rob and Emma, surely you have some help in the house?" asked the female voice, angling for a slipup, a chink in the armor. "The shopping, the cooking, and the cleaning," the voice continued. "Do you do everything yourselves?"

Part of me wanted Emma and Rob to tell the interviewer what they constantly told me: that the family couldn't manage without me, that I was the lynchpin of Wycombe Lodge. But there was another part of me that knew authors, particularly bestselling authors of books on life management, and their clever media personality academic husbands, didn't make public confessions about their sloppy domestic habits just to placate the housekeeper.

"Nearly everything," said Emma.

"We divide it up," added Rob. I heard the smile in his voice, and I knew he was looking at the interviewer with that same steady gaze he fixed on me, the one that used to make me feel so much better about myself.

"But we stick to simple things during the week—casseroles that I've prepared on the weekend, or something quick like pasta," Emma continued. "As I say in my books, it's all down to priorities and organization, and valuing oneself and one's work, not being afraid to ask your partner for help if you need it."

A small creep of hurt made its way down my back until I

told myself not to be stupid. But I couldn't help feeling a bit cheated. It was my organization, not theirs.

"I'm not Superwoman," Emma went on. "We do have a cleaner, and if things get really frantic, I'm not above ordering a takeaway meal if we're having friends to dinner. I mean, life is to be lived, and family time is very important. Rob and I, our children, we're very close. Our lives are busy, so when we're together, we like to concentrate on just us."

There was talk of shared online diaries and weekly date nights. This last word was drawn out so it sounded lascivious. Family outings were just as important. Emma and Rob spoke like they were handing down the Ten Commandments for Happy Families. Were there times when Emma and Rob went out, just the two of them? Had I ever heard of any family outings? Again, I didn't recall, although there was the Majorcan holiday planned for next summer.

There was silence, and the other female voice, no longer seductive but businesslike, announced that all had gone very well. There was a sound of a mug being replaced on a tray. From my eavesdropping position in the hall, I did not move. Again I told myself not to be stupid. Did I expect that Emma and Rob would waltz out to the kitchen and introduce me as their very own Woman Friday, make sure I was included in the interview, hand over a recipe or two? Was I waiting for a declaration that I was a fully paid up member of the family?

I was the housekeeper, the hired help with a messy past who cleared up other people's messy present, the one who protected their messy little secrets.

22

The housekeeper must consider herself as the immediate representative of her mistress.

—*Mrs. Beeton's Book of Household Management*, 1861

Two hours later, Emma strode into the dining room, face scrubbed clean of makeup and wet hair dripping onto her shoulders. She hovered on the other side of the counter, not taking up her usual cupboard door bashing position.

"That chicken smells so good." She sniffed the air with what looked like elaborate appreciation, but I knew she would push most of it around the plate later. "What a nerve-wracking afternoon! All those lights blazing in my eyes and that scary woman telling me to relax. I was absolutely terrified."

"I'm sure you were terrific." I wiped down the bench, my default reaction to almost everything. Emma's face was silhouetted against the faltering light in the garden. At that angle, the resemblance to Jake was uncanny and I couldn't resist. It seemed the perfect quiet moment before everyone clattered into the room for dinner.

"Will Jake be back soon? He seems so busy these days." A breath, and then it rushed out. "I guess it's this interest in religion, you know, the different texts that he's studying."

"Religion?" Emma laughed, a loud honk that I'd never heard before. "Texts? What on earth do you mean? Jake isn't interested in religion or anything like that. I don't know where you got that idea from."

"Well, it was just . . . I mean I thought once or twice when I was tidying his room . . ." My sentence trailed into rebuffed silence and started up again. "I must have got the wrong impression. It probably was something to do with homework."

"Jake's like every other kid in his class," she said. "You know, they like music and parties and concerts. He's going to Glastonbury next year." Emma said this with a flourish, like a ticket to a rock festival was certification of a well-adjusted urban adolescent. "No, Jake isn't religious. None of us is. Now, time for me to lay the table and light the candles. Where did I put the matches?"

I produced them from a drawer and gave them to her.

"Thank you, Anne. I know I say it all the time, but I can't imagine how we'd cope without you."

There was something about her fulsome praise so soon after her swift retort that made me feel like a dog that had been kicked away and then patted. As for the matter of Jake, she'd made it clear that my concerns about him were not worth further discussion. It rankled. But maybe Emma was tired. It was hard to think clearly when you were tired.

An hour later, they were all at the table—Jake next to Emma, then Theo, the woman with the cat's-eye glasses from the party, and a portly man with a salt-and-pepper beard in between Lily and Rob.

The woman, who introduced herself as Sabine, was already onto her second helping. She had a quirky way of dressing—ankle socks with high heels. Their conversation drifted into the kitchen. "I'm not so sure about logical positivism anymore," she said. "I think Wittgenstein might have had his day."

"Hmm, maybe you're right," said Theo. "That's the problem with philosophy. Everyone has their own ideas." Emma was the only one who laughed. Theo took her hand. "You're the only person who truly understands me." He kissed her wrist, a smacking sound loud enough for me to hear at the sink as I scoured everything with extra vigor and rinsed with scalding hot water.

The man with the salt-and-pepper beard was called Terence. He was a columnist for the *Guardian*. "I don't understand why English people don't respect philosophers or psychologists. In France, they're treated like rock stars. I wouldn't mind being Bernard-Henri Lévy. Rich as Croesus, film star wife, on the telly all the time. Sounds good to me. And there's Dr. Phil in America, his own show on TV, plus all his other stuff. He'd have to get on a very large ladder to count all his millions. But no one here has cracked it like that."

Rob gave a hollow laugh. "Don't look at me. No one's knocking on my door."

After dinner, Jake and Lily retreated upstairs and everyone except Theo went into the sitting room. He wandered over to the sink and thanked me for dinner. "I wish I could cook, even just a bit," he said. "Then maybe I could find the love of a good woman. I've been told I'll never find anyone unless I learn to cook and clean."

I didn't smile and I made sure my eyes met his. "Maybe you're not looking for the love of a good woman."

He flung his arm around my shoulder and drew me to him. There was that close smell again, the one I remembered from the night of the party, when I saw him and Rob. "But I am," he said. "Truly I am." He grinned and turned to join the others. I switched on the dishwasher and went to leave, wanting fresh night air on my face.

In the sitting room, Rob was holding court, a little drunk. He caught my eye and waved good night, raising his glass in an extravagant salute. As I opened the front door, he said, "There goes our magnificent Anne. Dust and dirt have been banished from our house, and thanks to her concerns about such matters, not to mention her culinary skills, we dine like kings and queens every night." Sabine and Terence tittered as I closed the door behind me, blushing with embarrassment.

Part of me was flattered to be acknowledged in public like that. But as I walked to the bus stop, I felt put down as well. It was my work that allowed their blessed carefree life. It was my loyalty to Emma and my concern for Jake and Lily that kept Rob's secret safe. The cook, the cleaner, the online grocery shopper—everything I did, everything I took so much care about, so easily transformed into a tipsy late night joke, so quickly replaced by takeaway meals, domestic agencies, and websites with smart cookies.

The bus home was unusually full, the smell of musty clothes heavy in the air. I unlocked my front door and climbed the stairs, picking up an empty crisp packet on the landing. Tiny fragments smelling of stale grease, salt, and vinegar spilled into my hand. I wiped my fingers clean and felt around my handbag for my car keys. I didn't want the emptiness of my own flat right then. I needed to go somewhere.

My familiar friend, that sense of abandonment, is never just one thing. It doesn't happen in a vacuum. It just topples over sometimes and creates its own self-pitying trajectory, taking you back to places you know are a big mistake.

Even as I drove past Anton et Amis, I told myself I was over him and it was mere curiosity that had propelled me to Mayfair. I told myself again that the breakup wasn't his fault and that I should turn for home. But I didn't. I thought instead of the black, heavy punch of grief when he left me, how it had taken on its own life and reached back to the loss of Gran and my mother before that. All my losses had become one. I'd found it almost unbearable.

I parked around the corner and crept through the darkness between the streetlights. It had stopped raining, but the pavement was still slippery and wet. Every window in Anton's flat was illuminated, slices of light pouring onto the pavement. The woman he had left me for was standing in the kitchen, arranging flowers in a vase. Carefully, all the time in the world was hers. Standing back to see the wide-angle effect, moving forward to rearrange an awkward stem. What was it to her if a strange woman was lurking behind a lamppost across the street, taking care not to be seen? She knew nothing.

She looked away, appeared to hear something, and left the room. Perhaps someone had called to her. It might have been Anton, wanting her advice on something. The sensor lamp by the side door of the restaurant flashed on, and there was Anton, his dark, bulky figure outlined against the golden light, swinging keys in his hand, a gesture so familiar it hurt. "Hurry up," it said. "Don't keep me waiting." I almost forgot myself and ran to join him. Only her shadow on the steps behind him and the sound of the door shutting prevented me. I ducked down behind a car, but not before I saw them link arms and smile at each other. I couldn't breathe for a moment. There was the familiar iron wire feeling in my stomach, and I swallowed hard, crouching like a thief.

One image turned over and over in my mind: the way they linked arms, such an easy, affectionate gesture. Affection was steadier than fickle lust and obsession. It was kinder. It lasted longer. I may not have had much of it in my own life, but I recognized it in others.

Back home, I turned on the television and watched a ginger-haired man solve a murder in record time. Driving past Anton's house was a relapse, I told myself, like falling off the wagon or smoking a cigarette after years of nicotine freedom. It was a temporary weakness—one not to be repeated.

Just before bed, as I undressed, I noticed something sparkling on the floor of the wardrobe. It was a jeweled clip. Fake, of course, but it looked good in dim light. It had fallen off an expensive dress, black, well cut, and flattering. Others much like it hung on either side. Below the dresses were my pointy-toed shoes with thin high heels. I'd bought all of it for Anton, for our dinners together. I saw now that I'd made myself up into someone I thought he would prefer, someone I hardly recognized anymore. I hung the dresses at the front of the wardrobe, ready to take to the charity shop that weekend.

23

~~~

True friends are with you all your life, enriching
every experience. Make time to keep up with those
closest to you, not just a quick catch-up, but a genuine heart-to-heart connection. List the qualities
that make them dear to you and memorize them.

—Emma Helmsley, "Taking the Moment," October 2, 2016

A bright Friday evening with the scent of the last honeysuckle
flowers mingling with the smell of fallen leaves. The radiance
of summer was spent. Rob's gingerbread cottage was luminous
in the dusk. Above it, the glare of the London sky faded upwards into weak amber heights.

Emma arrived home early. "No dinner for me," she said. "Huge
lunch." I doubted it. Her watch hung slackly off her wrist. We were
in our usual positions in the kitchen—me at the sink and Emma
sitting on the counter banging her feet against the cupboards.
She appeared already slightly drunk, slurring her words and forgetting to end her sentences, jumping down to scrabble in the
drawer for a corkscrew and immediately opening a bottle of wine.

"I keep asking," she said, pulling out two glasses and offering one to me, raising an eyebrow. I shook my head, and she
filled her glass almost to the brim and sipped at it quickly, tossing her head up and down like a thirsty bird. She caught her
hair in one hand and wandered towards the sink. She leaned
over it, as if she was about to throw up, but then she straightened in that elegant way of hers.

"So good to be home, the end of the week. And to have the place to ourselves. What a triumph."

Rob was at a BBC dinner and Lily had gone to the cinema with her gang. Jake was out as well, but hadn't said where he was going. The fact that we were alone in the house wasn't planned, but Emma made it sound that way; that we had fooled the others and were now set to enjoy our own delicious conspiracy against the world. She raised her glass.

"Bliss, absolute bliss. I've been so on edge lately. Rob and his work. I wish I'd never heard of bloody Rowan McLeish. And now the school wants to see us about Jake. I suppose I'll have to work out a time. They're probably going to complain about his homework or something. Why can't the teachers just sort it out among themselves, the way they did when I was at school?"

She flopped her arms on the counter, a dull thudding noise. "Sometimes I'd like to give up the whole thing and move to Scotland or somewhere and live on my own."

"You don't mean that." After the television interview and her dismissal of my worries about Jake, I no longer felt valued as her kitchen confidante. In her eyes, my position as housekeeper might never have counted for anything more than dust-free surfaces by day and protein and three veg by night, despite her daily automatic flattery. I was annoyed with myself for being so readily seduced and forgetting what I'd told myself in the beginning. Friends, real friends, weren't paid by direct debit on the first of every month. I should have listened to Jude more carefully. "It's Friday and you're done in."

"Yes I am. But I've also had it up to here." She drew one finger across her neck and grimaced. "Living up to everyone's expectations, being the one-woman cheer squad. Always making out that everything is fine. Sometimes, you know, sometimes it just isn't." She picked up the empty glass and held it out like an offering. "Oh, won't you have a drink with me? Please, please. I hate moaning on my own like this."

There was no dinner to be cooked, no mess to be cleared away. All I had to do was return to an empty flat and watch the last remaining episode in the final series of *Wallander*. "Thank you," I said. "I'd love one."

Emma grinned in triumph and poured me a glass. "Let's not sit here," she said in a girlish rush. "We're always in the kitchen. My bum hurts after I've been sitting on the counter for a while. Let's sit at the table, like grown-ups." She waved the open bottle about. "I'll take this. Can you bring another one with you? "

She jumped down and walked past her usual place at the head of the table to sit in the middle, facing the garden. I picked up a bottle of wine and the corkscrew and followed her, choosing one of the rickety chairs on the end. I'd never sat here before with Emma. It felt odd and good at the same time. We were no longer separated by the stuff of kitchen life: saucepans in the sink and food in the oven, pots simmering and the soft hiss of the refrigerator door as it opened and closed.

The wine was good. I hadn't eaten much all day and its warmth quickly spread through me, creating a pleasant buzz. The doors were open and Siggy snuffled about happily, looking up every now and then to check that Emma hadn't moved. Vague shadows from nearby trees fell over the garden. Windows and doors of neighboring houses were flung open and the dusk seemed made more from their sounds than anything else. The tinkling of a piano, the muffled voices of the evening news bulletin.

"My mother would really disapprove of our lack of effort in the garden," said Emma. The first bottle of wine was already empty. She opened the second one and refilled our glasses.

"Does she come here ever? I've never met her."

"Not in the summer. We're only graced by her presence in darkest winter. She doesn't like to leave her precious garden, even for a day. Oh, my mother's garden." Emma raised her glass in a mock salute. "It is renowned throughout the county. Color-coordinated in supreme good taste and manicured from spring to autumn. Never a weed or a lawn without perfect stripes. She spends all of her time in it. She says it never talks back, unlike her ungrateful children."

Emma had never spoken about her childhood before, but that night it spilled out like a flood. The classic lonely princess, the youngest of three daughters. All the silver-framed photographs in her bedroom came to life, but it was a different existence to the one I had imagined.

"Everything was pretty hideous actually. When I was about seven, my father cleared off for someone who lived nearby, a widow. My sisters had left home by then, and they told me I shouldn't mind, because at least the widow was in the same circles as us. It was kind of in the family."

So both our lives had changed at about the same age. Emma and I had more in common than I'd thought.

"I knew the woman," Emma went on. "But it wasn't until I was an adult myself that I realized she'd been my father's mistress for years. She often came to the house and she was always so nice to me, really made a fuss. That's how I knew, later I mean, because there was no reason to pay me any attention, apart from trying to seduce my father through me."

She drained her glass and walked back to the kitchen, returning minutes later with another bottle, already open. "I thought she really liked me. She was a wonderful rider and sometimes she'd come over and give me lessons." She refilled our glasses again. "You know, keep the reins level, leg on, elbows in. Aren't children gullible?"

"Yes, I guess so," I replied.

"And after that, I was packed off to boarding school. God I hated it." In spite of everything I'd told myself, it was a thrill to hear her confide in me like that. The glow inside, like being a child again, hiding in the hedge and sharing secrets with Douglas.

The pleasant buzz of the first couple of glasses had turned into a careless languor. I'd drunk them too quickly and I spoke without thinking. "So did I. Absolutely loathed boarding school. I kept running away, until they gave up and kicked me out."

"Gosh," said Emma. In the nicest possible way, she was surprised. She tried to cover it up and hoped I hadn't noticed. But I had. Not that I minded, because I understood that people who worked as housekeepers hadn't often gone to schools where you packed your pajamas along with your textbooks.

"I got a scholarship," I said by way of explanation. "I always thought they must have made a mistake with the exam papers. Anyhow, it was a long time ago. I never made it to university. I went into restaurants instead. I don't regret it."

"I met Rob at university," she smiled. "So things got better. He saved me in all sorts of ways. And of course, the children."

A companionable silence.

"This is good, isn't it," said Emma. "Just us, no Jake and Lily, no Rob."

"It's nice when they're around too."

"Yes, but I meant what I said about living by myself. However, that's never going to happen. Rob will only leave this house and this family in a body bag, and even then we might have problems getting him out of the place."

I felt a slip in the air between us, a possibility of boundaries falling away, bringing us closer together. I could have told her about Theo and Rob right then. The memory of them together was so clear that I could almost smell it. The shape of them in the dim light of the bedroom. The wet slopping sound. Long shadows danced on the lawn. The moment passed.

Emma refilled our glasses. I forgot my earlier resentment

and concentrated instead on the part of me warmed by Emma's bloom. This is what I'd always wanted, my early dreams of confidences shared, the intimacy of family and close friends. In my mind, it had seemed something gilded and precious, but beyond my grasp until this evening.

"Rob delivers his manuscript next week—thank heavens," she said, leaning her head on her elbow. "Sometimes I wish he'd go back to teaching. It's not as if . . ."

Emma was about to say it wasn't as if they needed the money, but stopped short. She wasn't that drunk. "It's just that when you start out, you feel you can do anything—that you can carve a place for yourself out of granite, if need be. But as you go on, every year there's a new surge of graduates who feel just the same way. And in the meantime, we're just getting older and more tired."

"But I thought Rob said everything was going well—I ask him about it sometimes in the morning, before he disappears down into his office."

Darkness fell around us. I shut the doors and turned on the lights. Kamikaze moths thudded against the glass.

"Really," she said. Her words slurred together and she slopped some wine on the table. "I know I shouldn't, but I get so bored with all of it sometimes. I just stop listening. Marriage is like that. You love the other person, you want the best for them, but you get bored."

"I don't know, I've never been married."

She gazed at me across the table, holding her glass to her mouth, as if she was deciding whether or not to say something. "Well, it's hard work. You have to be strong." She studied the puddle of spilt wine. "I nearly left him once, you know, when the children were little. I was infatuated with someone else. We weren't lovers, but it was very deep. Rob doesn't know a thing, of course, and I've never regretted staying with him."

She wiped her mouth with the back of her hand. "Well, almost never." Her eyes were heavy-lidded with alcohol.

"Hey," she said. "I bet if we'd gone to the same hideous boarding school, we would have been best friends. We're simpatico. I felt it from day one."

Everything began to lose focus and take on a golden blur. "Tell me about yourself. I want to know. Really, we're friends, aren't we?" There was something so sweetly plaintive in her voice. Sitting on my side of the table, Siggy snuffling at our feet, it felt like that semiconscious moment between sleeping and waking when everything was about to change, when everything was possible.

"Nothing very unusual," I said, moving my glass about the table. The light shone through the smeared imprint of my mouth around the rim. "My mother was a bit of a hippie. She died when I was young and my grandmother brought me up. And then I went into restaurants. I liked it there—it was sort of a family."

Emma stroked my hand and nodded in a gentle, understanding way. "And now, you're with us," she said, her voice soft as a whisper.

I couldn't help myself. Tears ran down into my mouth, bitter and salty.

"You're family now," said Emma in the same soft whisper. "Our family. Don't ever forget that." She moved her hand away with a tender pat on my arm. "This calls for another drink. I'll hunt out another bottle."

"I'll get it," I said, uncomfortable with the idea of Emma waiting on me.

"No, you keep Siggy company. I need to go to the loo anyway." She stood and walked off in a slow, careful way. It was fully dark now. Under my feet, Siggy snored quietly amid the comforting creaks of the house as it settled itself in the night.

It was some time—I couldn't say how long—before Emma reappeared, clutching another open bottle and seeming, miraculously, almost sober. "Sorry to take such a while," she said. "I had to make a quick call. By the way, I like your new bag. Couldn't help noticing it in the study."

It was one of Jude's castoffs, a caramel-colored plaited leather pouch. "Thanks," I said. "A friend gave it to me. It was surplus to her fashion requirements."

Emma went to pour more wine. I leaned back in my chair. The slight movement made me giddy. "I think I should switch to water," I said. "I've got to get the bus home."

"But you could stay here," said Emma. "You know you could."

I was thinking how pleasant that might be when the front door opened and slammed shut. We both jumped. There was a draft of cool air and Lily was beside us with one of her stern friends. I could never get their names straight. She picked up one of the empty bottles and scrutinized the half-full one by Emma's glass. "At home drinkers—you're the sort of people newspapers write about these days. You've got your very own medical danger group. Hospitals are filling up with people like you." She glared at Emma and then at me, in that self-righteous way of teenagers who dig away at their parents' frailties. "Don't stay up too late."

The mood was broken and I jumped up, suddenly more sober. "I should get going. Thanks for everything, Emma." She reached over and took my hand again.

"It was great," she replied. "And remember what I said. I mean it."

It was only when I was on the bus that I realized our usual evening chorus had been reversed. I had thanked her, not the other way around. It was significant in some way that I was too tired to ponder, so I gave up and examined my fellow passengers instead.

Often I saw interesting people on the bus or the Tube and imagined their secrets. I still thought about the blond-haired girl I'd seen one evening, trying to calm her drunken father, begging him to stop shouting at the bus driver, then helping him along the aisle because he was barely able to stand. What happened to them? There was a beautiful boy I used to see on the bus on the way to the restaurant. He had black hair and milky-white skin and always wore just a singlet and jeans, no matter how cold it was. One day a pair of ballet shoes and a leotard fell out of his backpack, and he blushed as he picked them up and dusted them off. I still wonder sometimes if he made it as a soloist.

I walked home, stopping at the late night shop. Imran stood in the aisle, examining a bunch of brown bananas. "Hey," I said, clutching a carton of milk and a bag of apples. "How are you?"

"Very well, thank you. I think my sister might come to visit us very soon." He smiled. "That would be good, for Faisal and me."

"Nothing better than family." I grinned back from a wine-enhanced glow. "Nothing at all."

Later, dry-mouthed, with the shadow of a hangover headache lying in wait for the next morning, I regretted yet again the invitation I'd presented him with weeks before. I wasn't used to having people in my flat, not even Jude. I'd make some excuse the next time I saw Faisal. He'd probably be relieved.

24

⚭

```
Words are lies most of the time. Actions
tell the truth always.
```
—Rob Helmsley, *Madhouse: The Life and Times*
of Rowan McLeish

The weekend dragged. I did the laundry and some food shopping and cleaned the flat. After so much time, I still missed Gran and my fortnightly journeys to and from Somerset. I'd drive past Stonehenge, up the steep hill, and along towards the pig farm before the roundabout, slowing so I could see the families of animals wandering in and out of their different-sized huts scattered throughout the fields. Gangs of piglets rushed about as sows snuffled around them. I'd imagine gatherings at the end of the day, all held in tribal pig harmony. Then, the best part of the long journey, coming over the crest of the broad hill and dipping down. Always there in that exact place, it seemed that the horizon tilted its golden fields towards me and welcomed me back.

The last time I saw Gran, she was in the nursing home outside Shaftesbury. I pulled into the car park, expecting to see her perched on the window seat just inside the hall. But she was in her room, lying down with her eyes closed. Her hand rested on her forehead, the slack flesh of her arm gathered at the elbow. An angry bruise bloomed on her temple, visible between strands of hair matted with blood. Her eyes opened slowly, as if from a deep sleep.

"What happened?" The words came out in a rush. "Why didn't anyone call me?"

"For heaven's sake, don't fuss, girl," she whispered. "Although I wouldn't mind some water, now that you're here." I helped her sit up and poured a glass of water. She drank and lay back, sickly yellow pouches of skin under her eyes. I wiped the dribble from her mouth and straightened her pillow. Under the sheets, her legs made a harsh noise like sandpaper. I drew up a chair and waited.

After about ten minutes, her hand fluttered against mine. "Marianne," she whispered, fixing on a point at the end of the bed. There was a prickle of apprehension as if the room were held by a halt in time. "Thank you for coming, bless you, darling girl. Don't go just yet, Anne will be here, any minute now she'll be here."

Her fingernails dug into my wrist.

"Gran, it's not Marianne, it's me, it's Anne." I heard my voice, shrill and bouncing around the room. "It's Anne. I'm here already. There's no one else in the room."

Her head lolled to one side and she closed her eyes again. "So silly. I could have sworn she was here." She sighed. "They've given me so many pills. I feel half-dead."

Gran must have missed my mother so much. For all of my early life, she hadn't known where she lived. She only knew where her daughter had died. My online trawling had made me see for the first time the stigma that existed thirty years ago about mentally ill people, how cuts in funding left so many wandering homeless when care was handed over to the community. Gran had no one to talk to about her worries, no one to help her be a mother or a grandmother. I'd always thought it was petty snobbery that kept her quiet. For the first time, I saw that her silence about my mother's schizophrenia was intended to spare me the shame she had lived with for so long, about flawed genes and toxic inheritances and my own illegitimacy.

When I got to work on Monday, Rob was doing his usual mooching thing about the kitchen.

"Hello," I said.

"Hi." He glanced at his watch. "Can't believe the time I've wasted. I'm so late."

"I'm sure you'll catch up with yourself," I said. It was hard to work out, this thing with Rob. I didn't know it was possible to feel so many things at once. I missed the way we were, our morning talks, the way he made me feel safe. There was the crashing sense of abandonment and betrayal after I saw him and Theo together, and fear as well that what I knew could change so much. I wanted to go back to how it was, before the party, before I went upstairs to get my coat.

There was also that other thing I didn't want to think about and that hadn't gone away completely: my attraction to him, the power of that irrational brief moment when we stood in the door of the study and I wanted him so badly. And overlaying all this was the inescapable fact that I couldn't bear to leave the family I loved.

"Emma says the book is pretty much finished."

He stared right into my face, as if he had been a million miles away and had just registered me for the first time. "Yep, it's good. Everything worked out in the end." He picked up his bag. "Nearly forgot. Could I ask a favor? I need my signature witnessed for some BBC paperwork that has to be filed today, and Emma left before I could ask her. Would you mind?"

"Of course not," I said. He fossicked in his bag and produced a pen and folded a piece of paper. I wanted to tell him that there was no need to fold the page. I wasn't interested in how much money he earned or the details of his contract.

Instead, I scrawled my signature and the date in the two blank boxes at the bottom of the page.

"Thanks," he said and off he went.

In between my usual routine, I fretted about seeing Emma later. It was a myth that secrets drew people closer together. I saw it all the time in the restaurant, the after-service letdown accompanied by a drink or two, the things that tumbled out from people you didn't really know, apart from standing next to them during a twelve-hour shift.

It was different with Jude, because she really was my friend and we knew each other's secrets. But the others couldn't help themselves. The things they told you! Men sleeping with their stepmothers. Women deranged by lust for boys young enough to be their sons. And always the next day, they stared off into the middle distance as they greeted you awkwardly, remembering what they'd said the night before and hoping that you'd forgotten. I wondered how Emma and I would act towards each other, if she'd be embarrassed or pretend that nothing of any consequence had been said.

She came into the kitchen an hour before dinner (sumac and chili chicken with roasted peppers and sweet potatoes, and steamed green beans). Instead of taking up her position on the counter, she walked over to the sink and put her arms around me. "I enjoyed our drinks party for two so much," she said. Her hair brushed against my neck. "Let's do it again sometime soon. That is, if you don't mind."

Of course I didn't mind. I was grateful. Emma had captured in an instant my awkwardness after our evening together. And now she seemed to be telling me, subtly, that she understood. She held up a wineglass and offered it to me. I smiled and shook my head. She poured herself a modest half glass and began foraging through a bottom drawer.

"Have you seen that list of school parents?" she asked.

"Apparently there's a bus strike tomorrow, and here we are, both Rob and me non-drivers. Fiona tried all afternoon, and it seems there's not a spare car or driver to be had in the whole of London. God, I wish I'd made more effort at those ghastly parents' evenings. I can't think of a single person I can call and cadge a lift for Jake and Lily." She stood very still, as if the lack of motion would somehow conjure a name and a telephone number, with a car attached in the middle.

I was about to suggest that she drop Jake and Lily at school in her usual morning taxi and then go on to her office. It was a simple enough solution. But Emma would see that as time wasted in her busy day.

"Why don't I take Jake and Lily to school? I'll need to drive here anyway because of the strike. No problem to come a bit earlier."

"Oh, you absolute angel," sighed Emma. "Thank you so much. Saving my life yet again."

I arrived at Wycombe Lodge early the next morning, walking in to the muffled and intermittent sounds of their breakfast. Emma was buried in her computer. Rob stared into the middle distance while Jake and Lily gulped down cereal in silence. They might have been four strangers in a roadside café.

"OK," I said. "Ready when you are." Five minutes later, we set off on our circuitous route through the back roads, carefully plotted by me the night before to avoid traffic snarls. The school was in a large stucco house on the other side of Richmond Park. Probably after one recession too many, no one knew what to do with such a place. It was too big for a private house, and too out of the way for a company headquarters, but perfect for a small, independent school, commutable from the stockbroker suburbs farther out and a good section of the inner west.

I watched Lily and Jake walk through the gates, noting how

easily Lily fell into step with a trio of girls while Jake slid alone through the stream of students as if he was expecting someone to attack him. Everyone except him looked the same; members of some affluent tribe, with their tousled hair and their confident slouches, leads trailing from their earbuds down into their pockets. Somewhere in the crowd was the daughter of a famous actor, the sons of a former supermodel, and twins belonging to a lesbian couple, one of whom was a political broadcaster and the other a photographer whose work hung in the National Portrait Gallery. The common denominator was a bank balance hefty enough to afford the fees and to keep up with the extracurricular activities: tennis, riding, skiing holidays. I'd seen the lists in Lily's room.

Jake disappeared into the crowd. Groups of students straggled behind him. I was about to drive away when I saw his history book on the floor beside me. He'd been revising in the car for a test. I thought he might need it, so I got out and walked through the gates to find him. The square of tarmac was empty except for a lone teacher. She had one of those earnest scrubbed faces with pale eyes and invisible lashes.

"Can I help you?" she asked.

"Yes please," I said. "I wanted to get this book to Jake Helmsley. He left it in the car."

"Thank you." Her voice was high and girlish. "I'll make sure he gets it."

"That's kind. I know he was concerned about the test."

"Actually," she said. "Now that you're here, if you've a minute . . ." There was a moment's hesitation, from both of us. I should have introduced myself, said who I was and why I had driven Jake and Lily to school. But I didn't.

She looked young enough to be a student herself, although I wouldn't have mistaken her for one. She was too dowdy in her serviceable green sweater and tartan skirt, her hair pushed back in an old-fashioned headband. "I'm Margaret Stiles, Jake's form mistress. We haven't actually met. I know how busy you must be—of course I know about your work—but I'm wondering did you have a moment to read my email? We were most concerned."

It wasn't too late to back out and say I was the housekeeper. Clearly she never browsed photographs in the society pages, because there was no way in which I resembled Emma. But I liked the look of respect in her eye. I told myself this was something I could deal with.

Margaret Stiles coughed, then cleared her throat. "As you know, this is a liberal school, and we try to encourage all points of view, from every one of our students. But . . ." She faltered. "But recently Jake wrote an essay for his History of Art class that we found, well, rather alarming. His teacher gave it to me, and I'm afraid I felt it necessary to hand it over to the headmaster. It caused quite a stir. I mean, the views he expressed in it."

"I'm sorry, but I'm not aware . . ." Even then, I could have said who I was. I still could have made it sound plausible. But I thought of Emma slumped on the table with her glass of white wine and her quick dismissal of my concerns about Jake. I'd have a better understanding of whatever this woman was about to tell me. Emma might not even need to know.

The teacher continued. "Perhaps my email went astray. They often do, don't they, you know, go into the wrong box. But I did leave a message on your mobile, asking if we could talk to you and your husband."

"I'm sorry," I said. "I don't know anything about this." Actually I did. Emma often recharged her mobile in the kitchen, so I knew she rarely returned calls that weren't to do with her work, or listened to her messages. The teacher looked over my shoulder. A raw blush was spreading up her neck and she chewed at her lip.

"There was an essay set on Caravaggio. They'd been study-ing his pictures, and Jake wrote that all work by homosexual artists wasn't worthy of public display, or discussion, because homosexuality was . . . the exact word I think that he used was an abomination. I mean, as a school, as an educational com-munity, we can't condone those kind of views."

"I read the essay." She had gained confidence while she was talking. The blush had receded into a series of pink blotches and she spoke more strongly. "He was quite emphatic about it, dredging up versions of biblical quotes to support his argu-ment. I mean, I'm sure you're aware that we are a gay-friendly educational community.

"We have openly gay students, gay teachers, and gay parents. And Jake would not see his own intolerance on this matter. He would not retract anything that he'd written. He said it was his right to speak freely, and that homosexuality was wrong. And the thing was, all of us here thought that Jake . . ."

Her voice trailed off. She was about to say her tolerant, gay-friendly, educational community had thought that Jake, with his golden hair and his long eyelashes, his distaste for sport, was gay. Doubtless they were anticipating his coming out. It was that sort of school. Part of me admired Jake's courage and wanted to applaud him for standing up for his right to an opinion, but that opinion came from intolerance and hate. Was this all that church's doing?

"I'll talk to Jake tonight, and call tomorrow to make an ap-pointment." I couldn't think of anything else to say.

"We'd very much appreciate it if Mr. Helmsley could come to the school as well," said the teacher.

"Yes," I said. "We'll come as soon as possible." By now I was embedded into my playacting, making a show of giving her a firm handshake as I said goodbye. I drove back to Wycombe Lodge, trying to justify my behavior. I could pass on some version of the conversation to Emma and ask her to contact the teacher. I could say the teacher was confused. And really, I was helping Emma by talking about Jake. She wouldn't have gone into the school with the history book. She would never have noticed it lying on the floor.

Even so, when I picked up Jake and Lily, I waited for them outside the school gates in the safety of my car. "Everything OK?" I asked Jake after they squeezed in.

His face was suffused purple with embarrassment or anger. It was hard to tell. "It would be, if people stopped asking stupid questions."

Lily opened the window. A motorbike roared past, a flash of black leather and chrome. "You can't keep a lid on things forever," she said.

Jake shot her a furious glance. "Sorry I'm such a letdown to you and your politically correct friends. More like the Stasi, if you ask me."

I turned on the radio, and we drove back to Wycombe Lodge accompanied by the gloomy crash and bang of a Mahler symphony.

"A bit of a mix-up," I told Emma cheerily that evening. "For a minute Jake's form teacher got confused and thought that I was you. Anyhow, she wants you to call her, said she'd left a message." Emma blinked in her bewildered way. "Oh, yes, she did contact me. I forgot about her. I'll put it on my list. "

25

Psychological scars have a memory all of
their own. It's called the truth. If a
person has a fear of abandonment, it's
probably because they were abandoned.

—Rob Helmsley, *Madhouse: The Life and Times
of Rowan McLeish*

Through all this time, I kept writing. As I burrowed past other memories, more came trailing up. I became intrigued by the concept of memory; where it began and how reliable it was. For a while I stopped watching detective series on TV and began my own online investigations. I spent the better part of a week reading articles and papers by Elizabeth Loftus, an American academic who'd spent her life studying memory. I watched her TED talk, admiring the way she calmly explained why she'd concluded that memory wasn't the most accurate recording device. She'd conducted studies in which a childhood memory of being lost in a shopping mall was suggested to a group of people and one quarter of the group then believed it to be true, although it was completely false.

Other people believed they'd nearly drowned as a child or been attacked by a vicious dog just because the memory had been suggested to them. There was Jean Piaget, the beaming beret-wearing, pipe-smoking Swiss psychologist who died in 1980, the same year I was born. He believed someone had tried to abduct him from his pram when he was being taken for a walk by his nurse. Piaget vividly remembered every detail: the man trying to grab him, the nurse beating him off, their eventual escape. The Piaget family was wealthy, so it made sense. But when he was about fifteen, the nurse, who'd left the family many years before, wrote to confess that the story was a complete lie. She'd made the story up to ingratiate herself with the family, but after becoming a member of the Salvation Army, she came clean and offered to return the valuable watch given to her by the grateful parents.

All this made me doubt my own memories. Were they only imaginings, examples of Elizabeth Loftus's false memory syndrome? But all the studies I'd read about involved suggested memories, false recollections that had been planted by another person. No one had suggested anything to me. I'd never been in therapy for my dreams to be interpreted as childhood memories, and there were no family friends to suggest things might or might not have happened. Everything had begun with the photograph of Kinghurst Place that Rob had produced during dinner soon after I'd started working for them. I'd looked across at that house and that strange tune, the one that wouldn't let go, had started up in my head.

I couldn't make sense of it. Not that that stopped me writing more and more each day. I got into the habit of keeping my notebook and pen in my back pocket as I worked my way through the house.

The haunted look on her face as she sits alone all day and all night, calling out her own name. Marianne . . . Marianne . . . like she's trying to hold on to herself. Then she nurses me in her arms like a baby. "I'm sorry, I'm so sorry," she weeps, and I run outside to pick wild strawberries from the hedge and make her a mud cake. But when I take it to her, she has disappeared. Everyone has disappeared except for the man with the carved face who bangs saucepans together all the time. I'm scared of him, but he teaches me to count. One day. Two days. Still she doesn't come. Three days. I eat windfall apples and hard bread. Four days. Five days. She is back! Her face is covered with blue patterns like lace. But she's blinking and her knee is jumping. There's that rotten smell like something inside her is waiting to explode, and she leaves me again, even though she's sitting right beside me. The other man tells me to get lost, but I won't. He slaps me hard, and I run away, right up to the roof again, where no one can find me.

As always, I turned to Jude, my beloved stalwart provider of psychological stabilizer wheels. "One thing's for sure," she said. We were walking back to her house after an early screening of an incomprehensible art house film. I'd told her about my latest notebook entry, the verses I'd found in the recycling bin, and the faint indentations that I thought might be the letters of my mother's name.

"You couldn't make it up if you tried. But what it all means is another matter altogether." She hitched her bag onto her shoulder and stopped abruptly. "Look at me," she said, grabbing my arm and putting her face right in front of mine. "It's a bit weird and fantastical at the moment, but it will make sense one day. It has to." She laughed. "You can't go on like this forever, cleaning up other people's mess and scribbling in that very nice Smythson notebook I gave you. Maybe I should blame myself for all this. It might never have happened if I'd given you a scarf."

I couldn't help joining her laughter. By now we were outside her house. She unlocked the door and stood in the hall. "Shall we stay here one minute and listen to this rare and beautiful sound?"

"Absolutely. But what exactly is that?"

Jude exhaled. "Sleeping children accompanied by noise of telly being watched by babysitter as husband toils away in Berlin again. Bliss on a stick!"

We stood for a moment in the dim silence before going downstairs. Jude snapped on the lights and opened a bottle of wine. I watched her move about the kitchen, gathering glasses and plates of salad, putting everything on the table in her elegant way. One of the pastry chefs in the Chiswick restaurant, annoyed that Jude wouldn't go to bed with him, had called us a pair of emotional lesbians. I wouldn't have gone that far, but her friendship was my Northern Star, the constant in my life.

"Thank you," I said as she handed me a glass. "Not just for the wine, but for everything. You give me so much, so much more than I give you in return. Your friendship makes me very happy and I'm so grateful for it."

"Good," she said. "Me too." Jude was always brusque in such moments. "Now, drink up and give me more inside stories of your adulterous employers."

"Nothing," I said. "Well, nothing much anyway." I gave a brief account of my evening with Emma, the church in Southall, and the incident at Jake's school.

"I knew it." Jude slammed her glass on the table. "Every time I see you, the web of that place and those people gets more complicated. So now, you not only still have the girl crush on Emma, you're also impersonating her at Jake's school. Also you think Jake is in the grip of some fundamentalist religious sect. And just after you realize you fancy Rob, you find him hard at it with the family friend! Oh, and I forgot. You've been promoted to chauffeur as well. I'm telling you, get out of there while you've still got some remnants of sanity left!"

I nodded. Both of us knew she was right, but also that I wouldn't leave. Not yet. I was too enmeshed with their lives.

After everything that had happened, Wycombe Lodge was still the place where I wanted and needed to go every day.

Nothing had been mentioned about Jake or the meeting at the school. Emma seemed to have let go of the topic entirely, just dropped it and let it skitter off. Rob did his usual morning perambulations around the dining room and then ambled off to his office or into the city. He appeared to have forgotten about our kaffeeklatsches altogether and I didn't want to remind him. I wasn't sure if he even knew about Jake's problems at school and I didn't ask. Only Lily was forthcoming during my evening visit to drop off her laundry.

"Everything gets to him," she said. She spoke like a village elder. Sometimes I thought she was the only sensible person living at Wycombe Lodge. "It's like he needs another layer of skin or something, and he doesn't help himself with all that ultra-right-wing religious stuff."

"Maybe that's what he believes." I handed over a pile of jeans and T-shirts. "Maybe we should respect that." I thought of my night at the church, the way the preacher controlled her audience. I didn't agree with Jake's views. But I recognized his need to belong somewhere. He didn't fit in at his school and he no longer seemed to fit in with his family. "Has anyone tried to talk to him about it? You never know, he might be pleased."

"It's not that kind of school," said Lily. "We're not that kind of family."

I didn't ask what she meant. I didn't want to listen to her criticize her mother. I might have put down my laundry basket to hear criticism of Rob, but not Emma. Jake's door was shut. I gave a perfunctory quiet knock and walked straight in, expecting the usual empty room. He was kneeling by the side of the bed, his hands clasped. His head was on the pillow. Something about the curve of his back and the angle of his head scared me. I found myself beside him, stroking his neck, his blond hair soft under my fingers as neatly paired socks and folded jeans tumbled onto the floor.

He whipped around. "What are you doing?" His face was scarlet as if I'd caught him watching porn.

"I'm sorry. You looked so sad and I was frightened that something bad had happened."

He stood up, kicking a cushion under his bed. "Like what?" His voice was wavering. "Like I'm going to get expelled for how I think? A guy in my class came to school completely drunk and they let him sleep it off in the infirmary. I'm not doing that. I'm not out there preaching to anybody about anything. I just want to be able to be who I am and believe what I believe. Is that so difficult?"

"It shouldn't be," I said. "But do you really believe that being gay is wrong? Can't you see the discrimination in that point of view? The way it breeds hatred?"

Jake made a sound somewhere between a snort and a sob. "It's more complicated than that. I can't explain it properly."

"The meeting at school, your parents and the teacher, what happened?"

"Nothing. They didn't have the meeting. Something about Mum's schedule and Dad's book. They've arranged a date after the book is published."

"So you're safe until then."

"That's just it," he said. "I don't feel safe. I don't feel safe at school or here for most of the time. There's only one place where I feel safe." He didn't need to elaborate.

"But—" I wanted to say that he could feel safe with me. Jake cut me off with a swipe of his hand.

"I'm fine. Just leave me alone." There was nothing left for me to do except retreat downstairs with my washing basket. Jake needed help, at the very least someone who tried to understand him. Yet every time I thought this, and I thought it often, there was the whisper of disloyalty to Emma, who had the time to drink wine with me but not to talk to her son. Still, after the book was published, perhaps everything would be different.

Each day was two minutes shorter than the one that went before. In the morning, the wan, gray air carried the threat of frost. The sun, when it appeared, was pale, like something spent.

Siggy waited for me in the hall every morning. It had taken almost a year of me dragging him across to the park or down to the river, stopping to encourage him to sniff lampposts and clumps of leaves, to enjoy the whole delightful business of being a small thoroughly spoiled dog. It had worked, and he had taken to trotting beside me with purpose. He'd even found a playmate in the park, an equally spoiled miniature poodle walked by an impassive Filipina maid. But for all this, his heart still belonged to Emma.

One Thursday night, she rushed downstairs to lay the table and light the candles. Her hair was still damp at the ends and there was that familiar woody scent about her.

"The last thing I want to do is go out after dinner," she said, holding a pair of shoes in one hand and a camera in the other. "But duty calls. One of Rob's things where I'm expected to tag along."

"You'll probably enjoy it when you get there," I said.

"I doubt that." She put the camera on the counter and slipped on her shoes, then grabbed a stick of carrot from the chopping board and nibbled around the edges of it like a rabbit before throwing it into the sink.

"What's for dinner?" she asked.

"Spinach and ricotta lasagna. Lily and I made it yesterday after school. It tastes better the next day."

"Really?" said Emma. She didn't sound convinced. "Lucky

Lily, having you as a cooking teacher. I wish I could cook," she went on. "I mean, I've tried, but I just can't. Maybe one day . . ."

She picked up the camera and turned it over in her hand. It was black, with lots of silver buttons, and looked expensive. "We got this for Lily's birthday last year. All these things that you give children that cost a small fortune. You think they're about to take up a new hobby, or discover a talent they never thought existed, but actually . . ."—she switched on the camera and the lens popped out with an efficient low whir—". . . they use it for a day or so and then leave it to gather dust at the back of their cupboard. I should take it for myself. She'd never notice and I could do with some more shots on my website."

"I never take photographs, even with my phone," I said. "I always forget and then it's too late."

Emma pointed the camera towards the garden. Click click. Siggy pricked up his ears. Click click. She moved the vase of autumn foliage I'd picked that morning from the center to the edge of the table. Click click.

"Your turn now," she urged. "Come on, apron off." I hated having my photograph taken, but she insisted. "You look so good through this lens. OK, smile."

I tried to grin in a casual photogenic kind of way. "Great," said Emma. "Now, a serious expression. You look so good. All your cheekbones are highlighted." Click. Click. Click.

"But I don't have any cheekbones," I said, getting back to the carrots and potatoes.

"Just one more," said Emma. I looked up, blinking at the sudden flash.

After dinner—Emma effusive about the lasagna without actually eating any of it—she and Rob left in a taxi. Lily and Jake helped clear the table. "Would you like to cook something one day with Lily and me?" I asked. "Name your dish, and we'll try it."

"Uh, maybe a bit later on. I've got a lot of homework at the moment." He had the same startled look on his face as he did when I surprised him in his bedroom.

"Sure," I said, biting back disappointment. "Anytime."

He disappeared upstairs. "Everyone is making his life hell at school," said Lily. "But he doesn't help himself. He won't listen to me, so there's nothing I can do." She put the leftover lasagna in the refrigerator.

"But you need to keep trying," I said. "Everyone needs to do that."

"If you say so." With that, she was gone. There was the sound of her footsteps clattering on the staircase, then her bedroom door closing with a bang. Downstairs, the house held its usual silence. I walked through the empty rooms, straightening cushions and piles of books in the sitting room and poking through some papers Rob had left on his desk. Nothing of interest.

I went back into the kitchen and through the side door to pull the garbage bins out onto the pavement. No recycling bags this week. Rob must have finished the book. I couldn't decide if I was relieved or disappointed. Probably both. Jude was right. I should leave Wycombe Lodge and find a job in another restaurant where fifteen-hour days would keep me too tired to think. Just move on, let things float by.

26

The Chinese word for crisis consists of two brush-strokes. One means danger. The other means opportunity. Work to recognize the difference. Be brave!

—Emma Helmsley, "Taking the Moment," October 28, 2016

My phone buzzed and I fished it out of my bag. Three missed messages from Jude, the first before 9 a.m. An odd time for her to call, smack in the middle of the nursery school run, accompanied by inevitable tantrums about the wrong-colored lunch box or a tangle in Amelia's hair. Jude was time management in motion in a restaurant kitchen, but a complete ditherer in her own home (something she and Emma had in common). Probably a misdialed number, I thought, or one of the twins had found her phone and played with it. The next call, an hour later, was probably to say not to take any notice of the first call. But the third?

I rang back immediately, not waiting to listen to her messages. "What is it?" I asked. "What's wrong? Is it the twins? I can come right now if you need me."

Silence. Never a good sign. "It's that man and that woman," she spat out. "I warned you."

I thought of Anton and the woman who'd replaced me. "What have Mr. Fancy Chef and his new lover done now?"

"Not him. Not her." There was an exasperated puff of air. "Your boss, the one who could do no wrong until you caught him having sex with his best friend. The one you were kind of in love with, not to mention the girl crush on his wife. The one you've been covering up for."

"I don't understand."

"Hang up and google Rob Helmsley. Then you might want to call me back."

The computer in the study always took far too long to start. Colored, whirling circles appeared in corners and stubbornly refused to move, often for minutes at a time. But the Internet connection was still better than the one on my phone, so I sat and waited.

What was Jude talking about? I imagined some kind of tabloid scandal, that someone had got wind of his affair with Theo. Tabloids loved to prick the façade of a family and see who bled. I pictured Emma at work, Fiona fielding telephone calls and emails; Jake and Lily at school with everyone sniggering around them.

Finally the computer spluttered into life. I typed in Rob's name. There was nothing recent in news. I clicked onto his website. Next to a photo of Rob looking earnest and intellectual, there was an image of a book cover with the gray and gloomy Kinghurst Place in the background. Superimposed on it was a photograph of McLeish with his heavy-lidded dark eyes staring out below the title. The book was called *Madhouse*. Each letter was printed in a different shade of neon.

There was mention of an accompanying program about McLeish and Kinghurst Place, to be broadcast at 11:30 p.m. that night. Nothing too odd about that. Just another of Rob's documentaries. Then I must have clicked the mouse by mistake, because another image swam into view. On the screen was a photograph of a young woman gazing pensively into the camera. Her face was almost out of focus and there was a series of quotations below the photograph. I didn't recognize the person at first. But less than a second later, everything stopped with a hollow jolt.

It was me, in my striped T-shirt and jeans, everything below my waist obscured by the kitchen counter. To one side was a crumpled apron. Underneath the photograph were words like "harrowing" and "psychological abuse" and "child neglect" and "extraordinary story." Each quotation was separated from the next by different vibrant colored dots: acid-yellow, lime-green, and shocking pink.

My breath rasped like chalk on a blackboard. Each thud of my pulse was a thunderclap. My sight closed in on itself and I couldn't see anything at all for a while. I sat very still. If I continued to do that, everything might go away. It might not have happened, might not be happening. I could go back to the night of Emma and me drinking wine when it was still warm enough for the doors to be open, with Siggy lying between our feet and the sense of a friendship found.

Friends gave you bits of themselves. They laid them down on the ground and said, "This is the part of me that no one knows and I entrust it to you." This is what Emma did that night, her blue eyes blinking through her fringe when she told me about falling in love with another man, about wanting to leave Rob all those years ago, when she told me that I was part of their family. Friends protected each other. This is what I did on the night of their party when I shepherded Emma away from the sight of Rob and Theo; what I had tried to do at Jake's school. My mind filled with memories that collided behind my eyes. I was shut outside, unable to get back in again. Searching for my mother, crying out her name. Alone in the dark, rustling sounds in the corner, the air in front of me thick with fear.

My phone rang again. It was Jude. "How did you know?" I asked.

"I was driving back from the kindergarten, listening to Radio 4, and it was a promotion about Rob's TV program tonight. No names mentioned, but it had to be you. Did you know, have any idea at all?"

"No, none."

"How did he get hold of all that stuff? You said you hadn't told him about it."

"I hadn't told him anything. He completely fooled me, said the book was strictly nonfiction and he couldn't include anything that wasn't completely factual and there was no proper record of me or of my mother being there. He said he couldn't write about something if he wasn't sure about it. Sounds so stupid now, but I always got the impression he was more interested in helping me than anything else.

"Emma and I had a couple of glasses of wine too many together a few weeks ago, when everyone was out. She told me I was part of their family. I know I drank too much, but I'm certain I didn't tell her anything about the notebook for the same reason that I didn't tell Rob. I was ashamed and I didn't want them to think less of me." My voice was heavy and slow. It seemed to be coming from a faraway place.

"Well, one of them got to your notebook somehow or other. And the pictures?"

"Emma took them, one evening. I thought she was just playing with Lily's camera."

Jude swore into the phone. "Why would she just play with Lily's camera when she could play with your life instead? I warned you about these people. I told you to watch out. But they can't publish photographs of you without your permission. They can't do that to you. I'm sure of it. I bet you could sue, take them down."

"There has to have been a mistake," I cried. "Someone must have taken the camera and posted the wrong photographs.

How could everything about me be plastered all over Rob's website?"

"I don't know," said Jude. "I wish I did."

I don't remember the sequence of events after that. At some stage Jude said I should find a match, set fire to the house, and leave, taking their spoiled dog with me. I think I slumped in the chair for an unknown length of time, paralyzed by an unseen force field.

I remembered the carefully casual way that Emma had brought the camera into the kitchen that evening and taken photographs of Siggy and me and the vase of autumn foliage. Did she take them deliberately? Or had Rob found the camera and the photographs and sent them to his publisher without telling Emma?

I thought of Gran, how upset she would be, all her life trying to obscure everything to protect me. I thought about trying to get another job, with people thinking that I'd sold my life story for a few shabby pounds; everyone knowing about my mother and looking sideways at me, wondering if I was like her, if her illness was about to explode inside me. Every now and then I repeated to myself, like a chorus, "It was my life. They didn't have to do that."

When Lily and Jake came home, I managed to say hello. "Are you OK?" asked Lily. "You look a bit pale."

"I just need a bit of air," I said, clipping Siggy's leash to his collar. "I'll take a quick spin around the block, and then I'll be good." I walked in a giddy blur, weaving from the gutter towards front lawn hedges and fences and back again. At the corner of the street, I stopped and slumped against a tree trunk, remaining completely still until its sharp knobs pressing into my spine forced me into movement.

Back in the kitchen, I waited for Emma. Every car that passed I imagined to be her taxi. Every sigh and creak I heard,

I imagined to be her about to open the door, to walk into the hall, when I would hear the clack-clack of her shoes on the flagstones and then her muffled footsteps on the rug. I don't know how long I waited. Finally, she was in the kitchen, flinging off her jacket and flicking her hair to one side in that careless elegant way I had once tried so hard to copy. Under her fringe, her blue eyes held mine in an unbroken clear gaze and she smiled. Even then, I couldn't help thinking for a second that it could all be OK, that there had been a mistake and everything could be returned to the way it used to be.

"What a day," she said, pouring a glass of wine. "Can I tempt you?" She waved the bottle in my direction. I shook my head. "Are you sure?" Again, I shook my head.

She circled the kitchen, sipping her wine in that birdlike way of hers. It was like every other evening. Maybe it was. Maybe nothing had happened. Maybe I had dreamed the whole thing.

"Cottage pie for dinner! How yummy. I'm going to go up and take a quick bath. I had to go down to Hoxton this morning and walk around for hours with some daft committee. It was so windy. I need to get the grit out of my hair."

Even when she came downstairs, hair dribbling in wet patches on her back, in her tracksuit and neon trainers neatly tied in childlike double bows, when she sat on the counter and began her evening drumroll against the cupboards, there was still something inside me that didn't believe what had happened. But when I shut the oven door and turned towards her, I felt tears scratching at my eyelids. There was the dissociated question of why should tears scratch when they're only water?

Emma cocked her head to one side. "Are you all right? You don't seem yourself."

"How did you do that?" I burst out. "How did you take my life and give it away like that? Just for a TV program and a chapter or two in a book? Or was it Rob? Whose idea was it? Did you think I wouldn't notice? Or that someone wouldn't tell me? It was on the radio this morning, an announcement for all the world to hear."

Her eyes darted off to one side. "I meant to say something, truly I did, but it never seemed to be the right time. I was going to tell you tonight, right now, before the program goes to air."

"Really." I polished the sink tap. Why are you doing this? I asked myself. You should leave, right now. But I couldn't seem to make myself move.

"Please don't be cross, I couldn't bear it," Emma said in a small, tentative voice. "It was so silly of me, I know, not to have told you before this. I didn't mean to, honestly. Please, please forgive me. I mean, it's not so bad, is it? Everyone will forget about it in a week or two. And we both want the same things. Anyhow . . ."—her voice fell to a whisper—"I was going to talk to you, really I was."

"And the photographs?" I asked. "You were going to talk to me about them as well?"

Her hand flew up to her heart, a hollow knock where it landed on her chest bone. "You have to believe me, Anne, that was just a coincidence. I wouldn't do that to you, you know that. That was a misunderstanding between Rob and me. It wasn't meant to happen like that."

"I don't understand," I said, gulping back the sadness. "I didn't tell you about my life because I didn't know the truth of it myself. I still don't. Yes, I wanted to find out more, and yes, I hoped Rob might help me do that, but I was so happy here. I didn't want all that to come between us. So I don't understand. It's not like you need the publicity, or the money, or anything. You and Rob have everything—why would you want more?"

Emma studied the sink. "I can't explain it just now. I really can't. You need to understand, we didn't intend to upset you. We're all in this together, really."

I turned on the oven for the cottage pie. Why? Even as I set the timer, I asked myself the question with no idea of the answer.

"Look, Rob will be back by dinnertime—why don't we talk about it afterwards, just the three of us?" pleaded Emma. "You know, we've been meaning to ask, Rob and I, if you'd eat with us every night. I know you said you didn't want to before, when you first started here. We'd like that so much, we'd feel more equal. You know how fond we are of you. Since you came here, it's been the most wonderful time for all of us, the children too.

"We felt you'd want Rob's book to be successful. I thought you would want to help him. I said you were part of the family, and you are, and families, well, we all pull together, don't we?"

"And the payoff is that I get to sit with you at dinner instead of washing the pots and cleaning up?"

She poured a second glass of wine and drained half of it in a gulp. "It's not like that. Surely you understand. Sometimes things come along and you have to take them."

"I'm not a thing," I said. "Last time I looked, I was still a person."

There was sadness and disappointment in her face, a crumpling of her features as though she was about to cry. A couple of seconds longer and I might have fallen for it, the way I might have fallen for it with Anton if he had kept protesting his innocence. I might even have gone to comfort her. But then she started talking to me, like I was a child who didn't understand the rules.

"Anne," Emma said. "You approached us about this job, remember. That was your choice, your decision. Let's try and be clear on this one. We could just as easily argue that you used us. Surely you can see that. You tried to mine Rob's expert knowledge, all his academic expertise—you tried to infiltrate that for your own ends. You wanted to find out about your childhood and your mother from Rob, and yet you weren't prepared to be open and honest with him about your own memories. We understand you didn't want to tell us because you were ashamed. Rob says that's not uncommon in families where members have some kind of mental illness. There is still such a stigma surrounding these things. So we've forgiven you for that."

She stopped suddenly and cocked her head to one side. "Sorry. I thought I heard either Jake or Lily on the stairs. I don't want them involved in this at the moment." Her trainers made a short drumroll on the cupboard door. She slid off the counter and stood at a sharp, straight angle. Instead of waving her arms about in that elegant casual way of hers, she folded them and stared at me, like a busy executive concluding a particularly tiresome meeting.

"Look, why don't you finish up now, go home, and have an early night. You'll feel better in the morning—we can talk about this at another time, when you're calm. OK? You'll see that nothing needs to change. We can go on as we were. In some ways, it might even be better. It always is when you've come through a difficult time. Everyone understands each other so much better. It makes for a stronger relationship."

My hands fumbled as I tried to untie my apron. The knots held steady. I ended up pulling it over my head and throwing it on the counter, where it landed in almost the same place as it was in the photographs.

"I know that it's come as a bit of a shock," said Emma. "I really do. But the most important thing you need to tell yourself is that Rob and I, and the children, we care about you very much and we want you to remain part of our family."

Without looking at Emma, I hurried out of the house. I strode past the woman walking her Labrador in the comforting blanket of dusk. All the way home in the bus, I pressed myself into a corner, refusing to acknowledge what was so obvious.

I scurried back to my flat, past the kebab shop with its cylinders of shaved lamb turning on their spits and greasy potatoes mounded under yellow lights, rushing past Faisal without stopping to say hello.

It was only when I pushed through the front door of my building and ran upstairs, desperate to unlock my front door, to shut it behind me and draw in some comfort from my own small sanctuary, when I threw my bag down on the coffee table and everything spilled out—my keys, a tattered cookery magazine, and my notebook—that I acknowledged to myself what had happened.

27

❦

People only betray those who trust and love
them. And then they turn against them. It
happens all the time.

—Rob Helmsley, *Madhouse: The Life and Times
of Rowan McLeish*

At some time, or times, the actual hour or date never to be
made clear, Emma had found the notebook in my bag. She
had picked it out and read it. She had either taken photographs of each page on her phone, and later transcribed
them, or transcribed them on the spot. Then she had given
them to Rob.

Or had it been the other way around? Had Rob found my
notebook and then persuaded Emma to take the photographs?
I wanted to think it had been Rob, but it didn't ring true. Rob
wasn't the sort of man to fossick about in a woman's handbag.
It wouldn't have occurred to him.

The inescapable fact was that it was Emma. None of these
details mattered much in the end, but I still wanted to know.
They mattered to me. Did she find my notebook on that night
when we were alone in the house, lolling about in the dining
room and drinking wine? When she was in the study, making
her phone call, was her eye caught by Jude's expensive cast-
off, the sort of expertly crafted item that someone on a housekeeper's salary could never afford? Did she pick it up and sniff
its intricately plaited surface to check if it was genuine leather,

or the chemical-smelling plastic of a cheap fake? Is that when she saw my notebook and read it?

But she was gone for less than ten minutes. Was that long enough for her to read it through and make a copy of it there and then? Or had she discovered it days, even weeks earlier, and dipped in and out of it, taking her time to photograph each page on her phone while I had my head in the oven or the refrigerator, while I was folding their laundry or loading their dishwasher? Most of the time when I was alone in the house, I kept the notebook in my back pocket, so I could scribble things when they occurred to me. But I usually put it in my bag before I started preparing dinner.

However Emma found my notebook, she must have given the photographs to Rob that weekend. Emma would have known that photographs taken on her mobile wouldn't be as good for broadcasting or publication as an almost professional camera.

I paced my sitting room, too agitated to sit. Up and down, up and down. I must have stamped about for some time, because at some stage the man from downstairs banged on my door. Before I could open it, he said he had a migraine, his ceiling was shaking, and could I please stop. I sat down on the sofa, too taken aback to move.

The thought of food made me nauseous, although I hadn't eaten all day. It also made me imagine the four of them, probably Theo as well, in the dining room, cocooned in warm candlelight, eating cottage pie and chatting in that clever, witty way of theirs. Emma would have explained my absence to Jake and Lily. They wouldn't have thought twice about it. They never watched Rob on television. They might not even know what had happened. If they did mention it, Rob and Emma would have dismissed the necessary sacrifice of the hired help who had a nifty way with herbs and ironing shirt collars. Rob would probably have turned everything into one of those moral maze arguments that he was so good at.

"Who was the more honest or dishonest person in all of this?" he might have asked. "The woman who maneuvered her way into a job in a place where she snooped about in bedrooms, where she went through people's garbage and developed an unhealthy crush on someone's husband? Or the husband and wife who discovered the snooping, who were prepared to forgive and let the woman keep her job? Surely she shouldn't mind that they disclosed parts of her life to the outside world? After all, it was in the pursuit of genuine academic inquiry.

"And where lay the greater good?" I pictured Rob leaning across the table, helping himself to more cottage pie. He might have spilled a bit on the table and wiped it up with his finger. He might have licked his finger clean with those sloppy table manners of his, and then rubbed his brow, the way he did when he talked.

"It's unhelpful to hold on to secrets," he'd have said. "They fester and they're corrosive. And the person's experiences could help others."

At this point Rob might have mentioned the number of people who have some incident of mental illness each year. He was good at producing statistics like that. As well, he would have added, the pool of academic knowledge would be that much bigger. Emma would have been sitting at the other end of the table, nodding agreement as she drank.

"The important thing here is," Rob might have said, "is that the person who snooped was not exposed in the usual definition of the word." Rob loved dissecting minute layers of meaning. "Their real name, where they live, and what they did for a living—all this has been protected."

I'd almost have fallen for that argument myself, particularly when spoken in that delicious chocolate voice of his, except that what I did, what I was trying to do, was never going to hurt anyone. I only wanted to find out about my mother and why she had left me. Was that so despicable?

I didn't plan on drawing so close to them. I had no idea that I'd fall in love with them, longing for their presence in my working day and their approval of everything I did, so much that I became too scared to tell the truth for fear of losing them. It wasn't in my job description to go upstairs in the middle of a party and find Rob and Theo clawing at each other, and then hiding it from Emma, so life at Wycombe Lodge could go on as before. Nothing like this was covered in *Mrs. Beeton's Book of Household Management.* It was just what had happened to me. I knew that I'd found myself sucked into my own version of a cult and had been brainwashed by their picture of a perfect family, until I drew back the layers of what was beneath. But knowing that didn't stop the hurt and the anger and, again, the feeling of abandonment.

Somehow the hours passed, every minute dragging as if under wet cement. I wanted a drink, very badly, but there was no alcohol in the flat and Ahmed's shop was closed. At last it was time for Rob's program. I turned on the television, my fingers shaking as they moved about the remote control. The opening credits swam onto the screen; a picture of a plaster head, with sections of the brain marked off for attributes or failings. The part for secrecy, I noted for the first time, was just above the ear. There was the opening sound track, the sound of a lone, wavering cello. The picture faded away, replaced by a shot of Rob walking in front of Kinghurst Place. "In this house behind me, now privately owned," he said, "once flourished a community—or a cult—led by one of the most controversial and famous psychologists of the twentieth century—Rowan Donald McLeish. McLeish believed that what we see as madness was merely a response to a crazy world, and he set up his own community of mentally ill runaways and schizophrenics right here, in the middle of East Sussex."

The image of the house faded away, replaced by photographs of McLeish playing the piano, giving lectures, and receiving awards. There was a David Bailey black-and-white portrait of McLeish staring at himself in a mirror. Just looking at it made me dizzy.

"It was a place with no boundaries," Rob's voice continued. "Orgies and wild parties were the order of the day. McLeish spurned legal drugs in favor of illegal hallucinogenic drugs like LSD and mescaline. He encouraged bizarre experiments, like attempting to drill holes in his followers' skulls to let light into the brain, an ancient practice called trepanning. And among all this lived a small girl of five years old, uncared for and mostly unnoticed, surviving on scraps of leftover food and sometimes left alone for days on end. After her schizophrenic mother died, the girl was finally rescued by her grandmother. Here, for the first time, is her remarkable story. We've used the voice of an actress to protect her identity."

I shivered, as if someone had ripped off all my clothes. Dread stirred inside, uncoiling like a lizard. The same blurred photograph of me I'd seen on the website appeared on the screen, accompanied by a female voice speaking in a sort of Scottish accent. The caption below the photograph read: "Anne X, now in the hospitality industry."

> "Sometimes, when I was allowed to join them, I sat on
> McLeish's lap, imagining or hoping that he was my father.
> Most of the time, I was banned from going anywhere near them.
> McLeish said children were able to look after themselves, that
> their parents damaged them. So I was left alone pretty much all
> of the time."

I pressed the freeze button on the remote control and peered into the screen. They'd used some special effect to make the photograph of me grainy and faded, so that it matched photographs of McLeish and his followers at Kingsley House. I would be recognizable to people who knew me, but not to a casual observer. It didn't make me feel any better. The photograph was replaced by one of the group at dinner at Kinghurst Place, the photograph I'd seen online and that Rob had showed me. The room was candlelit and the table was littered with empty plates and glasses.

"I was only five," the voice went on. That was when it hit me, so strongly that I lost breath. My love for them, combined with my yearning to find out what had happened to my mother, was such a convenient combination for Emma and Rob. For the past year, I'd been useful in so many ways.

"I was left on my own for days on end, just wandering around the house eating stuff out of cans and crying for my mother. Sometimes I was so scared, I wet myself. No child should have to live like that." On it went. The rhythms of my speech rang around the room. I couldn't remember writing some of it, although the sense of it was accurate. It was as if Rob had mined my brain. There were interviews with other psychologists, experts on psychedelic drugs. Some spoke of McLeish as a misunderstood, caring genius who went astray. Others described him as a manipulative sociopath. I lurched into the bathroom and vomited. Jude rang after I'd rinsed my mouth.

"There must be a way you can sue the bastards," she said.

"How could I do that?" I asked, still too numb to weep.

"They can't use photographs of you, however fuzzy, or quote your words without your permission. So we'll see about that," she barked. "Take a pill and go to bed. Right now."

I did as she said. The next morning, still groggy, I ran along the towpath, past the Hanwell asylum and Isambard Brunel's ingenious construction of three bridges that allowed cars, boats, and trains to pass all at once on different levels. If only my own life had been so efficiently designed. I ran almost all the way to Southall, until my legs began to ache and made me forget the other pain.

I walked back home, where I nearly collided with Faisal and Imran, carrying bags of vegetables from the local market. "There you are," said Imran. Faisal rested his bag on a ledge outside the kebab shop. The man inside stopped tending his giant cones of meat long enough to frown and make shooing motions. We ignored him.

"I was worried about you yesterday," he said. "You looked so pale and you were rushing. I thought maybe you were ill." A concerned look came over his face.

"I was tired," I said. "You know, the end of the week. I just needed a good night's sleep."

"Did you get it?" he asked. "The sleep?"

"Yes," I lied. "Everything is much better now."

"Good," he said. "I have had news from my sister. So . . ." He hesitated. "We can have the meal together, like you said?" It was more a question than a statement. My invitation, offered in unthinking and tipsy haste. It was the last thing I wanted to do. But there was his trusting, eager face right in front of me, nodding with enthusiasm.

"Of course," I said, as much to convince myself as him. "It would be lovely to meet her. Let's set a date when she gets here."

"Thank you, thank you." Faisal tugged at his sleeve. Imran smiled apologetically. "Yes, I'm coming now. We must go. The cinema. I promised him."

I walked back to my flat to find four plaintive bleats from Emma on my phone. "We need to talk, the three of us," she kept saying. "We can't just leave it."

Jude had other ideas. "Yes, you can bloody well leave it," she muttered. In the background, Amelia shouted that she was a naughty mummy for swearing. "Please, quiet in the backseat. Now listen. You leave all this where it belongs, in the gutter with those hypocritical rich lowlifes. You can get a great job, probably even better than the one with Anton. It's only been a year. People haven't forgotten how good you are in a kitchen."

"But what about Jake and Lily? Particularly Jake. I don't want to leave, just walk out of his life without saying goodbye. He's having trouble at school and he's getting sucked into another kind of cult. I can see it so clearly and it's terrifying. He needs help."

"Write him a letter then. You can say goodbye like that. OK?"

"OK," I repeated. I wasn't totally convinced. "I'll think about it."

28

Sometimes the only way forward is to make an ending. If this is inevitable, consider these three words—grace, honesty, and love. Keep them in your heart at all times.

—Emma Helmsley, "Taking the Moment," November 14, 2016

I went back to Wycombe Lodge. Not the next week, or the week after, but soon after that. Emma had kept up her barrage of messages, and finally I gave in to their sheer force and number. There was a part of me that wanted to have it out with them as well. What Emma and Rob would call closure. I rang the buzzer one Tuesday morning like a stranger and walked to the open front door. The gravel was covered in rotting leaves, and the olive trees in their pots looked dead, the soil dried out with deep cracks.

In the hall, Siggy danced around my legs, thinking it was time for his walk. I patted his head, running my hand along the soft down behind his ears to the rough fur on his neck. Everything looked the same: the hall table with the vase of overblown roses and the pile of letters, the faded red rug and the shaft of light from the dining room at the end of the hall. But it smelled different. There was a stale fustiness that made me want to fling open the French windows.

"Come in," said Rob. He and Emma were standing on either side of the fireplace. I wondered if they'd decided on talking to me in the sitting room the night before, if they'd rejected the kitchen as a place where I might feel more comfortable. Rob's theory of emotional geography. They'd have wanted to choose the room where they felt superior and safe, surrounded by their pictures and their things, all the subtle emblems of their life.

"It's good to see you," said Emma. She stood by the fireplace, wearing one of her trailing skirts and a shrunken pilled sweater. Her eyes were puffy. "Thank you for coming."

"Yes, thanks for coming," repeated Rob, pocketing his phone. He had on his preppy uniform. His shirt collar was creased. "We wanted to see you while Jake and Lily were at school," he said. "We told them you weren't feeling well and were taking some time off. It seemed better that way, until everything is sorted out." He made it sound like an agenda for a meeting, or a guest list that had to be decided upon. "Shall we sit down?"

They chose the sofa while I sat in one of the rickety cane chairs facing the French doors. All the times I'd gazed through those windowpanes, noticing the way my perspective changed whenever I moved my head. Now I saw nothing, except specks of dirt and pockmarked raindrops. I shifted in the chair. There was a sinking feeling, as if the seat was about to give way. Split strands of cane dug into my buttocks. We sat perfectly still, not speaking. Our eyes bounced off one another, up to the ceiling, and into the corners of the room.

In my mind I saw so clearly that first day I met them, standing on the corner of their road to catch my breath, brushing mud off my shoes before walking into this house where Rob and Emma stood, about to welcome me into their wonderful, magical life.

Rob leaned towards me, his hands clasped in front of him. He had on his best chocolate voice. "What we need to do here," he said slowly and clearly, "is try not to get too emotional. It's obviously a tender subject for all of us."

"But . . ." I interrupted.

"Now," Rob said, "let me finish. We're very upset as well. Frankly, it's a bit of a mess."

Again, I remembered so clearly those mornings when Rob and I sat in the kitchen, the way I felt myself bend towards him like a plant towards the sun. Their eyes fixed on me dolefully, as if their domestic pet, the one they were used to dancing attendance on them, had suddenly gone feral. "We would have told you," continued Rob. "We would have told you at the right time. But, as Emma has told you, we've been under pressure and so busy, and we haven't been thinking as clearly as we might have done. So now, I think the best thing to do is for you to take another week off and then let's try to get everything back to normal, so we can allow the trust between us to grow again."

I couldn't help it. "How can anything grow again? How can it go back to normal, after that program and after the book is published?" I hadn't realized, but I was shouting. "You have used me to promote yourself. You told me you were writing a book of record. You told me you didn't know anything definitive about my mother and me, but you'd try to help me. But you weren't helping me. You were helping yourself to me and my life. It may not have been that much of a life, but it was mine. If I wanted to write about it, I would have done so."

There was the suggestion of a sigh from Rob. "Yes, your name is in the book, but not your surname. And Anne is scarcely an unusual first name, I think you'll agree."

"But all that time, all those chats, why did you pretend you didn't know anything when you did? You knew so much more than you let on."

"Anne, accuracy was important, is important. If I'd told you everything I knew, it would have colored your own images and recollections. You wouldn't have delved quite so deeply into your own consciousness. And you have to agree that's always beneficial."

"Beneficial for you? Or for me?"

He ignored my question, continuing in the same calm tone that he used in his programs. "I think your mother was the woman in the photograph, the one they called Mary, but I can't say that definitively. McLeish had many mistresses. For all the reasons we've already talked about, there was no reliable record of a child or children living there. There was the odd mention, but nothing absolutely definitive. It was very much a floating population. I think you did live there, because your recollections are pretty accurate. But again, I had a duty to my readers and to the memory of McLeish to be fair towards him."

"But your duty to be fair didn't include me. It's all right for you to say I was subjected to abuse, I was left locked up for days on end . . . It was all exaggerated, turned into something that made you look good."

"Anne, dear Anne," said Emma in a low, clear voice that was new to me. "You have said yourself you had no clear recollection of what really happened, so you can't really say what Rob wrote wasn't the truth. The words in his book are your words after all. Rob didn't make anything up."

A flush was rising in my face, spreading along my cheeks. "Did it make you feel good? Copying it all down from my notebook?" Everything was on fire. "When did you do that? That night when we were on our own, or before?"

"I'm not sure that really matters." She ran her foot up and down Siggy's back. He rolled over and she began to rub his stomach. "Life is all about timing. Synchronicity. I saw the notebook in your bag that night when I went into the study to make a call. Well." She shrugged. "There it was, right at the top. It didn't take that long to read and I did have my phone with me. It's not like I had to take notes or anything."

"I still don't get why you did this."

Emma scuffed her shoe on the rug. "I thought you would have understood by now, how hard we have to work to maintain everything. It doesn't happen by chance."

Jude's words came back to me, about the photographs and my words, and how they needed my permission to use them. "I could sue you if I wanted to!" I shouted. "I may not be rich and well connected, but I have legal rights. You can't steal my life like that. I could go to court and let a judge decide."

"We didn't steal your life," said Rob. He was so sure of himself. "Go to court, by all means, if you have the money for a lawyer. But you will find everything is in order."

"You never got my permission," I said. "You needed my permission and I never gave it to you."

A look of victory crossed Rob's face. "But you did give permission. My publisher has your signature."

I remembered the folded piece of paper, the one Rob said was his contract, and my signature. I gripped the arms of the chair. "You tricked me into doing that!" I shouted.

"It would be your word against ours," Rob said. "And we do have a certain public standing between the two of us, Emma and me. We are responsible, credible people. So you might want to think about that, and also you might want to think if you've got the money to pay our legal costs when you lose the case. Because you would lose."

"Rob is right," sighed Emma, moving closer towards him. "It would only make things more difficult for you. And the irony is—it would probably give Rob's career a boost." She took his hand and stroked it.

There was the thick, ugly thing of Rob and Theo in front of me. "How can you?" The anger rose out of me. "Why are you sticking up for him?"

"Because we're a family," said Emma. "And because he's my husband and I love him."

"But does he love you?" I burst out. "If he loves you so much, and values your family . . ." I couldn't help it. The words erupted out of me. "Why is he having an affair with Theo behind your back?" I pointed my finger at Rob. "Why are you lying, pretending you're straight? What's the point of that kind of deception in this day and age? I saw you with him, in the bedroom, at that party. I saw what you were doing and I wanted to save Emma from it. I practically forced her to go downstairs so she wouldn't have to see you."

The corners of my mouth were clumped with spittle. I fell silent. Infinitesimal bubbles of my saliva floated along the light flickering through the windows. I started up again, even though my throat was hoarse from shouting. "You hypocrite! To do that in your own bedroom, in your own house! Did it thrill you? It disgusted me."

They didn't bother with any fake notions of embarrassment. Again, there was that effortless superiority, with no need to look caught out or to disguise an inconvenient expression. Rob shrugged, leaned back, and crossed his legs. Emma sat up and leaned in front of him. There was nothing tentative about her now.

"Your lack of understanding here is disappointing." There was that patient, slow tone in her voice again, as if I were a particularly dim student. "I am married to Rob. I will always be married to Rob, whatever the situation. Being together is so much better for both of us, for our lives and our careers and reputations and for Jake and Lily, than being apart. I hoped that your time in our house would have taught you something, got you out of your conventional little ways of thinking."

"You're the ones who are being conventional, pretending like this. Who cares? People can sleep with who they like and not lie about it. Being homosexual is legal in this country, haven't you heard?"

Again, I recalled my first meeting with them in this room, when they moved together and smiled, when I felt that they believed in me, that they liked me more than I liked myself; that I was worth something. The things that happen in the air between people, after dull, gray nothingness.

Emma moved forward, so close that I could smell that woody herbal scent she always wore. "Did you imagine that I didn't know? Well, you're not as smart as I thought. All that has nothing to do with our marriage, how we are as a couple and how we are as a family, nothing at all. You haven't understood a thing."

"I could go to the newspapers—tell them the truth about the so-called power couple." I was floundering by now. We all knew it.

"Oh, puh . . . lease," sniffed Emma. "You wouldn't get past first base and you know it. That is a rock-bottom empty threat."

Things blurred after that. I remembered it only as a series of sounds. The clink of my set of house keys as I flung them on the hall table. Rob's audible puff of annoyance. The clack of Siggy's toenails on the hall floor. The squeak of the gate leading onto the street and the slamming of the front door behind me. I got myself home and lay on the sofa and wept.

Isabella had written that a housekeeper had to consider herself as the immediate representative of her mistress. But didn't the mistress have responsibilities as well? It seemed an unequal equation.

Jude came the next evening, on her way to Heathrow to pick up Philip. She hugged me, a fierce embrace. "It won't always be like this. Keep telling yourself that. Have they called, begging you to come back?"

"Not again. They put a month's pay into my account."

"Blood money," said Jude. "And Theo?"

"He rang, left a message saying he was sorry that he wasn't going to see me again. No mention of anything else."

"You need to get working," she said. "Find a job. Keep busy. The other stuff will solve itself if you just give it enough time. You have to stop worrying at it like a dog with a bone." She produced a bottle of wine, something from Philip's enormous cellar, and surveyed my kitchen. "When was the last time you cooked a meal in here?" She foraged about for a corkscrew. "The oven looks straight out of the box." She opened the bottle with an efficient twist and poured us half a glass each. After her first sip, she opened the oven door. "You've never even used it."

"That's not true," I said.

"How come the labels are still stuck on the trays?" That was the thing I loved about Jude. She always made me laugh. "Seriously," said Jude. "You've got to do something." Her bracelets clinked as she stood up. "I need to go—don't want to be late. The Heathrow run is part of my occasional wifely duties. It makes Philip go all warm and fuzzy when I'm there instead of a chap with a cap. You should try it one day."

"What? Being a chap with a cap at the airport?"

"No. Being with someone who likes you, who's your mate, and you stick with them for life. It's not so bad."

29

For a month I moped and wept. It seemed I'd returned to the same dismal place I'd inhabited a year ago after Anton, except now there was no daily message from Emma to brighten my life. For the first week, I pressed the delete button each day with a stab of fury. Then I unsubscribed from her emails, which made me feel even more desolate.

I'd like to say that I managed to forget all about Rob and Emma and Jake and Lily, but I didn't. Particularly I missed Jake. I missed Siggy, the way he rolled over for me to scratch his stomach, his rough fur and his meaty breath. And I kept thinking about my mother and Kinghurst Place and McLeish. I thought about all of them every single day. Not all the time. But at night before sleep, and in the morning, I indulged in my fantasies.

I saw myself setting off on my own hunt for information about McLeish. I would find someone else who'd lived at Kinghurst Place, someone whose mind was still clear, who remembered my mother and me. Somehow I would make sure that Rob and Emma knew that I had proved to be the better detective after all.

I imagined Wycombe Lodge falling to pieces without me, a slovenly set of rooms with the sour smell of dust and flaked skin and damp towels everywhere. I conjured up images of burned food, dirty dishes piled in the sink, and soiled clothes heaped everywhere. Each morning I checked my mailbox in case Jake had replied to the letter I'd written to him. Each morning it was empty. I sent him a message through Facebook. No reply.

There was the irresistible Google alert. I was surprised how often I was notified, even before the book was published. I couldn't bring myself to watch any of Rob's programs, but I read about his guests, their reminiscences and regrets. I knew about Emma's regular appearances on that daytime television show and also that she was planning a new book on househusbands. There was a photograph of them on the opening night of a National Theatre production, smiling at their new friend Dominic Butler, the star of the play.

I avoided the corner store in case I ran into Imran and Faisal. The thought of making jolly chitchat with them was too much. But I knew I couldn't go on like this forever. Apart from anything else, I couldn't afford it. Jude was right. I needed a job.

A week later, I had an interview in a Richmond restaurant called Gunya. It was small and tucked away in a pedestrian lane near the Green, owned by an Australian couple with broad smiles and a ferocious appetite for hard work. "Gunya means 'home' in the Wiradjuri language," said Mimi as she deftly plucked pin bones from a fillet of cod. "They're an Aboriginal tribe. Their land was near where I grew up." She put the fish to one side and swept the bones into a bin. "So what do you think? We don't go in for that traditional old-world kitchen hierarchy thing. It's more a team effort. We take it in turns to decide the menu and to work the pass. You happy with that?"

I nodded. "Good," said Toby, her husband. "It might feel a bit chaotic to start with, but it works for us." His clear green eyes looked me up and down. "Do you want to begin now, or tomorrow?"

I laughed, but he wasn't joking. I started the next day.

The kitchen was tiny and poorly equipped compared to the one at Anton's, with its enormous Rorgue range and its walk-in refrigerators full of vegetables and perfectly hung pieces of meat. Gunya had Ikea tables and chairs, and battered second-hand ovens and commercial hobs. Mimi and Toby scavenged nettles and dandelion leaves from Richmond Park, grew herbs in their allotment, and scorned city bankers' favorites of beef fillet and turbot.

"Why would you want to cook stuff like that?" asked Mimi, wrinkling her freckled brow. "A person might die of boredom." Local residents must have agreed with them. The restaurant was always full and I liked the look of the customers. There was no one famous or particularly well dressed, and the prices were low enough for young couples and sometimes even entire families.

Within a week, I was back into my old rhythms of fifteen-hour days, chopping and braising and roasting. I liked their style of cooking. It was honest and unpretentious. They didn't concern themselves with delicate arrangements of herbs or swirls of sauce. They served their version of good family food and it happened to be mine as well. I started early and finished late. At the end of my shift, my muscles ached. I was worn out, but in a good way. There was a kind of pleasure in being too busy to think.

But I didn't stop missing Jake and Lily, and I didn't forget about Rob and Emma. I certainly didn't forget about the book, due for publication any minute now, according to the most recent Google alert. Sometimes, flushed from late night glasses of wine with Mimi and Toby, I conjured up a photograph in a glossy magazine of us accepting our first Michelin star. It would be proof to Rob and Emma not only that I had survived, but that I had triumphed.

Then the next week, as I walked to work, all the shops full of fake snow and Christmas baubles, I saw the book, *Madhouse*, in the window of a bookshop. I stopped, almost tripping up the person behind me, and made my way into the shop slowly, like someone who'd been attacked. I picked up the book. The inscription on the front page read: "To Emma, always." I stood there, not moving, not flicking through the pages until someone bumped into me, breaking my trance. The woman at the till glared at me. I bought a copy and hurried out of the shop.

There was a moment when I strode along the Green, past the theater and the elegant terraced houses, when I wanted, more than anything, to turn around and rush home. But I remembered Jude's advice. Sitting inside my own walls doing nothing would be futile. I needed the oblivion of a hard day's work that wouldn't allow the luxury of anger or despair. There had been enough of that. I didn't stop all day. In the lulls between lunch and dinner, I scrubbed shelves and cleaned refrigerators and mopped floors.

"What's got into you?" asked Toby. "You're like a whirling dervish."

"Just feel like it," I muttered, looking up from my bucket, annoyed that the hours had gone so quickly. Now I had to face everything all over again. On the bus home, I opened the book and turned to the blurred pictures of myself. A girl about eighteen sat beside me, smelling of wine and cigarettes. She leaned towards me and I snapped the book shut, not wanting her to see the photographs. For a mad moment, I thought she had recognized me, and that she was about to turn and shout to the other passengers and tell them who I was. But she was only pulling her phone from her pocket.

At the corner shop, I bought a bottle of wine. I swallowed

half in one gulp and poured the rest into the sink before I could finish it. An hour or so passed in a blurred haze before I dozed off. I woke just before midnight with my head squashed between two cushions. I levered myself upright and picked up Rob's book. Jude told me not to read it, but I couldn't just leave it on the table unexamined. And why had I poured the last of the wine down the sink?

The windows were closed, the noise of the city shut out. Everything around me was silent except for the sounds of a building closing down for the night; the sigh of settling timbers, the hum of appliances. Straightaway I opened the book at the sections devoted to Kinghurst Place, to my story. Hope and dread sprang up in equal measures. I read it scrupulously, turning each page with a shaking hand. But there was little that hadn't been covered in Rob's television program or in newspaper and magazine articles.

It was after 1 a.m., but it would be impossible to sleep now. I read on, to the recollections of McLeish's followers and their stories of why they came and why they stayed. Everyone mentioned McLeish the savior, McLeish the daddy they never had, and McLeish the man who opened his arms when the world shut them out.

"I was in hospitals or institutions all my adult life," said one man, who called himself Johnny. "They said they could fix me, or that I could stay, and then they told me I could leave when I wanted to, which was their way of telling me to get out, that I didn't count for anything. McLeish was different. He cared. In the beginning he really cared about all of us."

The recollections turned grim. McLeish was not always the loving father of the extended family, the benevolent caregiver. After a while, he spoiled some and spurned others. "It got bad towards the end," said another follower. "The drink was getting to him and the drugs too. I see now that it's better to take the meds, so you know what's going on. I didn't think like that back then. I was keen on going with the madness. We all were. But it turned sour. Weird and cruel, especially the dancing thing. McLeish took to humiliating this woman who'd been one of his favorites, as much as he had favorites. He told her she was getting old, that she'd lost it. He said it was time for a bit of a jiggle up, whatever that meant. I only remember because after that she tried to kill him. She just flew at him. I didn't see her much after that."

This time, I didn't need to reach for my notebook or wait for an image to surface. Everything was there, right behind my eyes.

Summer and I'm playing outside, no clothes on, the grass warm under my feet. I'm dancing with Marianne in the sun and then there's that tobacco smell. He sits beside us and draws on his cigarette. "She's a pretty little thing," he says, and I'm pleased, because he always used to call me a brat and tell me to go away. Now he lets me sit on his lap. "I think she'll enjoy it. Children do, you know. I've been reading about it. They get to love a bit of jiggling." And Marianne is between me and him, and her arms are around me and there is that fierce metallic smell rising from her, and we run away as fast as we can.

Something was making a noise. It was my teeth, chattering. Something was moving. It was my knee, jumping in a jagged rhythm that wouldn't stop until I hugged my legs to my chest, my whole body shaking with the force and clarity of the memory, clear as if it had happened yesterday. I prayed to any and all gods who had ever existed that Rowan McLeish was not my father.

Work became my Prozac, numbing the unspoken thoughts that had knotted in my mind. Gunya was busier than ever and we barely had enough time to sleep. It was a month before Christmas, overcoat weather, and we cooked golden food: saffron risotto, osso buco, and slow-cooked stews with thyme and lemon zest.

"We've been thinking, me and Toby," said Mimi one Friday after lunch. "You're doing a third of the work, so you should get a third of the profit. As I said, we don't go in for hierarchies. Too old-world for us. What do you think?"

Behind her, Toby grinned. "So, are you ready to commit? Don't go all English on us and say you have to think about it."

I heaved the last of the baking pans onto the overhead rack. "I am thinking about it," I said, my back towards them. "Very hard." I turned towards them. "OK. I've thought about it now. My answer is yes." There was the unfamiliar feeling of the stretch of a smile across my face.

30

I have always thought that there is no more fruitful source of a family's discontent than a housewife's badly cooked dinners and untidy ways.

—Mrs. Beeton's Book of Household Management, 1861

Mimi's menus over the past weeks had been full of traditional English food, tasty but without a hint of chili or what I called a proper spice. It was time for a trip to Southall. I drove past the Church of Eternal Truth. The sign outside the church read: DEATH. THE END OF EXCUSES. THE BEGINNING OF ETERNITY. Could it get any cheerier?

Still, the thought of perhaps seeing Jake again was irresistible. I parked the car and crossed the road. Inside the church, near the table of cups and saucers, I saw the old man with the tombstone teeth. "You came back." He beamed. "How splendid."

"Somehow I just couldn't help myself." I sat at the back, where I could watch everyone walk in and out. The church was already full. There was the same airless atmosphere, the same group of teenagers at the front, the same sea of red caps. Only the preacher was different. This time, a skinny man with a Northern accent stood on the dais with his cordless microphone. He was dressed entirely in black and looked like Johnny Cash. I didn't listen to his words, just to his voice as it rose and fell with rhythmic monotony. Every few minutes, the congregation murmured approval. Occasionally they clapped.

I wasn't so put off this time. I almost envied them—the way these people were able to walk into this broken-down hall, dump their faculties of reason, their doubts, and their failings at the door, and emerge an hour later refreshed for the week ahead. I could only imagine the joy of that. Then I must have nodded off, because the next thing I realized was that my head was jerking up and down and people were walking past me. Jake was one of the last to come out. He stopped when he saw me. His face was expressionless and I thought he was about to walk away. I followed him outside.

"I'm not stalking you," I blurted. "I wanted to see you." My breath condensed into frosty puffs that wavered between us. "I was so sorry not to say goodbye to you and Lily. Everything happened all at once. I sent you a note, trying to explain things and asking how you were. And then some messages through Facebook."

"I never got the note," he said. "But that's no surprise. A load of stuff gets lost in our place. And I don't do Facebook anymore. But I'm fine, thanks." Even in less than two months, his voice had deepened, and there was much more golden fuzz about his chin. "It's good to see you, really good. Lily and I, we've missed you." He didn't ask, but the question was there, unspoken.

"It's hard to explain," I said. I wanted to embrace him, to tell him how much I'd missed him and how often I'd thought of him. "Maybe it's best not to try." A man wheeling a pram came up from behind us and we moved away to let him pass. "I'm getting a curry across the road. Want to join me? And then I can drive you back home."

He waggled his head about for a bit. "Sure. Why not?"

I'd never been properly inside the restaurant before. I'd just hung around the front counter until my takeaway was ready. The dining room was like every other old-fashioned In-

dian restaurant: flocked red wallpaper, statues of Hindi gods
and goddesses, and an enormous flat-screen television blaring
from the back. Jake looked around warily.

"Don't worry," I said. "The food is good. And I'll make sure
it's not too hot."

"I'm good with heat."

After the waiter had left with our order, I asked him about
school. "What happened with the parent-teacher meeting? You
know, the one you were going to have after the book was published."

Jake shrugged. "Everyone jumped up and down for a bit
and then the form teacher asked me not to write essays like
that again. That was it."

"So you didn't have to leave, or anything like that."

"Nope. I told you about that school. I told you about my
parents." His air of nonchalance disappeared. His eyes glinted
with scorn or anger, or both. "They're not going to expel the
kid with the well-known father who's on the telly every week
and the well-known mother who writes successful books. They
need parents like mine. They're like bait to get new students
into the school. The teachers just had to make a bit of a fuss
about it, to settle the natives."

The waiter arrived with our food. We arranged bowls of
steaming rice and miniature pots of meat and vegetables on
the table. Everything crowded together. In my anxiety, I'd ordered far too much. I shouldn't have asked, but I did. "And
Rob and Emma? What did they think?"

Jake's fork of rice was halfway to his mouth. He held it there.
Grains of rice slipped and fell into the curry, slowly subsiding
in thick brown sauce. "They didn't think anything. They were
just relieved to get the meeting over and done with. They'd
postponed it three times." He scooped more rice onto his fork
and slowly chewed on it. "We know they stitched you up," he

said. "We saw Dad's book. We knew you wouldn't have agreed to it. Lily said you weren't the type who would want to talk."

"She's right about that," I said.

"They said you'd given your consent, but it was too much of a coincidence. Dad's precious book coming out and the next minute, you've gone."

"I didn't want to leave," I said. "I loved it at Wycombe Lodge. Even now, I think it was maybe the best job I ever had. But it wouldn't have worked out—me staying."

We ate in silence for a bit. "Lily and I get on better now," said Jake. "Although it probably won't last. Anyhow, we reckon you found out. We think you were too smart not to have noticed. After a while, it gets obvious."

"What gets obvious?" My fork slipped against the side of the bowl. Sauce flecked with chilies slopped on the table.

"Them. Dad and Theo. It's our little family secret, the one we never talk about. But we all know. I've known ever since I can remember. I mean, no one ever said anything. Maybe I saw something when I was a kid, or overheard something. It doesn't really matter." His voice gathered strength. "So you see what I meant about irony. You can see why I wrote that essay. I get so angry sometimes that I lose all reason. And then I calm down.

"I'm just so against the hypocrisy. I reckon it should be our family motto. It would work well. It's OK for them to ferret out your secrets and destroy your right to privacy, because your life is a boost to their career as the power couple. But their little secret—well—that would damage their currency, so it's all under the carpet and always will be. That's the thing I like about the church. There's no falseness."

He pushed his bowl away. "Lily's going to a sixth-form college in Oxford soon, so she doesn't have to put up with it much longer. I've asked if I can go to boarding school then. I think they'll agree."

"Boarding school? Are you sure?" I asked. "Take it from me, it's not for everyone."

"It'll be better than home," he said. "I suppose you think I'm a coward for not standing up to them. But if I did confront them, they'd just deny it. They'd never admit the truth."

"I'm sorry," I said. I reached for his hand. This time he didn't pull away. "I disagree with McLeish on pretty much everything, but maybe he had a point about families. Maybe they do send people around the bend."

We walked out into the wind, a shock after the warm fug of the restaurant. I drove back to Petersham, retracing that familiar route along the fields from the town towards Richmond Park. The road was empty. In the distance, someone walked their dog. It might have been the old woman with her Labrador, but she disappeared before I could see properly.

I pulled up near Wycombe Lodge. "I wish I was still here," I said. "Like it was at the beginning. I wish it could have gone on like that."

"Me too."

"Give my love to Lily. Don't forget. And you can call anytime. You have my number. Please."

"Sure."

I reached over to hug him, but he was already out of the car, walking up the street in that jerky way of his, shoulders squared as if he expected someone to attack him. My hand fell on the seat, still warm from his body. I kept it there until the heat had ebbed away and all that remained was the clammy feel of imitation leather.

31

Pay, pay anything rather than go to law.

—*Mrs. Beeton's Book of Household Management, 1861*

My Google alert kept me up-to-date with Rob and Emma. Reviews of the book were published. The *Guardian* said it illuminated the life and work of a controversial yet brilliant psychologist. It went on to note that the human cost had been high, particularly to the mysterious child who had been neglected and forced to spend too many of her formative years in the company of mentally ill people. The *Spectator* said it was a sensitive portrayal of blighted lives and regretted that Rob hadn't been able to track down the young girl's real family. It wasn't a commercial bestseller, but in their world of upmarket newspapers, literary magazines, and late night talk shows, Rob's book had made its mark.

Rob was interviewed in a popular psychology magazine. There was a photograph of him in his study, looking thoughtful behind the desk where I used to order the groceries each week, all his books on the shelves behind him. "Of course, I had a duty of care to these people, the former residents of Kinghurst Place who are so fragile and therefore vulnerable," he said. His false high-mindedness instantly enraged me. "And also, I had a duty to tell the truth about McLeish. He was a hero of mine when I was a student, and it wasn't easy to reveal his shortcomings, how he distributed dangerous drugs to the residents.

"I've tried to steer a middle road here," he went on. "There's still a real stigma about mental illness. That's why I've gone to such lengths to protect the identities of people. People keep asking me about the young girl, who she really is and where she lives now. She wanted to tell her story, very much, but she also wanted privacy and I would never betray her confidence."

On and on the article went: about his television programs, his other books, his clever wife, and his happy marriage. I threw the magazine across the room. Then I got up and tore it into tiny pieces. It didn't make me feel any better.

It was Jude's idea, of course. Sensible and sane, like all her suggestions. "I know you can't afford a London lawyer. Philip says a decent one costs about five hundred pounds an hour, and that just for starters. Often the firm asks for a retainer of thousands of pounds before you walk in the door. But didn't your grandmother work for a firm of solicitors in Shaftesbury for all those years? Why don't you call them and make an appointment and see what they say about all this? There must be something you can do, despite those bastards getting your signature like that. You might even get a cut rate. It's worth a try, surely."

It was my day off and we were having lunch in the Greek restaurant in Primrose Hill. It was full as usual. Waiters flung down our plates of slow cooked lamb and salad and rushed off. "You have to forgive such bad service when the food is so good," I said, using my napkin to wipe slops of sauce from the table.

"Yes, it is delicious," said Jude. "But you're doing your usual thing by obsessing about food and avoiding the point. Will you, or will you not, make the appointment?" She had that stern look again. There was no stopping her.

I rang the solicitors that afternoon and spoke to Jeremy Rylance, the man who'd handled Gran's will. I'd met him briefly after Gran died, when I had to sign all the various papers. He was the son of the solicitor Gran had worked for. His name had been Jeremy as well. It was that sort of firm, owned by that sort of family for two hundred years. No deviations from the norm there.

"I need to ask your advice on something," I said after we'd exchanged pleasantries. "It's to do with signatures and contracts. It's a bit complicated, so probably best to explain everything in person. Could I see you next week? It would have to be Monday, because that's my day off."

"Of course," said Jeremy. "Of course." He had the type of easy good manners able to disguise any surprise that I was calling him out of the blue like this. It was like we played tennis or golf every week, or that I was married to his sister. "It would be good to see you again. My father was very fond of your grandmother. Shall we say ten o'clock? At the office?"

"Perfect," I replied. "And may I ask about your hourly fee?"

"Oh," he said. "Your grandmother worked here for years. We won't need to worry about that just yet. Let's meet first and talk. If we proceed, then we'll discuss fees."

I reported back to Jude and booked into a B and B just outside Shaftesbury for Sunday night. I didn't want to meet Jeremy Junior rushed and jangled from a three-hour Monday morning drive from London and so set off on Sunday afternoon instead.

How many times had I made this journey? I couldn't remember. I was only aware of that familiar feeling seeping through me: breathing more expansively as the city disappeared and the country emerged from the endless rows of houses huddled together. Along the motorway, the snowberries had lost their pearled bloom and shriveled into brown husks. The crops in the fields had been harvested months ago, but wisps of golden straw still clung to the hedges on either side of the road. A few remaining giant bales of wheat dotted the horizon. At Stone-henge, the pig farm was empty, but new huts had been built and a crew of men were nailing down roofs and installing more water troughs for the next generation.

My B and B was old-school, with a lumpy double bed and a faded chintz-covered armchair looking out over hills shrouded in afternoon mist. The walls were hung with school photo-graphs of tennis and lacrosse teams, dusty and fly-stained. A closer look at the netball team showed it to be Stanton Hall. The owner, a disgruntled-looking woman in her late fifties, probably thought I'd be impressed.

The next morning, I passed on the full English breakfast and paid my bill. I drove into Shaftesbury, found a parking spot, and walked through the cold morning fog to Gold Hill. It was too early for tourists, who would arrive later to marvel at the cobbled street's photogenic quaintness. Apart from shop owners, I had the place to myself. Rylance and Sons had their offices above a tea shop. I rang the bell, pushed through a small door, and went upstairs. The place was like Tardis, extending backwards in a series of tiny interconnecting rooms. Nothing had changed since my occasional visits there as a child, parked in a corner by Gran and told not to move while she typed and directed phone calls from a small switchboard.

Jeremy, a younger version of his father, wearing the same kind of pin-striped suit, kissed me on both cheeks and ushered me into a paneled office overlooking the street. Files cluttered every surface and cobwebs hung from a disused fireplace.

"Tea? Coffee?" I shook my head. Jeremy dusted off a chair with an old newspaper and gestured for me to sit down. "I've got some papers for you, from your grandmother's file, but they can wait until we've talked." There was a spot of shaving foam in his ear and a cluster of bristles under his chin.

I smiled, although I wasn't keen on going through more

documents. There had been so many after her death, each one requiring a signature, each one reminding me that she was gone. Being back here again, in this office, made me feel stripped away, like an orphaned child.

"Now, how can I help you?" He leaned back, clasping his hands and looking up at the ceiling. "Don't mind me," he said, the bristles on his chin glinting in the light from the lamp on his desk. "I happen to think better when I'm looking at this spot up there." He pointed to a blotch of damp and closed his eyes.

In a shaking voice, I began my story, about Emma and Rob and Wycombe Lodge; about my mother and Rob's book and my notebook, and the folded piece of paper; Rob and Theo and the photographs and the program. Every now and then Jeremy shook his head and put his hand up to ask a question.

"So you're quite sure you didn't show either of them your notebook?"

"Think carefully. What exactly did Rob say when he handed you the piece of paper?"

"How many photographs were used? Was your face just blurred or totally obscured?"

"Hmm," he said at the end, after what seemed like a long silence. He opened his eyes and tipped himself forward. "Hmmm. Don't know about you, but I'm ready for a cup of tea." He picked up his phone. Five minutes later, a young man walked into the office carrying a tray. "My son, Jeremy," said Jeremy proudly. "Learning the ropes. Shall I be Mother?"

Without waiting for an answer, he poured tea into cracked china cups. "Well, when I hear stories like that, I'm pleased I live a quiet country life. But that's no help to you. Biscuit?"

"No thanks."

"Of course, parts of this story are not entirely unfamiliar to me. My father was aware of your mother's . . . problems . . .

and your grandmother sought his advice on various occasions, most specifically when your mother passed away in such tragic circumstances." He tapped a file on his desk with his finger-nails. "But back to the matter at hand. The man, Rob, was right when he said you would probably lose if you brought a case against them, and yes, costs would probably be awarded against you. So, I can't advise that course of action."

Disappointment rushed through me.

"There is, however, another way to kill the cat. A letter could be written, outlining certain, shall we say, discrepancies in their domestic arrangements, and asking for some kind of financial settlement in return for your cooperation, so to speak."

"Wouldn't that be blackmail?" I asked.

"Of course," replied Jeremy. "But strictly legal and above-board. And these people sound as if they could do with a bit of a shake-up. Up to you, naturally."

"I'm not sure. I know I don't want their money—it's poison. I don't want to sink to their level, but I do want some kind of justice for myself, just to get it behind me." I placed the cup down on the saucer with a clatter. "The one thing I do know with complete certainty is that I will never forgive them. Never."

From behind his desk, Jeremy surveyed me with a sharp but kind gaze. "You don't have to, my dear. But generally speak-ing in these matters, the passage of time provides its own solu-tions. Think about it and let me know what you want to do. Now . . ."—again, he tapped the file on his desk—"to this other matter, concerning your grandmother."

"I thought I'd signed everything," I said. I was wrung out from telling my story, and flattened by Jeremy's response to it. More than anything, I wanted to leave. I didn't want money obtained by subtly worded legal threats, and I certainly didn't want another file to do with Gran's death.

"This is a matter that doesn't require a signature," replied

Jeremy. "It's a closed file, which means I haven't read it, only the instructions concerning it, which state that it should be handed over to you if you came to us over any matter relating to your mother or your early life. And I think this visit fits that category.

"It's something your grandmother wanted kept for you, but for reasons of her own, she didn't want you to have it immediately after her death. She always worried about you and didn't want you to know the more . . ."—here he paused—". . . difficult details about your mother and your early childhood, before you went to live with your grandmother. My father advised complete transparency, but your grandmother was very determined on this matter." He handed me the file. "It's all yours. I'm sorry I can't be of more help," he said. "I know we look fussy and behind the times, but we try to make up for that by looking after our people. And by the way, there won't be an account, even if you decide to proceed. It's the very least we can do."

I couldn't help it. I burst into tears. Jeremy patted my shoulder in an awkward way. "Try not to worry too much, and call at any time if you have any questions about anything."

"Thank you," I mumbled and stood up to leave.

"Aren't you forgetting something?" He handed me the file. My fingers slipped over its dusty surface. "Your grandmother was very proud of you, always," he said, shaking my hand. "Remember that. It's important."

On Gold Street, the fog had cleared. A silver sun hung low in the sky. It was cold with a fierce wind. I scurried back to my car and tossed the file towards the passenger seat. It could wait until I got back to London.

32

Children love their mothers unknowingly and without measure, realizing only at the final separation how deeply rooted that love is.

—Rob Helmsley, *Madhouse: The Life and Times of Rowan McLeish*

I missed the seat and the file fell to the floor of the car. Four fat envelopes and a photograph of my mother slid out, a faded Polaroid of her laughing, her arms outstretched as if she was waiting for someone to run towards her. An unseen breeze lifted her hair off her shoulders. It was suddenly so cold. I turned on the engine, switched the heater to its highest setting, and picked up the envelopes and the photograph. Someone had written a date on the back. 1984. The year before Gran came to get me.

All the envelopes were addressed to her. The first was puckered with age and the seal had disintegrated into sticky strings. Inside was a receipt for £225.87 from a company called West Country Investigation Services. A rusted staple attached a typed page to the receipt: "As per your earlier letter, please note that the Coroner's Report stated there were no personal items left by the deceased, apart from clothing which you have asked this agency to dispose of. Any further correspondence from the Coroner's Court will be forwarded directly to you."

The second envelope, identical to the first, was thicker. The corners were worn away and the pages inside peeked through. I tore it open and pulled out the contents. Another short note about further correspondence. Another receipt stapled to a sheaf of pages, the rust bleeding into the paper. Probably a list detailing their expenses.

Later, I returned to this moment again and again, examining everything about it. Was there a sense of excitement, a shiver that so many unknowable spaces might be filled? But I only remember thinking that the West Country Investigation Services might have bothered to type up their list of costs instead of writing it out by hand.

> *I'm coming back for you, next week or soon after that. We'll be together for Christmas! Imagine that. I'll catch the train. I'm feeling so much better. Did you mind, little one, about going to Gran for a bit? She's a real softie under that hard shell. This time, when I come back to you, things will be different. I'm going to take my pills, the proper ones, and not drink, not even coffee. It's all going to be good.*
>
> *It's so cold here. Sometimes it makes me dizzy and I have to go back to bed. I should have left weeks ago. I'd be with you now, reading you a story, doing something nice. Sometimes I think it must be pride keeping me away from you and my mother—either that or shame. Probably both. Mothers and daughters, how tangled it all is.*

The heater whirred erratically over the thrum of the engine. I turned it off and pulled my coat around me. Through the silence, I heard my mother's voice so clearly through the pages. She sounded like honey. I'd always thought of her as something like mercury, mesmeric but impossible to contain. Now I glimpsed the person. She had longed for me just as I'd longed for her.

*I am coming ... , I promise, darling Annastasia. Any minute
now. I think ... ht take the bus instead of the train. I couldn't
come before Christmas. I had this cough that wouldn't leave.
I'm still sick, but I had to write to you anyway.*

*I won't insult you with apologies and pleas for
understanding my weaknesses—who I am, the fractures of
my mind, the holes in my heart, the gaps in my life. I will not
do that to you, the only one I have loved truly, the only one
I wanted to be someone for. So when I tell you this, I want it
unvarnished by the need for explanation. I want you to know
what happened. I was McLeish's patient in London. I thought
he could save me and for a while I think he did. After maybe six
or eight months, we became lovers. All this happened long before
we went to Kinghurst Place.*

*Did you ever think he might be your father? Sometimes I saw
you looking at him and wanting his attention. Darling girl, he
is nothing to do with who you are. You were already born by the
time I met McLeish. I wish I could tell you that your father was
a kind and lovely man. I wish I could tell you his name and
where he lives. But I can't, because I don't know. So hard to say
this to you or even myself. I don't know. I wish I could tell you
something else, but I'm trying to be truthful.*

*I'd like to tell you that I loved McLeish, that part of me
cleaved to him, but that would be a lie. He wanted me, you see.
And I saw that as power. I was still young then, and thought
that an accidental collision of genes along a cheekbone or
an eye was a special gift, a sign that you were chosen for an
extraordinary life. But it was just another cage, another set
of bars. I knew I was beautiful. Very few people want you for
yourself when you are a beauty. Very few are interested. I hope
you realize that one day, if you ever read this—I hope you do
and I hope you don't.*

Rowan, what to say about Rowan? The way he managed to

control everything about me, down to the way I spoke, the way
I lay in the bed, while all the while telling me he was freeing
my creativity, that I was his muse, that I made him fly, that
together we would be free to soar. Everything was so seductive, so
wonderfully exciting, and it was a while before I realized what
he was doing—making me crazier than I already was. I'm sure
it was by design, not by accident.

I couldn't work it out for a while, because it was so casual,
so slight. There would be this perplexed look if I told him that
I thought this or that. He would lean back in that way of his,
and tilt his head. "Really," he'd say. "Do you really think so?"
Then, "Are you sure?" And then "Are you quite sure?" After a
while, everything began to blur and collide with each other and
make a terrible noise.

And then he would lie beside me, and curve his body next
to mine, the same way he used to do with that stinking woman,
and tell me that he would save me. And then he would read
aloud poems he'd written for me, and give me those tablets that
made me feel like I was wrapped in clouds and floating high
above everything, like a goddess. But then the clouds turned
into ropes and I couldn't get free. I couldn't think anything or
do anything. It was like being imprisoned where no light could
reach. In the end I pretended to take them then threw them
away. That's when I began to realize that everything about
Kinghurst Place was bad. I hope you never remember any of it,
that it took me so long to see that Rowan was sicker than all of
us put together, sick in an evil, hideous way, and I had to get
you out of there.

It was nearly one o'clock in the afternoon. I'd been poring
over the pages for almost two hours, reading each one again
and again, tracing the outline of each word with my finger.
The pages had yellowed, and some were smudged with what

looked like earth or grass. Perhaps she had written them out-side, warmed by the last of the autumn sun.

The car park was full. A woman in a beanie knocked on my window and asked when I was going to leave. "Oh, I'm waiting for someone," I said, hardly able to tear myself away from the pages. "They might be a while." She disappeared in a huff. I settled back down in my seat. One of McLeish's poems flitted through my head.

You will not go
I will know.
My will grows as
Yours does slow

It wasn't academic and abstract, a way to convey McLeish's philosophies. Rob was wrong. It was written for my mother. McLeish had tried to control her through therapy and destabilized her with drugs. He'd abused her and was threatening to abuse me. My mother ran away to save us. I went through the pages again, noticing how often she'd mentioned feeling tired and breathless and giddy—all symptoms of untreated heart disease. Maybe her death had been a tragic accident after all.

I looked in his eyes and thought I was drowning. I think you know I have this illness. It started when I was 17. The doctors gave me so many pills. I stopped taking them because they made me feel half-dead. Better to die on my feet than live on my knees. You see, I thought then, I thought I could talk myself sane, or that McLeish could talk me sane. But I don't want to lie to you. I loved the madness. I loved it so much. It was an eternal rainbow, the angel voices, everything glittering and this power and energy rushing from me, like I could fly. I forgot about everything that followed, the weeks of weeping and not

being able to move, every muscle weighed with cement blocks,
wanting to end it all. And then I would return to myself and see
your little tin plates beside my bed, the mud cakes cracked and
collapsing, the berries no longer scarlet and sweet but gray and
molded, and your dear sad face trying to make everything better.
Well, it will be, I promise you. Soon, I'll be coming for you so
soon. I just need to get well again.

My back was stiff from sitting for so long. I felt a disturbance
in the atmosphere, almost imperceptible. The cramped interior of the car was suddenly full of tiny noises. The rub of my
jeans against the seat, the intake of air through my mouth, the
crackle of hair against my scalp as I shifted about. The sound of
my mother's voice came up again through the yellowed pages.

Everything is clearer now. Everything will be clearer when I
come. I'll find us a house, just for us, where you can invite your
friends from school. I know you want to go to school. I won't get
anything too big. A little cottage where we can grow vegetables
and flowers and be like everyone else. I'm so tired of being
different. The effort exhausts me. I'm going to sleep now. I feel
very faint. It must be the cold.

Outside rain began to fall. The quiet jubilation of that moment, the tide coming in at last. Suddenly, I had to see the
place of her death for myself. It was the only way I could make
sense of it all, to accept what had happened. I turned again
to the letters from the detective agency, sure that one had
mentioned where my mother had died. Yes, there it was, at
the bottom of the page. The exact location was a clearing off a
trail called Lower Oak Path in a wood outside Cardiff. If I left
Shaftesbury now, I could be there before nightfall.

Two hours later, pushing past lorries on the motorway, I

pulled into an almost empty car park with three unmarked trails leading off it. I had no idea which one to take and walked over to a group of hikers drinking mugs of steaming tea. "Don't suppose you'd know where Lower Oak Path is?" I asked. "I'm looking for a clearing somewhere along it."

A bearded man examined the darkening sky. "You'll need to get your skates on, but you'll make it, just. There's a clearing a quarter of a mile down, near a group of five oak trees. It begins over there." He pointed to a trail at the side of the car park. "There used to be a map here, with everything clearly marked, but vandals got to it. Kids around this area . . ." I didn't have time for a speech on rural delinquency. "Thanks," I said, already walking away. "You've been a great help."

The day's light was nearly gone. I strode along the trail, blowing into my hands to warm them and counting my steps. Two hundred, three hundred, and finally four hundred and forty. There was the group of oak trees, just as the hiker had said. I left the trail and walked through the ancient wood until I came to a small empty circle. A deer snuffled at a tree trunk. It froze when it saw me, eyes wild with fear, before turning and racing for cover.

I was alone again. Everywhere was the smell of dank leaf mold. At the edges of the clearing were scooped out hollows dug by animals seeking shelter and warmth. I couldn't be sure that this was the exact place where my mother died, but still I imagined her here, alone and shivering. I was deathly cold and I couldn't seem to get enough air. I was overcome by sadness that she had died here alone in an abandoned trailer, with no one to help her. I stood there until it began to rain, great gouts of water rushing through the bare branches of the trees and splashing up from the mounds of leaves. I ran back to the car and drove back to London. With the sound of every passing car and the flash of every headlight came the chorus, warming me like a blanket. You were loved. You were loved. Your mother loved you . . .

Your mother loved you.

I stopped at the corner shop for bread and milk. Imran was ahead of me in the queue of late night shoppers. "You look happy," he said. "You look refreshed and happy."

"I drove down to Dorset today and then to Wales," I said. "It was very good."

"Dorset. I don't think I know that part. Or Wales." He moved up a place and lifted his basket onto the checkout. "My sister is here. She's staying until after Christmas. It's wonderful to see her again."

"Great," I said. "I bet she'll have a great time." He looked puzzled and a bit offended. The dinner. Of course. I couldn't get out of it now. "You must come over then, the three of you. We'll make it a pre-Christmas thing. Maybe next week?" He smiled and began unloading his groceries.

A couple of days later, I ran into Imran at the pulses section, studying the small print on a packet of red lentils.

"What about next Sunday for dinner? Would that suit?"

"Yes, that would be wonderful. Thank you." He looked pleased.

"How is your sister enjoying England?"

"She likes it, although she says it's cold."

I laughed. "Good job she didn't come in February."

He tossed the packet of lentils into his basket. "So everything is better now? You look more rested."

"Yes, everything is much better," I said. "I like my new job. So it's all good. Now, what do you like to eat? Everyone has so many allergies these days."

"We eat anything," he said. "No food allergies where we grew up. We were grateful to have a meal every day. But since you ask, maybe, something plain, something you would cook for your own family."

"Got it," I said. "See you on Sunday then, around seven thirty."

I'd never had anyone to dinner in my apartment before, not even Anton or Jude, and I didn't know what to think about that, except that it felt odd and good at the same time. It would be a squash around the tiny table, but we'd manage. We'd eat something simple, but with a bit of spice. I still had my pestle and mortar, my Le Creuset casserole dishes. I could prepare everything ahead of time so I wouldn't get flustered greeting my first ever guests.

Jude rang just as I opened my front door. "I'm in a very good mood!" she shouted.

"How come?"

"I bring you good news, my little kitchen fairy friend. Oh, such good news. Where are you?"

I told her.

"Go back to the corner shop and buy the *Guardian*. Page six. Ah, I see His Majesty my husband coming with his prince and princess. Let's talk later."

It was immediately apparent what Jude had been calling about. An article about Rob was at the bottom of the page. I read it standing on the corner, buffeted by the slipstream from passing buses. Apparently he'd resigned from the BBC with immediate effect. Something about personal reasons. But Rob didn't have personal reasons, only public ones. Maybe he was ill. Something could have happened to Emma. Or Jake or Lily? For a moment, I was back in Wycombe Lodge again, wanting to fashion order out of mayhem, making myself feel better. Then I remembered. They weren't my family. They never had been.

I retraced my steps to my flat and opened my computer. There was a picture of Rob at a book signing in Hatchards that weekend. Emma had told her followers to stick to a two-color palette for work. It made for an easier life, she wrote. Nothing else.

But the next morning, there was another story about Rob, this time in all the newspapers. A retired professor from Princeton had accused Rob of plagiarizing a paper he had written on McLeish twenty years ago for an academic quarterly. Not just the odd phrase or paragraph, but great slabs of words without changing even punctuation marks. Rob had refused to comment, but his silence only fanned the furor. The *Huffington Post* showed a page from Rob's book next to a page from the quarterly. Every word was identical. The BBC said that Rob's program would not be broadcast that week and that the series and his contract had been canceled with immediate effect. Rob's own website had disappeared overnight. I went into the kitchen and looked out over the rows of rooftops, the sky swimming like water over the jagged horizon.

Faster and faster I run down the towpath, each breath hammering against my chest before I settle into a pounding regular stride. My leg muscles strain. My arms punch the air. I think of the things and the times that almost undid me. Gran's toxic secret. Her shame about my mother. Her love for me. Her misguided efforts to turn me into someone that I wasn't. I think of my love for Douglas and then for Anton, always wanting them to fill in my unexamined spaces. My love for Emma and Rob and Jake and Lily, and yes, even Siggy. How I'd yearned to belong to them and to Wycombe Lodge in my futile way. How that yearning fed into my search for my mother and myself and the truth about McLeish. How I'd been overcome by grief and howling rage when Emma and Rob betrayed me. How blind I had been to the way they were, and the way I am. A month ago, even two weeks ago, there would have been a sense of triumph and righteous revenge about Rob. I would have gloried in his downfall, Emma's as well. I'd imagined it often enough. For a moment, the old fury and despair flare up, bright as flames.

I pick up pace and sprint past the asylum. The small bronze plaque glimmers in the dull light. I don't stop. I know what happened behind these stone walls. I know what happened in my life. Not everything that happened. No one can say that. But I know enough to leave it behind. The relief is enormous, like I've let go of a half-ton weight.

Air rushes past, chilling my cheeks. There is the smell of snow, something cold and clean—something that belongs to a new season.

Acknowledgments

I'm very grateful to Sarah Branham, Judith Curr, Haley Weaver, and everyone at Atria Books; to Kerry Glencorse, Susanna Lea, and all at Susanna Lea and Associates, and to Anna Dorfmann who created such a wonderful cover.

A huge thank-you to Liz Houghton, who unscrambled so much, both in my brain and on the page.

Thanks to the staff of Le Gavroche restaurant, and its chef patron, Michel Roux Jr., who patiently explained the operation of a professional kitchen to me.

Thanks also to Lyndall Crisp, Jenny Cullen, Jeanie Evans, Kylie Fitzpatrick, Elisabeth Gifford, Susan Haynes, Corinna King, Angela Lett, Liz Loxton, Michael Lynch, Jennifer McVeigh, Jude O'Donovan, Chrissy Sharp, Tricia Wastvedt, and Helen Westlake.

Nicholas Dainty and Laura Dainty encouraged me throughout. As always, I owe so much to my wonderful children and I could not have completed this book without them.